UNMASKING THE CURSE

BOOK ONE OF THE ARALIAN SERIES

CHELLE CYPRESS

CHELLE CYPRESS

Cover Design by:
Jacqueline Kropmanns
https://jaqueline-kropmanns.de/

Edited by:
Taryn Page (Developmental Editing)
Lynsey Griswold (Copy Edit)
Beth Lawton (Copy Edit/Proofread)

ISBN: 979-8-9891185-0-2

First edition printed 2023

DEDICATION

For those who made themselves smaller
to fit other's expectations.
You were never broken. You were never too much.
You were never a burden.
You are loved. You are valued.
You are worthy of wonderful things.

MAP

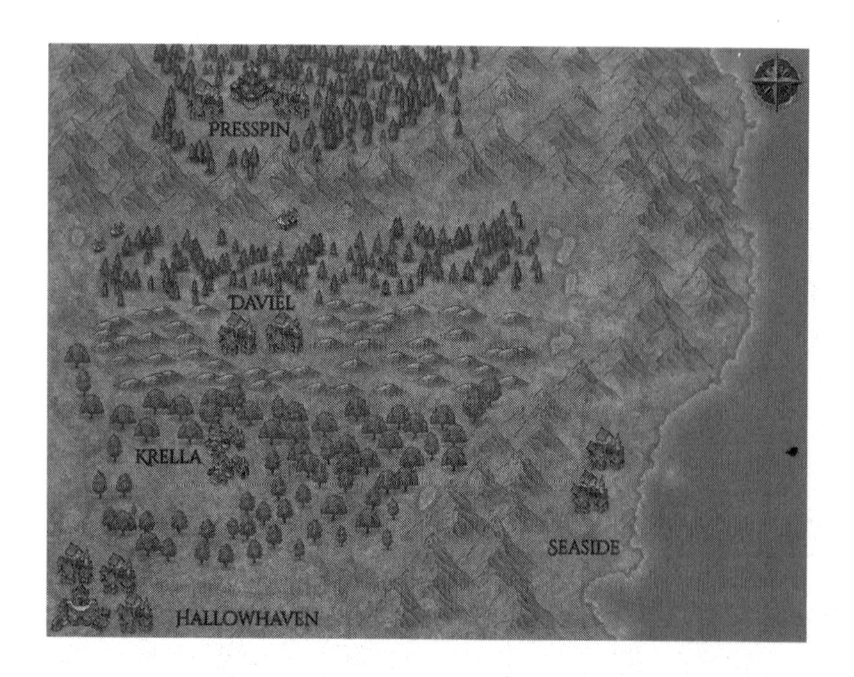

CONTENT WARNING

THE BOOK CONTAINS ELEMENTS of: abuse and neglect, abusive relationships, animal death, anxiety attacks (panic attacks and social anxiety), arranged/forced marriage, attempted rape, blood and gore depictions, burns, captivity and confinement, mentions of child abuse, mentions of childbirth, death, emotional abuse, explosions, mentions of eyeball trauma, nightmares and night terrors, parental abuse and neglect, physical abuse, physical injuries, poverty themes, religious abuse and trauma, unwanted sexual advances (groping/fondling/kissing), verbal abuse, mention of whipping.

CHAPTER 1

ARIANNA

"*CURSED MONSTER...WICKED WOMAN...MASKED NOTHING.*" The villagers' malicious whispers whirled around me. I was the wretch roaming their world, and my existence served as a reminder of the gods' displeasure. My presence in the square acted like a match to kindling, setting gossip ablaze. As I passed by the vendors' wooden carts brimming with wares, they glared at me with thinly veiled disgust. Their once boisterous shouts to lure customers died, and the bustling farmers' market halted in near stasis while they waited for me to pass. I attempted to pay them no heed and continued toward home.

A woman scowled as I approached, distaste coating her expression. She stepped off the broken cobble path and into the grime-covered road. Mud leached into the hem of her skirt, and I grimaced. She, like every other person in Krella, would rather endure trudging through the muck than share the narrow lane with me.

I quickened my pace, hoping to avoid confrontation, but a young mother turned the corner. Apprehension replaced her once cheery smile. Then she yanked her son back to the street from which they came. My shoulders slumped. This reaction shouldn't surprise me, but it twisted like a knife in my gut.

After nearly twenty years, they should realize the mask I wore kept them safe. My curse was bound to its rules, protecting them from the devastation lurking within me. However, I held no illusions of being welcomed—the blight no one wanted.

I hated coming into the village, but Mama insisted I run this last-minute errand while she prepared for the dinner that would determine the rest of my life. My nose wrinkled from the stench of horse manure mixing with the stagnant moisture. Sweat clung to the nape of my neck from the humidity exacerbated by the late summer rains. With my free hand, I pulled my cloak tighter, while side-stepping potholes where water pooled. Despite the balminess, I needed this covering as my poor attempt to protect myself from the onlookers. But I still sensed their glares burning into me.

I clutched the bag from the bakery tighter in my other hand and tried to distract myself with musings of these delectable desserts, a rare treat. However, that was a mistake. My stomach soured; the tarts would serve as the finishing point to the evening that would solidify my engagement to a man I despised. My heart hammered with dread, matching the clopping of hoofbeats as a cart rolled by. Heat radiated from the mask into my skin, triggered by this outing and the uneasy feelings about my future. I stumbled, my knees weakening from this panic attack.

I couldn't rid myself of these emotions threatening to drown me. Not as the onlookers murmured amongst themselves. Their fear rippled through the atmosphere, and their hateful stares intensified my malaise. With each step, the vendors' voices crescendoed, the sound filling my head like swarming bees protecting their hive.

I sweltered under the blazing afternoon sun. Anxiety seized me. My vision strained. The world descended on me in a dizzying swirl of colors. The shoppers became hazy figures. I gasped for relief. Yet my mask tightened, pressing into my flesh. I swayed under the pressure of the suppression spell that forced my curse to stay trapped within me.

Despite my discomfort, I trudged on, desperate to return to my room before the extreme fatigue—a side effect of my feeble disposition—overtook me. I stumbled along the walkway, my hood shifting, and people darted off the path as if I embodied the plague itself. Disgust crossed their faces as I rushed toward the outskirts of the square. My aching legs burned as maintained shops gave way to dilapidated buildings. Home was just beyond, with few venturing into this impoverished part of Krella. Unwilling to slow my pace, I turned the last corner too quickly.

Thud.

SILAS

Thud.

A small body knocked into me, causing a whoosh of air to leave my lungs from the impact. The bag the person clutched tumbled and landed on the filth-covered road.

"Oh, goddess. I'm sorry!" a female voice said, yet the cloak blocked her face and muddled her words.

"Watch where you are..." My lecture caught in my throat. The hood fell back to reveal blue eyes peering through a fine porcelain mask portraying rosy-red cheeks and pink-painted lips.

Impossible. How could a cursed person be in this village? Flummoxed, I froze and took her in. The ratty cloak covered her thin frame. A mess of curls sprung from her blonde plait while the smiling veneer beamed at me. I shook my head as if the motion would dislodge me from this shock. Why didn't Beatrix mention this in any of her letters? Given our family's history, did she not think this information pertinent?

"Mama is going to kill me," the woman said to herself, pulling me from my spiraling thoughts. She lowered her gaze, assessing the crumpled sack in the muck, unaware that she had shattered my grasp on reality. Strawberry tarts speckled the ground, and mud drenched the bag with *Martin's Bakery* scrawled on it.

In an unladylike manner, she squatted and mumbled to herself. I should have left, but I couldn't. Instead, I gawked at her and tried to reconcile a cursed person in this desolate hamlet.

Before I could make sense of her presence, she stood abruptly. However, she didn't settle on her feet but teetered precariously on her heels. She gasped, stumbling backward. Time slowed. Her eyes widened with alarm and they locked on mine. Without thinking, I closed the distance between us. I grasped her waist and pulled her against me, halting her descent into the filth. My fingers soaked in the warmth of her frail body. A hint of lavender wafted off her and enveloped my senses. Her blue irises pierced through my soul as I held her, protected within my embrace, for a heartbeat longer than appropriate.

"Thank you," she said, breaking the momentary trance as I returned her to standing.

I opened my mouth to speak, but snapped it shut. What would I say? Instead, I released her and forced myself to stride toward the village center. I fought the inclination to glance back but failed. She shook her head, and the sunlight shimmered through her hair. Her shoulders rose and fell in an exasperated sigh. Then she continued on her way, unaware that I lingered. I brushed off this peculiar preoccupation and willed myself to move forward despite the desire to watch until she faded out of sight.

Rattled, I took a breath, attempting to steady myself. I resisted the urge to loosen my cravat as I choked on the stench of dung mingling with the scent of hay from the outlying farms. Nature settled me, but this place lacked the serene beauty of Presspin. The flat green fields surrounding the village provided little charm.

My boots crunched against the unkept path, where puddles lay in wait. Neglected store fronts with dull bricks, dusty windows, and roofs made of deteriorating wooden shingles lined the block. I rolled my shoulders, loosening the thick fabric of my coat, which now clung to me from the humid climate. Minutes later, the dilapidated buildings gave way to well-maintained shops. When I turned the corner, a hectic farmers' market came into view. Vendors shouted to catch prospective buyers. I had no interest in their trinkets and homespun goods. However, they reminded me of my original intent to buy a gift for my sister, Beatrix, and her new husband, Duncan. The woman had jostled all sense out of me when we collided.

I paused at a window with *Martin's Bakery* etched on it. The display brimmed with confections, and I pursed my lips as if I could seal my questions within them. I shifted on my feet and vacillated between forgetting about the masked lady and delving into my curiosity. I shouldn't go in, but Beatrix loved sweets, I reasoned.

A bell chimed overhead, and the space gleamed in stark contrast to the bustling vendors. Scents of fresh bread and spice mingled in the air as I drew near to a glass display case with various pastries. An older man with graying hair and rimmed glasses placed biscuits on a tray behind the counter.

"Hello, how can I help you?" he asked as I mused over the selection.

"Do you have any strawberry tarts? I saw a young lady carrying a sack full," I asked, though I didn't care about the actual desserts.

"Sorry, all out."

Perusing the case's contents, I pointed to the cinnamon buns. "Three of these."

An uncomfortable silence stretched as he placed them in a sack. He shouldn't be unaccustomed to strangers. Krella acted as a waystation, located halfway between Hallowhaven and Daviel. I cleared my throat to draw his attention from the pastries, but he remained fixated on his task.

"The young lady with the strawberry tarts wore a spelled mask. I have heard tales, but I've never seen one of them."

The lie flowed, cutting through the quiet. My face stayed neutral, conveying that this was a passing observation and not niggling intrigue. However, his focus didn't sway from his work.

I stifled a groan. My curiosity remained unsatiated as he put the last bun in the bag and handed it to me. Resigned, I withdrew a few gold Aralian crowns for the sack. As I took it from him, his grip didn't relent, and his expression soured.

"From your clothes, I assume you are not from around here. Stay clear of Arianna Park. She is cursed. A harbinger of death and destruction. It is best if you forget all about her."

He released his grasp on the twine handle and plastered on a saccharine smile, his subtle signal to discontinue my prying. I nodded in solemn agreement, and left. The bell chimed behind me as I reentered the noisy crowd. My jaw clenched in frustration as I walked through Krella to my carriage. *Cursed.* They knew nothing of the truth of her curse.

CHAPTER 2

Arianna

I ran a hand along the decaying fence. The wood swayed under my fingertips, ready to give way with the slightest pressure. Our farm lay just beyond, and my stomach twisted in knots. Mama was going to kill me. I should have hurried home to beg for her forgiveness. Instead, I ambled. Sunshine broke through the leaves overhead and the birds sang, soothing my fraying nerves. I tilted my head back, wishing I could feel the sun on my face. Wishes were ridiculous, yet the peculiarity of this afternoon affected me. Perhaps my anxiety over my inescapable betrothal or the handsome stranger whose intense amber gaze lingered in my mind had shaken my resolve. For a heartbeat, I allowed myself to fall into foolish fantasies.

Our broken farmhouse, nestled amongst the apple orchards, pulled me back to reality, where my impending future awaited. Linens hung to dry, crisping from the blazing heat. I dodged pockets of mud that seeped into the path leading to our old brick home, decades past its prime. The two-story house had seen better days, and sprigs of straw poked out of the busted clay tiles crumbling from wear. My reprieve was short-lived as I reached the entrance. My hand trembled, hovering over the iron knob. With a shaky breath, I summoned courage and opened the old wooden door. A shudder crossed through me as a high-pitched squeak reverberated.

"Goddess above. Arianna, what took you so long?" Mama called from the kitchen. My pulse raced.

I removed my muddy boots and lined them against the wall. The paper had peeled, the floral corners twisting upward from where shoes had rubbed against it. The fresh scent of cleaning polish wafted through the air, dampening the mildew stench permeating the parlor. I dodged the rusted buckets, brimming with water, that dotted the floor. They had caught the rain from yesterday's unexpected storm, which leaked from our poorly thatched roof.

The last year had been catastrophic for our family: first Father's death, then the meager harvest, and now our ceiling threatening to collapse. Though I loathed Theo Terrell, he desired me, and his father possessed the funds to save us from financial ruin.

I entered the kitchen, where Mama leaned over a large pot. Heat billowed throughout the tiny space, laced with the scent of burnt grease. She muttered to herself as she stirred vigorously, but from the acrid smell, there was no saving the concoction. I remained silent, waiting at the doorway. She spun toward me, clutching the wooden spoon so tightly her knuckles turned white.

"Where are the tarts?" she asked, taking in my empty hands. Nervous, I folded them behind my back to hide the truth.

I opened my mouth to speak but snapped it shut. The truth never mattered, not when it came to me. Mama closed the distance between us, her blue eyes blazing with rage. Even her sable curls flecked with gray seemed to coil tighter from her displeasure.

She pointed the spoon at me. It was coated in a thin layer of putrid goop. "I can't believe you did this. You ruined this dinner, you disobedient child. Goddess above! I should have sent your sister, but she insisted you venture into town instead. Yet you failed at the simplest of today's tasks. All the while, Naomi scrubbed the floors and put the parlor to rights. You are a disappointment."

The burning scent intensified, pausing her reprimand. Her nostrils flared. She whipped her head to the source of the stench and growled in frustration. Thick brown gravy bubbled over the sides of the pot, coating the stove, and smoke filled the tiny kitchen.

She rushed to the rear entrance, flinging it open, and the hazy plume seeped out. The heat of the woodstove mixed with the summer humidity intensified the sticky sweat clinging to me. Mama returned her attention to the unsalvageable sauce. I slowly retreated, hoping she had forgotten about me, but she spoke before I could flee.

"Goddess! This is a disaster. The parlor reeks, the meal is near ruin, and there is no dessert." She pivoted toward me with a scowl. "Since the moment your curse awoke, you doomed this house. Now get out of my sight before I take that damned mask and keep you locked away until you are no longer my burden."

I fled up the stairs. The sound of grumbles and clanging cookware drifted off as I reached my room. My feet crossed the threshold, and I shut the door. The mask detached itself from my face, freed from the magical bond sealing it to my skin. I leaned against the doorframe. My shoulder pressed into the ancient Aralian language etched in the wood that locked me and my destructive power within. A spell that only affected the cursed, solidified through Aralia's divinity.

I yanked off the heavy porcelain, which acted as the key to allow my exit, and placed it on the dressing table. It mocked me with its painted placid smile, as if it knew of my inability to leave this room without it. I flipped the mask, unwilling to view its taunting grin. Exhausted, I moved to the window seat and sat on the threadbare green cushions. Leaves danced throughout the apple orchard while my sister, Naomi, hauled a large bucket of water from the well. Sunlight cascaded over her golden locks, highlighting her youthful beauty. However, her shoulders slumped from the hours of intense labor. It was torture watching her lug buckets while I did nothing.

Needing a distraction, I stood and perused the few books lining the small shelf on the wall. The fraying leather bindings crinkled under the pressure of my fingertips. Each novel bore the sign of being lovingly reread. I caressed the pristine golden spine of the *Book of Aralia,* the lesser-loved tale in my meager collection. I grabbed the storybook and settled back into the seat. Reading about the goddess was part reminiscent and part self-inflicted torture, a reminder of the girl I once was and the monster I had become.

As I flipped through the pages, memories of when I was Mama's beloved child, curled in her lap, filled me. She had read me the tales of ancient gods and the toll their displeasure took upon the world. I had clung to Mama, terrified at the pictures of the dark deities. They damned bloodlines with a curse that caused death and destruction. During my first six years of life, we had been unaware that this affliction dwelled within me, lying dormant, awaiting a trigger of turmoil to awaken its wrath.

"There is always hope. In the Goddess of Light, Aralia," Mama had said.

As I turned the page, the glossy artwork of the beautiful goddess replaced the beasts that had once terrified me. The gold-flecked pages highlighted the goodness she used to protect us. A gruesome battle played out until she defeated the dark gods with her disciples, the Aralians. She imprisoned these destructive deities centuries ago with the power of light.

However, she couldn't remove the blight lurking in our blood. Yet she didn't allow death to befall the damned. She provided the Aralian disciples with the ability to suppress our curse. They used her divinity to create masks and boundary spells to contain the destruction within those like me.

Memories from the fateful day when my devastating darkness awoke crawled forward. My heart pounded, and my focus strained on the words as I blinked at the blurring letters.

"What are you doing?" Naomi asked, and I glanced at the doorway. Until now, I was unaware she had entered.

"Reading." I shut the text and set it down.

Her lips twisted in a grimace. "Why that one? Aren't you torturing yourself enough by going forward with this betrothal?"

I fiddled with the loose thread on the cushion. "Is that why you didn't knock?"

She approached, picked up the book, and chucked it onto the rug that hid the marred wood from when my curse had awoken. The thud echoed through my tiny quarters. The space was no bigger than a closet in an estate. She sat beside me and grabbed my hand. Her fingers were rough from toiling away, and the faint smell of polish mingled with the lily salve she used.

"Partially. I heard Mama shouting and wanted to make sure you were all right. Also, why should we spend our hard-earned coins on desserts for the Terrells? I'm glad they will have to choke down the burnt supper."

My thumb ran over her rough skin, and guilt consumed me. Naomi often attempted to intercede on my behalf.

"I'm fine. She is just overwhelmed by tonight's events," I said, but when was Mama not overwhelmed? A harried frenzy seemed to be her typical state of being. A long silence lingered. I expected her to leave to help Mama with the preparations, but she stayed.

"You can stop this. Tell her you will not marry Theo." Naomi's logic was sound, but she didn't understand Mama's disdain for me. Mama loved her. If Naomi objected to a proposal, Mama would listen.

"I'm twenty-five, and no one else wants me. What should I do?"

"Stay here. Nothing has to change." Her words contained a naivete matching her nineteen years of life.

I lacked the energy to argue with her again about my looming engagement.

"You can visit Terrell Estate whenever you please. Perhaps, they have a conservatory filled with exotic flowers for you to sketch," I said, eluding her pleas.

She leaned her head on my shoulder. Naomi, my only companion, brought light, friendship, and joy into my lonely existence confined by these walls. Birds near the window sang a mournful tune, as if they knew our futures were bleak without an influx of funds. Naomi was too young to wed, and in our current state, she had limited prospects. However, with my bride price from the Terrells, Mama could fix our failing farm, providing Naomi with stability.

Before either of us spoke, Mama bellowed, "*Naomi!* Come here at once. I need your help with this damned sauce."

With a sigh, she stood and smoothed her stained apron. She paused to speak.

"Naomi, make haste!"

She pursed her lips, sealing whatever she wanted to say behind them. Her boots clanged on the hardwood floor as she left. A twinge of grief tugged at my heart. I would soon be married and parting from my sister. I gulped down the knot in my throat, willing myself not to cry. Though I dreaded the evening to come, I held on to a sliver of hope that this wretched match granted me. Mama would no longer consider me a burden, and I could provide Naomi with a better future.

CHAPTER 3

THEO

WHERE IN THE GODDESS was she? Hadn't I waited long enough? I shifted on the stiff, aged sofa, peering at the stairwell for the hundredth time since our arrival. This dank hovel lacked charm, smelling of must and lemon polish. Even the cheap swill posing as wine Mrs. Park plied us with didn't hold any amusement. Mother sat stone-still beside me. Dressed in an ornate gown, she had a grace that mimicked a fine lady, despite her status as the offspring of a wealthy merchant. She served as a beautiful show of Father's vast wealth, yet tension flowed off her as she clutched her hands. Father chatted about this year's herd and other frivolities, delighting the enthralled Mrs. Park. I rolled my eyes as he bellowed a laugh, lacking in sincerity. The daft Mrs. Park tittered with him, unaware, as he calculated the desperation of her situation. His jovial act was the perfect costume to hide his ruthlessness.

Goddess, I hated this house, yet my reward would come for my patience. I had met Arianna four summers ago and had counted down the days until she was mine. Last month, I turned twenty and entered into my majority, making me old enough to wed. I lounged on the sofa and huffed an exasperated sigh, then crossed one leg over the other, bouncing it in impatience.

"Theo, manners." Father gritted his teeth, breaking through his congenial persona for a second, then returned.

I folded my arms over my chest. Despite my restlessness, tonight I took a step closer to claiming my prize. I had been a lad of sixteen during our first meeting, and I had delighted when Mrs. Park instructed Arianna to sit under the apple tree with me. She had listened to my stories, nary speaking a word, as Father gathered supplies for our trip to Hallowhaven. Fate intervened when I stumbled upon this masked creature, as if guided by the hand of the goddess. I had spent years acquiring any item related to Aralia, and she would complete my collection.

Arianna was a priceless commodity. She was protected under the Aralians and possessed an ancient bloodline. Despite her blight, she would serve as a chess piece to Father's games. Last year, a seat on the high council became vacant in Hallowhaven, which ruled over Hallowhaven, Krella, and Daviel. Father, having grown bored with amassing wealth, had shifted his sights to obtaining what had always been just outside of his grasp: power. However, as the son of a pauper, he lacked prestige. Once I married Arianna, our union would provide Father with the connection he needed to be viewed as worthy in the eyes of the nobles.

Mother seethed at the impending betrothal, her full lips pulled into a thin line of displeasure. But she didn't speak of her grievances. Father ruled with an iron fist, expecting total obedience, and decades of cutthroat dealings had made him a shrewd businessman.

"Good evening," Arianna said as she entered the parlor, bringing me back to the moment. My gaze drifted to her. Goddess, I would do anything to have her satiate this unquenchable need. I tried. Aralia herself knows how I bedded wench after wench to clear Arianna from my soul. My hunger for her remained. I clenched my jaw in displeasure as she walked toward the chair by her mother.

"Sit by Theo," Father said.

Mother's mouth hung open like a fish, but his dark stare flashed cold in command. Mother sprang from the sofa and sat across from us, relinquishing her spot. Mrs. Park smiled, seemingly unaware of the exchange between my parents. Arianna perched herself on the edge of the cushion beside me and folded her trembling hands.

She tempted me in that gown, displaying her thin frame as the neckline dipped to the valley of her breasts, drawing my attention to her delicate cleavage. The worn azure fabric highlighted the sole feature I could see of her face, her blue eyes. Her mask had a pleasant smile and apple-colored cheeks.

Her light scent of lavender enticed me as it filled my senses. I shifted again; my arousal heightened as thoughts of our wedding night entered my mind. I wanted nothing more than to bite her bare neck, marking her as mine. My pet. My property.

"Let's cut to the chase and begin negotiations for the bride price. No need to spoil dinner with talks of business." Father enjoyed rattling his conquests by changing strategies abruptly. This kept those around him off-kilter, affording him the upper hand.

"Fine, Fletcher, but be quick. We don't want such a hearty supper to grow cold with drawn-out discussions." Mrs. Park squared her shoulders. I held back the urge to laugh at her comments about the meal. From the burnt scent that had emitted from the kitchen earlier, I doubted it compared to the feasts in which we partook.

"Of course, Clara." Father flashed a calculating grin. Like a cat playing with his food, he relished the fighting spark Mrs. Park exuded. Maybe beneath her placid demeanor, Arianna possessed the same whisper of defiance, but it was unlikely.

"Arianna is a lovely girl, and I can overlook her circumstance since my son's heart is involved. Despite her curse, she holds some value, which I intend to honor." Father scanned the space, taking in the Park women's faded dresses, the fraying sofa, and the condensation on the ceiling, indicating an issue with their roof. The faint scent of mildew saturated the air. His smirk widened at Mrs. Park, who beamed in return, too stupid to realize his plan.

"I'll give you five sheep for the girl," Father said, undercutting the settlement. Arianna was worth a flock. However, he never paid full price for anything, and especially not for a cursed bride. No matter how much I wanted her.

Arianna shifted, and her knuckles on her folded hands whitened. Did she realize Father's game? Was she more intelligent than I suspected? I shook my head and smirked at the ridiculous thought.

Hair prickled on the back of my neck from my mother's displeasure. I flicked a glance at her. Her lips pursed in disgust as she glared at Arianna. She believed Arianna was a debt we were accruing because of her curse. She did not agree with compensating Mrs. Park for the blighted offspring.

"That is quite the offer. However, she is my most precious daughter, and parting from her for such a meager amount would break my heart. I will take no less than ten sheep."

Father paused, leaning against the rickety chair, which groaned in protest, the feeble legs threatening to snap beneath his bulky frame. He was a hulking man with an imposing form that matched his larger-than-life demeanor. My antithesis in appearance. I was lithe and lean, with features much more delicate, similar to Mother's. It was a difference he often mocked me for. A thick silence clung to the air as he ran his fingers along his graying beard. His intense stare held Mrs. Park's in a battle of wits.

"Seven sheep, and we will host a ball for the couple. Think of Naomi and this perfect opportunity for her to meet wealthy suitors. She is going to reach her majority in a few months, making her eligible to wed, if I remember correctly." Father flashed his most charming smile. It almost warmed his frigid stare. I resisted the urge to laugh at his performance. He planned on having a masquerade regardless, eager to flaunt our new tie to an ancient bloodline that had influence in Hallowhaven.

Mrs. Park grinned, her chin tilting in triumph, as if she was still a lady of good breeding and not a simple farmer's widow. "And you will purchase our full attire, with no cap on the expenditure. You don't want your future daughter-in-law and her family to show up as paupers, do you?"

Father cackled, causing Mother and me to flinch. An accompanying titter came from Mrs. Park, easing the tension. He smoothed his countenance. I relaxed as his dark eyes crinkled along the edges, showing they held a spark of amusement instead of malice. My mother released a breath, her tense shoulders lowering as he cleared his throat and his practice smile returned.

"Very well. You drive a hard bargain. I swear, Henry should have had you running his finances and farm before he died. Fortune would have shined on you, Clara. But let us leave them so Theo can propose." Father rose without waiting for Mrs. Park's answer. Our mothers followed him into the dining room, and the door closed behind them.

Arianna stood to flee, but I leapt to my feet and pulled her against me. As I wrapped my arms around her petite body, pleasure surged through me, sending chills coursing down my spine. My cock stiffened as I sniffed her blonde hair.

She didn't move, ready to submit to me. She was obviously grateful for this marriage, and she should be. I was the sole heir to a wealthy businessman and had a striking appearance. She should consider herself fortunate to be my future wife, and from her stillness, I sensed her unspoken understanding. My pulse raced with eager anticipation. Unable to restrain myself,

I lowered my mouth to her ear and whispered, "I can't wait to have you. I'm impatient to see your face."

She tensed. Perhaps she was hideous and feared displeasing me. "Don't fret. If you are ugly, I can bed you with the mask on. I may prefer it. Either way, what fun it will be."

I wanted to ravish her here on this couch. Yet the clang of dishes reminded me of our lack of privacy. Anyone could enter, and I was not inclined to incur Father's wrath. We'd best leave our games for another time. I licked the slope of her neck. She shivered. I released my hold, then walked past her to join the others, leaving her behind.

CHAPTER 4

SILAS

"SILAS, SILAS, SILAS," THE voice cooed from the pitch-black landscape on this moonless night. I blinked in the lightless world, straining to see.

"Silas."

My feet acted of their own accord, pushing me toward the wraith who called my name.

"Where are you?" I shouted in panic, the darkness consuming me as I walked deeper into the void.

"Silas," the voice whispered, drifting farther away from me.

"Where are you?" I yelled. My heart raced as I sprinted, searching for whomever beckoned me. I gulped down my unease. I had to find the ghost to lead me out of this misery.

"Silas," it crooned in the distance, the sweetness of my name ringing in my ears. But the specter eluded me, no matter how fast my legs moved. I could no longer muster the strength to call out or give chase. The darkness leached the life from my soul.

Exhausted, I sat on this bleak space's cold, hard ground, lost in the abyss. I placed my head in my hands as fear consumed me. "Where are you?" I whispered through a shaky, disheartened breath.

"Silas," it crooned as warmth grazed my shoulder. I turned and...

I gasped. Air rushed into my lungs as I jerked into a sitting position. The blanket tumbled off me from my hasty motion, crumpling onto the floor. I panted with panic and searched the room. A plush sofa, a small table, and an unlit hearth occupied the guest suite of my sister's home, Archer Estate. But there was no phantom here. I scrubbed a hand over my face as sweat trailed from my forehead to my fingertips. The sticky heat of Krella made sleeping difficult. When I had eventually fallen into a slumber, the wraith had inhabited my dreams. For the fortnight since my arrival, the faceless, eerie voice haunted me. Yet I found no one.

I hated these tiresome nightmares and had forgone bringing a specialized sleeping draft on the journey. Brielle would chide me for my short-sightedness when I returned to Presspin. They hadn't plagued me for years. However, I felt unsettled here, and something dormant within me triggered these dreams to creep into my soul.

Unable to remain still, I swung out of bed. The dry flavor of cotton clung to my mouth. I poured a glass of water, warm from the humid night air, from the pitcher sitting atop the nightstand. I drank the contents, then settled the cup. It clinked against the mahogany harder than I intended.

I approached the window and pulled back the curtain. Sunlight cascaded over the horizon, yet the dawn didn't comfort me as light stretched over the orchards and lush garden. The crawling energy creeping beneath my skin remained even as the golden glow washed over me.

Agitated, I dressed in haste, ready to rid myself of this pent-up tension. The parks on the property were scenic enough to settle my whirling thoughts. My goal set, I slipped out of the suite and ventured to the gardens.

I ambled the ornate hallway lined with portraits of the old Krella lords who no longer oversaw this area. They were of no relation to Duncan. Yet he hadn't removed the artwork. Instead, he relished that he was now the owner of this manor without a drop of noble blood coursing through his veins. He prided himself on his business acumen and his ability to rise in the ranks from the son of a butcher to a sought-after estate advisor. Walls with paintings gave way to windows, and sunlight illuminated the manicured gardens. Escape was just around the corner.

"You're awake already?" Duncan asked from behind me.

I held back an exasperated groan, my intentions for a quiet morning slipping away as I pivoted to him. Duncan's gray irises brimmed with eagerness. I loved my brother-in-law. He had acted as my estate advisor when I transitioned to becoming the overseer of Presspin after my uncle's death, and I often relished our lengthy chats. But I wasn't in the mood.

"I was heading out to the—"

"Nonsense! Come join me for breakfast before I leave for Hallowhaven. I'll be gone for a few days, connecting with investors for the trade route I am spearheading from Hallowhaven to Seaside." Duncan grinned, and I couldn't fight his gregarious pull.

"Very well."

I followed him around the corner in the opposite direction of the exit. He chattered, leaving little space for me to interject, but I had no inclination to speak right now anyway. He filled the silence with plans for the trade route that would cut through the treacherous mountain range that made Seaside unreachable by land.

The smell of coffee wafted through the air as we reached the dining room. Duncan pushed the carved door open. Sunshine streamed through the oversized windows, highlighting the crisp colors of the floral wallpaper. A smile flickered across my face as I took in my sister, Beatrix, sitting at the oak table large enough to seat twenty.

I slunk into the chair across from her and perused the plates brimming with food. Like our other meals, breakfast was served with an overstated opulence. Artfully arranged pastries and fruit of various colors filled silver trays. A footman in beige livery waited by the wall for directions. Beatrix paid us no heed as she flipped through a stack of letters.

"My dove, I thought you were going to get some much-needed rest and dine in your suite," Duncan said to Beatrix with a wink and a roguish smile.

She glanced at him. Pink bloomed along her cheeks, highlighted by the rose-colored day dress she wore. I cleared my throat, uneasy over the insinuation.

The honeymooners were overly affectionate, even though they had been wed for six months. I was happy for my younger sister. However, some innuendos made me uncomfortable. They had always acted composed in Belmont Manor when around me. Yet we were no longer in my domain.

Duncan leaned over and placed a kiss on the top of Beatrix's head and sat next to her. Then he picked up the newspaper beside his plate. It crinkled as he unfolded it and began reading, ignoring us even though he had sidetracked me from my original plan to venture outside for solitude. I glared at him in exasperation, but the paper blocked his face. His fingers lingered under the headline and drew my focus: *Businessman Opts for a Vacant Seat on High Council.*

I shifted my attention to my sister. Beatrix beamed at Duncan. It pleased me that she had found a love match with my closest friend, but I felt a pang of sadness. These last two weeks, I realized something had been absent in my life: companionship. I missed my sister—her lively conversations, her nagging questions, and even how she strewed books around my study. These behaviors that had once grated on my nerves now felt endearing since her absence from Presspin. My time at Archer Estate stood in stark contrast to the silence in my expansive manor in the far north.

The footman shifted on his feet, pulling me back to the present.

"Tea, please, Jenkins," I said, and the servant scurried off.

I rolled my shoulders. I should have declined Duncan's invitation and headed outside to search for solace instead of sulking here. Hopefully, the chamomile would soothe my jumbled mind and emotions. I thrummed my fingers against the solid wood table while I waited.

Beatrix turned her attention from her letters to me. Her brow wrinkled. "You didn't sleep well again?"

Before I could answer, the footman placed the tea before me. I picked up the cup and sipped the hot beverage, but my shoulders remained tense.

Beatrix assessed me, likely taking in my haggard appearance that reflected my tumultuous sleeping habits. My black hair lay askew, and I had kept the collar of my shirt unbuttoned. The tight fabric had been choking me.

"I think you may need a change of scenery, dear brother. Perhaps Krella doesn't suit you." She shuffled through the envelopes and pulled out an embossed invitation. Gaudy gold etching flashed before me. My glance caught on *Arianna* in calligraphy. I stiffened.

Before me was the name of the woman I dare not mention. I gaped at the lettering. Why was she, too, haunting me? Over the past two weeks, her piercing blue eyes and the mask she was bound to often permeated my mental reserves. I had contemplated divulging my curiosity about the lady to my sister. Yet her obsession with romance novels would lead her astray. She'd take my inquiry as one of love at first sight and not of the blatant shock I felt at the discovery that a cursed lived within this tiny village.

"Give it to me." I opened my palm.

Beatrix's bright smile faltered as she passed me the invitation. I scanned the delicate scrolling, reading over the words once, twice, and a third time: *Arianna Park engaged to Theo Terrell.* Against all reason, I gripped the card too tightly, and the edges wrinkled under the pressure. I smoothed my expression and returned it to her. She glanced at the crinkled card, then arched an eyebrow at me. I could almost hear the multitude of questions bubbling in her mind.

"Is that the invitation for the Terrells' masquerade?" Duncan asked as he lowered the paper.

"It is, dear. I was hoping Silas would accompany us," Beatrix said. She ran her thumb along the bent corner of the card, then placed it on the stack. Her focus returned to me. She cocked her head, and the wheels in her mind spun behind that familiar smile.

"I am aware that you despise socializing, Silas, but Duncan plans on spending the entire night talking business instead of waltzing with his beautiful wife. Please, save me from being a wallflower." Beatrix pouted.

"I hate dancing," I said to end the conversation.

"I am sure there will be many attractive, eligible young women to catch your eye. You are Lord Belmont of Presspin, and you are past marriageable age at thirty. Isn't it time to secure a bride?" Duncan asked, gesturing to the footman for his coffee.

I winced at the statement. I had no intention of marrying.

"Weren't you thirty-six when you wed?" I asked. I sipped my tea but held Duncan's stare. He had been a bachelor far longer than I, and his constant hints about matrimony were exhausting.

Duncan folded the paper and placed it on the table. Then he grabbed a shiny red apple and bit into it; the crunch echoed through the strained silence.

Beatrix peered at the two of us in our silent battle of wills. She lowered her cup with a clink, breaking our stare-off.

"Yes, dear. What took you so dreadfully long to declare your love for me?" She grinned and elbowed him playfully in the side.

Duncan let out a chuckle, switching his focus to her. "My apologies. You were very young when we met, and I didn't want to rush you."

They seemed to be well suited. Initially, I had been reluctant to give them my blessing because of their ten-year age difference. Duncan's break in protocol by forgoing formally requesting my permission for her hand in marriage hadn't helped matters either. However, after he proposed, Beatrix made a rousing speech about her undying love for him. She reminded me that she was well past her majority and would do as she pleased.

"Let's not be distracted, my dove," Duncan said.

I reached for a plump purple grape and popped it into my mouth. But the tart flavor added to my unease as he focused on me yet again.

"You must venture out beyond your routines and Presspin. Think of the bevy of beauties who will attend, happy to please you for a chance to become the lady of Belmont Manor." He smirked.

I almost choked on the fruit, which stuck in my tightening throat. But he held my stare; he had expressed his wishes and now he expected me to agree with his judgment.

I swallowed roughly. All the while, Beatrix beamed, her face alight with optimism. Any argument caught on my tongue. Why should I disregard my sister's and my brother-in-law's desires? I didn't want to disappoint them.

"Fine," I said. Yet reality hit me. I had no affinity toward attending a soiree, to be chased around by matrons wanting to secure me for their daughters. However, that wasn't my sole hesitation. The idea of crossing paths with Arianna Park again unsettled me.

Duncan lifted the gazette, the pages rustling as he flipped through them. His subtle sign that our conversation was over. I tensed with tightly coiled apprehension over this turn of events. I stood, and the chair scratched on the hardwood floor from my sudden motion. Beatrix studied me, concern crossing her expression.

"Where are you going? You hardly ate anything."

I ignored her question and strode out of the room. Feet scuffled behind me, and I picked up my pace, hastening down the hallway. I didn't stop until Beatrix tapped my shoulder. I paused, my focus on the exit ahead that offered solitude full of fresh air instead of the stifling expectations that clung to this morning.

"Wait. Are you ill? You have seemed unsettled. I assumed homesickness, but I dare say it is more than that. What is wrong?"

I fixated on the door. I didn't have a coherent answer. Why had the dreams begun again? Why did I care that a cursed woman, Arianna, lived in this town?

"I figured your mood was from not being in your normal routine. However, you have become more surly with each passing day. What is going on with you?" Her words were gentle, but whatever composure I had dissipated. My disjointed emotions roiled through me, and my fatigued brain could not stop the words from leaving my mouth.

"Why didn't you tell me a cursed person lived here?" I asked, whipping around to her. Her brown eyes widened in shock, and her olive skin flushed, creating a stark contrast to her raven-black hair. She was an excellent secret keeper, but I'd never expected her to keep secrets from me.

"How did you—"

"I ran into her, literally, on my way here." I clenched my fists into tight balls.

"Oh...why haven't you mentioned it until now?"

"Your mind is always running amuck with romantic notions. You would think it was some sort of...gods, I don't know, I don't read that drivel. Did you at least plan on telling me before I went to her engagement ball?" I bit out and ran a hand through my hair, fighting the urge to storm off.

She lifted her thumb to her mouth and gnawed on the nail, her worst tell. She indeed intended for me to go without this vital piece of information.

"No, I assume she will blend in with the guests. It is a masquerade. There was no reason to—"

"You should have told me." Not waiting for her answer, I strode for the exit and searched for relief in nature.

CHAPTER 5

Arianna

The unsettling sound of violinists tuning their instruments coursed through the air. I traced a finger along the shimmering crystals on the gown. It hung on the golden rack, and the wire hanger bent under the weight from the detailed beadwork. I should have been ready, since the Terrells expected me downstairs in half an hour. My engagement ball tonight felt like the last nail in my coffin, and I couldn't stomach stepping into that dress to seal my fate.

Instead, I sat on the velvet bench beside the window and watched as the sun descended behind the rolling hills that dotted Daviel. The sky turned beautiful shades of violet and pink, and the vibrant colors stretched beyond the knolls that would soon succumb to the darkness. I pressed my forehead against the glass, and a chill crossed through me, despite the temperate weather.

My vision strained as the last whispers of light faded away. I needed to prepare. Instead, I opted for procrastination. My gaze shifted toward anything but the awaiting garb. I took in the gaudy bed and the pink perfumed rugs, then settled on the words freshly carved in the door frame. The Aralian disciples had cast the suppression spell on the suite before my arrival. It acted as a symbol of their blessing on my upcoming nuptials. My heart pounded and my palms grew sweaty as the gravity of my decision to wed Theo came into sharp focus in this rose-colored prison.

Downstairs, below my room, the chatter of arriving guests pulled me to the present. Their boisterous greetings mixed with the calibrating violins created an eerie tune. My skin crawled at the disjointed sound which mimicked my barely tethered feelings. I wrung my hands, attempting to soothe myself, but a knot formed in my throat, threatening to choke me.

A knock sounded on the door, and Naomi entered. "Why aren't you ready?"

For a moment, I gaped at her. She was lovely, clad in a crimson gown. Her golden locks were woven in an elaborate design. She possessed a beauty that would break many hearts, yet agitation rolled off her.

"No one came to help you? With the coin being poured into this farce of a celebration, Mr. Terrell should have hired you a lady's maid," she said.

My lack of a servant didn't surprise me. Even the modiste refused to see me in person, preferring to create gowns from the measurements Mama provided.

Naomi closed the distance and removed the dress from the hanger, then held it before me. This bedazzled garment felt akin to a costume, showing that I blithely accepted my plight.

However, since we'd already received my bride price, there was no retreating. Resigned, I lowered my robe and stepped into the gown. The expensive blue fabric made my eyes sparkle with an unaccustomed vibrance. Naomi worked her fingers over the row of buttons, binding me to my destiny.

She stepped back. I caught my reflection in the window. The satin clung to my thin frame, hiding my bony figure and making me appear more like a blossoming lady than a frail woman.

"What do you think?" I asked, pivoting toward her.

"What do I think? This entire evening is ludicrous. Do the Terrells really believe they can hide your curse in plain sight with a masquerade? What is more ridiculous than this ball is your unflappable insistence on marrying Theo."

We'd had this conversation ad nauseam over the past few weeks. I skirted around the truth, but she was persistent. Yet she didn't realize that Mama saw me as nothing more than a bartering piece. My feelings were irrelevant. However, I would serve as the sacrifice for Naomi's future. Even though a sliver of me longed for freedom.

I repeated my mantra internally. *This is the right choice. This is the right choice. This is the right choice.*

Marrying Theo was the right choice. Mama would no longer view me as the harbinger of doom who brought misfortune upon her. Instead, I'd darken his home, and perhaps he would get far more than he bargained for. As a cursed bride, I was the blight he chose.

The violins struck a mournful note, punctuating the silence that settled between Naomi and me.

"He is vile, and you hate him." Her lips pulled into a frown, and her cheeks flared with a tinge of red. She held my stare and heaved out an exasperated breath.

"Please. This is already hard enough without you chiding me for my decisions. I can't remain at home, a spinster draining Mama's dwindling savings. At least here, I'll eventually be the mistress of this estate. I'm certain there is a library here where I can spend my days lost in books. Don't worry. Theo will grow bored and leave me alone. I suspect him to venture out to Hallowhaven by spring for some torrid affair with a stranger."

I hugged her, attempting to comfort both of us. She remained rigid in my arms. Her shoulders rose and fell with indignation. Eventually, she relaxed, her body capitulating to my embrace.

"I won't be able to change your mind, will I?" she asked.

I shook my head, the soft curls bouncing about. She pushed out an exasperated sigh. "Fine, let's get this over with. Sit, and I'll fix your hair."

I moved to the vanity and sat. She wove my dull blonde tresses into an intricate pattern. However, there wasn't relief in our silence as she pinned crystals into my locks. My mind dwelled on my future in this place with Theo as my warden. I kept the swell of tears that threatened at bay, unwilling to show Naomi the internal battle that raged within me. She secured the final adornment and stepped back, her head cocked to the side.

"Shall we?" she asked. No joy filled her gaze, but she plastered on a smile.

"Give me a few moments."

She pursed her lips but didn't argue. The door shut behind her. In my solitude, in this rose-colored nightmare, I granted myself the smallest moment to wallow in the truth. I picked up the new mask, a gift from the Aralian disciples, and hurled it across the suite. It clattered to the floor, and the smooth porcelain face stared at me from the carpet. It mocked me. The mask and suppression spells were unbreakable, while the only thing broken in this room was me.

CHAPTER 6

ARIANNA

"CONGRATULATIONS ON YOUR UPCOMING nuptials," a man with streaks of gray peppered through his dark hair said.

I nodded in acknowledgment. He paused as if to speak more, but another gentleman pushed forward in the receiving line, replacing him.

Guests greeted Theo and me with the same hollow felicitations. My ears rang from the revelers' chatter. Their voices bounced off the high ceilings, causing my head to pound. Sweat beaded along my back from the body heat of the crush.

Theo smirked beside me, unaware or uncaring of my discomfort. His inky hair was slicked, and his green irises shone through the half-domino mask. He grinned at the ladies, who fanned themselves to hide their flirtatious glances. They obviously thought him handsome. He had high cheekbones and an olive complexion that matched his mother's. However, his almost delicate features made him more menacing, like a monster who lived in the skin of a striking boy. I blinked as yet another guest shuffled in front of me, jarring my awareness back to this endless reception.

An hour later, the last attendee strode into the ballroom, and silence fell over the foyer. I should have felt relief. Instead, nervous energy prickled along my spine as Theo smirked at me. Mama fiddled with her fan on my other side.

"Only half of those we invited from Hallowhaven have come. How am I to gain influence with a mere fraction of the noblemen here?" Mr. Terrell exclaimed through gritted teeth. His jovial smile pulled into a thin line. Theo flinched beside me, taking a step toward me and away from his father. My stomach soured at the closeness and the scent of spirits that rolled off him.

Mrs. Terrell soothed her husband, but their words were indiscernible to my hazy mind. An ache blossomed in my skull. I swayed under the weight of the beaded gown and the pressure of this evening's expectations.

"Excuse me. I need fresh air." I hurried away without waiting for a response.

"My apologies, Fletcher. Arianna is unaccustomed to large crowds and conversing with strangers," Mama tittered behind me, her cheerfulness blatantly feigned. Though I sensed her icy glare, I hastened, ignoring her remark.

I entered the ballroom, and its opulence hit me. The gold-crusted wallpaper twinkled, and the marble floors gleamed. The Terrells' garish manor was a sign of their desperation for acceptance by the upper crust. Swirls of colors overwhelmed me as I swerved past women in lavish gowns and men in crisp formal attire. They ignored my petite frame as I wedged through the clusters of people.

There were too many people here. At least I blended in—just one in the sea of masked revelers. The gaudy room gleamed under thousands of candles. However, this dreamlike scene felt akin to a nightmare. Laughter bubbled from a gaggle of ladies, and groups formed, their conversations cresting over each other, causing my pulse to surge. I needed to escape.

I snuck out the side door. A breeze laced with the sweet smell of roses soothed my fraying nerves. The shadows consumed me as I rushed to the balcony railing for balance. I clutched the edge, and the cool stone beneath my fingers anchored me. I forced my breathing to calm. With each heartbeat in this empty space, the panic lessened.

Minutes passed in solitude, but I couldn't hide here forever. Resigned, I straightened and willed myself to return. Yet the air caught in my lungs as a person pressed against me. I gasped as they wrapped an arm around my waist, pulling my body into theirs. I squirmed to free myself from the possessive grasp, but it was to no avail.

"What a smart pet you are, to run off where no one will see us," Theo whispered. Distress seized me.

"Please don't. Anyone could come out here." It sickened me that my intentions for venturing outside were wildly misread.

"You expect me to wait to play with you? The exquisite toy my father purchased for me and wrapped like a pretty present." His tongue glided over the shell of my ear. "Maybe I should bend you over right here and claim you."

I struggled against him, wriggling my shoulders, trying to break out of his clutches. With each futile attempt, my energy dwindled. His vise grip tightened. My soul cried to the goddess, to the gods, to whomever would listen. I didn't want this, and I didn't want him.

"I hoped you had some spirit."

Already fatigued, I was too weak to fight him off. He spun me to face him with ease, then pressed me against the rail, trapping me between him and the cold stone. He licked his lips.

I wiggled in a final attempt to escape, but I was no match for him. His hot breath reeked of whiskey, making my nose wrinkle. I had avoided his advances for years, claiming my chastity as a gift from Aralia that only my husband could claim. As his intended, my past argument was now futile. My stomach dropped as I realized my terrible miscalculation. I closed my eyes, unable to watch my fate unfold before me.

Suddenly, his weight pressing against me ceased. I let out a ragged breath of relief. When I opened my eyes, I gasped. A man stood between Theo and me. My rescuer's shoulders rose and fell, and he expelled a rattled exhale. His righteous indignation was almost palpable.

"How dare you?" Theo yelled.

I gaped at the unflinching stranger. His raven locks curled at the nape of his neck, and his trimmed black coat clung to his broad back, blocking my view. I peeked around him as Theo lunged. The man placed his hand on Theo's shoulder, halting his forward movement.

"The lady isn't interested in your advances. Best be on your way. We wouldn't want anyone to get hurt," the stranger said.

Theo flinched, and his lower lip quivered. To my surprise, he muttered something inaudible. The stranger let go, and Theo scurried away. My rescuer didn't move until the door swung open, slamming into the wall, and my betrothed disappeared into the crowd.

The adrenaline that had surged through my veins moments prior dwindled, and fatigue seized me. I teetered, unable to hold my weight, then leaned against the ledge for support. I summoned the dregs of inner strength. I should have thanked my savior, but words eluded me. Sadly, his valor served as nothing more than a temporary reprieve. Theo would find many ways to express his ardor for me once I became his wife. The realization caused bile to burn in my throat, and the meager contents in my belly threatened to expel from me.

"Are you going to be all right, miss?" The man's voice cut through the terror, soothing me. Like warm honeyed tea easing my anxiety.

I willed myself to my full height. The man was far taller than I. He stared down at me and the flicker of dim candlelight caught in the gold flecks of his irises. My unsteady knees trembled. How could this be? I would recognize those eyes anywhere; they brimmed with the same compassion as when he stopped me from falling. I had buried that memory in the recess of my mind, but in my weakest of moments, that brief kindness had stirred a longing within me better left forgotten. Yet here the stranger was, protecting me again, despite my curse.

I took in the black mask adorned with gold leaves. It completely covered his face, but I suspected who was beneath. For a heartbeat, I forgot about the pain, the ball, and my betrothed. "Thank you, I—"

"Arianna, oh." Naomi stepped onto the terrace. She froze for a second before she continued. "Sorry, but it's time for the first dance."

Yet I didn't look at my sister. Nor did my legs heed her request. I remained still, staring at this mysterious man. The red of her dress broke my trance as she approached. She yanked me out of my stasis, then guided me into the crowded ballroom. Despite my desire, I dared not glance back at my rescuer. Instead, I focused on my steps toward Theo, readying to face his wrath.

CHAPTER 7

SILAS

I CLENCHED MY JAW and gripped the rail where the woman had been pinned. The urge to hurt the rake who had touched her churned within me. However, it was unwise to draw attention to myself, even if my mask made me unrecognizable.

I gazed into the night and inhaled, the sweet scent of roses filling my nostrils. A breeze wafted through the air, cooling my fury. I flexed my fingers, and a smudge of marred stone laid beneath them. The onyx ring I wore gleamed in the moonlight, a reminder that I must remain in control at all times. However, I couldn't shake the primal rage at seeing her in such a precarious situation.

Arianna. Gods, I would recognize those eyes anywhere. They were the same ones that had haunted me since my arrival in Krella. I exhaled, pushing out my vehemence, but the whispers of anger remained.

"Silas, there you are. Why are you hiding out here? Too afraid that I'll force you to dance? Don't worry. I know you have two left feet."

I turned to view Beatrix, yet no coherent words formed on my lips. She beamed and closed the distance between us, her violet dress swishing from her hasty steps.

"Did you hear me?" Her smile slipped as she assessed me and tilted her head, unable to read my hidden expression.

"I'm fine. Just needed some air," I said, not wanting to worry my sister.

She sparkled with merriment, and I dared not dull her excitement. Instead, I walked past her and into the crowd. She called out after me, but her voice was lost in the clamor.

I settled in an alcove, tucked away from the revelers. Irritation swirled under my skin as a gaggle of women adorned in gaudy dresses flirted with gentlemen just beyond my hiding spot. I gritted my teeth in frustration at their simpering laughter, tempted to leave this wretched place. Then my focus caught on Arianna. I froze as she stood beside the rake in the center of the dance floor. The hairs on the back of my neck prickled, and a bitterness laced my tongue. A hush fell over the room.

"Welcome, honored guests and friends. Thank you for joining us to celebrate my son Theo's betrothal to Ms. Arianna Park. They will commence the festivities," a bulky man I assumed to be Mr. Terrell said.

He signaled to the string quartet in the room's corner. Music filled the space, and I tensed as Theo swept her into his arms, ushering her through the waltz.

My glare burned into her betrothed, but he was unaware of my ire. He clutched Arianna possessively, pulling her in too close for propriety. The action caused me to clench my jaw hard enough to break a tooth. A footman passed by, serving wine. I grabbed a glass, shifted my mask, and downed the contents in one gulp. However, the sweet liquid didn't quench this visceral reaction. I couldn't look away as he rushed her through the steps with little grace, the movements charged with his earlier intent. With each agonizing minute, my grip on the goblet tightened, the cut crystal indenting into my fingertips. Finally, the song reached its climax, then faded off. Arianna's intended kissed her hand and released her to a man waiting in the wings for the next set. Yet I felt no relief.

Instead, I remained transfixed by her as she floated through the waltz like a spirit in a dream. I bristled in the shadows, and time quickened with my heartbeat. Unsettled, I feared spiraling out of control if I continued to watch her. I needed to leave. As another server passed by, I placed the glass on his tray.

Yet I found myself stalking toward the center of the ballroom. The violins crescendoed, signaling that the song would end soon. In my haste, I bumped into patrons, my body moving of its own volition. Ladies whispered behind their fans. They mused over me, likely curious about my intent and mysterious identity. I ignored their chatter, cresting the edge of the dance floor just as the music ended. I stepped in front of a balding gentleman waiting nearby for his set with her, positioning myself as her next partner. I stood far too close to Arianna. Her skirts rustled when she pivoted to me, her pupils dilating as she took me in.

"May I have this dance?" To my surprise, the question tumbled from my lips. I bowed and awaited her answer.

Her expressions were unreadable beneath the porcelain mask. A pang of empathy reverberated within me. What discomfort she must have suffered, bearing that gruesome contraption for hours on end without reprieve. All the while, the attendees ate, drank, and reveled. They paid no mind to Arianna.

"You may."

I took her hand and secured her against me. The violins struck a somber tune. We spun through the steps. Her blonde curls shifted from the quick motion, and a hint of lavender enveloped my senses. The air crackled with an unexplainable intensity as we swept through the waltz. I held her gaze, but even I sensed the murderous scowl from her betrothed. She glanced at him, where he was seething from the sidelines. She trembled. Fear radiated off her and into my bones, as if I shared in her pain.

"Are you all right?" I asked.

She remained silent, yet her shoulders rose and fell in quick succession. Regardless of being mere strangers, I wanted to soothe the storm that roiled within her sky-blue eyes. I drew her closer, caging her in my protective embrace. Her breathing steadied, but I lost myself in the unfathomable depths of her gaze, as if she were gravity itself, keeping me from drifting away. She mesmerized me. My soul compelled me to speak, and the words tumbled from me. "Let me help you. I can show you the way to freedom."

Arianna

"Let me help you. I can show you the way to freedom."

My heart raced at his statement. How could I ever wish for freedom? This evening sealed my fate to become the bride of Theo Terrell. Yet he held my gaze, the amber of his irises glowing amid the too-bright room. The gossiping guests fluttered in my periphery, becoming streaks of vibrant colors, then nothing but a distant memory. Even the music became muted. All I could hear was the stranger's heartbeat. In his arms, time stood still, and I relaxed in his protective hold.

Trust him, something whispered deep within me. Hadn't he already come to my aid not once but twice, despite my curse? I shouldn't trust him, but I did.

"Meet me in the gardens."

I flushed as his hot breath tickled my ear and the warmth of his touch soaked through my gown, melting me to my core. Before I could speak, the last note ended. Reality snapped back into sharp focus.

He bowed over my hand, then released it. He didn't wait for my answer before he pushed through the crowd. I remained unmoving as he disappeared from sight, my body frozen to the spot.

Someone grabbed my wrist, breaking my trance, and yanked me into the throng. My heart pounded in terror as I stumbled from the suddenness of the movement. My dress caught around my feet, and I bumped into a woman, causing her wine to slosh. I whipped my head to Theo, who was pulling me through the crowd.

"You said you didn't know him. You lying bitch," Theo sneered.

"I don't."

He had peppered me with questions about the stranger during our dance. He seethed, assuming the man to be my lover, yet even he realized the absurdity of the claim. I vowed that my rescuer was indeed no one to me, and I had no clue about his identity.

Unsatisfied by my answer, Theo gripped me tighter. I shrank under the pressure of the pain that would likely bruise. His fingers dug deeper into my flesh, and panic flooded me. I winced as the mask seared into me, triggered by my fraying nerves.

"I believe you owe me this set." Naomi's voice cut through the tension. I attempted to pivot but couldn't. Theo's hold anchored my body. "Or more accurately, your parents have insisted. We don't want to disappoint them, do we?" She gestured to the Terrells as they glared at us from across the hall, likely having watched the scene unfold. Whether her interference was because of their concern or their desire for a scandal-free engagement, I didn't know or care.

Theo cocked his head toward them. His father sneered in disapproval. His breath hitched, and he released me instantly. He stepped back. His focus wasn't on me, but on his father. His brows were knitted together, and for a heartbeat, he appeared younger than his twenty years. Akin to a boy awaiting a harsh punishment. Those near us spoke in hushed tones, soaking in every detail of the argument for future gossip about the pauper's son marrying the cursed girl. He returned his attention to us, that brief glimpse of a trembling child was replaced with a fuming man. He grabbed Naomi's hand. Her fingers turned white under the pressure of his hold as he took his frustration out on her. Naomi appeared unfazed by his brutality, plastering on a serene smile, but her blue eyes flared with hatred. I flinched as he pulled my sister away. Her ability to handle any circumstance baffled me, but I didn't have time to dawdle.

I weaved through the guests toward the exit. Something in my soul beckoned me to venture into the gardens. Despite my better judgment, I left to find the stranger who promised freedom.

CHAPTER 8

SILAS

HIDDEN NEAR THE GARDEN entrance, I waited for her. The path we would take lay ahead of me, with arches of white roses to usher us into the darkness. I shifted on my feet in impatience as music drifted from the ballroom. Had I lost my wits? Duncan didn't know the truth, nor did Agnes, Peter, or Mrs. Potter.

My reeling thoughts halted as Arianna descended the stairs and an eerie thrumming pounded in my chest. She glided like a goddess surrounded by glimmering stars. I couldn't help but watch her as she walked into the garden. Compelled by her, some persistent instinct overruled my logic. *Show her who you are.*

I emerged from the shelter of the shadows. She gasped but steadied herself and smoothed her hands over the beaded dress. Without glancing back, I followed the trail leading away from the manor. Her heels clicked behind me in quick succession, and I slowed my long stride.

Moonlight filtered through the trees, dimly lighting the way. The music drifted off, replaced by her labored breathing. A gentleman would have offered his hand to assist her, but I didn't. I teetered between certainty and terror as I battled with my internal struggle. *Show her,* my inner voice insisted, repeating in a never-ending loop.

A gazebo came into focus, surrounded by ancient oaks providing cover. Soft candlelight served as a beacon for couples searching for a secluded spot for an interlude. I cared little for such frivolities. No, my blood boiled from containing this suppressed secret. It clawed to be released, as if it controlled me.

"Stay here." I held out a hand, halting her forward motion to follow me. I entered the pavilion. Turning to her, I removed my mask and clutched it.

She waited at the entrance. I exhaled, wishing I could see her expression as I revealed this truth. My rattled brain wasn't in control. No, an impulse far greater than I ever felt compelled me to act. Unable to stop myself, I summoned what lurked within me.

Arianna

A breeze flowed over me, cooling my flushed skin. I took in his familiar face and a twinge of a smile tugged on my lips, rubbing against the porcelain that hid my satisfaction. Would this man help me find freedom? How did he know my deepest desire? A hope I had buried sparked anew. I spun my engagement ring, waiting for him to explain, but he said nothing. He furrowed his brow. His shoulders rose and fell in a steady rhythm.

The atmosphere stilled, crackling with a pressure akin to a forming lightning storm. The candles flickered in response to the friction filling the space. My chest tightened as time slowed. Fear swelled in my belly, but my instincts whispered *trust him.*

His once unblemished olive complexion transformed, as if ink rushed through his veins, painting jagged lines where his blood pulsed. With each heartbeat, the transmutation crawled along his flesh, racing up his neck and covering his face. I gulped back bile, and a shiver of terror settled in the pit of my stomach. He closed his amber eyes, and when they reopened, they were bottomless pits of black. A smoky aura wrapped around him. I no longer beheld a handsome stranger, but a man harboring a devastating power.

Goddess, help me. I should have run, yet I remained paralyzed. *Trust him*, my soul cooed. I now felt foolish for leaving the ball with him and entering this isolated area where no one would hear my pleas. Apparently, my instincts were not toward self-preservation. Perhaps he planned on liberating me from my plight through death. A maddening laugh bubbled in my throat. I hadn't expected to be murdered.

"Arianna." My name rolled off his tongue. The timbre of his tone contained an otherworldly quality. It soothed my jagged fears. "We are the same. I am cursed, too. Don't be afraid. I won't harm you."

My breath hitched. We were the same? Cursed? Was this how I appeared that day when I became a monster? How was this possible? Before I could form coherent sentences, he exhaled, extinguishing the darkness, which dissipated into the air.

He blinked, returning his gaze to shades of golden brown. His once marred skin smoothed to his sun-kissed complexion; his veins no longer drenched in ink as he returned to normal.

How could this be? Didn't he fear he would destroy everything around him? Our curse was akin to unstable dynamite, ignited by the faintest of negative emotional triggers. That was why we needed the suppression spells, but he walked this world unincumbered.

My legs wobbled like a harvest pudding, but I forced myself to approach the stranger. A cascade of questions flooded me, but only one formed on my lips: "Who are you?"

His stare darted past me as I, too, heard the scuffling of boots approaching. He lifted his hand and snapped wisps of crackling energy, smothering the candles. He grabbed my wrist and yanked me into the shadows. I yelped in surprise, staggering in tow.

"Shh."

We crouched behind the bench at the rear of the gazebo, consumed by the night. His hot breath tickled the nape of my neck. I inhaled his untamed scent. It was similar to the groves on the outskirts of Krella, with a sweet undertone intertwined. Chamomile, perhaps?

"Someone's coming," he whispered, causing a shiver to snake along my spine. I resisted the urge to lean my weight against him, but my legs burned from this uncomfortable position. I swayed. He wrapped his arms around me, pulling me against him. His heartbeat pounded in my ear. I stiffened as footsteps approached.

"Arianna! Where are you? Playing hide-and-seek?" Theo's voice boomed through the quiet. I flinched.

"Arianna!" Theo seethed.

Wood creaked under his boots. I counted his steps, each one coming nearer to where we hid behind the high-backed bench. *One...two...three.* I burrowed deeper into the stranger's tightening embrace. A branch snapped in the distance. Theo stopped, looming only feet away. I held my breath.

"Ready or not, here I come." Theo stomped off.

I trembled against the man until Theo's agitated growls faded. In the stillness, he lowered his lips to my ear.

"My name is Silas. Silas Belmont."

He released me, and despite the temperate weather, I felt cold without the warmth of his touch. Standing, he offered a hand and assisted me to my feet. My fingers lingered in his, and my pulse thrummed as I attempted to search his face. Shadows obscured his features, with only a hint of moonlight cutting across his gaze.

"I'll contact you. Speak of this to no one. Go." His command broke my temporary trance.

Without saying a goodbye, I fled, running along the trail, uncertain whether Theo would catch me and make me his prey. Adrenaline raced through my blood, fueling my frantic pace. I panted as light crested through the trees and emerged from the edge of the garden. Exhausted, I scrambled onto the patio. I leaned against the rail for balance, wheezing for long minutes. My vision swam, and reality tilted. Fatigue threatened to overtake me. The clicking of heels and the swishing of fabric kept me from falling into the sweet darkness.

"Oh goddess. What happened? I have been searching for you everywhere." Naomi's voice cut through my spiral into unconsciousness. I blinked up at her, sweat beading between my face and the mask. My gown clung to me from perspiration.

"Theo...he...and I...and then..." I gasped for air.

She rubbed soothing circles on my back as my pulse steadied. Finally composed, I wanted to elaborate but stopped, remembering Silas's words. *Speak of this to no one.*

"Theo was playing a twisted game with me, a more lecherous version of hide-and-seek. I somehow evaded him," I said. I shifted to stand, but my legs buckled beneath me. Naomi grabbed my elbow, hauling me up to my full height.

"Don't worry. I'll make excuses so you can rest in your room. Mama is too preoccupied with the festivities to notice your absence. She is bragging to her old acquaintances from Hallowhaven about the funds she will receive once you wed."

I leaned against Naomi for support. She guided me into the manor and through the crush of revelers. They were far more interested in their own pleasure to pay us any heed. Each step ached along the long trek to my suite. Relief filled me as I crossed the threshold and the mask clattered to the floor. I shooed her away, needing her to return to the ball to work whatever magic she possessed over Mama. As she closed the door, I peered down at the porcelain. It stared at me as if it wondered what choices I would make. Would I choose freedom or a life bound to the rules I had grown accustomed to?

CHAPTER 9

ARIANNA

THESE PAST THREE DAYS, since returning home, had dragged on. I had little to occupy myself as I waited for Silas to contact me. In need of distraction, I curled up on my bed with my favorite novel and flipped to a riveting chapter. However, instead of focusing on the words, my mind drifted for the hundredth time to him.

Too preoccupied to read, I lowered the book to my chest, where my heart thundered. I closed my eyes and slipped into daydreams of being in Silas's embrace. My body melted into my bed, and I could almost feel his warmth. I shouldn't have dwelled on the unlikelihood that he would indeed reach out, but he had ignited a spark of hope within me.

However, these reveries triggered an onslaught of dread. Theo had come so close to discovering us. I had eluded my betrothed by leaving the morning after the masquerade ball. According to the gossiping staff, he had passed out drunk from the festivities. Soon, there would be no avoiding him. A shiver cut through me. Unwilling to dwell any longer, I lifted the novel and relaxed into the familiar story.

Half an hour later, harsh steps bounded up the stairs and pierced through the comfortable silence. My door flung open. I flinched, causing the book to tumble out of my grasp.

"Come with me," Mama said, then rushed away with a frantic energy.

I stood, grabbed my mask, and followed her without protest.

"A new customer is coming, and your sister hasn't returned from the village. Prepare a tea tray."

I scurried past Mama as she muttered to herself and rushed about the parlor. She shuffled through the clutter, gathering the items she needed for the appointment. Customers entering our home had become a common occurrence over the last year since Father died. Her seamstress work had barely kept us afloat through the lean months. However, the savings had now dwindled to nothing more than a handful of Aralian crown, with hardly enough for two weeks' worth of food during winter.

I stepped into the kitchen. The kettle sat on the wood-burning stove as the fire roared beneath. I searched through the hutch for suitable unchipped cups but found none. Instead, I settled for one with a minor flaw on the bottom. I reached for the metal canister and wrinkled my brow at the sparse contents. With any luck, this mystery client would likely provide us with funds to at least restock the dwindling supply. I scooped the last of the leaves into the tea strainer. A knock sounded at the entrance. The front door creaked open.

"Hello. Come in. Come in," Mama said.

"Thank you. It was so, so fortunate that we met at the Terrells' masquerade," a chipper woman's voice said, followed by the rustling of skirts.

The kettle whistled, and I completed my task of preparing the refreshments. With the meager offerings in hand, I walked to the parlor.

The woman came into view. She stood a head above my mother. Her smile was bright and accompanied by rosy cheeks, making her appear good-natured. She wore her black hair in an immaculate chignon, and her moss-green dress accentuated every curve of her full-figure. The detailed embroidery along the soft fabric highlighted not only her wealth but her tailor's skill, giving me pause. Why, then, was she here for alterations? Based on the stitchwork, her tailor looked to be a painstaking perfectionist. I studied her, and a prickle of recognition pulled at me. Did I know her? Perhaps she had attended my engagement ball. However, her cheerful demeanor and elegance would make her difficult to forget.

"Hello, you must be one of Mrs. Park's daughters." She tilted her head, but she didn't flinch with unease. Nor did the warmth leave her smile. She reacted differently from those who viewed me for the first time.

"I am her eldest, Arianna." I lowered the tray to the small table between the sofa and the chair. Then I glanced sidelong in search of Mama, who spoke with a footman.

"I believe we are near the same age." The woman approached me.

I poured the weak brew, unsure of how to answer. She could be in her mid-twenties, yet she possessed a confidence that I lacked, making her seem older.

"It has been lonesome since I moved here. There are so few young ladies of our stature here," she said.

"We don't have any sugar, but I have strawberry preserves, if you would like." I avoided the topic of the village because I had no clue about the people of Krella. I spent my days sequestered in my room. I only left our farm on the rarest of occasions.

"Plain will do."

I turned to hand her the beverage. She didn't take it, but she beamed and stepped closer. I searched her face and swore that I had met her somewhere.

"Perhaps we could be friends?" she asked, undeterred by my lack of conversation.

I peered at her in deep confusion. Why did she want to be friends? She likely possessed a morbid curiosity. Some, like Theo, were obsessed with Aralia, and they believed my curse connected me to the goddess. I remained silent, but she continued to prattle on, ignoring the tea I attempted to give her.

"I haven't made many acquaintances since I married Duncan. Fortunately, my older brother, Silas, has graced me with his presence."

Silas. My hands shook at the cursed man's name, causing the teacup to rattle on the saucer. Silas's sister raised an eyebrow. Her smile shifted to a mischievous grin.

"Arianna! Serve Mrs. Archer at once," Mama said through a clenched jaw. I forced myself to steady.

Realization dawned on me. She possessed the same nose, full lips, and bone structure as Silas. Their resemblance was uncanny. Though her eyes were not the same whiskey amber as her brother's. They were a deep brown, the color of rich, dark chocolate.

"Here is your tea, Mrs. Archer."

"I insist you call me Beatrix." As she took the cup, she slipped something into my palm, and I clutched the tiny folded piece of paper. Then she winked before turning her attention to Mama.

"Excuse me," I whispered, then hastened to my room for privacy. Mama's muffled apologies for my uncouth behavior and Beatrix's giggles floated behind me as I crossed the threshold of my quarters. The mask fell to the floor. I opened my fist and unfolded the letter in haste. My heart skittered as I read.

Arianna,

I can show you how to control your curse. If this is your desire, then send your response with Beatrix. She will serve as our cover by arranging for you to come for tea at Archer Estate. We must keep our training secret.

Silas

I rubbed my sweaty palms on my dress and gulped down the swell of emotions. My brain swam with indecision. Yet memories of his mastery played out in vivid detail. It was foolish to hope, foolish to dream, foolish to desire for more, but I did. *Trust him, trust him, trust him,* that nagging inner voice whispered.

I went to my vanity and grabbed a pen. My fingers trembled as my intuition responded for me. *Yes,* I wrote. I folded the paper, mimicking Silas's precise lines. I picked up the mask and re-secured it to my face. The steps groaned beneath me as I rushed downstairs. I entered the parlor.

The footman had brought in a trunk of dresses that Mama was sorting through beside the sofa. With her back to me, I headed toward Beatrix. She grinned conspiratorially, giving me her empty cup. Under the cover of the saucer, I slipped the note into her palm. She cocked her head in question, and I gave a nod of agreement.

"What about this one, Mrs. Archer? Perhaps some lace embellishment?" Mama spun and lifted the rose-colored garment. She furrowed her brow as she spotted me.

I busied myself gathering the used dishes and strode out of the parlor.

"Lovely idea. It is my favorite dress for tea. Speaking of tea..." Beatrix's words drifted off as I entered the kitchen, relieved that Mama was none the wiser to our schemes.

CHAPTER 10

ARIANNA

BUTTERFLIES FLUTTERED IN MY belly as I grabbed the soft gray day dress from the small cedar chest. Shaking out the wrinkles, I wished for something less bland than the simple frock for my meeting with Silas. Yesterday had been a whirlwind, beginning with Beatrix coming into our home as a client, and ending with Mama agreeing to allow me to join her for tea today.

The door opened, and I pivoted. I gaped as Mama entered. She rarely came into my space. My stomach dropped in fear that perhaps something terrible had happened. Was she revoking her permission for me to go to Archer Estate?

"Is everything well?" I clung to the gray dress. My heart pounded. Had she realized the ruse?

"It's fine. I'm going to help you prepare for this afternoon." She crossed her arms over her chest. Her discomfort at being around me rolled off her.

"Where's Naomi?" I asked, and neither of us moved.

She pinched the bridge of her nose. "She headed to the village this morning. Again. Some nonsense about her ailing best friend. She scurried off before she finished her chores, flighty girl."

Naomi had been venturing into Krella more often than usual, but I hadn't realized it until now.

The door clicked closed behind Mama. Her brow arched as she took in the frock in my hand.

"You can't wear that. Mrs. Archer is a fine lady with immaculate tastes. No, that will not do."

She squeezed past me and shuffled through the chest. My lips pulled into a tight line when she removed the blue gown I'd worn for my engagement dinner. It was the finest garment I owned, and it was woefully inappropriate for an afternoon tea. Yet I didn't argue with her. If I showed any sign of defiance, she would lock me in here.

I lowered my robe. It pooled on the floor, and I put on the dress. Her fingers moved along the row of shimmering buttons. I soaked in her touch. I couldn't remember the last time she had embraced me. It had been well over a decade.

She finished and stepped back, leaving me cold. "Sit."

I sat at the vanity, and she tugged my hair into submission. I fought the urge to wince. Despite the pain, her fingers weaving through my locks reminded me of when I was a little girl. She used to brush out my tangles and hum lullabies from her childhood. My reminiscing was short-lived, though, replaced by the harshness of reality.

"I know you think I am too hard on you, but given the circumstance of your curse, I am more than fair." She twisted a strand and shoved a pin into my scalp.

I studied her in the mirror. The wrinkles on her face had grown more prominent since Father's passing. Gray hairs streaked through her sable locks in thicker chunks. She let out a long, exasperated sigh, and focused her attention on my curls.

"Your curse has created complications. Yet I have prevailed by the grace of Aralia. I have worked a miracle in finding you a wealthy husband."

I shifted my gaze off Mama and to the vanity, where the dried flower Naomi had brought me from the fields rested. I held on to the memory of Naomi's smile as she presented me with the bouquet of colorful wildflowers in hues of pinks and purples. However, I couldn't escape into blissful reveries as mother continued.

"The opportunities for me are coming to fruition. This invitation proves that our family will hold honor in Krella. I'll no longer be a simple farmer's widow, but a lady of good standing once again. Like before I wed your father. What a stupid girl I was, marrying a frivolous man for love rather than money. You know, I feared his impulsive nature filled your blood, but being under the Aralians' supervision at least made you obedient." She returned to her ministrations with less vigor, and the ache in my scalp dulled to a tingle.

I bit the inside of my cheek, then plastered on a smile of placid acceptance. Silence dragged as she finished the last sweeps of the too-elaborate chignon.

"I am not allowing you to go today for your benefit, but for you to secure an invitation from Mrs. Archer for Naomi. Supposedly, her brother is the lord of a vast estate, and he is the overseer of the village of Presspin. It is located somewhere in the northern mountains past Daviel. The territory is not under Hallowhaven's sovereignty, and I hear they don't worship the goddess Aralia. Yet he is wealthy and obviously of a noble bloodline. He will make a fine husband for your sister." Her blue eyes held mine through the reflection, searching for my compliance.

I willed my expression to remain steady, but distaste arose in me at the thought of Naomi and Silas together. Despite the turmoil churning within me, I nodded, and a hint of a grin crested her lips.

"Good, I am glad we understand each other."

She didn't wait for a response before she left in haste. I picked up the mask that stared at me as if it had watched the entire interaction. I placed it on my face, the magic sealing it to my skin, and headed downstairs to await Beatrix's carriage. Mama hummed in the kitchen as I prepared myself to meet with the man she intended for my sister to marry.

CHAPTER II

SILAS

I HANDED THE LETTER for my steward, Vincent, to the servant and exited the library. I should have hastened to join the women in the sitting room, but I ambled the corridor instead. My mind raced. I vacillated, again, between helping Arianna and returning home to forget all about the impetuous behavior she stirred within me.

Though I felt compelled to train her, a pit of uncertainty gnawed in my gut. Would it be enough to give her these skills? I doubted it. My pulse pounded at the thoughts of her impending life, and memories of Theo's hands on her slipped into my mind, causing anger to swell. I clenched my jaw, which ached from the constant grinding of my teeth. Her future wasn't my problem, but I found myself drawn toward her at this juncture.

Laughter filled the corridor as I reached the sitting room and opened the door a crack.

"You are funny," Arianna said. "I'm curious. Tell me about Presspin."

"It is cold, dark, and covered in snow half the year." I froze.

Arianna regarded me. She looked ridiculous—here for mid-day tea but dressed in the blue evening gown—but still alluring. I gaped as her gaze locked on mine. A heartbeat passed, and she ensnared me again, like a fly to honey.

"Doesn't she look lovely today?" Beatrix asked, cutting through the charged silence with her biting tone.

"I can't train her in that," I said.

"Silas, sweet mercy. What is wrong with you?" Beatrix folded her arms over her chest, bunching the crisp fabric of her pink dress.

What was wrong with me? Arianna's presence unsettled me to my core. As if she were the harbinger of my destruction as well as the angel who would save me. I should have apologized, but I didn't.

"How am I supposed to teach her breath work when she's dressed for a formal dinner?" I strode to the chair across from the pair. I took a seat and resisted the urge to unbutton my collar. It was as if her presence made the air thinner and harder to breathe.

Beatrix's eyes narrowed to slits. "We can't have her return home now."

"It's fine. This was a mistake." Arianna sprung to her feet and scurried to the door.

"Wait," I said, surprising myself, as I stood, then strode to her. She was such a petite woman. Her head just reached my shoulders, and her willowy frame leaned more toward sickly than delicate. She paused with her hand on the knob, mere seconds from fleeing.

"There is much to discuss. We can go over some of the basic information about mastery instead. If you are not afraid, that is."

"The presence of fear doesn't equate to me lacking courage," she said and spun to face me.

The corner of my lip quirked in a half smile at the hint of her fighting spirit. My pulse quickened under the magnitude of her presence. I had capitulated to this force at the masquerade, which led us here. She intrigued me, but I feared this reaction she stirred in my soul. Beatrix cleared her throat, and we shifted our focus to her.

My sister gave me a knowing grin, and I glared at her. The morning after the ball, I had unburdened myself to her, but I had omitted the information about my closeness to Arianna in the gazebo. It had shocked her, almost as much as I had surprised myself, that I had revealed my most guarded secret. She hadn't even told Duncan because of the promise we made to our uncle on his deathbed. However, from the twinkle in her eye, she was already running amuck with romantic notions, which was likely why she'd helped. Yet I didn't begrudge her motives, since her clever brain had coordinated this ruse.

Arianna settled beside Beatrix as I sat in a chair across from them. My fingers unlatched the chain around my neck where I always wore my uncle's onyx ring.

"This belonged to our uncle. He, too, was cursed. The mask suppresses the curse within you, but the ring allows the wielder to siphon it while keeping us from being overwhelmed by the intensity of our power. Our darkness would become too volatile to control without a conduit."

I opened my palm to Arianna, and she leaned so close that if I wished, I could stroke the porcelain covering her face.

"Who taught him how to wield his curse? I didn't know this was possible until I met you." Arianna traced a finger along the onyx, and I held still at the featherlight touch.

"Ophelia," Beatrix said.

I closed my fist around the ring, almost catching Arianna's fingertips. She drew her hand back, and her pupils dilated.

"Who is she?" Arianna asked, turning her attention to my sister, who beamed.

I slipped my uncle's band into my pocket and slumped into the chair. My fingers thrummed against the floral-patterned armrest. I hated delving into this part of our lives, but Beatrix relished in the story of our uncle and his beloved.

"Many years ago—" Beatrix said.

I shifted in annoyance, a gruff sound leaving me.

"Hush, Silas. This is an important part of the story. Anyway, when our uncle, Oliver, was a young man, he lived in seclusion after our grandparents died. Our mother resided with our father in Hallowhaven. They wed prior and—"

I coughed, sensing her veering off track. Beatrix ignored me. As Arianna pivoted in her seat toward my sister, I watched her. However, that damn mask inhibited my ability to discern her. Did a smile pull on her lips at the story, or did she wrinkle her nose when she laughed? Gods, why did I care? Beatrix's voice cut through my ruminations.

"One day, he ventured into the woods and stumbled upon a woman. She lay near death, collapsed in the snow, and Uncle Oliver did not recognize her. In our town, it is rare for foreigners to venture into town, and the trek through the mountains is deadly during the winter. But he wouldn't allow anyone to suffer, not even a stranger. He possessed a kind heart and spent months taking care of her. A fondness formed between them. She had been a disciple of Aralia's but sought shelter in Presspin. As repayment for his kindness, Ophelia forged the ring for him. When we came to live with them after Silas's curse awoke, she made him a ring as well. Silas has never donned a mask."

My breath quickened, and memories laid siege, permeating through my mental defenses. My father's words floated through my thoughts on a loop: *A monster, boy, you are nothing more than a monster.*

I focused on the clock in the corner. I matched my breaths to the ticking, but the onyx against my skin heated. A sign that my unsettled feelings would fuel the devastation lurking within my body.

Waking nightmares flickered into existence against my will. *The clopping of hooves. The taste of ash on my tongue.*

I gulped down the fear I had felt as a child attempting to keep the darkness at bay as we traveled to Presspin.

I didn't want Beatrix to die. Not like—

"Silas."

I blinked at Arianna as she stared at me, her head tilted. Her mask smiled at me with a sickening grin, as if it knew the torment I suffered. Overwhelmed, I stood and made a beeline for the window. Tension churned as I took in the park's view. The stone steps led out to the lush yards brimming with fruit trees and dotted with flowers of every color. I would find peace by the pond later.

"Where is she now?" Arianna asked, but I could feel her stare on my back.

"She ran off one night without a word. About fifteen years ago," Beatrix said.

I attempted to ignore their conversation, focusing instead on the outside world. The leaves rustled in the wind, the shades of orange and red threatening the green hues as autumn neared. But the tight seal that held my memories at bay had loosened this afternoon, allowing them to spring free.

Uncle Oliver had gripped my hand. His once bronzed skin had grown sallow as illness claimed him. His cries for Ophelia rang within my ears as if he were here, calling her name from the great beyond.

Love had been such a foolish choice. When Ophelia left, Uncle Oliver had been a shell of the man he had once been. Even his warm smiles had hollowed. I wouldn't suffer a similar fate if I remained unfooled by the lure of romance.

"Silas?" Arianna's voice cleared the haze of my mind.

I pivoted to her, having been too lost in the past to notice her approach. She stood beside me, and her gaze searched mine with unspoken sympathy. I fought against being further mesmerized by her. I smoothed my demeanor to a stony expression and acted not as Silas, but Lord Belmont, who oversaw an entire territory.

"Tomorrow, I'll show you how to master breath work. It will strengthen your resolve when you're overwhelmed by negative emotions that may trigger your darkness. Hopefully, you'll be a quick study. We don't have time to waste."

Her shoulders slumped, and I regretted the words, but I needed to get control over myself. I brushed past her and called out, "And wear something more appropriate tomorrow."

"I am sorry. Silas can lack social grace, even though he knows better than to be rude." Beatrix's voice echoed along the hallway, loud enough for me to hear. A gentleman would return and apologize, but I was no gentleman; I was a monster.

CHAPTER 12

ARIANNA

HOOFBEATS CLOPPED ON THE drive of Archer Estate as the carriage rolled by, leaving me at the entrance. I froze at the carved, cream-colored door and traced my fingers along the swirling pattern in the wood instead of rapping. I took in the white-washed brick of the massive archway secured by pillars easily twice my height. The grandiose home touted modern updates, according to Beatrix. However, I had visited it once as a very young child and could say with certainty that the renovations made it feel washed clean of its previous charm. I gulped back the unease I'd felt since last night when Mama chided me for failing to secure an introduction to Lord Belmont for Naomi. Beatrix's invitation for tea brightened Mama's mood and strengthened her matrimonial hopes for my sister. I feared Mama might soon limit my opportunities to venture here if she didn't get what she desired. I raised my fist to knock but paused, wavering in my resolve. Perhaps it would be wise to return home. I was unsure of how to handle this taciturn version of

Silas, whose demeanor had been diametrically opposed to the man I met at my engagement ball.

With the carriage gone, I couldn't stand here all afternoon. I lowered my fist but connected with a broad chest and not the door. My cheeks heated, hidden by the thick porcelain. Like a fool, I didn't move my hand, which soaked in the warmth of the hardened flesh it pressed against.

"What are you doing?" Silas said as he brushed my fingers away as if I were an insect.

"Sorry," I murmured. I waited for him to allow me in, but instead, he stepped out and closed the door behind him.

"Follow me." He breezed past me and down the stone steps.

My lips pursed, rubbing against the porcelain, but my confusion slowed my brain's ability to process. Fixed to the spot, I gawked at him. Where was he going and why wasn't he dressed in his well-tailored black coat? No, today, he wore a linen tunic that clung to him. Tucked under his arm was a worn floral quilt. At the base of the steps, he stopped and pivoted to me. His appearance was akin to a roguish prince. He didn't flash me a charming smile but rose one eyebrow in impatience. I hastened to join him and followed in tow.

We weaved through the parks. The sweet scent of honeysuckle and gardenias floated through the gardens. Trees lined the trail, brimming with fruit ready to be harvested. Yet my focus wasn't on the beautiful scenery but on the whispers of glimmering olive skin peeking out from beneath the thin fabric of Silas's tunic. I took in his broad shoulders, the raven waves that ended at the nape of his neck, and the lean muscles of his back. My mouth dried, and a fascination with him blossomed inside me.

"Here." He halted, and I stopped shy of crashing into him.

He placed the quilt on the ground, which padded the damp grass. We'd trekked farther than I'd realized, having ventured out of the manicured gardens. We were now in a meadow encircled by dense maples, with neither a soul nor the manor in sight.

"Isn't Beatrix joining us?" I asked as I fiddled with my ring. The afternoon light caught on the diamond.

Silas's brows drew together as he settled on the blanket. "No, she won't be attending our lessons."

I opened my mouth to speak but decided against it. Resigned, I sat beside him and focused on the maple trees ahead and not on the handsome man next to me.

"To wield our curse, we must still our minds," he said, flicking a glance at me, unaware of how my heart raced because of our nearness.

I expected him to instruct me, but the only sound breaking the quiet was the breeze whistling through the leaves. I peered at him, searching for additional instruction. But his eyes were shut as he inhaled and exhaled in measured beats. His tense jaw loosened, and I studied his face as if the answers to stilling my mind lay in his features. They didn't, and I hadn't the faintest of ideas about how to achieve this peace he alluded to.

He blinked at me, and I snapped my gaze forward. He sighed and ran a hand through his hair, which rumpled the once immaculate locks.

"Concentrate on your breathing," he said. Then he returned to his mental exercise, ignoring me.

I did as he instructed, but nothing happened. Irritated, I squirmed, hoping a more comfortable position would help me. Unwittingly, my shoulder bumped into his arm.

"Be still," he bit out through clenched teeth.

This time, I attempted to mirror his breaths, yet the calm eluded me. I rarely found comfort in stillness. I often kept my mind occupied until the sweet release of sleep stifled the cacophony of my thoughts.

The noisy squirrels chattering in the branches above mixed with Silas's breathing. Minutes passed as I searched for serenity. Instead, dormant memories rushed forward. My body went rigid, and I clenched my fists, attempting to keep them at bay. In the sprawling silence, they multiplied, filling me with horror. Like cards being shuffled, they came out one by one at random. My fear of Theo ravishing me against the stone railing. The hours I wept alone after Father's death. My mother's ire. They crashed all at once. My stomach churned, and I gulped for air, drowning in my ruminations.

"Arianna." Irritation edged Silas's voice, startling me to the present. "You need to relax."

A maddening laugh escaped me, a reaction to the creeping panic, the nightmarish flashbacks, and his physical proximity. I pivoted to him, my knees knocking into his. He glared at me, his nostrils flaring.

"Relax? I haven't had a minute to relax since the Aralians bound me to this thing." The bitter truth rolled off my tongue.

His features softened, and he blew out an exhale. "Mindfulness can be difficult at first, but—"

"I don't understand. I'm just supposed to sit here?" My words came out clipped, and his body heat beside me felt akin to a furnace. My temperature and annoyance were climbing.

"We don't have time to argue. I'm leaving at the end of harvest, and you—you need to master control before then. Until you accomplish this, you will be bound to that damned contraption. Go find peace."

I shook, agitated by his sheer lack of understanding. Why did I think he would be any different from anyone else? He didn't understand me; no one did. The mask tightened as my frustration boiled and fatigue seeped into my bones. However, I held a withering stare, pulling from some dormant remnant of fighting spirit I'd thought long gone. I stood and stomped off, heading toward the house. The gravel path crunched under my boots. The chipper flowers leading back to the manor were too bright and joyous, given my anguish. Sticky tears dampened my cheeks, and I wished I could wipe them away.

"Wait," he called out. I hastened my pace, but he grasped my shoulder, stopping me. His soothing touch radiated into me, but I sagged in defeat. I would never be free. I had been wiser before I met Silas, resigned to my fate as a bride of the man-child in a rose-colored prison.

"Let me go; this is pointless."

With my back to him, I studied my worn boots; the toes were scuffed to a measure that no amount of polish would fix. They were like my life: damaged beyond repair. The past, the present, and the impending future overwhelmed me. I trembled as hot tears trickled from the edge of the mask down my neck. His warmth left me, and I expected him to leave me to my blubbering, but he spoke.

"I almost killed Beatrix when my curse awoke. My mother's death triggered it."

A pit gnawed in my stomach, hollowed out by the understanding of our similar histories. But I couldn't look at him, so I focused on the cobble trail ahead.

"We were happy once, living in Hallowhaven. My mother was lovely, and she held our family together. But when I was seven, the sweating sickness swept through the city, and she fell victim. Days prior, she had taken us on a picnic in the park. She'd woven crowns of flowers for Beatrix and me. But within a week of that cherished outing, she succumbed to the ailment and died in my father's arms. The shock of seeing her limp body and unseeing stare caused my agony to ignite."

"I am so sorry," I said. But I remained still, too afraid to view him while he shared.

"I remember little other than the horrific shrieks and the darkness leeching from me, destroying our home in Hallowhaven. I turned it to ash, and my father barely escaped with Beatrix in his arms. After my rampage, I saw the fear on Beatrix's face, and I took hold, wrestling the curse back into me. My father then decided Beatrix and I would live with our uncle."

I pivoted to him. As if lost in thought, he stared beyond me. A cloud loomed overhead, shading us under its gloom. Silence lingered, fraught with sadness. I couldn't let him wallow in this vulnerability alone.

"I was six. My mother almost died. My memory is just fragments of my awakening. The nursemaid weeping as she cradled Naomi. Mama shrieking. The blood, there was so much blood. I wanted so desperately to crawl into bed with her, but her sallow skin and wheezes gave me pause. Then she slipped into unconsciousness. The midwife shouted, Naomi cried, and I fled to my room. Then I snapped, and the curse awoke. The darkness leached from me. I can nearly smell the charred wood even now. Something whispered in my mind, clawing for release, but Naomi's cries anchored me. If Mama perished, she would need me."

I breathed out heavily from sharing one of my darkest moments. An ache burned in my chest, and the following words were bitter as I continued. "Time was irrelevant. It could have been minutes or hours, I don't know. My father fetched the disciple, and after she enchanted my quarters, she considered me lucky. I had only damaged the floor and the furniture. She said that the minimal destruction meant Aralia had blessed me with favor. My mother survived, but by sundown, I transformed from someone who was once cherished to a burden relegated to my spelled room."

His gaze held mine. My lips parted as my anguish loosened its grasp around me. A heaviness hung between us, filled with the sorrowful stories we shared. I felt relief. Piece by piece, he freed bits of me that had been locked away, and I doubted he realized the effect he had on me.

"I promise you, it is not hopeless. We can try again tomorrow." His shoulders fell, his words laced with the sadness coating both of us.

Did I possess the strength to continue? To dive deeper into my pain?

"The choice is yours," he said, sensing my hesitation. Without another word, we headed to Archer Estate.

CHAPTER 13

ARIANNA

SUNLIGHT STREAMED THROUGH THE canopy of trees surrounding us, warming me. How would the sun's warmth feel on my face? A memory of walking through the orchards before my sister's birth flickered. I could almost smell the scent of apples and sense the balminess on my forehead. I longed for the sun's caress instead of this porcelain. Hadn't that been why I returned? For the summer heat to radiate into me, to sip tea at the local shop, or to walk in the village without onlookers glaring.

However, last night, the suppressed memories I kept at bay chased me in my nightmares. This morning, I'd been unsure whether I would continue with my lessons, but my curiosity and desire beat out my trepidation. Despite the recklessness, a seed of hope had taken root, pushing me forward.

Silas shifted beside me on the quilt. He breathed in a steady cadence that soothed me. The silence today was not fraught with tension like yesterday. Somehow, a mutual understanding had formed in the shared vulnerability of recounting our most horrific memories. A gentleness had radiated off him as we walked to this spot, the harshness of his manners having evaporated.

This afternoon, I felt lighter. I had never spoken of my awakening with anyone, not even Naomi. By relinquishing this secret to him, I took a step toward freedom.

"I want you to close your eyes. I will guide you through the exercise to open your senses." His words were as gentle as a caress. I should have relaxed, but I stiffened, worried about the flashbacks.

"Close your eyes," he said again, unfazed by my hesitation.

Regardless of my apprehension, I did as he instructed. Sunlight warmed my hands, my hair, and my neck. The heat loosened my tight muscles, and my tense shoulders dropped. My palms rubbed over the blanket we sat on, and the soft texture soothed me.

"Inhale and exhale slowly. Release everything you have been holding. Ease your tension with each breath."

Minutes passed as I inhaled and exhaled. Oxygen flooded me, and my respiration found a cadence of its own—my heart beating in slow and steady measures. My muscles slackened and I relaxed.

"Open your senses to the world around you and release your burdensome emotions. Your fear, doubt, worry." His voice reverberated through me.

I surrendered my pain: the mocking stares of the villagers, Mama's harshness, Naomi's cracked fingers, and Theo's malicious smirks. One after another, my worries dropped from me like stones from my grasp. With each exhale, the unspoken weariness I lived under lessened. Tears flowed from me, washing the afflictions I carried away. I exhaled through the ache of sadness, allowing my despair to exist in this moment.

"You can let go of your burdens. You are safe here with me." His tone radiated compassion and anchored me.

I released my heartache until my sobs steadied. I exhaled, dispelling the discomfort until I no longer clung to the past. I absorbed the breeze rustling through the trees and the faint scent of chamomile and pine rolling off Silas. As I settled into the ease, his soothing commands ended and the subtle change in his breathing synced with mine.

In the silence, everything fell away. Time was irrelevant. I delved into myself, where my curse dwelled, visualizing its inky depths. I should have been afraid, but I wasn't. I dove into the vastness. Something tethered me to the outside world. This connection had always been present, though I'd never noticed before. A compulsive need to explore the limitlessness consumed me. I delved closer to the well of power beckoning me, yearning for complete submission. With each exhale, I advanced toward its siren call. But the cord to reality threatened to snap, causing my breath to hitch, and panic flooded me.

The abyss's once soothing embrace became ominous, and I searched for a way out. It sensed my turmoil. The darkness consumed me, turning heavy, as if black tar weighed on my soul. I gagged for air. I was suffocating. I couldn't see. All I could do was sink farther into the depth of despair. But the thread wouldn't allow me to submit under this weight as it dragged me to the present.

Gasping, my eyes flew open, and my senses assailed me as everything snapped into sharp focus. The gentle rustling of the trees turned into a harsh howl. The once soft sunshine blazed, and my skin crawled as if my blight was attempting to break free. The mask seared, and I feared the suppression spell would melt into my face. I cried in agony, pulling at it, trying to rip it off to no avail. I screamed, then collapsed. My fingernails dug into where the porcelain and flesh met. My brain boiled under the heat until nothing remained.

Silas

Shrieks cut through my soul, making my blood run cold. I whipped my attention to where Arianna sat beside me. She screamed in anguish, and she worked frantically to find purchase between her face and the mask. Angry red marks appeared along her chin. The stillness I'd felt seconds prior evaporated, and terror snaked down my spine.

"Arianna."

She collapsed and stilled. An unnerving silence replaced her screams. Even the once chipper birds stopped singing, as if they too watched in horror. My heart pounded. I reached for her, shaking her gently.

"Arianna!"

She didn't answer. I pulled her against my chest, but her head lolled and her blue eyes rolled back. A thick fog entered my perception, as if I were in a living nightmare.

"Arianna! Arianna!"

She lay as limp as a rag doll. A choking sensation clutched my throat. I placed my ear against the mask. There was nothing, no sound or trickle of heat to indicate life.

"Arianna." Her name came from me, like a guttural plea so tender it was unfamiliar to my ears. I stroked her arms, the worn material of her dress rubbing against my hands, but she remained eerily still. Something deep within me sparked an unrelenting compulsion to keep her safe. Then the scene before me crumbled, along with my sanity.

I stood and ran with her tucked in my embrace. The gardens whirled past me as I dashed through them, her head secured against me. Gods, she was so frail. My footsteps echoed through my addled mind as the ground beneath me changed from gravel to the marble floors of the manor. She needed to be all right. I promised her she was safe with me. I choked on a heartache so intense it burned. Reaching my room, I searched, hoping it possessed some sort of magic to revive her, but none existed here.

I lowered to the bed and cradled her. I rocked as if the motion could soothe me and coax life into her. My fingers grazed the wild curls that sprung from their braid. She didn't stir or breathe. Lifeless. A strangled groan escaped me, half plea and half guttural sob. My heart pounded and power pulsated within, attempting to break free from its internal cage. It could sense my despair and tempted me to relinquish my body to its desires.

Anguish consumed me, forcing the barely tethered control to unfurl like strands unraveling. I blinked as my vision heightened. I could no longer withstand the panic as my curse seized me, akin to a match setting the dormant fire ablaze. Darkness leached from me, moving of its own volition. Inky tendrils enveloped us both in a protective cocoon of shadowy current. A crackling energy emitted from me and crawled over her. I dreaded it would sizzle her flesh or turn her to ash. Yet it flowed over her and permeated the mask, as if it could resuscitate her.

"Please, please." My lips pressed into her hair. I choked on this raw emotion. I begged whatever god would listen with every fiber of my being for her to return to this mortal coil. Then a flicker ignited within me, as if I'd bargained a piece of my soul for her life.

A gasp pierced the air as Arianna's chest rose and fell. Shallow wheezes escaped from beneath the mask. I stroked the cool porcelain as I willed myself to steady. But relief did not come because consciousness continued to elude her. As I embraced her, the rhythm of her painfully slow breaths anchored me. Time became irrelevant. It could have been mere minutes or hours which passed as I held her against me, unable to release her, as if I tied her to this mortal plane.

Footsteps clicked from outside the haze that encompassed Arianna and me, pulling me for a heartbeat into reality. Yet as the steps grew louder, I growled with ferocity. Arianna's head bobbed as I yanked her closer in an attempt to shield her from whatever threat approached. My curse thrummed in response, ready to strike a killing blow to protect her.

"Silas!" Beatrix's voice pierced through this primitive instinct that possessed me. Unwilling to harm her, I used her presence to force myself to leash the unruly energy. I would not destroy her home again. I tethered myself to my past guilt and regained control. Long minutes passed until the shadowy cocoon that protected Arianna and me dissipated.

Luckily, the room remained undamaged. The bed suffered minimal issues, with only the blanket having been scorched under the crackling energy. The scent of charred cotton hit me, a reminder of how close I'd come to lighting this manor ablaze.

"What happened?" Beatrix stood rigidly in the center of the suite.

I struggled to ground myself. Sweat beaded on my forehead, and my brain throbbed from the whispers wanting to consume me. But Arianna was alive, and I clung to that knowledge almost as desperately as I held her.

"What happened?" Beatrix asked again, her tone gentle. She approached with tentative steps, and the fog in my mind continued to clear. She stood before the bed, concern written on her face. Tentatively, she stretched out a hand to Arianna. That primal instinct surged in me as I pivoted my shoulder, serving as a blockade between Arianna and Beatrix. A guttural growl pressed through my lips.

Frightened, Beatrix lurched back and stared at me. Apprehension lined her features. Yet my pulse raced, and I curled Arianna deeper into my embrace. I was too preoccupied with this primal desire to protect her to care about my sister's bewilderment.

"Let me see her," she said in determination. I hesitated, but she didn't relent. She held my stare, her jaw rigid as she waited for me to yield to her.

My knuckles blanched, but I exhaled and loosened my grip on Arianna. Pain flooded me as I laid her on the bed. I hovered only inches from her, unable to leave her side. Beatrix stepped beside me and assessed Arianna. Her mouth twisted in concern, and she grabbed her wrist. "Her pulse is weak. She needs help. A doctor, an herbalist, or an Aralian disciple—"

"No! I won't let them touch her!" I snarled over her as static buzzed in my ears and I reached for Arianna, tempted to curl her into me again.

"Fine, I'll tend to her, but you need to leave. Go. Get ahold of yourself," she said in exasperation.

I couldn't force myself away from Arianna. Yet black spots flickered in my vision. I worried I'd combust in an explosion of destruction. My skin ached from the strain of containing the devastation coursing through my veins.

"Go now!" she shouted, pulling me from my thoughts as I left Arianna's side. I dragged myself from my suite. The door slammed behind me, and as I leaned against it, my legs shook. I closed my eyes and grappled with the power that threatened to burn this entire house down to protect Arianna.

CHAPTER 14

ARIANNA

"ARIANNA...ARIANNA...ARIANNA." A VOICE BEGGED me to rise. However, I was exhausted from the weight of living. The weariness settled in my bones as I accepted my fate, ready to drift into the sweet nothingness that beckoned me.

"Please, please, please," someone mourned. The tether linking me to my mortal coil tugged against my ribcage and would not let me succumb to death. My heart swelled with life as the connection binding me to the world yanked me from the darkness.

I blinked, gazing at a dimly lit ceiling rather than the crisp blue sky I'd anticipated. Where was I? I shifted in the comforter that cocooned me in this four-poster bed. My fingertips grazed the blanket and caught on a scorched hole, and the mild scent of burnt cotton hit me. I rubbed my thumb over the charred fabric as I tried to remember how I ended up here.

An ember popping dislodged me from my thoughts. I attempted to sit to take in my surroundings, but my vision swam. A clammy, cold sweat washed over me. I collapsed onto the pillows and groaned. My tongue rolled in my dry mouth, tasting metallic.

"Sweet mercy, you are finally awake." A soft voice spoke from just beyond my field of vision. I dared not attempt to sit in fear of tumbling. Quick footsteps clicked against the wood floor, then Beatrix leaned over me. She didn't brim with effervescence but frowned. A sober aura consumed her lighthearted nature, causing a pang of worry to swell within me. Wordlessly, she pressed her fingers against my wrist. Seconds passed before her brow smoothed and a sigh left her.

"Thank the gods." She removed her hand but hovered like a nursemaid. She straightened the skewed comforter and tucked me in with fervor.

"What happened?" I asked as she stepped back.

A thick silence lingered. The rose-colored day dress she wore didn't match her somber mood. Instead of answering, she scurried off. The shuffling skirts forced me to heave myself into a sitting position. She fluttered about the suite, stacking books and papers neatly on a table beside a deep green fainting couch. Then she grimaced at an empty crystal snifter as she lowered it next to the other items in a tidy order. She muttered to herself, as if she were figuring out a challenging problem.

Minutes passed before she stopped mumbling. Then she released a heavy sigh, and her shoulders slumped. She returned to my side and straightened the pitcher on the nightstand. "You lost consciousness when you were training. Silas, he brought you here, and he..."

She shook her head and picked up a glass. Her lips pursed as she examined it. I inhaled, searching my mind for answers, but only darkness welcomed me. A shiver crawled along my spine, and I shuddered.

"Silas isn't making much sense since I found both of you." She placed the cup on the nightstand. "He's not acting like himself."

A whisper of a memory prickled but was unable to be unearthed. Questions popped into my mind in rapid succession. Why was I in this suite? Why did she appear out of sorts? Why had I slipped into unconsciousness? However, I couldn't piece the events together. My temples throbbed as a migraine formed. The mask heated against my skin, making my discomfort even more difficult to bear.

"He carried you here and—"

The door burst open, smacking against the wall. We flinched. A disheveled Silas barreled in, his hair askew and his eyes wild. His once crisp white tunic had wrinkled, and he had unbuttoned the collar. His countenance was not that of an aloof gentleman, but of a ruffled rogue. A frantic energy rippled off him as he approached. He stood next to the bed, and his gaze locked on mine.

"When did she wake?" He studied me. Raw tension leached off him, filling the atmosphere, and my pulse surged.

"You'd best calm down. We wouldn't want a repeat of this afternoon, would we?" Beatrix asked through straight-lined lips.

Silas pivoted to her and held her withering glare. A battle of wills crackled between them in this standoff. Whatever had transpired between our training at the meadow and now had caused a strain between the siblings.

Beatrix did not cower. Silas's shoulders shook as he relented, and his rough edge softened. He returned his attention to me, and an untamed intensity glowed in his amber irises. He took a ragged breath, and I flushed. Who was this man? Certainly not the terse teacher from earlier in the day. No, something had unlocked this primal pulse. I gulped, transfixed by him. The world around me became hazy as I searched his face for answers. For a heartbeat, I forgot about Beatrix's presence. But then her cough drew my focus.

"I have arranged for you to stay here tonight. I informed your mother that you stumbled and hit your head while we were strolling the gardens," Beatrix said.

I glanced at her but sensed Silas's intense stare on me. She crossed her arms over her chest as she studied us. What had occurred while I was unconscious? The friction between the siblings was palpable. However, I didn't have time to figure out the answers to these questions. I needed to return home immediately or Mama would be furious. My stomach twisted over the punishments that would await me if I remained here. They were unaware that my ability to attend tea had only been because of Mama's desire to snag an invitation for Naomi. She would not abide me staying the night.

"I have to go home." I flung the blanket off and attempted to stand. The world tilted at the sudden motion, and dizziness seized my senses. But before I could tumble to the floor, Silas's muscular arm wrapped around my waist, steadying me. I froze, caged in his embrace. Heat rushed through me, from embarrassment at my weakness and from the closeness of this man who, despite all reason, appeared concerned for me.

"You are not going anywhere." He secured pillows behind my back, propping me against them. He embraced me a second longer than was appropriate, and I held my breath at the surprising tenderness. Then he released me and sat on the edge of the mattress. "Do not get out of this bed. You are not well enough after..." He fisted his hand into a tight ball, then unfurled it as he exhaled. "After you...You are not to leave this spot. Do you understand?"

I nodded, unable to speak to this unaccustomed and fierce version of Silas. "What happened?" I whispered.

"Yes, please do explain," Beatrix said, wearing an unamused expression.

Without a word, he stood and began pacing. His footsteps were punctuated by his grumblings. Agitation rolled off this rattled man while he prowled the space. My eyes darted back and forth, following his frantic steps. Beatrix remained frozen in place, gnawing her thumb nail. Moments later, he stopped, then pivoted to us.

"It might have been your mask that caused the issue. I assume the suppression spell attempted to contain your curse. It must have put a strain on your body, and you...and you...fell into unconsciousness."

He paused and stared out the window. I tracked him with my gaze and gasped, registering the dark night sky.

Beatrix halted her nervous fingernail biting and smoothed her hands over her dress. She diverted her attention from her brother and onto me. "I have a guest suite prepared for you."

"No, she won't be leaving my bed." Silas whipped toward her with a scowl, but she did not cower at his domineering tone.

"Get a hold of yourself." She squared her shoulders and carried an edge of authority in her demeanor. She tilted her chin. "You can have the room instead. Your actions have already caused enough impropriety."

"I am not—"

Beatrix held out a hand, halting his argument. Silas clenched his jaw but remained silent.

"I'll give you a few minutes," she said. Then, without awaiting his answer, she left.

He vibrated beside the window with a tension like a pot seconds away from boiling over. He raked his fingers through his hair and huffed an exasperated breath. To my shock, he sat again, settled on the corner of the mattress near me. His demeanor softened in Beatrix's absence.

"How are you feeling?"

I gaped at him. My brain swam with an odd mix of confusion and fascination. I rubbed my fingers along where the mask and my flesh connected. My thumb grazed a deep scratch, and I winced.

"I'm confused and have a pounding headache."

He scrubbed a hand over his face, then lowered it to his chest. His brow furrowed, then smoothed, as if he had reached some decision. He unfastened the chain that secured his uncle's onyx ring. It gleamed in the candlelight, illuminating the etched lines of the ancient Aralian language similar to the wards that bound me.

"I should have done this hours ago." He grabbed my hand and slipped the ring onto my thumb. The mask released from me, and the heaviness I lived under lifted. The porcelain shell smothered into the blankets, no longer controlling me, nothing more than an adornment I despised.

I stroked my bare cheek. My lip quivered as tears threatened to fall. I hadn't been unbound from the suppression spells outside my room since childhood. Emotions flooded me: fear, joy, elation, terror. Panic overruled them all as memories of my destructive abilities took hold.

"Please, I don't want to hurt anyone."

"You won't." The mattress shifted as he reached over and poured a glass of water. "Drink."

He gave me the cup, and I gulped the contents. The liquid triggered an awareness as I felt the depths of exhaustion, hunger, and thirst crash over me.

"As long as you can remain calm, you won't trigger your curse. I promise I'll keep you safe."

He took the cup and returned it to its place. The motion caused him to inch closer to me. My heart thundered at his nearness. His gaze roved over my features, as if he was studying each one independently. A blush crept over my face, and I felt hot despite the dwindling coals in the hearth. I wanted to apologize for my plainness, certain that my angular nose and hollow cheeks were not what he expected. Yet a charged silence crackled, and his shoulders rose and fell in quick succession. My pulse skittered as he leaned forward, his chin tilted to the side slightly as he took me in. I squirmed on the pillows. He inched closer, and a whoosh of hot air pressed through his parted lips. I could smell a faint tinge of brandy on him. Frantic breaths escaped me from the unexplainable pressure that coursed through my body as his eyes bored into mine. I gulped as his fingers stroked my cheek, and I melted into his touch. I fought an overwhelming urge to close the distance between us.

"That's enough," Beatrix said as she entered with a tray of food. He flinched as if burned by me and jolted to standing. Bewilderment crossed his expression. Whatever had surged between us, his sister had snuffed it out with her return. But he didn't move away.

"Arianna needs her rest. Join Duncan in the study. Now." Her tone was coated in authority. "Go."

He took his time leaving, and a stony demeanor replaced the gentleness he once bore. He glared at his sister as he strode past her, then slammed the door closed. Beatrix glided toward me and began her role as my caregiver for the evening.

CHAPTER 15

SILAS

I STRODE THROUGH THE corridor. Candles illuminated my way, and the plush rugs lining the wood floors dampened my heavy footsteps. I slowed, buying time to smooth my countenance. I had stalked between my suite and the sitting room for the hours Arianna had remained unconscious. Each minute that passed had been excruciating. However, seeing her awake didn't soothe my tumultuous emotions. I paused at the edge of the open study door, lacking the composure or ability to explain to my brother-in-law what had happened without divulging the secrets I kept.

"Silas, stop your lurking and come in," Duncan commanded.

I clenched my jaw at his terse tone. It reminded me of when I had been under his tutelage and a lecture awaited me. For years, I sat while he admonished me about the most minor mistakes, from miscalculations on my ledgers to not securing wheat at the cheapest price. Though his guidance had served me as I transitioned from a young man to the Lord of Belmont

Manor and overseer of Presspin, I was in no mood for his chastisement.

I squared my shoulders and entered. His face had a familiar stern expression, his firm, square jaw set in a line of dissatisfaction. We didn't exchange pleasantries as he gestured to the seat beside the mahogany desk. Instead, I walked to the drink cart and perused the etched crystal and expensive liquor. A sweet scent filled the air as I poured two fingers of brandy. I could feel his stare on my back as he waited impatiently for me. However, my jumbled nerves had not stabilized since the afternoon, and my curse thrummed like my pulse, ready to break free at any minor inconvenience. I took a deep breath, then sipped the contents, taking a moment to center the barely tethered angst sizzling just beneath the surface.

I turned to face him. His jaw ticked, and from my years of knowing him, I could sense his displeasure at my defiance. However, I was no longer a young man seeking his wisdom. I swirled the drink and remained standing by the cart.

A hint of a sneer twitched on his lips, then smoothed. He lifted his snifter of brandy and gulped the contents. This evening, he was my antithesis in every way. My locks lay askew, my tunic was rumpled, and a raw emotion had unsettled me. While Duncan, despite his thinly veiled displeasure, was the epitome of the collected businessman. His blond hair lay unruffled, his gray irises were sharp, and his shirt was still crisp. Even his study was painstakingly arranged, with shelves of leather ledgers, meticulously chosen artwork, and crystal liquor decanters neatly lined in a row. A stack of papers strewn about his desk was the only outward sign of disarray. I sipped my drink as a charged silence dragged out between us until he smacked his empty glass against the mahogany with a thud.

"I knew letting that woman into my home was a terrible idea. But your sister begged, and I relented because of my love for her."

I remained silent, and the truth of his feelings lingered as he stacked the papers, the shuffling punctuating the tension. I took a swallow of brandy, allowing the alcohol to unfurl the tight knot that had been sitting in my gut since the incident. His lips pulled into a straight line. He picked up the thick leather ledger and slapped it against the desk, then stuffed pages into it. Unflinching, I fortified my stony resolve.

"But instead of visiting Beatrix, she was out in the gardens with you. Then I heard from the gossiping staff that you carried her to your bedroom, where she remains unconscious."

"Duncan, let me explain—"

He cut me off with a mirthless laugh.

"What is there to explain? She is engaged. Her betrothed's father is the wealthiest man in Daviel. What were you thinking? You could have any woman. Any woman, but you pursued a masked monster?"

I slammed my glass onto the cart, and amber liquid sloshed over of the rim. I gritted my teeth and leashed my seething frustration at his blatant misunderstanding of the situation.

"You don't know what you are talking about." I stalked toward him. My blight delighted in my rage, and the ring heated against my finger. I gripped the back of the chair and leaned forward, speaking through clenched teeth. "She is not a monster."

He laughed, a grotesque chuckle, and the sound made my skin crawl.

"I never thought you'd be interested in a cursed woman, but everyone has their predilections." A lecherous grin spread across his face, and he crossed his arms over his chest, unswayed by my looming form.

"Your tastes are your discretion. Whatever this is between you, it stops now. I will not have you place my home, nor yours, at risk because you indulged in some peculiar fantasy."

Agitation boiled, and I fought desperately to hold on to my power. My fingertips heated, and the wood beneath them softened, ready to crumble. I released the chair before it gave way under the pressure of my darkness.

His gray eyes flared, unaware of the danger before him. How I wanted to ring tendrils of darkness around his bare throat for the words he had uttered. Family or not, my unhinged curse whispered of destruction.

I steeled myself against the burning anger. "She is not my lover, nor is she a monster. No one, not even you, will speak ill of her."

He lifted an eyebrow in challenge, and it took all my restraint to not react. Yet I held his glare, tilting my chin and donning the air of Lord Belmont, not Silas, his once youthful charge. Footsteps and a maid humming along the corridor broke the strained silence.

"Very well. I won't speak ill of the girl, but she may never step foot on my property again. Luckily for you, the staff are loyal and will remain quiet about our involvement in this unscrupulous matter. Beatrix has already woven a tale to the servants that you were merely carrying Arianna at her behest after she fell in the gardens. In your shock, you went to the wrong guest room: the one you occupied. It is our secret that you were alone with her."

He returned his attention to organizing the stack of papers and let out an exasperated sigh, ignoring me now that he had given his instructions. My lip twitched as I peered down at him. He was totally immersed in the maps and charters for his Seaside business venture, as if I wasn't standing here. He still viewed me as a youth who had barely crossed the age of majority. As if I still needed him to usher me through my mistakes.

Agitated, I stalked out of the study without another word. As I prowled the hallway, whispering maids scurried away from me and my less than amiable mood. I should have sought Beatrix, but my feet moved of their own accord, pulled to Arianna's side.

CHAPTER 16

ARIANNA

I SETTLED INTO THE mound of pillows Beatrix had rearranged. She had hovered, insisting I eat every bite of dinner. I devoured two slices of bread slathered in butter and the chicken stew before she scurried off. A smile flickered on my lips despite the oddness of the afternoon. She possessed a warmth that stood in stark contrast to her capricious brother, whose mood fluctuated from aloof to concerned.

However, occupying his guestroom was like catching a rare glimpse of this perplexing man. The furnished suite felt cozy yet orderly, decorated in shades of green. I leaned forward and squinted at the stack of books on the table. What did the mercurial Lord Belmont read? I assumed something dreary. Perhaps the annexation of Krella to Hallowhaven or mathematical practices for estates. I doubted he read for leisure.

Unable to make out the titles, I rested my head on the pillows. A blush crept up my neck and settled on my cheeks from the intimacy of being tucked into Silas's bed. Despite my virginity, I knew the precariousness of this situation. I had devoured plenty of salacious novels to fuel my fantasies. My heartbeat quickened, and a prickle of awareness coursed down my spine at the sheer impropriety.

A knock sounded. I sat up, pulled from my daydreams. Beatrix entered with a garment.

"You look comfortable." She approached and placed the white nightgown next to me. I ran my fingers over the nearly translucent silk and gaped at her.

"It is from my trousseau. It is far too small for me. Layla must have included it by mistake. She is a little scattered. Lucky for us, this is exactly what you need for the evening." She beamed, and a hint of mischief flashed across her countenance.

I nodded. How could I argue or request something more modest, given Beatrix's care?

"I'll check on you in the morning. I have squelched any gossip about your presence, but you should remain unseen."

"Thank you," I said, but I still studied the flimsy fabric.

"Duncan is waiting to speak with me. Good night." She smiled, then hurried out.

I worried my lip and held the nightgown. Despite the sheerness of the garment, I longed to be out of my sweat-laden clothes. I stood. My legs wobbled as I attempted to reach behind myself to unfasten the row of tiny buttons. Minutes passed as I struggled. Teetering from exhaustion, I gritted my teeth in determination until the top fastening came undone. Only a dozen left. I steeled myself, attempting the second button. I swayed. Swinging forward, I grabbed the poster before toppling over. To my relief, the door opened. Beatrix, my savior, would help me.

"What are you doing?" a male voice asked as I clung to the frame in a feeble attempt to stand.

I craned my neck to behold Silas, and embarrassment flooded me. My mortification continued when my legs buckled beneath me. I squeaked with surprise. I expected to hit the floor. Instead, I collided into the curve of a masculine body, and Silas's muscular arms wrapped around my waist.

"What are you doing?" he breathed into my ear, his words halfway between a whisper and a snarl.

A blush crawled over me as my body melted against the firmness of his taut frame.

"I'm trying to change, but these buttons," I said through a shaky breath.

A grumble came from him as he straightened me to standing. Then his fingers moved to the top button.

"W-what are you doing?" My pulse surged as his knuckles brushed along the cotton slip. Only the thin fabric blocked his touch from my skin.

"Unbuttoning your dress," he said, as if he were reporting on the weather.

I froze under his ministrations. My breathing quickened with each slide of his fingers. He disrobed me with an ease that showed his experience in undressing a woman. The realization sank within me like a stone. But why should it matter? I wasn't beautiful enough to tempt a man as handsome as Silas. Had he seen me as anything more than his pupil, he would have called for Beatrix to avoid the impropriety. He wouldn't allow himself to be alone with me; his gazes and this tension were just signs of his concern, weren't they?

His fingers left my garment, and he backed away. A shiver cut through me at the lack of his warmth against my skin. I sighed out my mixed emotions and waited for him to exit, but the door never opened. I twisted and viewed him. He was facing the opposite wall. He studied a painting of a mountain range and evergreen trees.

"Why are you still here?" I held my dress against my chest, keeping it from falling off.

He didn't turn toward me or leave. "I'll wait until I can get you back into my bed."

Arguing seemed pointless. I shimmied out of the dress, and the fabric crumpled with a whoosh to the floor. He cleared his throat. I took a steadying breath, feeling too aware of his proximity to me in this state of undress. Blood pulsed in my ears as I discarded the thick cotton slip. I pulled on the wispy nightgown and peered at myself. The sheer silk left little to the imagination, and the neckline draped, exposing the tops of my petite breasts.

"Are you ready?" he asked, an edge filling his voice.

I lugged my body into bed and gasped for air from the exertion. The effort of something this simple shouldn't have fatigued me. However, it did, given the exhaustion of today. I collapsed onto the mattress and tried to scurry under the blankets.

He didn't wait for my answer. Instead, he whipped around. In a few quick strides, he closed the distance between us.

"You should have let me help you." He grabbed the comforter as I squirmed, unable to hide my frail body from him. His gaze roved over me before he turned his head away and tucked me in. For a heartbeat, he hovered with an unrecognizable expression on his face, but quickly, his stony demeanor returned.

He pivoted to leave, and I called out, "Wait, I...I have some questions."

His shoulders rose and fell as he sighed. He eyed the exit and slicked a hand through his hair. Wordlessly, he walked to the couch and lounged on it. His long form barely fit on the green cushions as he stretched out. It seemed out of character for him to act in such a casual manner. Perhaps being in his domain allowed me this momentary glimpse into the man he truly was.

"Why did my mask come off?" I asked.

"Why don't you try putting it on and see what happens?" He leaned back and stared at the ceiling.

Uncertain, I reached for the mask on the nightstand and placed it against my face, but nothing happened.

"Now without the ring."

I gulped as he flicked a glance at me, but I followed his orders. As I removed the onyx ring, the familiar suction of the porcelain bonded to my flesh. Pain radiated through my skin as the heavy constraint clung to me. I put the ring on my thumb, and the mask fell off. Its face was smothered in the blankets once more, unable to mock me any longer.

"Suppression spells have their weaknesses and loopholes. The ring supersedes the Aralians' wards, which are not unbreakable." He paused for a moment, a deep crease forming between his brows.

"What can break the wards?" I asked, curious about the magic I thought to be infallible.

"Enchanted rings are the only physical component that I know of. Though Ophelia believed that there were ancient ties that could surpass the wards. Some drivel about destiny and love." His brow wrinkled, and he shook his head as if clearing the thoughts in his mind before proceeding.

"You should be able to sleep tonight without it. I'm one room over if you need anything." Yet he remained lounging on the couch with his head tipped back.

"Are you all right?" I asked, aware of the tension that had crackled in the air since I awoke.

"I have been wondering the same thing." He let out a wry chuckle. I shifted, and the rustling drew his attention. He sat up. His eyes widened, drifting over me, before he looked away. "You need your rest. I am sure you are exhausted."

"I'm not," I said a bit too quickly and snapped my mouth shut.

A quirk of a smile tugged on the corner of his lips. He stood, then walked to a large dresser at the far wall. He returned with a box and settled on the bed. I clutched the blanket. My heart pounded at his proximity while he pulled out carved figures and a board. I studied him in confusion as he set up the game on the mattress between us, arranging each piece precisely in deep concentration. "Have you ever played chess?"

I shook my head. I had only played simple card games with Naomi at night when she was too restless to draw while I read. His gaze held mine as he said, "I'll teach you."

CHAPTER 17

ARIANNA

I STRETCHED IN CONTENTMENT. For once, no nightmares had haunted me. My hand ran along the thick quilt as I let out a sigh. Peace dwelled within the cocooned safety of Silas's bed. I couldn't help but smile as my thoughts drifted to the time we'd spent playing chess. An ease had settled between us as we focused on the board with our conversations solely on the game, as if nothing of note had happened earlier that day. He beat me, but with each round, I began understanding his strategies. He possessed a boyish charm as he studied my moves, which he said were unpredictable, causing him to wrinkle his brow. Hours had passed before he noticed my long yawns and called it a night.

A knock jolted me from my musings. I sat up and adjusted the skewed nightgown. My pulse skittered. Was it Silas coming to check on me and how I slept?

Anticipation overtook me at the thought. However, as the door opened, Beatrix stepped in, carrying a tray of food. My heart steadied, and I chastised myself for my foolish optimism. He had only shown me kindness because I had fallen ill under his supervision.

She approached and placed the platter on the bed. She beamed, her soft yellow day dress highlighting the return of her chipper nature. "Did you sleep well?"

"Surprisingly, yes." It had been the best night's rest I had ever experienced.

I poured a splash of cream into the coffee and savored the blissful aroma. It had been years since we could afford such a luxury. As I sipped the hot beverage, the flavors danced and swirled. I couldn't remember anything tasting this good in my entire life.

Beatrix drew the curtains open, and light cascaded through the space. Then she pivoted to me and brimmed with excitable energy. I drank, uncertain as to why she was so chipper but also relieved that the worried aura had dissipated.

"You must have been exhausted. It is half past ten already. Silas, too, rose late." She gave me a knowing smile, and I choked on my coffee.

"Yesterday was overwhelming for everyone," I said and lowered the cup. She sighed and sat on the edge of the bed beside my feet.

I turned my attention to breakfast, and my mouth watered over the plate. I piled eggs on the butter-slathered bread and took heaping bites, one after another. As I ate, Beatrix chatted about her recent visit to the bookstore and the titles she acquired. I nodded and chewed but didn't interject. My ravenous appetite was uncharacteristic, but the food was remarkable.

As I finished, she stood to take the tray.

"Wait. Before you go, would you mind helping me? I struggle with buttons."

She froze mid-step and turned. Then she raised an eyebrow at me with a catlike grin. "How did you manage such a feat alone, then?"

A flush crossed my cheeks. I looked away and tugged on the thread of the blanket, twisting it as I burned under her scrutiny.

She lowered the platter to the small table by the sofa. She picked up my clothes, which had remained pooled on the floor. Her lips pursed as she shook out the fabric, then handed me the petticoat. I stood and pulled the slip over my body, then shimmied out of the nightgown.

She held out the dress, and I stepped into it. I straightened, and she fastened the buttons in seconds. She stepped back, and I smoothed my hands over the creased material. I turned to Beatrix, who assessed me with a satisfied smile.

"You really are lovely," she said.

I chuckled at her politeness. My skin was sallow from my face never seeing the sun, my locks were a dull blonde, and my nose was not petite. I was plain.

She grabbed the platter. "Silas is in the library. It's the third door that way." She shifted the tray and gestured to the right. "The staff are too busy preparing for luncheon to venture upstairs for at least an hour."

She exited, and I spun my engagement ring, vacillating between going to him and remaining here. Uncertain of what to do, I ambled toward the books on the table. They were not business texts or legal tomes, but mystery novels. I flipped through the pages and settled on the fainting couch. I melted into the soft fabric, and the faint scent of Silas filled my senses. That woodsy, wild aroma. I could almost hear him calling my name. This unrelenting draw to go to him overwhelmed me. Perhaps being in his room had rattled my logic.

Resigned, I stood and returned the novel to the neat stack. I unfurled my braid, and loose curls fell past my shoulders. I sighed. I likely looked a fright, but an incessant need to see him propelled me forward.

Leaving the comfort of his room, I scurried to the library and froze at the threshold. Silas lounged in a leather chair. He had returned to his composed self, but this morning, he compelled me. Sunlight caressed his masculine profile, glimmering across his olive skin. It highlighted his solid chin, his symmetrical nose, and his full lips. Light played through his wavy raven hair, and I wanted to run my fingers through his locks.

He turned toward me, as if he sensed my presence. My heart skittered at the hint of the roguish smirk he gave me, but I remained paralyzed. He arched an eyebrow, and his smoldering gaze beckoned a piece of me deep within my soul. A shiver crawled down my spine as he gestured for me to sit in the chair next to him. I forced my shaking legs to move and sank into the seat.

I breathed in the scent of leather and ink. The atmosphere soothed this erratic sensation that pulsed through my body at being so close to him.

He lowered his book to the small table. “How are you feeling?”

"Despite what happened yesterday, I feel better than I have in years." I wanted to expand, but he transfixed me, and the words caught behind my parted lips. His eyes locked on mine, and he anchored me to this new reality, where everything seemed more alive.

Seconds passed as we remained in this trancelike state. But he broke the connection as he shifted his focus to the empty hearth. His brow furrowed as he combed his fingers through his hair, causing the once tidy locks to spring about. "The wards don't just suppress your powers, but often pieces of who you are. Your senses, your feelings, your resolve. My uncle spent his early life bound to his mask, like you, and said that without the suppression spells, the world brimmed with possibilities."

I opened and closed my mouth, the truth of the statement reverberating through me. Since being freed from the suppression spells, there had been a lightness. Colors appeared brighter, food tasted better, and Silas—goddess, Silas was a sight to behold. An unaccustomed boldness came over me, and I placed my hand atop his. The desire to touch him was overwhelming. I expected him to pull away, but he didn't. Instead, he remained still as his eyes roved over my face. My pulse raced as the warmth of his skin radiated through my palm. "Thank you for everything. I would have never known."

His gaze held mine, and I relished in this unspoken thrumming energy that lay between us in the silence. He frowned, and a crease pinched between his brows. "No, don't thank me. Not when I have to tell you—"

Beatrix burst in, and I yanked my hand from his. Panic crossed her expression. "Go get your mask and come downstairs. Your mother has arrived." She rushed away, her frantic footsteps clicking down the corridor.

I didn't want to leave, but I had no choice. I walked toward the door. Giving Silas one last glance over my shoulder, I left the warm comfort of the library and headed into the coming weeks that would change everything.

CHAPTER 18

ARIANNA

I LOWERED MY BOOK to the bed, having read it three times in the last week. I slumped into my pillows and rubbed my temples. There was nothing else to stave off the boredom. Since being trapped in my room, I'd devoured my minuscule collection of novels more than once. They were gifts from my sister when she'd possessed a meager allowance before our father's death. The long hours of these days stretched in isolation, with my mother having barred Naomi from visiting. This punishment would allow me distraction-free time to reflect on my impropriety and lack of prudence in spending the night at Archer Estate—at least that was Mama's reasoning. My only contact with the outside world occurred when Mama brought my lackluster meals with a grimace on her lips. Yet I should have considered myself lucky she fed me, given her mood.

These days were lifeless. I sighed, thumbing through the book. These adventures no longer enthralled me. My sanctuary felt like a prison since experiencing the invigorating freedom of life devoid of the suppression spell. The wards dulled everything. The comfort of my quarters seemed hollow, and the food was bland. Even that draw toward Silas dampened, as if this room severed the rawness that swelled within me at Archer Estates.

My heartbeat quickened at the mere thought of the man. Closing my eyes, I envisioned Silas's handsome face. Foolishly, I allowed myself to dream, another of my primary mental escapes. I replayed the moments with him, the feel of him unbuttoning my dress, the warmth of his hand beneath mine, and the hours we spent playing chess. Despite reason, I fantasized about leaning forward and kissing him. Heat flushed my cheeks at the silly notion.

Silas only cared for me as his pupil. If he had possessed an inclination to kiss me, the opportunity had passed. But I didn't allow logic to ruin my escape into my fantasies, where I recalled how the light shone on his flawless skin and his amber irises.

As I ran my fingers over my lips, the cold metal of my engagement ring brushed against them. I peered at the diamond, a reminder of my future. I wiggled my empty thumb, where the onyx had once gleamed. Naturally, I had left it on Silas's nightstand before I'd departed. When I clenched my fist, the silver band dug into my finger and the stone glimmered. It reminded me that though Silas possessed my thoughts, soon I would wed another man.

The door opened, and I flinched out of my musings. I expected Mama, but the Aralian Disciple, Ester, crossed the threshold. She entered, as she had done for many years, her crisp white dress swaying with each step as she approached. I pursed my lips in displeasure. I'd hoped Mama hadn't reported my indiscretion to the Aralians when a week had passed without Ester making an appearance. My hope had been futile.

She waited in expectation in the center of my cramped room. I stood from the bed and lowered myself onto my knees. The position was second nature to me when an Aralian graced me with her presence. I bowed my head and studied the swirling pattern of the knots within the wood, daring not to lift my gaze.

A swish of fine silk fabric cut through tense silence, which dragged on longer than it should. My knees ached, and I stole a glance at Ester as she took her time removing her ornate white hood, and her disdainful glare beat down my back.

"Blessed be Aralia. Goddess of Light, the bringer of peace and harmony to this world. May those who walk in her glory be favored with abundance. Merciful Aralia, who cherishes even those tainted in cursed blood, a blight on her pristine beauty. We shout your name in praise," she said over me.

"We shout your name in praise." The phrase left my lips as it had at the end of every prayer. Empty words to appease the woman who oversaw my blemished soul.

"Cursed one, your mother has informed me of your incident and punishment. Do you have anything to say?"

I flinched internally. Stating my cause would be fruitless. Instead, my focus drifted to the black markings on the floor that peeked out from the rug, a physical remnant of the monster lurking inside me. I had learned long ago that the best course of action was to accept my punishment without argument.

"No, Disciple Ester. I was clumsy, as my mother informed you. The fault is mine," I said, repeating Beatrix's story. I hoped the lie sounded convincing enough for her to let me stand as I resisted the urge to fidget in discomfort.

"And you stayed the night in Mrs. Archer's home?" Her curiosity colored every word.

A thin layer of perspiration formed beneath my dress. "I lost consciousness and did not wake until the next morning."

She paused for a long moment as my legs trembled. I would not move from the position, which was expected of me, despite the discomfort that shot through my body as my knees buckled on the solid wood floor.

"The next morning," she repeated to herself, as if testing my answer.

I tried not to gulp as sweat formed under my slip, making it sticky and slick.

"Rise now, cursed one."

I rose, but my gaze remained on my feet, despite my desire to search her face for any inkling that she didn't believe me. But the truth was more preposterous than the lie. She wouldn't suspect a cursed man had discovered how to roam the world unbound by suppression spells.

I locked my questions away, and she expected me to remain silent. As a cursed person, I served as evidence of the ancient gods and their destructive nature. I was not allowed to speak nor make eye contact with the pure, with the disciples—a lesson I learned upon Ester's arrival at our home all those years ago. Nor could I ever enter the temple in Hallowhaven, the sacred city, to pay homage to the goddess as Mama and Naomi had after my father's death. No, my presence would sully the purity of the holy shrine. I was to remain humbled before them in every way possible.

"Your mother's punishment was wise. It is best you remember your place in our world. You are the embodiment of everything Aralia hates, and yet she shows mercy on you. Providing you with a room to live in, a mask so you may walk amongst her people, and soon a marriage to a fine young man whom we have sanctioned. Are you unaware of how blessed you are? So many of your kind perished when their darkness awoke. You survived and are allowed to exist because of Aralia's clemency. Don't forget, you owe the goddess your life."

Her words should have felt harsh, but they didn't. I'd heard similar speeches from the pious disciple since my blight emerged, and when my wrongdoings spurred visits from her.

When I was seven, she placed me on my knees before her for complaining about the weight of my mask. It was my first infraction of many until I learned to endure in silence. She whipped me for my lack of gratitude to Aralia and the mask her disciples provided. At ten, I snuck out the window and wandered into the village. My presence unsettled the whole of Krella, and Ester once again punished me. Lessons upon lessons taught me the only choice was obedience.

"Praise be to Aralia, Goddess of Light." I tensed, expecting the blow of a whip. Nothing came but long moments of silence. I held my breath; perhaps she believed me. She leaned close, her porcelain-white skin nearly as pale as the adorned dress and cloak she wore. The faint scent of begonia wafted to me. I focused on her feet, surprised that despite the dusty streets of

Krella, her robe was pristine, as if she had floated to our home. "Don't forget your place, cursed one."

I closed my eyes as soft footsteps pattered away and the door clicked shut. I peeked, yet remained frozen, fearing that moving in any way would signal her to come back and delve deeper for answers that were best kept secret.

CHAPTER 19

SILAS

"SILAS, YOU'RE ABOUT TO lose your queen," Beatrix said.

I flicked my gaze from the leather chairs beside the hearth to her. She raised a manicured eyebrow at me in question.

"W-what did you say?" I asked, lost yet again in my thoughts.

"I'm going to take your queen. It is so unlike you to be unfocused, especially when we are playing chess," she said.

I tried and failed to force my attention off the chair where Arianna had once sat, but I couldn't drag myself from the memories of how vivacious she was without her mask. Her soft blonde curls had framed her face, her blue eyes had sparkled, and her pink lips had worn a gentle smile. Her features were lovely, with high cheekbones, a narrow jaw, and a slightly angular nose. She was ethereal and out of place in her faded brown dress, which didn't match the spark of spirit igniting within her that morning, here in the library.

Gods, she had left an imprint on this entire estate, and I couldn't seem to escape her. Our first meeting at Archer Estate tainted the sitting room when she wore that tacky ball gown unsuitable for afternoon tea. The once peaceful gardens were now filled with the horror of her shrieks, which haunted my soul. My guest suite no longer served as a respite; her sweet lavender scent lingered for days on the pillows she'd once lounged on. I should have considered myself fortunate that I hadn't had nightmares about the abyss. Instead, Arianna's lifeless body plagued my dreams every night. I'd hoped a game of chess with Beatrix would help me focus; alas, it didn't. Not when Arianna's presence lingered in this space. She had timidly touched my hand and thanked me for showing her a sliver of an existence unencumbered by the wards. In retrospect, I had put her deeper in harm's way.

Offering to assist her had been the epitome of my hubris. I had trained for years, yet I assumed I could teach her these skills in a matter of weeks. My focus on the present had overshadowed the broader scope of the reality awaiting her.

"Silas, your move." Beatrix gestured to the chessboard but didn't chide me for my absentmindedness. Instead, she tilted her head in observation, and questions likely formed in her mind. Ones I couldn't answer.

"My queen." I shifted my focus to the board. She was indeed cornered and would soon be out of play if I failed to act. I removed the queen from harm's way. I gritted my teeth as Beatrix slid her rook into an offensive position.

"Check." She flashed a smug smile.

"You haven't won yet." I slid my king out of harm's way. Yet my strategies were unfocused from days of fitful sleep and a deep unease that I hadn't shaken since Arianna had left Archer Estate.

"Checkmate," she said in triumph.

I gaped at my glaring misstep. I'd walked right into Beatrix's trap. Despite her jovial exterior, she was cunning to the core, with a mind for details, making her a ruthless chess player.

"You baited me to move my queen."

"No, I tried to help you! You should have moved the piece here." She pointed to the square where she indeed would have been safe.

"You did the opposite. You may have saved the queen, but you sacrificed the king. Such a simple mistake, and so unlike you." Her gaze roved my face, likely taking in the dark half circles under my eyes and my messed hair.

"Nightmares?" she asked.

"You are not sleeping well either. I hear you rising before dawn, and Duncan..." I pressed my lips together, not wanting to delve into the chaos I had caused in their marriage.

Since the incident, their conversations had lacked the ease from when I arrived in Krella. A discord reverberated through their relationship. Duncan's displeasure rippled onto Beatrix far more harshly than I'd expected. He suspected that she, the romantic at heart, had been the architect of my alleged tryst with Arianna. He had remained in his office for long hours, focused on work, and our meals were polite but stiff. Duncan's once gregarious nature had turned icy. Guilt racked me at his irritation as he had spent the last week and a half keeping us at a distance.

"This is all my fault. I shouldn't have involved you." I began resetting the game. I lacked interest in playing yet another round but was unwilling to continue staring at my defeat.

"No, it's not. You always possessed a chivalrous streak, and helping Arianna is what Uncle Oliver would have done. He would be proud. Duncan will calm down. He departed for Seaside this morning to work on the trade route. I'm sure when he returns, he will have forgotten about the whole incident. He just needs some time." She reset her side of the board.

The door opened, and a butler entered with an envelope in hand. He flourished a bow, handed it to Beatrix, then exited the room. She pursed her lips as she scanned the contents. A line between her brows furrowed, then deepened with each passing second. Finishing the letter, she passed it to me.

Dear Mrs. Archer,

Thank you for the letters over the past week and a half. You are far too kind to inquire about Arianna's health and invite her to tea. Yet your politeness is unnecessary. I assume, because of your upbringing in Presspin, that you are unaware of Arianna's circumstances as a cursed being. She won't be leaving our home as her wedding day approaches. After her nuptials, you may attempt to correspond with her if her husband allows it. You seem to be a woman capable of finding friends of your own station. Do not waste your time on her.

Sincerely,
Clara Park

I crumpled the letter, and the ring burned hot against my finger in warning as power seethed beneath my skin. I hated the note. It reminded me that despite any training, lessons, or help I provided her, she would be married and under the constraints of her husband's wishes. My hand tensed around the flimsy sheet of paper bunched in my fist as my memory drifted to his lecherous intent on the balcony. Soon she would be his bride, and she would...no. I could no longer ruminate over the inevitable future in front of Arianna. She was engaged to another man. She would be bound to him and the mask for as long as she lived.

The once tight reins I held against my curse seeped out of me, and the letter dissolved into ash in my fingertips.

Beatrix gaped at me. "Silas, you need to calm down."

Though she did not fear me, she knew firsthand the destruction my power invoked when my base instincts took over.

I peered at the chessboard. It had needed to be reset, much like my life. I had to remove myself from Krella and the turmoil my presence caused. Unable to look at my sister, I stood and walked to the window, taking in the lush gardens. There was no peace here, not where I had failed Arianna as her teacher, failed Beatrix as her brother, and failed Duncan as his friend. "I have decided to leave tomorrow."

"Silas, everything will be fine. You don't—"

"It's for the best for everyone. When Duncan returns, you can settle back into your life as newlyweds. And I...It is time I return home and find peace again."

I couldn't wholeheartedly admit the truth. Nor could I tell Beatrix about the nightmares of Arianna's limp body in my arms or divulge how close Arianna had hovered near death. I dared not expand on how her presence followed me throughout this house. There was no solace here for me.

My curse was unruly, and I wouldn't risk hurting my sister. No mindfulness training, breathwork, or even running could settle the darkness threatening to break free. However, I hoped my return home would soothe me. The crisp fall air, the mountain ranges, and the tall evergreen trees might bring my power the solace it required to become manageable again. I trusted the distance between Krella and Presspin would be enough to stop the memories of Arianna from haunting me.

I sensed Beatrix readying herself to object, but I couldn't allow her to sway me. I stalked out of the library, searching for anything to provide relief until I departed.

CHAPTER 20

ARIANNA

MY FINGERS MOVED DEFTLY as I attached a lace trim to a mauve day dress. Mama had spent the morning altering in a tizzy for a client who would pick up their order tomorrow. She had procrastinated yet again and needed my help to finish the garments in time.

Sewing was one of the few talents I possessed that Naomi lacked. My stitches were impeccable from hours of making little dresses for my favorite doll, Ms. Matilda. I had created them out of scraps of discarded gowns as a child. Fortunately, Mama had taught me needlework, language, and arithmetic. Even a cursed daughter needed some abilities to snag a husband.

Sighing, I paused and flexed my aching fingers, yet it felt rewarding to do something other than read.

Over the past few days, Mama had loosened her grip on my punishment. Ester had unintentionally softened Mama's resolve by praising her for her diligence. Yesterday morning, I stepped foot out of my room for the first time since the incident.

Mama had permitted me fifteen minutes to fetch water. I had welcomed the cool breeze and the soft ground under my boots as they sank into the dirt. The sensations were a needed respite from the monotony of my quarters. Last night, she even allowed Naomi to deliver my dinner. I had peppered Naomi with questions about town and her best friend, Tabitha, who she'd visited frequently. But our reunion was short-lived, as Mama called her away. However, I was thankful for the intervention. Naomi's stories had turned into inquiries of my visits to Archer Estate. I was uncertain how much to divulge to my sister about my misadventures with Silas.

"Arianna, you have a guest!" Mama called out from downstairs. Shocked, I pricked my finger with the needle.

Not wanting to sully the fabric, I moved the delicate gown to my nightstand. I sucked the blood from the prick and watched the door. Who would Mama allow to see me in my confinement? A pang of optimism swelled. Perhaps she had permitted Beatrix to visit.

I lowered my hand and stood. I smoothed my dress. The gray fabric was worn but suitable. Wild curls popped out of my messy plait, but Beatrix had seen me in worse sorts and wouldn't care about my appearance. Hope renewed, I thought of Beatrix bursting through the door with her beaming smile, pleasant conversation, and a plan to get me back to training at Archer Estate. A knock sounded.

"Come in." My cheer diminished as Theo strode into my sanctuary.

His lips quirked, then smoothed to an expression of disinterest. He adjusted the crisp green cravat that matched the jacket clinging to his slender frame.

Mama fawned over him. "What a dutiful betrothed you are to travel to check on Arianna. She is much better and—"

"Leave!" He waved her away as if she were a servant and not my mother. She froze, her eyes wide at the request. He whipped his head toward her, and an eerie smile cut across his face. To my horror, she scurried off.

I gaped at the closed door. My shock vacillated between Theo's presence and Mama locking me in with my betrothed. Hadn't my nearly two-week punishment been because of my lack of propriety in staying the night at Archer Estate? Yet she didn't hesitate to leave me alone with a notorious rake.

He stepped closer, and his gaze wandered over my body. My stomach churned at his predatory grin as his intense stare settled on my face. I wrapped my arms around myself, grateful for this shapeless gray dress. I needed to run or hide, but my tiny room offered no space as he closed the distance between us in two quick strides.

I gasped. He pushed his body into mine, pinning me between him and the edge of my bed. I wanted to step back but feared I would teeter onto the mattress.

"What are you—"

"Shut up!" He wrapped a hand around my throat. His thumb tilted my chin upward as he studied my face like a farmer examining a horse for purchase—with nothing but cold assessment. His breath rushed out, reeking of whiskey. Was this man ever sober? The luncheon hour had barely passed, and the stench of a tavern rolled off him, only intensifying my gagging sensation. I tried to squirm out of his clutches, but his grasp tightened with each movement.

"Stay still and answer my questions. Don't make me punish you more harshly by lying. Why were you at Archer Estate?"

I blinked back tears as his soulless green eyes stared at me, wide with rage, and his nostrils flared. Panic rose within me, and my mind scrambled for some suitable response. But the truth would send him into a jealous fit, which I feared I would not recover from.

"I visited Mrs. Archer. She wanted a friend. We met recently, and she invited me to tea," I said with a trembling voice.

"Why would she want to be your friend?" He laughed mirthlessly, as if someone befriending me was hilarious.

"I don't know." I gulped, the motion tightening the pressure on my throat.

"Stop playing dumb and tell me. Why were you at Archer Estate?" A sneer crossed his lips.

"I think she wants to be my friend because of you," I lied, hoping the statement would boost his ego enough to sway him to release his brutal hold.

"Because of me." He rolled the statement over with a lick of pleasure in every word. His grip loosened a fraction, and he smiled with satisfaction. "Explain."

"She desires a connection with me because I am to be Mrs. Terrell, and you will one day take over your father's estate. I thought forming this friendship would make you happy. To have me building connections that could help you in the future."

His lips pursed. I expected him to release me, but his grip on my neck didn't yield. Instead, his jaw clenched.

"I heard Mrs. Archer has a brother staying with her. Did you speak with him?" The edge of jealousy reverberated through his words. Theo had been furious when the stranger intervened on my behalf at our engagement ball and when he had later led me out onto the dance floor. Silas had been unidentifiable in his all black attire, and he'd left after our moment in the gardens. Yet I worried Theo had pieced together that Silas and the stranger were one and the same. I needed to dissuade Theo from any suspicion.

"What brother? Why would I ever notice another man when I'm marrying you?" I asked with a saccharine-sweet tone. I kept my features soft and attempted to flick what I hoped to be a coquettish glance. It felt preposterous given his grasp on my neck.

But he took the bait. His smile widened with each word that padded his vanity, and he released me. I coughed and sputtered, collapsing to the floor and gasping for air. My throat burned, and my eyes stung with unshed tears.

Before I could get myself back to my feet, he yanked me by my shoulders, lifting me like a limp rag doll. His countenance shifted from rage to lust. He pulled me against his chest, melding my body to his. Unable to move, I could not avoid his lips crushing against mine in a brutal kiss. The way his tongue darted into my mouth was akin to a hissing snake. I wanted to scream, but this fate was inevitable. He pulled away, smirked, and placed his thumb on my chin, tilting it skyward so I held his gaze.

"You are never to visit Mrs. Archer again; do you understand me? You can't comprehend the ways of the world. Foolish pet, she isn't your friend. She's a social climber hoping to ensnare you into future favors. Don't forget, no one else wants you. You are a cursed nothing, and I alone am willing to bear the burden of marrying you."

He released my chin, and his focus shifted to the bed. His lips brushed my ear. "I think we have time for some fun. Just a taste to tide me over."

He pushed me back, and I tumbled onto the mattress. He leaned over me with a hungry gaze and tugged at his cravat. I trembled in fear.

"It is best you leave." Naomi's voice cut through my terror. In the commotion, she must have stepped in, unbeknownst to either of us. I let out a breath as Theo turned his attention to her.

"Or shall I call my mother up here and inform her of the liberties you are attempting to take with my sister under her roof? You don't want to risk displeasing your father. Those maids you've bedded are quite chatty about your strained relationship."

He stalked to her until they stood toe to toe. Fury rolled off them, their stares locked in an intense standoff.

"You wretched minx!" He gritted his teeth.

"Gods, did you drink our tavern entirely out of whiskey, or did you just bathe in it? Go home. I'm certain you wouldn't be able to get it up right now anyway."

I sat on the bed, gaping in astonishment as my sister dressed him down with her quick wit.

"Shall I teach you a lesson instead?"

Naomi didn't flinch. Her eyes flared with challenge. "Mama, Theo is ready to depart," she said over her shoulder. "And don't you dare step foot into our house again."

She held his withering stare, lifting her chin in defiance.

"Theo, your carriage is waiting," Mama called up the stairs, her soft footsteps pattering toward us so she could accompany him out of our home.

"You may have won today, but don't forget that your sister will be mine in nearly two weeks, minx. Then I can do whatever I please. You won't be able to stop me." He slammed the door behind him.

Like a taut bowstring, I snapped. The emotions I held poured out as hot tears flowed from me. I pressed my face into the pillows and choked back my sobs, fearing Mama would hear me. I had already suffered enough this afternoon without her critical assessment of my emotional state. As I curled into myself, the bed shifted with Naomi's familiar weight.

"Please talk to me. You have been shutting me out since the masquerade," Naomi said.

She stroked my scalp, soothing my fraying emotions. I remained buried in the cushions as I mourned the life ahead. A reality that no amount of daydreaming or pretending could stop. In nearly two weeks, I would be that horrid man's wife.

"You can't marry him."

Her statement was simple, yet complicated. I didn't look at my sister as I spoke through my sobs. "I am a burden. Marrying Theo will provide you and Mama with the funds you need. He's right. No one else wants me. No one."

My cries filled the tiny room. Long minutes passed, but I didn't move. My cheek brushed against the worn cushion that absorbed my tears. At last, I attempted to steady myself as my sobs softened to shaky breaths. Naomi halted her fingers' soothing circular motion and finally spoke.

"Not even that stranger? The man I saw standing between you and Theo at Terrell Estate? The one you danced with and whom I suspect you ran off into the gardens with?"

My heart pounded at her implications, but I didn't sit up to view her. I rolled to my side and peered out the window.

"Silence instead of a denial. Interesting. Did you know there is also gossip spreading throughout the village about a very wealthy and dashing bachelor who is visiting his sister in Krella? To my surprise, I found out that he is Mrs. Archer's brother. The same Mrs. Archer that you have been meeting for tea, even though you cannot drink anything with your mask on."

She paused, but I didn't speak.

"No, still not wanting to answer? Then let me take my curiosity further. I have wondered since hearing this rumor if her sibling and this mystery man were indeed the same. Are they?"

I sat up and gaped at her. Goddess above, had she been male, she would be the sharpest runner in Hallowhaven. I rubbed my itchy eyes, which felt like I'd rolled in sand. Dread replaced my shock. My stomach twisted in a knot at the sudden realization. If Naomi had deduced this information...Had Mama? Had Theo?

"Goddess, does *everyone* know?"

The old wooden headboard creaked as she leaned against it. She crossed her arms over her chest and pursed her lips. I waited with bated breath, terrified that my last-minute rebellion would bring even more doom to my doorstep.

"I doubt it. Mama is far too self-involved; she didn't ask after you once at the ball. She spent the night bragging to lost connections and prancing like a peacock, showing off her new dress. And Theo lacks the foresight to put the two together. Thank the goddess your betrothed is more interested in rutting with maids and drinking himself half to death. Mrs. Archer's brother lacked anything to distinguish him from any other person. Mrs. Archer's immaculately tailored dresses tipped me off. A lady's maid could have easily added such frivolous trimmings. Then the invitation came for tea. I suspected you were up to something. Luckily, Tabitha is quite the gossip and divulged everything she knew about the Archers and one Silas Belmont."

"You are cunning," I said in exasperation, my heart pounding in my chest. How long had she known about my outings? However, she had only discovered half of the truth. Though I swore to keep this a secret, I trusted Naomi with my life. Summoning courage, I smoothed my hair and dress, wishing it would also smooth my composure. I searched for the strength to share what I had withheld from her since the masquerade. "You are mistaken. Well, at least partially."

Her eyes widened. She was brilliant. Yet her blind focus on what she believed to be the truth kept her from seeing other aspects of reality.

"Silas was the man from my engagement ball. He, too, is cursed. His sister arranged for us to meet and train..." I released a heavy breath and placed a hand on my aching neck, feeling the strain from the afternoon. "He learned how to control the blight. Without the wards."

Naomi pinched the bridge of her nose, taking in the new information. Moments passed, and I fiddled with the vine embroidery on the quilt. She gasped and turned to me. "Does this mean you don't need these suppression spells or the mask? Could you live a normal life?"

I let out a harsh snort despite the earnestness of her question, a hopefulness highlighting the youthful naivete she clung to. These past weeks had reminded me of the impossibility of a typical existence. My fingers skittered over my sore neck. I swallowed. I couldn't escape the doom awaiting me.

"I had two catastrophic training sessions with Silas. During the last lesson, I fell unconscious. Even if I can learn more from him, I'll soon wed another. Could you imagine Theo allowing me to master my curse under the guidance of another man?"

I repressed a harsh laugh. No, Theo planned on locking me away for the rest of my life. I would be trapped in that rose-colored prison for him to play with as he pleased. Silas...Goddess, I would never see him again. I grabbed a pillow and clenched it to my chest. There had never been hope. The moment I had run into Silas, I allowed myself to give in to my fanciful notions, but dreaming only led to disappointment when reality beckoned. My shoulders slumped.

"He was just your teacher?" A knowing implication filled Naomi's tone.

"Whatever he meant to me in those few brief interactions doesn't matter. He is a stranger who showed me a glimpse of an unobtainable life. I am to be wed, and he will return to Presspin.

Our lessons were a ridiculous fantasy, and I have paid dearly for this last-minute rebellion. It is best I resign myself to my fate. My only comfort is knowing the funds received will keep you well cared for."

Naomi glared at me. "I don't want you to marry Theo for my well-being. We can figure this out. There has to be another way."

"Please, I'm too exhausted to talk any more." I collapsed onto the bed and stared out the window. The colors of foliage were transforming; the once green leaves swayed in the breeze, but their vibrance was succumbing to decay. My heart sank. I would never be part of the world. I was nothing more than a spectator to the living.

Instead of pushing further, Naomi lay beside me, and the light scent of her lily salve soothed me as she pulled me against her. I relaxed, comforted by the sister who loved me, the sister I would die for.

CHAPTER 21

SILAS

"WHERE ARE WE GOING?" I asked as the carriage jostled along the unmaintained path on the outskirts of Krella. I flicked a glare from the window to Beatrix. She plastered a saccharine smile on her lips. I leaned into the seat and crossed my arms against my chest, grateful to be leaving for Presspin tomorrow, which would free me from the complications here. However, I had somehow been talked into accompanying my sister on an errand, thus delaying my departure a day. She had cajoled and pestered me with pleas of sibling duty until I capitulated.

Minutes passed as I thrummed my fingers in impatience against my arm.

The carriage slowed. It turned in to a long dirt driveway, stopping before a dilapidated farmhouse settled on a large parcel. Well-cared for yet sparse orchards lined the property. The ramshackle house seemed out of place. The roof bore gaping holes patched with dry straw, which would be problematic once the rains came. Layers of dust covered the faded brick home.

"Where are we?" I attempted to piece together why we were at some impoverished farm on the edge of town. Perhaps Beatrix planned to help me procure supplies before I left for Presspin? However, why would she be secretive about our destination?

"We are at the Park residence." Beatrix raised an eyebrow and grinned. She wore the same triumphant expression when she achieved checkmate, when she lured her opponent into a trap. I should have realized her machinations when she insisted I stay for one more day. She lacked a poker face.

"Why are we here?" I clenched my jaw and shot her a withering glare.

Unmoved by my bluster, her eyes bore into mine as she lifted her chin in challenge. "The simplest answer, dear brother, is to pick up the dresses Mrs. Park altered for me."

"And why bring *me* here?" I leaned deeper into the seat, wishing to the gods I had not fallen for her pleas and pouts. Now, I understood the fanciful ideas dancing in her mind instead of the harsh reality we lived in. How was I supposed to step into that home and face Arianna, knowing the fate awaiting her? I had no control over her future, and I wouldn't torture myself waiting for the inevitable to occur. It would be best I left before—

"There is something more between you and Arianna, whether or not you care to admit it," Beatrix said, cutting through my ruminations.

I didn't speak or look at her. Instead, I assessed the dilapidated farm, taking in the window on the second floor above the door. Where were Arianna's quarters? The room that was...

"I know you are ready to depart from Krella, but you will regret leaving without at least saying goodbye." She patted my hand, soothing my apprehension. I hated to admit that she might be right.

She rapped on the ceiling, signaling for the footman. I tensed as we exited. A chill crawled along my spine as the light breeze wafted over us. The air cooled as the sun began setting. Shades of pinks and purples filled the sky, and the large trees cast shadows over the home, as if something ominous lurked within. The hovel suffered from years of neglect. It had chipped paint on the trim and windows thick with dust. The path was more dirt than stone. I gulped, feeling as if my damnation loomed here, and fought the urge to return to the carriage. Beatrix grabbed my arm, pulling me forward with each step.

I was not a coward. I would face Arianna and say goodbye, knowing I would never see her again. Beatrix's grip intensified. Did she, too, sense what awaited Arianna? The realization rattled me, and a truth neither Beatrix nor I would dare speak ached within my chest, causing my shoulders to nearly collapse in on me. Arianna would...no, I couldn't allow my mind to dwell on her future or lack thereof. Instead, I pulled my arm from Beatrix and smoothed my composure. We stood before the entrance, my fingers tapping against the worn wood. The door swung open, almost smacking into me.

"Come in, come in." A graying lady cut a toothy smile. She took me in, ignoring my sister despite the greeting.

"May I introduce my brother, Lord Belmont of Presspin," Beatrix said.

"I am Mrs. Clara Park. It is truly a pleasure to meet you, Lord Belmont." The woman bobbed an immaculate curtsy, which felt odd in this failing farmhouse.

We entered the home. I gave Mrs. Park a curt nod and peered past her at the silhouette in the stairwell. I gulped against the tight knot in my throat and hoped it was Arianna. A different young lady, likely a sister, came into view. She was tall and pretty, with braided blonde hair and round, rosy cheeks. Despite myself, I felt disappointed. She froze on the steps. Her eyes widened. She turned and headed back up the stairs, disappearing into the shadows.

"Come and sit, Lord Belmont. How truly kind you are to accompany Mrs. Archer on such a humble errand." Mrs. Park directed me to a faded sofa in the small parlor. Somehow, I managed a curt nod as the woman scurried away.

I sat, my rapt attention locked on the staircase. Why would Beatrix do this to me? She knew, at least I suspected she knew, of the fate that awaited Arianna. I couldn't bear this. No, feelings led to pain. It was best I left before...

My breath caught as Arianna descended the stairs, and my inner thoughts ceased. I inhaled sharply, the air palpable in her presence. I stood, my body moving of its own accord until I reached the base of the staircase. Her gaze locked on mine as I offered my hand to assist her with the descent, pulled closer by her spell. Warmth radiated into me as I caressed her fingertips. I guided her forward. Her feet touched the landing, but I couldn't break the compulsion I fell under when she was near. Instead,

I stayed there for a heartbeat longer than I should, soaking in these last moments with her. Her wild curls flowed over her shoulders, untethered from the typical braid. Her vibrant blue eyes pierced through the porcelain. She captivated me. Why couldn't Beatrix let me leave in peace?

A slight cough sounded from the stairwell. I darted a glance to the young woman who descended. She said, "Mama, don't you think Arianna and I should show Lord Belmont the farm?"

I blinked in confusion as the sister gestured for me to take her hand. I grabbed her fingertips and guided her down the last step when Mrs. Park's attention drifted to us. It served as a well-executed tableau. Me assisting the eligible daughter. The young woman flashed me a calculating smile.

"Yes, Naomi, I think a walk around the property with Lord Belmont is a delightful idea. Take Arianna with you as a chaperone. She is nearly a married lady. I believe her presence is sufficient." Mrs. Park beamed at me. She likely hoped I would form some sort of connection with the sister I suspected she favored based on the quality of her day dress.

"Indeed," Beatrix said sarcastically while examining a gown.

Naomi clung to my arm with fake interest as we exited. She walked beside me as she stared forward in silence with Arianna in tow. As we drew farther out of sight, Naomi released me and allowed seconds to pass before ambling behind, giving Arianna and I space to converse alone.

"What are you doing here?" Arianna asked as she led me into the apple orchard. The trees here provided further privacy from the house. Shadows clung and wisps of light from the setting sun peeked through the branches, catching on the mask, which smiled blithely at me, uncaring of her future.

"Beatrix asked me to join her on an errand. I was unaware we were coming to your home. But I wanted to say..."The words caught in my throat.

I couldn't look at her. Instead, I assessed the orchard. The trees were not bountiful but bare. The once green and lively leaves were fading, turning to shades of red and brown; soon they would fall and decay, succumbing to the inevitable. I breathed in the sweet smell, but the hint of rot had already taken hold.

I turned to Arianna. I wished I could look upon her face one last time, then I could choke out a farewell. The words were bitter on my tongue.

The breeze blew through her hair. Wisps of curls shifted, drawing my attention to the smudges of purple hidden behind the blonde tresses. My stomach sank at the necklace of bruises covering her creamy flesh.

I closed the distance between us, certain my suspicions couldn't be correct. She froze as I brushed her locks back and delicately traced a thumb against her throat. Disbelief swelled, but what did I expect would happen to her? Wasn't this just a piece of the fate she would endure? Rage superseded my shock, and my finger trembled against her skin. My chest rose and fell from heaving breaths. These bruises ignited a blazing fury within me.

"Please don't." Her words stung as I removed my fingertips from her neck.

These bruises were the last straw. Everything since I'd arrived in Krella felt like it had converged on this moment. My tenuous control over my emotions faltered. The churning anger boiled over my thick inner walls like molten fire burning through metal. The trees swayed from the pressure of my curse threatening to break free.

"Who did this to you?" I asked through my clenched teeth. Yet I suspected I already knew the answer.

Arianna stared beyond me, silent, her arms wrapped around her chest as the wind blew again. I doubted her threadbare dress offered any warmth as summer released into autumn. Shivering, she rubbed her hands over her sleeves. However, I wasn't certain if her trembling was because of the cold or fear.

Stepping back, I gave her the space I assumed she desired. I rolled my neck, trying to loosen the building tension. My curse delighted in my anguish, and energy crackled around me with my killing intent. I wanted to murder whoever harmed her, watch them turn to ash in my hands until they were nothing but dust in the wind. Yet, I didn't want our last moments laced with her fear because of my base instinct. I gritted my teeth, forcing long, slow breaths until the power dissipated and the air stilled.

"Arianna, please look at me." My lips trembled, and the words were a plea.

Her eyes locked on mine, and agony lived within their depths. A melancholy aura rolled off her. I resisted the urge to comfort her, fearing even the slightest touch would be my undoing.

"Who did this?"

She flicked her gaze to me and let out a long breath. Then she stared at the ground, focusing on her scuffed boots.

"Theo," she whispered.

"Theo." His name tasted bitter on my lips. "I should kill the bastard. Arianna, I am serious. I will destroy anyone who'd dare lay a hand on you." I expected her to agree as she wilted beside me under the pressure of her intended's abuse, but she didn't.

"What difference would it make? Look around you. Mama would sell me off to another husband. At least the funds received from the Terrells have insured Naomi's future." She slouched, resigning herself to this fate.

"Sell? What do you mean?" I asked through clenched teeth.

Had the Terrells purchased Arianna like chattel at the market? They still exchanged bride prices in the areas under Hallowhaven's control. In Presspin, we viewed the practice as barbaric. I pieced together the new information: the dilapidated farm, her worn clothing, and her willingness to marry that bastard. She would be the martyr her family sacrificed for their salvation.

She turned away. For a heartbeat, I feared she might flee to her room and accept the life that circumstance had dealt her. However, hadn't I come here to bid her adieu, despite what I already knew?

Before I could rationalize what was happening, she walked toward the edge of the orchard. I strode after her. I grabbed her arm, halting her forward progress. Her shoulders dropped as I anchored her to the spot.

"My marriage is securing my family the funds they need to survive. I have no other choice. Please let me go."

"Is that truly what you want? To marry a man who will abuse you? All for your family's well-being? Do they not care that he already laid his hands on you? I hope your bride price was a fortune for what you will endure as his wife."

Her breath rushed out, and she trembled. I waited. The wind rustling through the trees cut through our tense silence.

"How much did they pay for you?" I pulled against my standing as Lord Belmont, lacing my tone with command.

"Seven sheep."

Seven sheep. For the impoverished Parks, seven sheep must be a fortune. However, Arianna was worth far more, especially under the circumstances she would bear. My head pounded. Darkness threatened to leach out of me with each new revelation. I wanted to burn this farm to the ground, and my curse promised retribution on her behalf, tempting me to delight in the carnage it would leave in its wake. Then I would kill Theo. He would writhe in agony. They would all succumb to my blight's predilections. And then Arianna...gods, and then Arianna...

Releasing her, I withdrew, creating a space between us. My focus shifted away from her as a red leaf drifted, falling to its death. Time was running out, and an understanding crashed upon me so swiftly it nearly brought me to my knees.

She had been my harbinger of doom. I should have run in the opposite direction after I collided with her on the street. However, our fates converged as I beheld this bruised and broken woman whose family would trade her for their comfort, uncaring of what the future held for her.

I paced, but there was no walking away now. I sensed her watching me as leaves crunched beneath my boots. What I had to do tightened around me like a noose, and I unbuttoned my collar, hoping it would soothe this choking feeling. It didn't. Arianna had only one solution to all her issues. I dreaded this truth and couldn't allow myself to fall under her spell. Yet I wouldn't leave her to wither into nothingness, locked in Terrell Estate, married to Theo.

"Come to Presspin with me." I turned to her and wished I could see beyond the placid smile of the mask.

CHAPTER 22

ARIANNA

GO TO PRESSPIN WITH him? He must have been joking. I blinked, unable to piece together what his intentions were. I was engaged to another, my bride price paid, and he wanted me to flee as if it would fix everything? Go with him as what, his servant or a traveling companion? Or as someone he met in Krella? Then what? I had no money and few skills to survive. I shook my head, an ache forming in my mind as I attempted to comprehend his logic.

"I don't understand." I peered at him, and he stopped the pacing he had resumed after his statement.

He paused before me. His face was a mix of rage and worry. The frustration he bore seeped off him. For a moment earlier, I had feared his curse might come to life, ignited by his wrath toward Theo. Despite his displeasure, I wasn't afraid of him as he stalked the orchard like an agitated cat. Silas had always shown me kindness. His gold-flecked gaze burned into mine, laced with fury and something else I didn't understand.

"The only way to break an engagement is to become someone else's wife." His shoulders rose and fell with his quick, tense breaths. A palpable tension loomed in the air.

Despite my better judgment, I wanted to agree. However, I admired Silas. Marrying me would be a horrible mistake. I would not bring my curse, my doom, to his doorstep.

"No, I cannot accept your offer. I don't want to become your burden and ruin your life."

He stepped away, taken aback as if I had slapped him. I remained firm in my resolve.

He studied me. I expected him to leave, relieved that I had released him from whatever chivalrous code he must live by. But he didn't. Instead, he arched a brow and his lips pulled into a humorous line.

"You are being foolish," he said, but I held his stare.

A breeze whipped past me, an icy chill cutting through my dress. The setting sun immersed us in the shadows of the soft light of dusk. His presence had been unexpected, but I was grateful to say goodbye. To see him one last time and thank him for showing me a glimmer of peace. Naomi had arranged my hair around my neck to hide the bruises; it had been my misfortune that the wind ruined my plans of hiding Theo's malicious actions. I assumed it would displease Silas, but I never expected this level of protective anger. He was like a knight in a romance novel, gallant despite his stony exterior.

He resumed his pacing, and I soaked in every detail. Once the last dregs of light disappeared, he would leave my life forever. My mother had already informed me of her intention to keep me locked away in my room until my wedding day. Naomi tricking her into allowing me these brief moments with Silas was a gift I would cherish.

Footsteps crunched behind me, and I sensed Naomi's approach, but I couldn't move. She had likely come to inform me that this interlude must end. Instead, I watched the fading sun cling to Silas's black hair, his high cheekbones, and the slope of his nose. I would treasure his last act of kindness toward me for the rest of my life.

"Arianna!" He bellowed my name like a command, and he faced me, still a few feet away. "I cannot leave you in this...in this...situation."

His eyes transformed from golden brown to wholly black, the whites consumed as the darkness permeated them fully. Power crackled around him. A smoky aura surrounded his body. The leaves on the trees swayed under the pressure, the ground beneath his feet charring whatever was underfoot. I should have been afraid, but I wasn't. In the core of my soul, I knew Silas wouldn't hurt me.

"You are leaving with me. Tonight. I cannot allow this to continue," he growled, his voice taking on a richer tone under the control of his curse. His brow furrowed, and coal lines filled his skin, crawling along his flesh, a sign of his killing intent.

"Enough! You are being foolish. I am trying to save you from a rash decision you will regret. Don't you want to find love? To marry someone you desire?"

His labored breathing slowed. I watched in silence as he wrestled with his curse until he returned to normal and the crackling energy dissipated. Unlike the first time he showed me his power, he appeared to struggle with control this evening.

I let out a sigh, grateful he had finally accepted my answer, and I waited for him to walk out of the orchard and out of my life forever. Instead, he stalked toward me, leaving only a handbreadth between us. My breath caught at the closeness as the scent of woods and chamomile hit me.

"I had no intention of marrying and do not possess the capacity for love. My name will give you protection, and our marriage will be one of convenience. You could live your days in my manor, and I would be your teacher." He lifted his hand, his fingertips grazing over the painted apple-cheek of the mask. I wished he could touch my face instead of this contraption. His countenance softened, and a tremble entered his voice. "Let me set you free."

"Go with him, Arianna," Naomi said from behind me.

I had forgotten that she was there as I'd lost myself in Silas. He withdrew his touch, but his gaze searched mine.

Reluctantly, I pivoted to my sister. "Naomi, I can't leave you here alone and without funds." I moved closer to her, but she put up a hand, halting my forward progress.

"We can return the sheep, and we will survive. I am not as helpless as you believe, and I can't let you marry Theo." She peered around me at Silas, assessing him. "I won't be able to live with myself if you stay here. Please, go."

I opened my mouth to speak, but that stubborn streak had taken root in Naomi. Her eyes held mine, and a wordless plea filled her stare. How was I supposed to leave her to deal with this mess? How could I part from my dearest sister and friend? As I listened to the two people I admired most in this world, the truth settled into my bones—the truth I had been running from since my engagement dinner.

I didn't want to marry Theo. I wanted to escape this fate, and a defiant streak had taken hold. A spark of fight smoldered within me. When I stepped foot into those gardens, a series of events fell like dominos spurred on by my choices.

"I can provide your mother with funds above the asking price for the harvests."

I whipped my attention to Silas, shocked by the statement.

"They will be cared for. I promise." Earnestness crossed his expression and sincerity laced his tone.

My reasoning for staying disintegrated before me. Perhaps my base instincts were more inclined to self-preservation than I thought. Heaving a sigh, I turned to Naomi, but the wisps of light were vanishing, immersing her in the shadows as she nodded for me to agree.

"I'll marry you," I said, but I didn't feel relief. Instead, a knot churned in my stomach.

"I will return at midnight, and we will wed once we cross into the Presspin territory."

The orchard darkened, and I let out a breath as my future husband walked past me. No smile or relief shone on his features. Only stony acceptance that our fates were now intertwined.

"No one must know of our marriage or Arianna's whereabouts. It is the only way I can fully protect her." To my surprise, he offered his arm to Naomi, and she glanced back at me before taking it.

We walked from the orchard, appearing exactly as this ruse began. Silas, the wealthy bachelor, with my lovely and eligible sister by his side. My mother would be none the wiser that Lord Silas Belmont had indeed proposed marriage to her daughter in the fading light of the orchards. However, it wasn't the one he led home with an aloof expression on his face, but the daughter she despised who would soon be his bride.

CHAPTER 23

SILAS

I SLUMPED INTO THE carriage seat and rubbed my forehead where an ache throbbed. I shut my eyes, hoping my mind had trapped me in some sort of nightmare. Perhaps I would awaken and find myself tucked in my bed at Archer Estate. Yet the door clicked closed, reminding me that this wasn't a dream.

"It was generous of you to purchase the Parks' entire harvest at double the price," Beatrix said with a nervous titter in her voice.

I didn't answer her. Instead, I stared at the roof with my arms crossed against my chest. No words formed on my lips as I contemplated what had occurred. My life had irrevocably changed, but what should I have done? Walked away? Yet hadn't I known Arianna's fate when I entered her home? Those damned bruises made my desire to run feel cowardly. At the core of my soul, I realized I wouldn't allow her to fall into ruination. Like when I first saw her, my body acted of its own accord, keeping her from peril.

"Did you say goodbye?" Beatrix asked.

I sensed her assessing me and my terse mood. The carriage turned down the level path, returning to Archer Estate. The clopping of hoofbeats matched my pounding heart. Minutes passed in this awkward silence. She fidgeted in her seat, then let out a huff.

"Silas, what happened on that walk?"

A maddening laugh escaped me at the preposterous turn of events. I had been so close to returning to Presspin unencumbered. Now Arianna would be my bride and the lady of my manor.

"You know exactly what happened. You played me like one of your pawns." I tightened my grip on my arms, attempting to leash this fury. I glared at her through the shadows of the dark carriage.

"What are you talking about?" she asked.

"Don't play games with me. I am too tired, and I'm losing patience with this evening. You and your fanciful novels and damned romantic heroes have doomed me. You knew I wouldn't be able to walk away. I couldn't..." The choking sensation returned, cutting off my words. My thoughts filled with the agony I felt at seeing Arianna in such a precarious situation.

"Silas, you are not making any sense."

To my relief, the carriage pulled in front of Archer Estate, ending our conversation.

I leapt out of the conveyance. Consumed by the night, I gasped, choking on the inevitable future ahead. How would I survive with Arianna under my roof? During our interactions, I had been a moth to a flame, unable to resist her. Restless, I didn't wait for Beatrix to pepper me with questions. Instead, I hastened up the steps to the entrance. I pushed the heavy door open with a smack. Then I stalked through the manor until I reached the sitting room and beelined for the liquor cart.

I had avoided this place. Gods, I had avoided most rooms where Arianna once dwelled. Yet given this evening's events, I required a drink. I poured two fingers of whiskey and downed it. The alcohol didn't loosen the noose around my neck. I needed more. I tipped the decanter. Amber liquid sloshed into the glass. My hand gripped the crystal so tightly I thought it might crack.

"Silas! What is going on with you?"

Beatrix rushed to my side and grabbed the snifter out of my clutches. She scowled at me. "Uncle Oliver always said overindulgence in spirits could affect your control over your curse."

Agitated, my body shook with a mix of overwhelm and frustration. Ignoring my sister, I stalked toward the window and peered at the bleak darkness. Tension pulled through my shoulders. I seethed. Beatrix had led me like a lamb to the slaughter, my life the sacrifice for Arianna's. Trapped, I yanked off my jacket and flung it to the floor. The motion allayed me, freeing me from the coat but not my future.

The glass clinked against the cart, then Beatrix's soft footsteps approached. She placed a hand on my back and rubbed soothing circles. "Please talk to me. What happened?"

"You already know what happened," I said through gritted teeth.

Her palm froze, confirming my suspicion. I stared into the darkness instead of turning to her.

"Why did you do this? Was it a fun game for you? You knew if I entered her house, I wouldn't be able to endure witnessing the truth. It killed me."

I choked on my words and combed my fingers through my hair, but the motion failed to calm me. Agony swelled within me, replacing my rage. The flash of purple contusions flickered in my mind. My shoulders shook as I let out a ragged breath.

"Theo, he strangled her, left a necklace of bruises on her throat. She didn't plan on revealing them to me. I only glimpsed them because of the fortune of a light breeze."

Beatrix took me in, and her gentle gaze cut through me. The expression gnawed at my soul. I had no interest in her sympathy. Instead, I focused on the window and the night awaiting me.

"Arianna and I are leaving tonight, and we shall wed when we cross the border. Peter can perform the binding ceremony." The words felt strange coming from my mouth, as if I were disconnected from this reality.

"This elopement is the best course of action for Arianna. And for you," Beatrix said.

My shoulders shook with a maddened chuckle. I brushed off her fingertips and pivoted to her. "Gods, Beatrix, this is my life, and you meddled yet again. We are adults, and your interventions have consequences. This isn't like when you tried to help me become friends with Layla, or when the youths convinced you that farmer Martin's daughter pined for me. Everything has changed because of your inane whim. I came to Krella a bachelor, and I'm returning with a lady of the manor. The servants...how am I going to explain this?"

She didn't answer me. Instead, she sauntered over to the drink cart, grabbed the discarded glass of whiskey, and downed the contents. I gaped at her. Beatrix was a lightweight with alcohol, preferring wine to spirits and only at dinner. Her glare burned into me, and she tipped her chin in defiance, challenging me.

"Enough. Did I suspect you needed a push toward doing what we both knew was right and declaring your feelings for her? I did. However, you made the choice. I still don't understand why you are agitated. She accepted your proposal, and you are leaving Krella with a bride you're obviously in love with."

I bellowed a laugh, knocking my head back. She jolted. "Gods! Those novels really have muddled your thoughts. We are not in love. How could we be? I hardly know the woman. No, our marriage shall be one of convenience. Belmont manor is large enough for us to avoid seeing each other, except for when I train her to control her curse. Once she achieves mastery, we can live separate lives."

Beatrix's mouth hung open. She rubbed her crinkled brow and shook her head. "Do you hear yourself? Sweet mercy, I knew you were stubborn and a bit daft over matters of the heart. But this? Did Father really—"

"Don't you dare speak about Father. Not now. He has nothing to do with this."

She didn't bristle at my agitation. Instead, she flopped onto the floral sofa, her green day dress pooling around her.

"Fine. I don't want to argue, not if you are leaving tonight. Can we stop bickering before I'm left here alone?" She let out a weary breath as she slumped farther into the couch. Her brown eyes were sorrowful, and that damned trembling pout pulled on her bottom lip.

I heaved a sigh to release these disconcerting emotions. Moving toward her, I sat in the chair. Weeks prior, Arianna had lounged across from me, curious about Presspin. Now she would be its lady. This visit had been so hopeful. I had planned on spending time with Beatrix and perhaps enjoying some of the local produce while securing supplies for the winter. I could have never predicted the chaos this trip would cause.

"Are you worried the Terrells will discover your connection to Arianna?" Beatrix asked. She fiddled with an appliqué on her dress. The pink silk flowers dotted the green fabric, making her seem like spring itself.

"Our marriage should supersede her betrothal. At least once Arianna and I consummate our union. Yet the only way I can guarantee her safety is through complete secrecy. If anyone suspects our connection because of your recent teas with her, I assume you will lie?"

"Yes, of course. If anyone asks, you only met Arianna in passing. Actually, you were far more interested in her sister, the young Ms. Naomi. It devastated me when you left on urgent business. Though it can't be helped. You are the overseer of Presspin." She tilted her head, and her countenance shifted as a mischievous smile crossed her lips. "I'll also swear that you would never carry an engaged woman into your room and secure her in your bed. You most definitely wouldn't help her undress."

"You knew?" I asked. How had she known, and did she think we...?

"We played chess. Nothing more. She couldn't sleep and neither could I."

"You will have plenty of evenings to play games with her now. Hmm. Or not, since it's a marriage of convenience. So no late-night recreation for you."

"Enough. We shouldn't speak of this." I found my footing in the conversation, pulling against the stony demeanor I relied upon. Yet Beatrix's jest soothed the fraying edges of my nerves.

"Fine, I won't tease you." Beatrix sighed. The lighthearted moment faded, replaced with the charged silence over the topic neither of us wanted to broach. A minute passed before Beatrix relented.

"Duncan is not a dunce. He thought you were intimate with her." Her lips flattened into a tight, thin line as she mentioned her husband.

"As far as he knows, I have respected his wishes. He still views me as a young man he trained, following him with blind obedience. I have never opposed him. Nor have I given him any reason to expect I would. Especially given his extreme displeasure with the situation."

Beatrix let out a heavy sigh and began chewing on her thumb, lost in momentary thought. But she stopped her nervous nibbling and lowered her hands to her dress, folding them tightly.

"When Duncan returns home, we can explain everything. He will understand, and it is past time we shared the secret of your curse with him. For now, he intends to stay in Seaside through the autumn, working on securing a trade route with the seafaring town behind the jagged coastal mountains. There isn't an established road or post. When he returns, we will inform him of the good news, and he will soften to Arianna. We are a family, the three of us...and soon the four of us."

I nodded instinctively, but the idea of Arianna being referred to as our family felt off-putting. Exhausted, I stood to leave.

But she reached out and grabbed the cuff of my sleeve. "Are you worried about them searching for her in Presspin or coming for you?"

I rolled my neck, then glanced down at my sister. Worry flashed across her expression, as it should. We both understood greater forces were at play. Powers far more insidious than even the Terrells, and if they found Arianna, I couldn't guarantee her safety or mine. Neither of us spoke this secret into existence.

"Let's hope they assume she ran off and is dead in a ditch somewhere. As long as our connection remains hidden, no one should suspect she became my bride. A cursed woman traveling masked without stopping at a spelled room would seem impossible. My wife won't be bound to one. No one will know of her true identity or the blight she carries. Please, lie well." I grabbed her hand, and she squeezed it in return.

I released her and left to plan for my sudden departure.

CHAPTER 24

Arianna

Mama's joyous humming drifted to my room. Her mood had turned from sullen a few days prior to elated since this evening. Naomi had played her role well when we returned home from the orchard hours ago. Mama had chatted delightedly at Silas when he entered the parlor with Naomi on his arm. My sister, in turn, shot him coquettish glances. Yet Silas remained stoic, showing not a hint of the truth in his countenance as he offered double the price for our meager harvest. The promise of gold sent Mama into a delighted tizzy as she peppered him with praise and flourished a ridiculous curtsy as they departed.

"He is besotted with you, my dear girl! Why else would he pay such an exorbitant amount for the produce? With his fortune, I doubt he is a poor businessman. Yet he is from Presspin and might be unaccustomed to haggling. Either way, I suspect he is half in love with you already." Mama had beamed at Naomi.

I left as Mama focused on her darling daughter. Her wishful thinking drifted up the stairs as she dreamed of my sister being the future Lady Belmont of Presspin. I repressed a wry laugh, realizing that I would hold the title.

Mama's humming stopped, pulling me from my thoughts of this afternoon. An eerie silence filled the space as I took in the small dressing table where I ate my meals as Naomi would gossip about the happenings of the town. I slumped onto the bed. My palm rubbed over the worn green quilt, smoothing the fraying embroidered vines. I reminisced over the nights I spent wrapped in this blanket and the gentle feel of my mother brushing my hair when she once loved me. The hummed tune from earlier reverberated in my soul, the same melody she used to sing me to sleep.

But I couldn't allow myself to dwell here, not when I needed to collect my meager belongings. I pulled out the four day dresses from the trunk and shoved them into the burlap sack, along with my underthings and a nightgown. The small pack brimmed full, forcing me to pick only a single story for this journey. I pivoted to the wall that held my novels. My fingers traced the titles on the shelf. They had served as my escape, my only portals to the outside world. Now a real adventure awaited me. I grabbed the pirate princess novel and flipped through the worn pages. The scent of faded ink soothed me. As I clutched it to my chest, my focus drifted to the dressing table, where the dried pink and purple wildflowers sat. I plucked one and examined the crinkling violet petals, a gift from Naomi's summer romps in the outlying fields.

I closed my eyes and envisioned Naomi in this existence, where I was Lady Belmont. In this future, she danced amongst the wildflowers, adorned in a beautiful day dress with her blonde locks braided into a crown. She lived without the financial burden weighing on her shoulders. A pot clanged downstairs, pulling me from my reveries. With a sigh, I slipped the flower behind the cover and placed the novel beside my possessions.

A certainty filled me. Silas, though stoic, seemed honorable. If my family fell on hard times, I knew he would provide for them. Maybe this arrangement would give Naomi more security. Whereas Theo wouldn't have intervened if my sister suffered.

A shiver snaked along my spine at the thought of my former intended. Theo would be furious. But Naomi had been correct: they would return the seven sheep to the Terrells. Theo was still young and handsome, despite his horrible personality. He could secure a new bride. Perhaps one with a greater tie to an ancient bloodline. Theo himself considered me a cursed nothing, but would he let me go? The memory of his jealous rage when he suspected I had merely spoken to Silas made me shudder. Instinctually, I traced the bruises along my throat. Would he come for me, even after I was married to someone else? Or would he forget about me and move on to torturing another? I hoped for the latter, but I feared his unhinged wrath would follow me to Presspin.

However, hadn't that been why Silas insisted we keep this a secret? To protect me from the Terrells until the dust of our elopement had settled? Or did he fear our nuptials would not abolish Theo's claim on me? Would the high council and the Aralians not see our union as irrevocable and force me to wed Theo anyway? But the act of consummation should supersede my betrothal, even if the ceremony occurred under Presspin law.

My ruminations spiraled away from Theo and onto more intriguing notions. My knees weakened and my skin flushed at the idea of my impending wedding night. I licked my lips as I imagined kissing Silas. I leaned against the wall, allowing a fanciful daydream that would soon become a reality to wash over me.

A knock pulled me from my musing. I straightened and fought the urge to blush as Naomi entered, carrying my dinner. She forced a watery smile, but a hint of melancholy lingered in her gaze.

"You need to eat before you go." She lowered the tray to the dressing table. Then she settled on the mattress as she had for so many evenings. Night after night, the pattern had been the same: Naomi brought me my meals, and I ate as she told me stories. This dinner would be the last. The heaviness of what I was preparing to leave behind bloomed within my chest, replacing my fanciful hopes.

My stomach sank, and I doubted I could eat a bite of the thin soup. The sureness I had felt moments prior became clouded with ambivalence. Had I lost my mind since seeing Silas, throwing me into a delusional state? I couldn't leave, I couldn't wed Silas, I couldn't risk Naomi's happiness. I collapsed onto my bed beside her. Her smile faltered, and her lips twisted into a frown.

"I can't do this. I can't abandon you here by yourself." I held back tears, tired of crying over circumstances outside my control.

"Aren't you curious about what I desire?" she asked, her brow wrinkled in consternation.

I nodded. A knot had formed in my throat, making it difficult to speak.

"I want you to live a full life. You don't have to sacrifice yourself for my happiness, and I already have plans for my future that do not require you wedding a monster. Moreso, do you not realize how much I care for you? How devastated I would be to see you tied to a man who would harm you?"

"I do, but—"

"I'm a grown woman and not your responsibility. Let me and Mama go. Start a new life. Trust me, all will be well." Her words were gentle. Naomi smiled wearily and patted my hand. Her inner strength amazed me. I wanted the world for her. Maybe once everything settled from this whirlwind elopement, I could give her all the things she deserved.

Instead of arguing, I studied her every detail. Her large round, eyes radiated with intelligence. A shade darker than my own, they were azure like gemstones. Her apple cheeks were rosy and her fair skin flawless. She possessed our mother's symmetrical and regal nose. I brushed back her unbraided tresses and tucked them behind her ear, and an ache tugged in my chest. I memorized the curve of her jaw and the arch of her eyebrows, painting a mental portrait of her to carry with me always.

I stroked her cheek, soaking in her warmth. My lips quivered as I locked the guttural cries behind them. She had filled this dreary world with so much light, illuminating my existence. I cherished her more than life itself. We had never parted, not since the day she was born.

I gazed upon my first love, my best friend, my sister, who meant everything to me. The impending loss felt like a hot knife cutting into my chest. The pain was unbearable as I entered an existence without Naomi by my side.

At the realization, sobs racked my body. Her frown deepened, and she clutched her folded hands so tightly her knuckles blanched.

"I don't know when we will be reunited." My shoulders shook as the repressed emotions broke free.

She pulled me into her embrace. I swear a tear rolled down her cheek, even though she hated crying.

"I love you," I said, her lily fragrance soothing my fraying nerves.

"I love you, too, and I will keep your secret," she said.

We held each other for long minutes, until my sobs stifled. Then we broke apart. I dried my tears and exhaled a shaky breath as I forced my mind to focus on the task at hand. I strode to the dressing table. I gripped a note and pivoted to Naomi. She stood and brushed her hands over her dress, smoothing out the wrinkles and her composure.

"I wrote this for Mama when she realizes I've fled. I hope to mislead her on her search. The note informs her of my search for refuge in Hallowhaven. And would you—"

"Lie? Yes, I'll keep this secret from Mama. If I am fortunate, she won't notice you are gone for days at worst, a week at best. When she finally discovers you are missing, I'll mention your sudden interest in visiting the Aralian temple." Naomi rubbed her brow and pursed her lips in thought, an expression she wore whenever she was piecing together something that puzzled her. “This secrecy Silas is demanding. It seems excessive.”

I opened and closed my mouth to argue but couldn’t. I too wondered about his adamance that Naomi speak of this to no one. Obviously, we needed a short period of time, but after we were wed and the bride price was returned, the betrothal contract with the Terrells should be null and void, shouldn’t it?

“He seems secretive, hiding his curse and the ability to control it from the world. Perhaps it is best we follow his lead, at least for now,” she said.

She brushed past me and placed the letter on the dressing table. Her fingers traced the pink flower, the dried petal cracking under her touch, and with it, so did her demeanor. Soft sobs escaped her. “I will miss you. More than you know.”

She didn’t turn toward me as she wept. Instead, she clutched the ledge of the vanity. I wrapped my arms around her waist and pressed my cheek against her back. Minutes passed before her cries softened. The cadence of her breath steadied, and I withdrew my hold.

She pivoted to me, and we wordlessly stared at one another. We lingered in this heartbreak as our paths diverged. Her eyes held mine as she backed away slowly. Then she left without another word.

The door clicked closed. Anguish seeped into my soul at the sudden isolation. I willed myself to steady, to breathe through this excruciating pain, because there was one last person I needed to see before I ran away.

The mask pulled against my skin as I exited my room. I crept down the steps and through the parlor in search of Mama. Walking into the kitchen, a pang at the familiarity tugged at me. She sat at the table, drinking tea out of a chipped porcelain cup, the last piece of her wedding dishes that hadn't been sold off to keep the farm afloat. Her cracked fingers gracefully held the cup with a delicate and faded rose painted on it, which reminded me of Mama. Despite her loveliness, there had always been undertones of fragility to her disposition. Over the years, sharp thorns had formed around her to protect the delicacy of this country rose.

"Arianna," she said, startled out of her routine as I approached where she sat in once relaxed silence. But her attention turned to me as I joined her, taking a seat on the stool across from her. She didn't question my appearance despite its oddity, likely still too elated with the afternoon to care. She lowered her cup to the table. Her usually tense demeanor smoothed as she smiled.

"You did well. You must have spoken your sister's praises when you were at Archer Estate for Lord Belmont to be so taken by her. He is smitten with her already, rushing past me when he saw Naomi in the stairwell. Then he perched on the sofa waiting with bated breath for her. And the gleam in his eyes when he led her down the stairs? I nearly swooned with excitement. I'm certain they will be wed by next summer. A mother always knows these things."

I smiled beneath my mask. She truly hadn't the slightest idea, and yet seeing her jovial was something I hadn't witnessed in ages. It warmed my heart, even though this interaction had been built upon a lie.

She examined me in a rare moment of genuine observation, trying to see the girl beneath the mask. A loose strand of hair crept across my covered face. She studied the lock before she reached forward. I froze as her fingertips grazed past the porcelain, tucking the curl behind my ear. Her gaze searched mine and softened for a heartbeat, reminding me of when she used to look at me as a child.

Her smile faltered as she lowered her hand and glanced at the purple bruises peeking out from under my collar. She reached out and gently grazed over them. I flinched. She pursed her lips, as if fighting internally to say something. But she only shook her head in resignation. A knot welled in my throat, and I stifled sobs, wishing desperately she would notice me. I longed for her to care for me, to intercede on my behalf and take the pain I carried off my shoulders. Yet she said nothing.

Instead, I absorbed every detail, line, and wrinkle on her face. However, she stood, breaking this rare interaction. "Goodnight, Arianna."

I watched my mother walk away until she faded into the dark shadows of the hallway leading to her room. Tears rolled down my face as I whispered, "I love you, Mama."

CHAPTER 25

SILAS

MOONLIGHT FILLED THE NIGHT sky on this clear evening as I rolled to my doom. The lantern attached to the front of the carriage pierced through the darkness, creating a path toward my future. As I slumped in the seat, a nervous energy pulsed through me. For a moment, I considered traveling to Presspin alone, leaving Arianna waiting at the side of the road. But in the depths of my soul, I knew I wouldn't be able to live with myself if I abandoned her.

I closed my eyes, and the occurrences of these few weeks in Krella played on repeat through my mind. I attempted to sort through the memories, certain a single moment served as a catalyst. Which of these whirlwind events had brought me to this juncture? Had I gone mad the instant I stepped foot in the village? No, my madness took hold when Arianna bumped into me, leaving a trail of ruined strawberry tarts behind her. Like that bag of desserts, she threw my tidy life into chaos.

The carriage halted as it neared the edge of the Parks' property. I heaved a shaky exhale as the conveyance swayed. I forced my hunched posture into a more appropriate position. My heart thrummed as the driver opened the door and Arianna entered. She pushed her hood back, revealing the porcelain that shielded her features. Moonlight cascaded over her through the window, catching on the mask, which blithely smiled at me, delighting in my misfortune.

She scurried to the seat across from me and stared at the floor as the door shut behind her. Seconds later, the driver flicked the reins, and we lurched forward. Silence remained between us, punctuated by the horses' hooves clopping on the broken path. With each hoofbeat, her breathing turned more ragged. Her shoulders shook, and sobs escaped her.

My throat bobbed at the painful sound. For the past few hours, I had dwelled on my misfortune. I had thought little of my future bride's feelings. But shouldn't she be elated? She no longer had to wed that brute. I couldn't offer her love, but she would have safety, freedom, and a home where my people would welcome her. Yet her cries intensified as we turned onto the smooth path leading out of Krella.

A guttural wail escaped her, piercing through my heart, causing it to ache for her as she fell into anguish. I was uncertain of what to do and gaped helplessly at this woman who broke into a million pieces before me. Her sorrowful moans transformed into wails of agony, and she tugged at the porcelain frantically.

"Get it off! Get it off! Get it off!"

Her pain was sweet nectar to her curse, which yearned to be unleashed, yet the mask served as the jail confining it. Panic emerged within me as I remembered the afternoon in the gardens when the suppression spell overwhelmed her and death had beckoned. At the memory, power prickled beneath my skin. I, too, would succumb to my dark impulses if we couldn't rectify this situation.

Without hesitating, I broke the chain from my neck and removed my uncle's onyx ring. I lurched forward, balancing precariously, then settled beside her. But my presence didn't soothe her as she tugged at the porcelain, and a painful moan left her. I grabbed her hand and slipped the ring onto her thumb. The mask tumbled off her and clattered to the floor. In frustration, I kicked the damn thing out of sight.

She peered at me, and tears glistened along her cheeks. I thought she would find relief without the spelled contraption. Instead, her wails intensified. If her emotions remained unchecked, she would summon the misery to life, and we would be in a dangerous situation.

Hesitantly, I wrapped an arm around her and pulled her into my embrace, hoping the contact would soothe her. She burrowed her face into my side, stifling her cries. Moisture pooled against my jacket. She trembled against me for long minutes with ragged breaths until her wails yielded to sporadic sobs. I shifted to move, but her fingers clutched my lapel, halting my forward motion. I leaned back with her curled against my side, nuzzling into me. My pulse surged as my fingers grazed over the soft curve of her hip. I gulped back the swell of intrigue that tightened my groin.

I clenched my jaw and pushed this physical awareness away. No, when we get to Presspin, I needed to create as much distance as possible between us in order to maintain my composure.

To my relief, her once shaking shoulders slowed and her respiration evened. She lifted her head and peered at me. The subtle moonlight highlighted her fine features, and through a trembling voice, she said, "I'm so sorry."

Despite my logic's protestations, I tightened my grip around her, and my lips grazed her hairline. "Go to sleep."

I reached for the curtain and drew it closed, enveloping us in darkness. Then I leaned deeper into the seat, and she settled her head against my chest. My heart thundered, feeling far too aware of her body melded against mine. I told myself, on this chilly autumn night, that she needed my warmth, which would keep her from spiraling into her emotions again. Instead of moving to the opposite seat, I relaxed and hoped sleep would take me as I held my future bride. A bride I swore to myself I could never love.

Arianna

A whisper of sunlight flickered over my skin. Gods, my bed had never been this comfortable. I nuzzled my cheek against the soft fabric, but the cushion of my mattress felt firm against my body. I inhaled the scent of something vaguely familiar, and my half-dazed mind registered Silas's woodsy aroma. My eyelids fluttered open, and I took in the empty crimson seat before me. I flushed with embarrassment. My head rose and fell against his chest as he breathed steadily in slumber. I gulped down mortification from last night. I had blubbered like an idiot against him, unwilling to let him go, clinging to him for comfort.

I gingerly extracted myself from his loose embrace and crept to the other side of the carriage, attempting not to wake him. Settled on the cushioned bench, I sighed with relief as he remained unstirred. He appeared more relaxed, looking far younger than his years in this state. But at that thought, my stomach dropped as I beheld my bridegroom. I didn't know how old Silas was. Though I despised Theo, I knew more about the man than I cared to admit, from his obsession with the goddess Aralia to his hatred of carrots. Silas and I were practically strangers. The knowledge gnawed at me, and my impetuous decision felt even more preposterous in the light of day.

To distract myself, I pulled back the curtain and peeked out as dawn crested over the rolling hills of Daviel. A shepherd guided his bleating flock through the lush greenery. The hoofbeats clinked along the stone streets as we entered the square. A few vendors rolled carts brimming with wool, heading for the bustling commerce center. Ashwood shops with red clay tile roofs lined the way. The lane appeared sleepy, but in mere hours, it would likely be filled with people hustling about. Grander than Krella, Daviel was the northernmost town under Hallowhaven's rule. From stories Naomi told me of her visit after Father's death, the capital city dwarfed even this sprawling territory.

"Close the curtain. We don't want anyone to see within." Silas peered at me with one eye open. He had shifted, taking up the space I once occupied, with his long legs draped over the cushions in a relaxed sprawl.

"Sorry." I dropped the heavy crimson drapery, and only a sliver of light peeked around the edges.

"And please stop apologizing," he said, but he didn't look at me.

I nodded, and the word *sorry* almost passed my lips, but I stopped myself. Instead, I asked, "Do you think anyone will realize we left together?"

He stretched, his hulking form filling the cramped space. I gulped, taking in the full view of him. His black tailored pants clung to his muscular thighs. His once crisp dress shirt gaped open, and his collarbone peeked through. I bit my lower lip. The usually composed gentleman appeared rumpled in the most intriguing way.

But he sat up abruptly and rolled his neck. His stony demeanor replaced the softness he had exuded seconds prior. "It depends on how long your absence goes unnoticed."

I smoothed my hands over my wrinkled dress and focused on the fraying fabric instead of him.

"No one should realize I'm gone for at least a few days. I rarely leave my room, and Naomi brings my meals and helps me dress. My mother, she doesn't care for entering my quarters, nor attending me. She likely won't check on me until the wedding date draws near." I slumped into the stiff cushions, making myself more comfortable.

"Let's hope your mother is as neglectful as you say. The longer your absence goes unnoticed, the better." Silas's jaw clenched, and he ran his fingers through his messy, wavy hair.

I nodded, thinking about the note I had left for my mother. It contained a few simple lines conveying my intentions to run away to Hallowhaven. I hoped sending Mama in the opposite direction of Presspin would slow her suspicions.

Turning his attention from me, Silas leaned toward the floor, rummaged through a small bag I hadn't noticed, and pulled out a loaf of bread. He broke it in half and handed me a piece without a word.

"Thank you." I took the offering and nibbled on it. We ate in silence, but an indescribable tension lingered between us. Perhaps we were both nervous about wedding someone we knew so little about. In an effort to bridge this gap, I asked, "How old are you?"

"Thirty," he said. Then he returned to eating, studying the baguette as if the flaky crust was the most fascinating thing he'd ever seen.

Seconds passed, and I furrowed my brow. "Don't you want to know my age? I am to be your wife."

"I suppose so." He finished the last bites of breakfast and dusted the crumbs off his jacket. Then he tilted his head back and stared at the ceiling.

"I'm twenty-five," I said, feeling agitated by his lack of inquisitiveness. Perhaps we needed to warm up to each other? But only silence fell between us. Sighing, I made a last attempt. Though I was awkward and rarely engaged in conversation, I had to try. He would be my husband after tonight. I searched for a question, anything, and settled on "what activities interest you?"

He straightened, and his stare bored into me, displeasure etched in his features. "This is unnecessary. As I said yesterday, we are to have a marriage of convenience. Perhaps you are unfamiliar with this sort of union? We will live separate lives under the same roof. Except for this evening, I'll never visit your bed, nor will I welcome you into mine. We don't need to form a friendship. Think of our arrangement akin to a master and apprentice: I'll teach you the skills required to control your power and provide you with a home, nothing more."

I opened and closed my mouth, wanting to argue, but the terms were fairer than I had received under Theo.

"Very well. When can I invite my sister to visit Presspin, then? I know we must wait for everything to settle and for my mother to return my bride price, but I am certain that in a few weeks' time she could—"

"No." Silas's face hardened. I flinched at the statement, the word rolling through my mind.

"Why?" I twisted the onyx ring on my thumb, attempting to quell this nervous energy. Had I exchanged one prison for another?

His jaw twitched, but he remained silent for a long while. He let out an exasperated huff, then spoke. "If I am to protect you, then our marriage must remain a secret. You are not to contact anyone outside of Presspin. Not your mother, not Beatrix, not even your sister. It is the only way I can keep you safe."

I gulped at his statement and wanted to argue, but that incessant voice which had led me to the gardens whispered, "*Trust him, trust him, trust him.*"

Despite my uncertainty, I nodded in agreement.

"Good, let's not discuss any other trivial topics." He reached for the bag and rummaged through it, ignoring me. He grabbed a ledger and lounged back into the cushions. He flipped through the pages, immersing himself in his work.

Regardless of his terse nature, I couldn't look away from him. Naomi was right. He seemed to have many guarded secrets that I might never discover. Yet I should consider myself grateful that I was free from Theo's clutches and the grasp the mask possessed over me. I picked at the bread, no longer interested in eating as I worried about my upcoming nuptials to a man who was caring one second and aloof the next.

He flicked his attention to me, and I blushed as his amber gaze held mine. A sigh left his lips. "Eat. We won't be stopping for food again until we reach the inn later this afternoon."

I ate the bread. The buttery flavor danced on my tongue, but I cared little about the delicate texture. Instead, I studied this mercurial man, and a flutter of uncertainty filled my soul. But my hesitation didn't matter, not when our lots had already been set.

CHAPTER 26

ARIANNA

I LOWERED THE BOOK to my lap and stretched my arms over my head. My bones ached from the carriage's never-ending jostling as we bounced along dirt paths. We had stopped once after passing Daviel to relieve ourselves and trade out horses at a small outpost where rolling hills had given way to evergreens. Silas had been determined to cross the border out of Hallowhaven's control before sunset.

Wearily, I picked up the novel and thumbed through the pages to find my place. As I had done for hours, I trained my gaze off the stoic man who sat across from me.

"We are here," Silas said.

I let out a sigh of relief. Soon I would be out of this cramped carriage and able to stretch my aching body.

I blinked as we slowed in front of an inn more akin to an oversized cottage. It was made of smooth gray stone, with vines creeping to the tops of wooden shingles. Ancient evergreens surrounded the building as if it were part of nature itself. Yellow wildflowers sprang about the gardens and wove through the shrubbery along the path. My heart fluttered at the romantic spot. It looked as if it had jumped straight out of a fairy tale. We were the sole conveyance and likely the only visitors.

The carriage halted. Silas didn't wait for the driver to open the door. Instead, he burst out of the confined space. He strode away, with quick, heavy steps. I exited, and a shiver cut through me as a crisp breeze pierced through my ineffective cloak. The temperature had dropped at the base of the mountain range, leading to Presspin. The scent of pine and damp earth hit me, so reminiscent of Silas that my tense nerves loosened.

"*Silas,*" a woman's voice called out, and an elderly couple raced to him before he reached the entrance.

I froze, taken aback by their jovial nature as the pair embraced him. I ambled toward the group. Cobbles crunched beneath my boots, but despite the noise, they paid me no heed, the three of them lost in their own world.

Finally, they released him. The late afternoon sun washed over Silas, highlighting the flicker of a sheepish smile that softened his countenance and left me breathless. My heart thundered at this tender side of him. It was in such stark contrast to the stern and silent man I had spent hours with inside the carriage.

The plump woman placed her hands on her hips, assessing him. Her brown eyes crinkled with a mix of mirth and confusion. "You are early. I didn't expect you until the end of harvest."

The graying man with umber skin beamed and patted Silas on the shoulder. "It is such a wonderful surprise to see you."

Silas's face flashed with a brilliant joy. Against the background of the Presspin mountains and the wildflowers, he appeared like a fairy-tale prince, a knight rescuing a maiden. Goddess, I needed to stop reading such fanciful novels. But there had been flickers of this gentler version of Silas in our interactions at Archer Estate, even if his taciturn nature left me confused now. However, he had been more than clear about his intentions for our marriage, and these longings were best kept buried.

As I stepped closer, my boots clinked against the path. The couple shifted their attention to me, then turned back to Silas. Their expressions brimmed with unspoken questions.

"We require your assistance," Silas said.

The pair looked beyond Silas. They studied me, then exchanged confused glances. The man stroked his chin and cocked his head, assessing me. "Who is this young lady?"

"Arianna, my betrothed. And we need to be wed. Tonight." Silas gestured for me to join him.

The pair's eyebrows rose to their hairlines in near unison as I moved to stand beside Silas. I blushed as the couple studied me. I expected them to turn us away or argue.

The woman recovered first, and a wide grin painted her expression. "This is quite a surprise!"

She grabbed my hands and pulled me toward the cottage. "Peter, the boy has finally decided to wed. Let's not question him about this miraculous event. Blessed Cassius. I never thought this day would come. Now go prepare for the ceremony while I ready the bride."

She tugged me through the door and said, "I'm Agnes, dear. It's a pleasure to meet you." I peered behind me at Silas and Peter, who stood unmoved, as if Agnes's reaction had been far more shocking than our sudden request to be married.

Once inside, she guided me down a hallway with wallpaper depicting creeping green vines that mimicked the exterior. Watercolors of landscapes lined the walls, but I couldn't meander.

"This way, dear." Agnes led me into a room designed in chipper yellow colors that matched her sunny demeanor. Then she released me but didn't give me a second to get my bearings.

"Do you have something you wish to change into?"

I looked over my threadbare brown dress and wished I had brought the gaudy blue gown from my engagement dinner. I hadn't thought about my wedding attire before we fled Krella. Sensing my answer, she assessed me. Her mouth pursed, then she turned without a word and rushed out the door.

Nerves gripped me, and I slumped onto the plush mattress. Was I truly marrying a stranger? I fidgeted with the onyx ring on my thumb. Despite its strangeness, it suited me far better than the diamond band, which I had left behind with my letter to my mother. Instead of focusing on the impending ceremony, I took in the lovely space. The four-poster bed had a crisp buttercup-colored quilt, and fresh yellow wildflowers were arranged in a glass vase on the nightstand. The soft scent of soap and lemon filled the space. My heart pounded as I awaited my future. Minutes passed, and I considered venturing out in search of Agnes. But before I could, the door opened. She glided in with a genuine smile and something tucked under her arm.

"This was from my binding ceremony many years ago. I would be honored if you wore it today." She unfolded the fabric with a flick of her wrist. It unfurled to reveal an exquisite dress.

Her kindness shocked me. My fingers skimmed along the preserved sage-colored silk with tiny dark green embroidered flowers that were almost black. The beauty of it far surpassed any white wedding gown.

"Thank you, but I can't wear this. You don't even know me."

Her free hand caressed my cheek in a gesture so tender it nearly brought me to tears. "Silas is like a grandson to us, and you will become our granddaughter. Anyone he loves dearly enough to elope with in haste must be a veritable treasure."

She gestured for me to turn around without awaiting my answer. I stood facing the bed as she undressed me. In nothing but my thin slip, I took a steadying breath and stepped into the gown. My heart hammered with apprehension and tears threatened to fall as she laced me into my fate. The gorgeous dress didn't fit perfectly. However, it was beautiful beyond measure, with gossamer sleeves and a cinched bodice that flared out into silk skirts. The style had been popular decades ago, but it was far more vibrant than the gaudy white lace concoction that would have awaited me at Terrell Estate. Though Agnes was shorter than me and fuller in the bust, she secured me in the garment by tightening the laces to shape the fabric to my frail frame. She spun me to face her, and her gaze caught on my bare neck where the bruises lay. Her brow wrinkled and concern replaced her jovial demeanor. Instinctively, I placed my hands over them to shield the contusions, but she didn't comment.

"Now, I must make certain we are ready for the ceremony. Have a seat. I'll return soon." She gestured to the plush bed, and I perched on the edge, afraid of wrinkling the fabric.

The door clicked closed, leaving me isolated yet again. My heart thundered and blood pulsed in my ears. I willed myself to stand in front of the mirror to take in my reflection, but I couldn't. Instead, I felt the hollow ache of experiencing this day alone, without Naomi or my mother.

Many minutes later, Agnes returned, bearing a crown made of pine needles and a small satchel. She lowered the bag and headpiece to the nightstand. I remained still as she twisted her fingers through my curls, coaxing a spring into them. Satisfied, she placed the crown on my head and beamed. Then she rustled through the satchel. She pulled out a jar and brush. Then she dusted the fine powder over my face and neck, covering the bruises. She continued her primping as she lined my lids with kohl and my cheeks and lips with rouge. Finally, she took my hands in hers and guided me toward the mirror.

I gasped at the unrecognizable woman who peered back at me. The gown accentuated my tiny waist, and the sage fabric made my eyes appear richer in color. The powder lightened the bruises, almost covering them completely.

"Beautiful," Agnes said.

My lower lip quivered, and for once in my life, the compliment felt true. In this unorthodox sage gown, with a crown of pine needles, I was lovely.

"It's time, dear." She laced her fingers with mine and guided me out the door.

We ambled down the corridor. My pulse skittered faster with each step toward the sitting room. The hallway opened to the soft light of the hearth. My breath hitched as Silas came into view. He stared at the fire with his back turned to me. A fresh black coat clung to his broad shoulders, and his raven locks were slicked back, as if he had just bathed. He clutched the wooden mantle, unaware of my presence.

Peter cleared his throat. Silas pivoted to me. His countenance showed no hint of intrigue, yet his gaze burned into mine, beckoning me. Despite my brimming anxiety, he mesmerized me, and my mind quieted. I drifted forward until I stood next to this exquisite man. Agnes placed my hand in his and stepped away. Heat radiated into my skin from our entwined fingers. I studied every detail of his face: the slope of his angular chin, his straight, regal nose, his full lips, and the amber of his irises that glowed beside the firelight. My body pulled to him like a magnet until we were a handbreadth apart. I lost myself under this billowing pressure between us, as if he possessed me wholly.

"Let's begin," Peter said.

I couldn't break this connection with Silas. Even as Peter entwined an end of the cord around Silas's forearm. The soft leather wrapped over our joined hands, binding us to each other, then snaked up my gossamer sleeve. Peter stepped back, and Silas's lips parted as he let out a shaky exhale, which matched mine. I trembled, and my heart thundered in my ears. How could this simple touch feel like my undoing?

"Silas and Arianna. You have come before us to bind yourselves in eternal marriage. This cord symbolizes your everlasting bond from this day forward, joining you in an unbreakable covenant in this life and the next. Do you agree to binding yourselves to each other?"

My breath hitched at the strength of the spoken contract, which was loftier than the nuptials in Krella.

"I am in agreement." Silas nodded to me. My mouth dried under the intensity of his solemn stare, making me momentarily unable to speak. I swallowed hard.

"I am in agreement."

"May you share in your joys and sorrows in this life and the next," Peter said.

He passed a goblet to Silas, who drank from it. Then Peter gave it to me. I assessed the contents. Silas nodded in silent encouragement. I sipped sweet alcohol and licked the remnants off my lips. Silas's eyes dropped to my mouth.

Peter took the chalice from me, but I couldn't look away from Silas.

"With this wine and a kiss, your fates are bound for all eternity."

Peter's words rang through my head. *A kiss.* My pulse surged as Silas's thumb gently caressed my chin. He leaned into me, and my heart pounded so loudly I swore it would halt him. His soft, full lips brushed mine, the taste of wine still lingering upon them, leaving me with a whisper of a kiss. He remained mere inches from me, and his sweet breath rushed over my skin. He didn't release me, and his gaze pierced through me with an intensity I couldn't explain as a warmth fluttered in my belly.

"Now bound for all eternity," Peter called out as if exclaiming to a large group of onlookers instead of just his wife, our other witness. Silas shuddered. He dropped his thumb from my jaw and withdrew. A chill cut through me at the absence of his proximity. My arm tugged, a reminder that the leather held him by my side despite his attempt to flee. Silas's demeanor hardened as he unraveled the cord and released my hand from his. The absence of his touch left me cold, and the binding dangled from me as Silas backed away.

"Let's celebrate!" Agnes cheered as she clapped, cutting off Silas as he opened his mouth to speak. To my surprise, Silas offered his arm to lead me toward the small dining room.

CHAPTER 27

Silas

I clenched my jaw as I entered the dining room with Arianna's fingers laced in mine. Despite my disjointed feelings, I couldn't stop staring at her. When we had arrived at the inn, Arianna had scurried off as a mousy miss, but she had reemerged an enchantress—lulling me under her spell. An energy had buzzed between us since she emerged donning that gorgeous gown as if she had always been destined to be a bride of Presspin.

The scratching of a chair along the wood floor drew my focus. We approached a small oak table with a humble meal of roasted meat, potatoes, and fresh bread laid out on unadorned ceramic dishes. I released Arianna's hand and pulled the chair out for her, clutching the back tightly. She perched herself before the feast and gave me a murmur of thanks. Wordlessly, I settled beside her.

Agnes and Peter were seated across from us, beaming brightly at Arianna with a swirl of questions likely forming in their minds. Though I attempted to focus on them, I failed as my glance drifted over my bride's profile. She turned her attention to me and tilted her head slightly as she caught my stare. I didn't look away. Instead, I fell into the blue depths of her eyes that appeared a richer color against the green gown, like the crystal depths of the clearest lake.

"I would have prepared a finer meal had I known you were coming, especially for such a momentous occasion." Agnes sulked in mock agitation, and I forced my focus off Arianna.

A hint of a smile cut into the corner of my mouth despite my unease over the gravity of this evening.

"The food looks amazing," Arianna said.

Agnes grinned as she scooped a heaping serving onto Arianna's plate. To my surprise, Arianna didn't restrain herself as she took a large bite of the roasted meat. She let out a soft moan of satisfaction, causing me to shift in my seat. The sound was a reminder of events to come.

Agnes placed the food before me, but I had little interest in eating. I was far too aware of the woman beside me who stirred within me a mix of apprehension and desire. Instead, I watched Arianna as she delighted in her meal with a vigor I was unaccustomed to. Sighs of satisfaction escaped her after every bite.

"Silas, did you forget to feed your wife on your journey?" Agnes asked.

My focus shifted to Agnes as the weight of what I had done settled on my shoulders. *My wife*. Arianna was now my wife.

"I'm so sorry," Arianna said, and a blush bloomed across her cheeks.

I stifled an internal groan, far too aware that soon her skin would flush under my touch.

"I was only teasing Silas. Please eat to your heart's content. It gives me a sense of pride when my guests appreciate my food," Agnes said.

Arianna's posture relaxed, and she returned to eating. However, I couldn't. Instead, I picked at my plate, rolling a potato around in disinterest. Agnes's face pinched in reprimand. I shuddered at the familiar expression from when I was a child and she worried over my fickle appetite. Resigned, I shoved a piece of roasted meat into my mouth but couldn't fully enjoy the rosemary undertones.

Agnes likely feared that Arianna had been half-starved, given my wife's ravenous consumption of dinner and frail form. During the half hour, I choked down a few more bites of food. Finally, after devouring two servings, Arianna lowered her fork, and a satisfied smile spread over her face.

Peter placed his fork on his plate with a clink, cutting through the quiet. He folded his hands over his stomach and leaned back in his chair. "Now that we are all well fed. Silas, you must tell us the tale of this whirlwind romance. You left Presspin barely a month ago after swearing a lifetime of bachelorhood and now have returned in haste to elope."

My shoulders tensed. I wouldn't blatantly lie to them, yet I couldn't be wholly honest either. I wouldn't put them at risk. Searching for inspiration, I looked to Arianna. Her blue eyes held mine, unlocking a truth I hid.

"She knocked me off my feet." My posture relaxed, and a smirk tugged on my lips as I thought of our first meeting. "Literally. She crashed into me, and my life hasn't been the same since."

That damned blush bloomed on her cheeks, and she chewed her lower lip. A moment of tense silence lingered as I lost myself in her gaze until a short cough from Peter dragged me to the present.

"Oh, how lovely." Agnes smiled in elation and clapped.

Agnes chattered with excitement. She brimmed with fanciful notions of our futures as lord and lady of Belmont Manor. However, Peter was less easily swayed. He raised an eyebrow, his focus shifting between Arianna and me.

Peter turned his attention to Arianna. "My dear girl, you must be smitten with Silas to run off to Presspin and elope. With no family present and in such a rushed affair."

Arianna opened her mouth and then snapped it shut. Words seemed to elude her. Long moments passed, and even Agnes's musing about a house filled with Belmont children quieted as they awaited her answer.

Arianna twisted the onyx ring on her thumb. "I...I...I—"

"She was betrothed to someone else," I said in haste.

Agnes gaped in shock, and Arianna froze.

"I see." Peter stroked his chin as if he understood the magnitude of the situation.

Alas, he didn't. I loved Peter and Agnes like grandparents, but nobody from Belmont Manor was aware of my curse, a secret hidden from everyone. This half-truth would protect us all. They needed to remain oblivious to my true reasons for marrying Arianna. I couldn't bear losing them.

Peter's demeanor softened as he tilted his head toward Arianna. "Our wedding customs here are far simpler than those in the southern territories. Agnes and I served as your witnesses as you bound your lives to each other. Once you seal the marriage tonight, any prior betrothal contracts should be nullified in Presspin. However, those under the council's control in Hallowhaven do not always view our ancient practices as binding."

Arianna nodded, fidgeting again with the onyx ring.

"Arianna, I'll show you to the room and you can take a nice, long bath before..." Agnes paused and smirked. "You retire for the evening."

Arianna stood and followed Agnes up the stairs, leaving Peter and me alone. He was the only father figure who remained, and for a second, I swore he planned on lecturing me for my impetuous behavior. Instead, he left for the kitchen, returning with a bottle of wine.

He poured two glasses and gave one to me. "I thought a toast seemed appropriate."

I took the wine as he lifted his glass.

His voice had aged, but it still possessed the same authority from my childhood. "To Silas and his new bride, Arianna. A blessing upon your house. May it be filled with an abundance of love and tenderness, and many children to once again fill the halls of Belmont Manor."

I tipped the cup until I drained each drop, unwilling to think about the reality of the circumstance. I would never live this life Agnes and Peter hoped for me. For a future brimming with affection and offspring.

"A game of chess while Agnes fusses over your bride?" Peter asked, unaware of my inner struggles but likely assuming my tense demeanor was that of an antsy groom in need of distraction. Without waiting for my response, he stood and moved toward the hutch.

I thrummed my fingers on the table. A nervous energy pulsed through me. Peter returned and set up the board. We played in amiable silence as the clock ticked, punctuating the hour that felt like mere minutes before Agnes interrupted our game.

"Arianna is ready to retire," Agnes said as she took the seat beside Peter.

I opened and closed my mouth, uncertain of how to respond. So I said, "Thank you for everything."

The couple who had doted on me since childhood beamed as I exited and made my way to the suite Agnes had prepared for us. The stairs creaked as I ambled. My heart thumped erratically. I was no virginal boy, heading into my first time. Though not a rake, I had warmed women's beds before. I even had an arrangement. Gods. I gripped the railing, swaying under my absentmindedness. How could I have forgotten about Brielle? I couldn't think of her now. I shook my head and dislodged her from my mind.

I reached the landing and headed for the suite. The corridor had an eclectic yet cohesive style, with floral-patterned rugs lining the wood floors, vine-covered wallpaper, and scenic pictures dotting the hallway. Silence filled the space. Even my footsteps were muted by the thick carpet. I halted in front of the last room and gripped the iron knob. The cold metal pressed into my palm. Yet I hesitated. Once I entered, there would be no barriers between Arianna and me for tonight. The realization caused a gnawing ache to eat at my resolve. However, there was no turning back now. With an exhale, I opened the door.

I stepped into the suite. The fire crackled in the hearth, and the aroma of lavender wafted through the air from Arianna's bath. She sat tucked under a thick lilac quilt in an oversized bed. She wore her hair unwoven. Wild waves cascaded over her shoulders, glimmering in the candlelight that highlighted the rich amber weaving through her locks. Yet her relaxed countenance tightened in my presence. She yanked the blanket over her chest, her knuckles turning white from her tense grip.

I walked to the dressing screen. My nightclothes were folded on a bathing stool, likely laid out by Agnes. I undressed behind the opaque partition that left little to the imagination. The changes in Arianna's breathing punctuated the silence. I smirked. At least I was not the only one affected by this evening.

I emerged in my nightclothes. Arianna watched me, worrying her lip between her teeth. I hated to admit it, but she was beautiful, with creamy porcelain skin, bright blue eyes, and high cheekbones. Even the slight angularity of her nose only added to her ethereal features. But, taking in the bruises still on her neck, I sensed her apprehension. I would not force her into relinquishing her body against her will.

"Arianna, we don't have to. We can always claim we consummated. I am certain Agnes and Peter would corroborate our story. I am sure you are exhausted from the trip; you can sleep, and I—"

"No." She held my gaze. A hint of resolve played in her features.

For a heartbeat, I believed I misunderstood her.

"No?" I asked, confused by her statement and this spark of determination within her.

She shifted her focused to her hands as they wrung the blanket, and her shoulders slumped. "We must consummate. It's the only way to ensure I am protected in this marriage. I know I am not...experienced. If it's a burden for you to...to...do this, then I understand. But...but...I cannot risk our union being invalidated."

I closed the distance and sat beside her on the bed. I lowered my hand to hers, my thumb stroking over her smooth skin. Her eyelashes fluttered. That agonizing pull locked into place, and I gulped under the magnitude of her draw.

"If that is what you wish, then we shall. Do you know what to expect? Has anyone ever..." I allowed my words to trail off. She nodded, and a hint of a shy smile broke across her face.

"Naomi snuck me many salacious novels, so I have an idea. Though I never have..."

Thank the gods for small favors. At least she possessed some limited knowledge.

"What do I do? Shall I lie still? That is what Mama said in our talk after my engagement ball. To lie still until my husband finished." She leaned against the pillows stiffly, her body tense. I frowned. What kind of mother did Arianna have?

"No, I won't just be taking pleasure from you." I raked a hand through my hair. My pulse surged as my attention lingered on the perfect cupid's bow of her mouth. "I'll make certain that you are satisfied in our coupling as well. I promise."

A flush crept along her creamy flesh, and a whoosh of air pressed through her trembling pout.

"Sit up," I said in a voice laced with more desire than I expected.

She sat. I ran my fingers through her unruly locks. My hand grazed the nape of her neck, and I drew her into me, capturing her in a tentative, gentle kiss. My tongue slipped along the seam of her mouth, coaxing her. Her lips parted. She tasted of honey, a sweet nectar I could lose myself in. I teased my tongue over hers with languid strokes. She leaned closer to me, and a throaty mewl left her, causing heat to course down my spine.

I pulled her into my embrace and deepened the kiss. Yet she was so frail I feared hurting her and loosened my grip.

"Silas," she whimpered and pressed her palm against my chest. Breathless, she shifted and broke the connection. Her pupils dilated in the soft glow of the candlelight. Her reddened lips beckoned me to devour her.

"Do you want me to stop? I will—"

"Don't stop. I just didn't realize a kiss could feel this good." A rosy blush colored her cheeks, her shoulders rising and falling as she attempted to catch her breath.

I smirked at the exasperated look crossing her flushed face. Despite my need to keep this coupling as platonic as possible, I had an unyielding longing to send her into raptures.

"As you wish."

I nuzzled her neck and inhaled her lavender scent. My lips grazed along the hollow of her throat. She arched, giving me better access, and I sucked the sensitive flesh. Her breath quickened, and she melted against me.

"I want to see all of you," I whispered into her ear, and goose bumps formed along her bare arms.

I pulled away, certain she would deny me, but that spark of strength ignited within her gaze. She withdrew from my embrace, removed the tattered nightgown, and kicked off the quilt. The discarded clothing and blanket were crumpled at the edge of the bed.

She lounged bare before me in all her glory. She was gorgeous, with a narrow waist, smooth skin, and taut, perky breasts. My arousal hardened as I took her in. Yet I couldn't complicate this arrangement by growing too close. I lacked the capacity for affection. However, tonight, we would find ecstasy in one another's bodies. I may have been a monster undeserving of love, but I wouldn't ruin this by thinking of the future. I buried my worries, delving into the moment. I had desired her more than I cared to admit, and I couldn't fight this any longer.

"Lie back."

Stiffly, she did as I instructed. Her breaths were labored as I hovered above her, still clothed, unwilling to risk a loss of control before she was ready. My teeth grazed her collarbone, and I trailed kisses along her flesh until my lips found the peak of her breast. As I drew the taut pink tip into my mouth, she moaned and arched.

"Oh, Silas." Her fingers tangled in my hair, running over my scalp. The simple, innocent touch caused my groin to tighten further as she panted with urgency beneath me.

I skated my fingers over her hip, gliding toward her core. At her sex, I parted the damp curls, teasing the sensitive bundle of nerves. She mewled and arched against my digits' ministrations. Yet I didn't quicken my pace. Instead, my tongue lapped over her breast as I strummed slow circles on the gentle nub with my thumb.

"Silas...I...I need." Her words rasped in a breathy whine as she pressed against me. Her desire to reach the apex of pleasure was evident in her increased wetness.

"I'll give you what you crave." I glided my hand toward her opening and slowly slid a finger in.

She gasped and clenched around me, her body tensing at the intrusion.

"It's okay. Let me help you. Just relax." I flicked my tongue over the pebbled flesh of her breast.

Her muscles loosened as I stroked my thumb along the sensitive nub. She whimpered as I swirled my finger over her damp opening. Her breath hitched as I slid my knuckle in. I worked her core until I could push in the full length of my finger without resistance. The feel of her tightly wrapped around my digit was maddening. My hardened cock throbbed with anticipation, and I lowered my head against her chest, exhaling to uphold my resolve to not take her prematurely.

"Silas, please," she whimpered, pressing against my hand, her body searching for the release it desired. Her scent of arousal made my mouth water, and I fought the urge to lap at my virginal bride's folds. Gods, I wanted every aspect of her.

My finger plunged into her tight channel. She ground against me. I pushed a second digit in, preparing her for what was to come. She moaned, her hips rocking against my hand.

She gasped as I pumped into her wet depths, hitting that elusive spot and causing her to tumble toward euphoria. My thumb continued massaging languid strokes over the bundle of nerves, driving her closer to ecstasy. Seconds later, she tensed, straining for release. I nipped at her nipple. She erupted with a rasping cry of rhapsody and shuddered against me.

I removed my hand and knelt beside her. She lay boneless and satiated. The soft candlelight caressed every curve of her body and the cascade of wild curls toppling about the mattress. Her eyes were heavy-lidded with lust as she stared at me in reverence. She was a sight to behold, rumpled and panting on the mussed sheets. I inhaled deeply. The aroma of her release intertwined with the lavender fragrance intoxicated me. I stripped bare, unable to resist a second longer. My arousal bobbed with rigid desire. She gulped, and her pupils dilated at my disrobement. She clutched the sheets, causing her knuckles to blanch.

“Don’t worry. It will only hurt for a moment. I promise.”

I used my knees to spread her legs. Her breath hitched as I moved over her, positioning my body atop hers. I hovered on my forearms, unwilling to crush her with my weight. Then, slowly, too slowly, I slid the head of my cock into her core. Her thighs trembled, but her hands roved over my back, drawing me closer. She gasped as I worked my hard length into her, each inch at a painstakingly patient pace, allowing her body time to adjust. Her gaze never left mine, locking me into her inescapable magnetic pull.

As I thrust in fully, she winced, then relaxed as I seated myself inside her. Tingles snaked along my spine as her warmth enveloped my shaft. I groaned and nearly came like an inexperienced boy. She was so tight, so sweet, so beautiful. I rocked my hips, my cock rubbing within her core as new mewls escaped her, fueling my frenzy. This ache built, and the need for release became more unbearable with each stroke.

She wrapped her legs around me. Ragged pants rushed from her. She gripped my back, anchoring me into her, and the blue of her eyes beckoned me into a deeper connection. I shouldn't have given in to her siren call. Yet with her sheathed over my cock, my resolve crumbled.

As I chased my orgasm, something else stirred within my power, an unfamiliar yet ancient longing. I buried myself inside her, lost in her eyes, her scent, her body.

"Silas, Silas, please." Her breaths grew ragged, her head tipping back and her form arching against me.

Despite myself, logic eluded me. Her cries broke through my mental resolve, and I thrust harder and faster into her, unlike the composed man I strived to be, promised to be. But she responded in kind, her warmth tensing, urging me forward.

"Arianna," I growled, and I nipped at the shell of her ear. Her hips moved in response as she, too, chased her release.

"Come for me again." I sucked the hollow of her neck and snaked my hand between us, strumming the bundle of nerves. Her core clenched around me as I pushed her closer to the brink.

"Silas." My name came from her like a reverent plea as she hit the pinnacle and tumbled over. Her core pulsated as her body quivered beneath me.

I rutted mindlessly, heat and pressure building until I could last no longer. My completion came hard and fast. Yet as I held Arianna's gaze, something wild connected us, my power pulsating internally like a flame igniting, and I sensed a flicker of something else. No, not something else, someone else. This blissfully euphoric moment was quickly overshadowed by a looming, unshakable presence. Oh gods, what had I done?

Arianna panted beneath me, her chest rising and falling, her face flushed with the aftereffects of exertion. My curse stirred as I beheld her, whispering things I did not want to hear, but I pushed down whatever dwelled.

"Silas," Arianna purred as I rolled off her. I lay beside her as she caught her breath, but I couldn't look at her, unable to give her more than I already had.

"We should go to sleep now. We will have a long journey tomorrow." My voice sounded gruff despite the mix of unsettling feelings entangling within my curse.

"Oh," she whispered, then shifted away from me, leaving me cold. She blew out the candles. Darkness cast over us. She settled on the far end of the bed. Long minutes passed until the cadence of her breathing slowed as slumber took her.

I stared at the ceiling, my heart pounding as I attempted to sleep, but my father's voice entered my mind. *You are nothing but a monster, boy. A monster no one will ever love.*

CHAPTER 28

ARIANNA

SINCE THIS MORNING, SILAS and I had acted as mere strangers. We bathed in the tense quiet that stretched over our long journey to Presspin. With nary a word said between us, as if our bodies and souls hadn't intertwined. Despite reason, I peeked over my novel, scanning my taciturn husband, who had me in raptures the night prior but couldn't bear the sight of me in the light of day. My pulse surged as memories of our liaison flashed through my mind, making it difficult to focus on the worn pages. I fought the urge to blush as my gaze trailed over him. He became even more morose with each passing minute stuck in this carriage with me.

I lowered my novel and rubbed my weary eyes, as if the motion could scrub the delicious thoughts of our entanglement clear from my mind. I knew last night served as a means to an end for Silas to secure me to his name. Yet my wanton desire to re-experience our interlude lingered. However, Silas's sullen attitude made his lack of interest unmistakable.

A rustling caught my attention. He was no longer lounging cross-armed and staring at the ceiling as he had for the past hour of our journey. Instead, sunlight filtered into the carriage as he opened the curtain, and an opulent estate came into sight.

Without thinking, I, too, leaned toward the window, grazing my shoulder against his. He recoiled at my nearness, resuming his cross-armed, sullen vigil while I remained peering at the scenic view leading up a long cobble path. We rounded a bend.

I gasped as the grand gothic manor came into view. The massive mansion had multiple turrets. It was akin to a castle with intriguing sharp lines and edges that matched its master. However, updates appeared to have been completed, as two additions to the original structure spanned on either side of the principal home. It denoted hints of a more modern style yet blended the past and present harmoniously. Oversized windows gleamed, providing picturesque views of the nestling mountain ranges and the town below.

The austere manor matched Silas. However, untamed wilderness loomed at the estate's boundaries. It sprawled across acres. The gardens were meticulously maintained until they gave way to nature, where stone trails led to the woods.

My heart hammered with each hoofbeat toward the massive home. I felt like a pauper coming to live with a prince. I hadn't suspected Silas's wealth could overshadow that of the Terrells'. By the twice as grand estate, I had woefully underestimated his fortune. The conveyance came to a halt, jolting me off balance from my perched position.

Within seconds, Silas leapt out of the carriage. He walked down the path to the entrance, paying me little heed. The driver extended a hand as I exited. I craned my neck skyward, dwarfed by the pristine cut-stone walls that towered over me. While I gawked, Silas's boots clicked against the stone steps, followed by the clang of a knocker. Yet I couldn't focus on anything beyond the expansive castle before me.

"My lord, you're home unexpectedly," a woman said.

I shifted my attention to the enormous wooden door where she and Silas stood. Her brow wrinkled in confusion and her lips pursed, deepening the worry lines that settled around her puckered mouth.

Silas snapped his focus to me. A hard look of impatience flickered in his countenance as he gestured for me to join him.

The woman peered down at me. I rushed to the entrance and made my way to Silas's side. She tilted her head, yet not a hair of her ash blonde knot moved out of place. She assessed me, and I feared she found me lacking. I wrapped my arms around myself, mortified by my threadbare dress. However, a flash of understanding crossed her face and her posture softened.

"My lord, how gracious you are. I mentioned before you left I needed a new scullery maid, and you—"

"No," Silas snapped.

The woman straightened her shoulders and tucked her hands behind her back.

"This is my wife, Lady Arianna Belmont. Notify the staff of her arrival. When she is settled, you are to be personally in charge of seeing to Arianna's needs."

She opened and closed her mouth like a fish, but no words or sounds emitted from her.

"That is all, Mrs. Potter. I'll escort her to her quarters myself."

Silas's jaw ticked, but the woman didn't flinch at his stern temperament. Instead, she bobbed a quick curtsy, then she scurried away.

Silas rolled his shoulders, then entered the manor. I followed behind him but paused, awed by the opulent domed ceiling of the foyer. A crystal chandelier glimmered overhead. I worried my bottom lip between my teeth as the reality of my situation came into sharp focus. I wasn't Arianna Park but now Arianna Belmont, the lady of this lavish castle, but only in name. Yet I couldn't dwell as I hurried after Silas, who had already ascended the stairs.

As we walked the halls, there was no warmth one would expect, only cold civility. Even the lush rugs underfoot diminished the sounds of our steps. The silence between us echoed through the core of my being. Ancient tapestries depicting unfamiliar tales lined the corridors, but I struggled to take in my new surroundings. I focused on Silas's broad shoulders and swallowed down the fluttering feelings swirling within me. He stopped at a mahogany door and opened it with a slight creak.

"Your quarters." He moved aside.

I gaped at the large floor-to-ceiling windows and the ornate furnishings in icy blues and silvers. To my right lay the oversized bed situated against the wall. A silk canopy snaked along the four posters, and a mound of pillows was artfully arranged. An ornate silver rug sprawled over dark wood floors. To my left, two charcoal gray armchairs were directed toward a pristine, unlit whitewashed hearth. In the far corner sat a table for dining and walls of empty shelves that lacked trinkets and books. A desk was settled in the opposite corner, devoid of any personal effects. Though the room was clean, a faint mustiness lingered in the air. I froze at the entrance of the sprawling suite the size of our farm's first floor. I shook my head, uncomfortable with the grandiosity. There had to be something smaller and less lavish, perhaps an unused servant's chamber or a nook?

"I can't stay here...it's too much." My breathy voice punctuated the air, breaking the spell that had settled upon us since we awoke to our new life.

"It would be untoward for you to occupy any other suite. You are the lady of Belmont Manor." He fidgeted with his cravat, tugging at the crisp black fabric. His demeanor was like a taut bowstring, ready to snap at any moment. I dared not argue and test his temperament. Instead, I stepped through the doorway.

"This room adjoins mine. It is best for me to remain close..." A furrow crossed his brow, then smoothed. "In case your curse becomes uncontrollable."

"This suite isn't spelled?" I ran my fingers along the icy-blue-and-silver wallpaper. "Will you have a disciple come and—"

"No. I would never submit you to the suppression spells you lived under. I could never do that." An ache coated his words as I pivoted to him. His lips pulled into a straight line, and anguish filled his gaze. I waited for him to say more, but he didn't. Instead, he turned to leave, and I stared at him in confusion, in longing, and in loneliness. Though this manor was grand, it was not my home, and the pang of homesickness flickered through me as I stepped farther into this unfamiliar place.

"Mrs. Potter will provide you with what you need. We will train in the morning." Without waiting for an answer, he closed the door behind him. A deafening silence filled the vast space.

The silver rugs lining the wooden floors softened my steps as I walked to the large window. The mountain range insulated the quaint village below, and thick groves of evergreen trees covered the terrain. I placed my head on the glass and wished the coolness could soothe my jumbled feelings. It didn't. I blinked back unshed tears. In the stillness of my new quarters, the harsh reality crashed over me. I was completely alone.

I forced myself away from the window and stumbled to the bed. My body flopped onto the pillows, which muffled my sobs. I should have been grateful for my safety, for this home and a husband who wouldn't dare touch me. However, I broke into a million pieces. My heart ached from the whirlwind events that had led me here to this isolation. Time felt irrelevant as I lay on the soft mattress, numb. Eventually, the light shifted from the late afternoon sun to the whispers of sunset.

A knock pierced through my exhaustion, and foolishly, I hoped for Silas, taking long strides into my room and holding me as he had our first night in the carriage. The door opened. I jerked to sitting and wiped my hand across my face, where dried tears made my skin sticky. Instead, the slender Mrs. Potter entered, and a footman dressed in black livery followed, carrying my worn sack filled with my meager belongings.

"My lady." Mrs. Potter curtsied.

The footman lowered my bag to the small table. He assessed me for a heartbeat. Mrs. Potter cleared her throat. He bowed, then rushed away.

I stood and smoothed my dress, blushing at the frayed gray fabric, which was of lesser quality than her uniform. "Call me Arianna, please."

Her lips quivered in a flicker of a frown.

"Is there anything I can get you this evening? Perhaps a bath, or something to eat after your journey?"

I twisted the onyx ring on my thumb in nervousness, pulling her attention toward it. Within a heartbeat, she approached and grabbed the hand that bore the ring. The fading sunlight caught upon the dark stone, and symbols scrolled on the black band. Her chapped fingers ran over the onyx. The tight crow's feet lining her brown eyes softened.

"My lord gave this to you?" Her words were slow, as if she spoke of impossibilities.

"Yes."

She held my hand and tilted her head. She scanned my face. I froze under her weighty assessment. A flicker of a smile pulled on her lips, softening her harsh countenance.

"I see." She released me. Her once tense demeanor smoothed as she folded her hands neatly in front of the white apron covering her crisp black smock.

"I have been informed by my lord that you will be dining alone tonight. I'll bring up your meal and a bath." A gentleness entered her tone as I nodded absentmindedly.

"My lady, I'm at your service if there is anything you need." She curtsied, then left.

The sun continued its descent behind the mountains, and my heart broke yet again in the painful silence of this room. Naomi was not here; there would be no stories about town while I ate or even Silas's stony stares. A hollow ache formed within my chest as I collapsed into the soft fabric of the charcoal-gray armchair. My nose stung as fresh tears welled, and my shoulders shook with suppressed sobs, but I refused to cry anymore.

I had made my choice. I had resigned myself to this solitary life, married to a man who didn't want me despite the longing I harbored for him. To endure this agony and protect my fragile heart, I vowed I would indeed be nothing more than Silas's wife in name alone. I buried the flicker of desire for him deep within the darkest corners of my soul.

CHAPTER 29

SILAS

THE FIRE CRACKLED IN the study's hearth, warming the cool night air. I rolled my shoulders, which were tight from being hunched over my desk for hours, and shifted my gaze from the mounds of ledgers to the stack of petitions. I lowered the pen to the pad and raked a hand through my hair. My steward's work was impeccable, but many requests needed to be fulfilled before the winter. Yet the tasks served as a diversion, keeping my thoughts over Arianna at bay. Candlelight flickered from the short, waxy nubs that had shrunk since being lit at sunset. The clock on the mantel ticked minutes by, and I peered at the glass face reading midnight. I rubbed my weary eyes. They blurred from focusing on the records, as if the distraction could blot out the truth that I had married Arianna and brought her to my home on some inane whim.

I stood and stretched, then moved toward the small table beside the leather sofa. I contemplated over the dinner tray of roasted meat. However, it had grown cold long ago. Instead,

I moved to the window, taking in the moon-drenched night, breathing through the tension which lingered not only in my body but in my soul.

I should have found relief in depositing Arianna in Mrs. Potter's care since my return to Belmont Manor hours prior. Yet I could nearly feel Arianna's presence looming near as I greeted the staff, spoke with my steward, Vincent, and eventually settled into my study. As if consummating our marriage had granted her permission to haunt me.

The lateness of the hour felt heavy upon my bones, and I willed myself to go to bed. Ruminating over unchangeable events wouldn't provide me comfort. With an exhale, I exited, then ambled along the silent corridor. Suddenly, my blood ran cold, filling me with terror. Seconds later, a scream pierced the once still air.

Somehow, in the core of my soul, I knew it was Arianna. I sprinted toward her quarters but couldn't register why the manor remained undisturbed despite the shrieking that rattled within my skull. As I reached her room, I flung the door open.

The dwindling fire from the hearth cast a faint light as I beheld her. Raw anguish painted her expression as black wisps of power sizzled, threatening to decay and mar the mattress. Her blankets had tumbled off her and onto the floor. Regret gnawed at me; I should have stopped at the herbalist's shop to procure a sleeping draft. Yet I had forgone the option, not wanting to complicate my life further.

Her cries ached within my soul, pulling me into action.

"Arianna!"

Her eyes flickered open. They were not the pools of blue I had grown accustomed to, but pits of inky black. Her curse had taken root in her nightmares and used her body as its conduit for destruction. Unthinking, I rushed to her side and reached for her, hoping to jostle her from the trance. With my hands on her shoulders, I braced myself for the agony that awaited as my fingers touched the darkness. However, the crackling tendrils didn't burn me. Instead, they swirled against my skin in a caress.

"*Arianna.*"

She whimpered. Tears like tar streamed down her cheeks, and the agony etched upon her face tore into me, crumbling my walls of resolve. I gulped down a wild, primitive response as her curse beckoned mine forward, whispering promises of destruction and desire.

Without thinking, I crawled into the bed, pulling her into my embrace, and hoped the contact could soothe both our powers' untamed longings. Soothing hushes left my lips, the same soft hums Ophelia would make against my brow when I had nightmares as a boy. My chest heaved, and I could nearly feel her anguish seeping into me as I tried to coax the darkness to recede.

Time became irrelevant. It could have been mere seconds or hours before she relaxed against me. Our breaths synchronized, and the dark aura retreated into her. Afraid of a resurgence, I continued humming long after the energy dissipated into nothing more than a distant memory. The black orbs that once stared at me shut as sleep took hold of her. Despite myself, my gaze drifted along the curve of her face, and my heart pounded as her warmth soaked into me. She nuzzled into my chest, and her form melded against mine. My pulse surged, and I dared not close my eyes with her pressed so closely against me. If I did, only memories of our coupling would lie in the recesses of my mind.

Hesitantly, I unfurled her from me and slipped out of the bed. I gathered the crumpled blanket from the floor and placed it over her, tucking her in. She parted her lips, and a soft sigh escaped. I should have left, but I lingered, peering down at her slumbering form. My fingers moved of their own accord, brushing the springs of wild curls off her delicate face. A tingling sensation coursed along my spine at the simple touch. I removed my hand and clenched it into a fist, gulping down the desire to lose myself in her sweet scent and soft touch.

However, I couldn't complicate matters with whatever this was, so I fled from her room. I strode toward my quarters and vowed this wouldn't happen again.

CHAPTER 30

ARIANNA

DAWN PEEKED OVER THE mountain range, but despite the warm light cascading over the path, a crisp autumn wind blew, causing a chill to cut through me. Shivering, I clutched the threadbare cloak, wrapping it tighter around myself. My worn boots clomped over the thin layer of frost covering the forest floor. The morning larks whistled a merry tune, unaware of the tense silence between Silas and me as we walked into the woods on the outskirts of the estate.

I hastened my steps, attempting to keep up with his brutal pace. I dodged fallen limbs on the trail and prayed I wouldn't become entangled in the overgrown brambles. But he ignored me as I scrambled behind him. The same thick tension from the day before clung to his shoulders. Had he, too, suffered from a fitful slumber? For most of last night, I had nightmares of Theo finding me, but at some point, my dreams calmed. I awoke, oddly, to Silas's scent upon my pillow. Though I was certain his woodsy aroma must have lingered through many rooms of his childhood home.

We veered off the path and trekked farther into the forest until nothing but trees and echoing silence surrounded us. He halted and laid the blanket he'd carried in the crook of his arm on the ground. The thick fabric soaked in the frost from the dirt below. He sat and gestured for me to accompany him. Anxiously, I joined him. My shoulder grazed his as I settled on the narrow quilt. He tensed at my nearness. Nerves prickled beneath my skin, though I was uncertain whether they were from our proximity or the impending lesson.

"We will practice breathwork. It is an important tool for connecting the mind and body. Finding these moments of centering will grant you greater control over your triggers," he said.

I winced at the memory of our last exercise weeks ago, when I fell unconscious, and a knot formed in my belly. His terse features softened, and a hint of understanding colored his gaze. Despite his aloof attitude toward me as his wife, he seemed to hold some regard for me as his pupil.

"Close your eyes and follow my voice."

Hesitantly, I obeyed his command as he led me through the exercise, urging me to relax with each breath. At some point, I stopped ruminating over the anguish of my decision to marry him and flee Krella. Instead, with each heartbeat, my worries drifted away one by one.

No longer burdened, I absorbed the world around me. A chilly breeze whipped against my face. I inhaled the sweet scent of the pine trees, and warmth radiated from his shoulder as it nearly brushed mine. His voice was gentle as a caress, and his presence soothed me, lulling my mind into submission.

I fell deeper into his commands but didn't dive into the darkness within myself. Instead, I approached the inky depths like a child at a pond, dipping my toe into its shallows. Eventually, his words halted as his focus shifted to his own practice. In time, our breaths aligned until my pulse and respiration matched his, beat for beat. Many minutes passed, and a warm peace soothed me, brought on by the comfort of his nearness. I released my uncertainty, relaxing into a trance.

In this state, something skimmed against my senses, as if an unseen entity surged between Silas and me. A palpable awareness hummed through me, acknowledging this oddly familiar presence in the depth of my soul that had lain dormant until now. Goose bumps rose along my skin, and the atmospheric pressure densified. This entity beckoned me forward, urging me to relinquish myself into its yearnings. Yet this sensation felt different from our last lesson. No, I was not being called toward the sweet release of death and destruction. Instead, a bone-deep longing existed, tasting of desire. Curious, I fell under the siren call. My breath hitched, and euphoric tingles coursed through my body, a reward for my compliance. My curse swelled in response, coaxing me into subjugation, as if it too craved this connection just within my grasp.

"Arianna, enough!"

Jolted out of the trance, I whipped my head to Silas. His lips quivered, and bewilderment crossed his expression. At what point had his steady respiration turned to quaking heaves?

"That is all for today." His shoulders rose and fell with his quick, clipped breaths. With a shaky exhale, he smoothed whatever emotions he wrestled with. What had unnerved him? But what occurred within him resolved just as quickly as it appeared, and his stoic countenance returned. Without a word, he stood and stalked toward the trail.

I scrambled to follow him, leaving the blanket on the hard ground. A shiver crept over me, but I was uncertain whether it was from the cold or the absence of the surging power which had kept me warm. I attempted to catch up to him, but the brambles caught on my hem, pulling on the threadbare dress. A rip pierced the air as the bottom of my skirt shredded. He stopped. A long, audible sigh escaped him. He turned to me, examining my bedraggled state, and pinched the bridge of his nose in exasperation.

"You'll need warmer clothes to survive a winter here." Without waiting for a response, he pivoted and strode off into the woods.

I hastened, no longer worried about the brambles, which yanked at the tattered material. We trekked along the trail that led us from the forest into the gardens and finally reached the manor.

He swung the large door open, and tension rolled off him as we entered the foyer.

Mrs. Potter rushed toward us, and a hint of concern played on her features. She curtsied. "My lord."

"Have the carriage readied; we are heading to town once Arianna has changed into something more appropriate." Silas brushed past her and headed up the stairs.

I gaped as he bounded the steps without a glance back and disappeared. I flicked my gaze to Mrs. Potter, and she assessed me with a heavy sigh, her focus on my torn fabric.

"Come quickly," she said as I followed her up to my room.

CHAPTER 31

Arianna

The carriage ride was achingly silent as Silas and I ventured toward town. Presspin differed significantly from Krella. Pristine cobbles lined every street, and shops showed no sign of wear. The air lacked the stench of old manure and sweat, which seemed to cling throughout the village center of Krella. Nestled within the mountain range, Presspin was picturesque, yet there was not a single Aralian temple. My mother's words about their lack of acknowledgment of the Goddess of Light flitted into my memory. But I had little love now for the goddess and her disciples. Especially when the onyx rings allowed our kind to walk the world undetected and unbound. A nagging question tickled in the recesses of my mind: why didn't the Aralians allow us to control our curse? Why did they suppress it with the mask? However, the conveyance halted at the corner of the square, interrupting my pondering.

Silas exited the carriage. To my surprise, he did not stalk off. Instead, he extended a hand to assist me. Despite myself, the brief touch warmed me, and a blush crossed my cheeks. But as soon as my feet hit the cobble, he strode ahead with me following in tow.

I ambled, fascinated over the two-story stone buildings that lined the streets. They were more romantic and less stringent than those of Krella. These shops were meticulously crafted. The stone and brick intertwined, creating a homey feeling throughout the town. Vines grew along the faces and the iron railings that led to the second stories. Windows were open, and townspeople bustled about with chipper faces. I smiled as we wandered under a large trellis where ivy and azure wildflowers hung.

But I didn't have the ability to meander as Silas pushed forward at a brutal pace. We turned a corner to a row of buildings tucked off the main artery of Presspin. I gaped at the architecture. Nature intertwined with the town as if it were a living and breathing thing. I nearly smacked into Silas as he stopped abruptly, having been far too absorbed in soaking in as much detail as possible. I panted for breath as I read the sign overhead: *Demetrius Designs.* A large window displayed elaborate gowns and pressed trousers. Yet Silas didn't wait for me as he stepped into the shop.

The bell chimed overhead as we entered. The scent of leather and fabric wafted through the air. Materials dotted the floor, haphazardly strewn about. Colorful bolts filled a crimson sofa along the wall. In the center were two worktables. One was covered with scattered patterns, thread, and buttons. This place reminded me of home, and a pang of sadness clenched within my chest. I had spent hours last night worrying about Naomi and whether my mother had already realized I was gone. Yet I wouldn't know, since Silas had forbidden me from writing to anyone.

"Layla," Silas called out to the empty room.

A woman emerged from the rear of the shop, dressed in tailored trousers and a crisp white blouse that accentuated her rich sepia-colored skin. She approached, brimming with energy, her tight black curls bouncing from her quick steps.

"How is Beatrix?" she asked. Her focus was squarely on Silas as she swayed from one foot to the other.

A slight smirk formed on his lips, the first smile I had seen since our arrival at Belmont Manor. Watching their exchange, I assessed her, curious about who she was to Silas.

"She is well settled in Krella," he said.

The woman's hazel eyes drifted past Silas, taking in my presence. I willed myself to straighten despite my nerves. In my experience, most considered me akin to the plague itself. I prepared for a distasteful stare or a tight, uncomfortable smile. Instead, she beamed and rushed toward me, practically pushing Silas out of the way.

"Layla Demetrius. It is nice to meet you." She offered a palm in greeting.

"Arianna." I grasped her extended hand, and tentatively shook it, then released it.

Elation coated her expression as she assessed us. "This must be your wife! The whole town has been abuzz over your sudden marriage."

Silas's jaw twitched, but Layla seemed unaffected by his reaction as she stepped back. Her gaze roved over my lackluster gray dress. Unexpectedly, she pivoted to him and flicked her wrist, shooing him away.

"You are not needed here. You may leave."

I flinched at her bluntness. Silas only gave a nod of acknowledgment and left the tailor's shop.

Layla, without hesitating, grabbed my arm and led me to a pedestal. I stepped onto it and stood still as a statue. She became lost in her own world as she paced around me with her thumb and index finger on her chin. She paused, making a humming noise.

"Are all your garments like this one?" She gestured to my ratty attire, but there was no judgment in her expression, only curiosity.

I nodded in response.

"A full wardrobe for the new Lady Belmont. Excellent, we must get started right away." She clapped and grinned.

Layla bustled about, pulling an array of fabrics in every color and draping them against me. All the while, she chattered about the town's comings and goings as if I wasn't a stranger who'd just arrived. What felt like hours ticked by as I remained stone-still. Yet her chipper demeanor eased my tension. That was until the conversation turned to questions about me.

"We were all astonished to hear of your arrival. You must tell me all about this whirlwind romance. Silas has always been so serious, without an impulsive bone in his body. Then again, apparently, he does possess at least one." She snickered at her own joke and picked up the measuring tape. "He must be truly smitten with you." She gave a wink as she measured my waist.

A deep blush heated my cheeks, and I held back the wild urge to laugh at the statement. From an outsider's perspective, our sudden nuptials would seem like a romantic affair. When I didn't answer, she pivoted to her desk, grabbed a pen and pad, and wrote my proportions.

"How long have you known Silas?" I asked instead, attempting to distract her from my unorthodox marriage.

She gave me a knowing smile.

"Since he was a little boy. We met when he came to live in Presspin with his uncle. Beatrix and I became close friends when we were children. I would visit her often at Belmont Manor. Though Silas was hesitant to play with us at first, I eventually wore him down."

She lowered the pen and pad to the desk, then resumed measuring me. I let out a huffing sigh, grateful when she didn't pry further into our elopement.

After she finished collecting my proportions, she led me to the sofa. She wrinkled her nose and sighed as she lugged the bolts off the cushions, clearing a spot for us to sit. She flopped into a corner, and I perched on the edge.

Hours passed as Layla peppered me with an array of patterns. She often pursed her lips as I opted for simpler styles than those she suggested. However, the grand designs and magnitude of garments she insisted I needed overwhelmed me. As we finished, my heart sank. Even with my modest choices, I didn't have any funds to pay for the likely exorbitant cost. My shoulders slumped in defeat.

"I can't afford any of this."

Layla's brow furrowed in confusion. "Silas isn't paying for the clothes? Surely, since you are his bride, he would be happy to lavish you with a new wardrobe."

I bristled at the thought of him purchasing these items. Already indebted to him, I couldn't bear the idea of owing him further. "I don't want him to pay for anything."

She tilted her head, her tightly coiled curls springing at the motion. "Do you have any experience sewing or cleaning?"

I nodded.

She grinned and gestured around the space. "I need an assistant. Someone to help me get organized so I can catch up on projects. Why don't you work for me as payment?"

A genuine smile formed on my lips for the first time since I had come to Presspin. There was comfort in this shop. Its harried state was like my mother's room, where she stored all her sewing. Familiarity tugged in my heart, spurring an aching loneliness as thoughts drifted briefly to my sister and mother.

"What do you think?" she asked.

I nodded, overwhelmed with gratitude. She looked me over once more. Her brow furrowed at my attire.

"Now, let's find you something else to wear. I can't send you back to Silas in those awful clothes."

CHAPTER 32

Silas

Uncertainty rolled through me as I stood in front of the oak door. I lifted my fist but paused. I peered down the steps that led to the apartment above the herbalist shop and considered pushing off this difficult discussion yet again. However, I'd spent hours evading this, having already completed my long list of tasks. The morning had passed since I left Arianna with Layla, and I could no longer avoid this conversation. I let out a heavy exhale and knocked. The door opened.

"You've returned early." Brielle stepped aside, allowing me in. Her hips swayed as I followed her into the sitting room, where I had spent many nights visiting. We entered the small space, and she gestured for me to sit in the chair I often occupied beside the hearth, but I remained standing. Instead, my hands clutched the back of the smooth leather as I tried to steady myself after the whirlwind events of the past few days. I focused on the floral sofa across from me and the intricately patterned wallpaper depicting wildflowers instead of on

Brielle. She lingered beside me instead of occupying the settee and tilted her head in assessment. Her long auburn locks shifted.

"Something is vexing you. What is it?" she asked, arching one manicured eyebrow.

My knuckles blanched, the leather indenting beneath my grip. With an exhale, I released the chair and raked a hand through my hair. I smoothed my countenance to a stony resolve, unwilling to allow Brielle or anyone to see my uncertainty about the situation. She waited for me to speak. Curiosity and a hint of worry flickered in her emerald eyes.

"I need an onyx ring."

Her brow wrinkled in confusion. Her gaze drifted to my hand, where my onyx ring gleamed on my finger, then snapped to my face. Her lips puckered, then tugged into a catlike grin. Wordlessly, she moved to the sofa and draped herself upon it. The grandfather clock in the corner ticked the seconds as she drew out this uncomfortable moment before she returned her stare to me.

"Yours seems to be intact. So pray tell, Silas, why do you need another one?"

She lounged in sensuous ease on the settee, her body curved to highlight her form. She smirked. However, I hadn't come to seek a casual carnal entanglement like I had sporadically over the past two years. I had at times found myself in Brielle's bed to quench the bouts of loneliness that accompanied being the lord of Belmont Manor.

"The ring is for..." I clutched the leather-backed chair again, the words catching in my throat until I choked out, "My wife."

Brielle unfurled from her languid lounging, popping into a rigid posture.

"So the rumors are true. I didn't believe it, but good for you, Silas. A new lady to grace the halls of Belmont Manor. Is it true, then? The gossip of your whirlwind romance with a peasant girl you wed in haste? If it is, then, well, how fortunate for you to find love and so quickly. But why would your bride need an onyx ring?"

I knew the rumors of my elopement would have moved through Presspin like wildfire. However, I assumed there would have been more time before the whole town discovered my impetuous decision. Tension crawled through my body. My grip intensified on the edge of the leather chair so tightly I feared it might snap. But Brielle must have suspected the truth of Arianna's presence, especially if I required another onyx ring. She opened her mouth to speak, but I wouldn't allow her to comment further.

"It's complicated. She needed protection and training."

I loosened a rattling exhale as my stony exterior wavered. That damned choking sensation returned, and for a heartbeat, the weight of my choices tightened along my chest. I unbuttoned my collar, but it didn't help.

Despite my efforts, exasperation entered my voice. "It was the only way to keep her safe. She is cursed. Marrying her was the only way..."

The mood shifted, and a strained silence settled upon us. Brielle's eyes widened in near terror as the bigger picture came into focus.

"Silas, have you lost your damn mind? How could you be so reckless, bringing her here and risking your safety? Do you want them to find you? They will come for her. Gods! Is some woman really worth your—"

"Enough, Brielle. I know...I know." My words were gravelly, coated with anguish. But if she'd seen Arianna at that farm, would she have been able to leave her to her fate? A pain formed in my skull. I was overwhelmed by my new life and the choices that had led me here.

"I know...but I couldn't...I couldn't..."

The truth tightened around my throat like a noose, and the same ache that had haunted me as I entered Arianna's home clung to me. My shoulders shook with tense breaths. I'd felt like a raw nerve ripped opened and exposed to the elements since this morning—no. Gods, since I arrived at that damned farm.

Brielle's brow furrowed, then softened as she examined me, her mouth agape in astonishment. Her tone smoothed from the alluring seductress to seriousness. "Silas, is she your—"

"Enough!" I snarled through gritted teeth.

I didn't have the resolve today for her antics or her preposterous ideas. Yet emotions bubbled to the surface of my hasty marriage, and I shoved them away, burying them in the abyss that dwelled within me. I recovered my aloof facade.

"Arianna is my pupil. My wife in name, yes, but nothing more. I will train her to control the curse, as my uncle and Ophelia did for me."

Her expression softened, and a flicker of a genuine smile played upon her lips as she shook her head.

"You always possessed a propensity for saving lost girls." Brielle stood; her brow crinkled as if a decision formed in her mind. "I will forge a ring for your lady."

She sauntered to me, the sensuous sway reentering her hips. She approached until a handbreadth lay between us. Her alluring gaze attempted to pierce through me. "Is there anything else I can provide for you, Lord Belmont?"

"A sleeping draft," I said, and took a step back. I was in no mood for a dalliance.

At my answer, she halted her advance, grinned, and cocked her head. I cringed inwardly as her eyes danced, as if she'd come to some realization that amused her. She withdrew.

As she departed, her hips lacked any sway, nor did her smile possess any allure. Despite knowing her for years, she had changed little since she, a runaway Aralian disciple, had found sanctuary in Presspin. Though she never completed her discipleship, she was well versed in the spells that worked in conjunction with our curse.

I sat in the leather chair. Silence filled the space, even though the apartment was atop the busy herbalist shop she owned. Given her attire and the quiet, she must have closed early. I sighed, my thoughts drifting to when she had arrived in town. Years prior, she had little to her name but possessed a skill we desperately needed in Presspin. I invested in the shop because of her assistance with medicines and knowledge of my curse. The decision had been equally advantageous, yet our mutual respect and sporadic interludes had been unforeseen benefits.

Brielle returned with the sleeping draft. I stood.

"Nightmares again?" She handed it over.

“They are not my nightmares.” My fingers wrapped around the bottle and tucked it into my pocket. I expected her to balk, but she raised an eyebrow, intrigued by the statement.

“I have work to do now. You don’t want to keep your wife waiting, do you? And don’t worry about me. My bed won’t be cold for long,” Brielle said. Then she sauntered to the hallway, leaving me to see myself out.

I left Brielle’s and headed to Layla’s, attempting my most composed countenance as townspeople grinned at me knowingly. Did the entire town already know of my marriage? Thankfully, no one stopped me to confirm the rumors. However, I quickened my steps, eager to be away from the curious glances and whispers as I reached the tailor in record time.

I opened the door, taking in the neat piles of fabric that seemed out of character for Layla’s chaotic style.

“Layla!” I called out.

“Coming,” her voice responded from the rear room.

I took in the tidy shop. Its appearance was in stark difference to the disarray from earlier. At a clearing of her throat, I turned my attention toward the sound as Layla and Arianna came into view.

I gaped momentarily as I beheld Arianna clad in clothes accustomed to Presspin. She donned a cream-colored blouse with a deep V at her breasts. Black pants clung to her legs and narrow hips, while knee-high boots adorned her feet. Her loose blonde waves cascaded over her shoulders. I fumbled for words as I noticed Layla standing behind her, smirking wickedly as she mouthed, “You’re welcome.”

Arianna's brow furrowed. "I hope this is satisfactory. I'm not used to clothing like this."

I glanced at Layla, who snickered into her hand.

My mind searched for words and failed. I nodded in curt approval. "Yes, it is...satisfactory."

Layla turned to her desk, then draped a cloak over Arianna's shoulders and handed her a bag brimming with clothes.

"See you tomorrow," Layla said as we exited.

We stepped onto the cobble path, and I took the heavy parcel from Arianna. "Do you have more clothing to discuss tomorrow?"

Arianna shook her head. "She offered me a job. I didn't feel right having you pay for the garments, nor did I like the idea of her just giving them to me, so we worked out an arrangement. I will organize the shop and help her sew in lieu of paying for the wardrobe."

I glanced sidelong at her, surprised by the plan, and wanted to argue. As Lady Belmont, she possessed unlimited access to funds and could easily find distraction with her responsibilities. Yet a flicker of determination rang through her being. Perhaps this was Arianna's attempt at finding her way in Presspin. I couldn't help the twinge of a smile as she strode with a wisp of confidence and sense of purpose.

Despite myself, this woman intrigued me in more ways than I cared to admit, and her curse fascinated me as well. I had contemplated for hours over how her darkness caressed me instead of marring me. Then this morning, in our meditation, a cadence formed in our breathing. I felt as if she pulled against my power, igniting something that lay dormant between us.

The unspoken beckoning had been deliciously intoxicating, but I couldn't allow myself to fall under her spell.

"Good afternoon, my lord," Mr. Johnson called out as he passed, tipping his hat to me.

I nodded, then searched for Arianna, who walked ahead of me. She brimmed with unbridled curiosity as she took in the town square, surrounded by my people who beamed at her. She paid them little notice. Instead, she turned to me with a coy, shy smile, and my heart thundered as her brilliant blue eyes crinkled with wonder. I nearly melted at the sight.

I forced a steadying breath, chiding myself internally. I was losing control, and that terrified me. Yet against my better judgment, I lusted after her, desiring to strip her of her new garments and taste of her skin once more. My well-reined curse possessed a mind of its own when in her presence. But I pushed those feelings deep within myself. Locking them away in a dark place, I reminded myself she was nothing more than my apprentice, no matter how much my blight and body yearned for hers. I strode past her without a second glance and headed back to the carriage with her in tow.

CHAPTER 33

Theo

I STRETCHED IN MY bed as the maid gathered her crumpled clothes. A flush still crawled along her tender flesh as she dressed. I lounged against the pillows with a satisfied smirk. The girl rushed out with her cap askew. She'd served as a delicious treat for my last night as a single man.

I shifted as I thought of my bride-to-be. Arianna had been a bad pet, venturing off, and it pained me to punish her, to train her. Yet I doubted she would step out of line again. There had been no reports of her returning to Archer Estate.

Restless, I stood. My feet hit the cold wood floor as I wrapped the velvet robe around myself, then walked to the small adjoining room where I kept my collection. Lighting the candles in the sconces, I took in my treasures. The possessions soothed me as I ran my fingers along a broken mask worn by a cursed woman long forgotten. Ancient texts were strewn about, with magnificent illustrations of the goddess Aralia. Arianna would be the ultimate piece locked away for me to play with whenever

I wished. I couldn't wait until tomorrow, for she would finally be mine.

"Young sir," a voice called out from the hall.

I stalked through my quarters and smoothed on an expression of disinterest. I opened the door.

"What is it?"

"Young sir, your father...he wants you in his study...immediately," Edgar, one of our most trusted servants, said. He wrung his hands, and I furrowed my brow. The anxiety in his hazel eyes gave me the briefest pause. What had unnerved our most unshakable servant? I pushed the thought away. I wouldn't be at my father's beck and call.

"I'll come when I'm good and ready."

"Young sir, please...you must—"

I shut the door before Edgar could finish his pleas. He often attempted to be the voice of reason. I was in no mood to listen. Based on Edgar's nervousness, Father was already in a piss-poor mood. I wouldn't jump at Father's demands. I wasn't his servant, but his son.

I took my time dressing in my most elaborate clothing, highlighting the stark contrast between us. A reminder that we were indeed different, a fact I emphasized like the armor a knight wore into battle with a dragon. When, in a foul way, he often mocked me for my lithe form. I wouldn't allow him to catch me off guard, not tonight, as my happiness was so close.

Satisfied with the trimmed jacket that highlighted the deep green of my eyes and my slender figure, I left my room. I sauntered down the corridor. The staff who were still awake darted out of my path. Their terror filled the air, a sign that Father's ire had hit a critical tipping point.

I reached his study and didn't knock before entering. Father sat cross-armed at his massive walnut desk. No moonlight peered into the space since the black curtain lay closed behind him. The only light came from the flickering lamps casting an eerie glow about the room.

I ignored him and went straight for the drink cart, padding across the thick carpeted floor. If I had to endure his tirades, I would at least enjoy his most expensive whiskey. I glanced sidelong and could sense his displeasure as he thrummed his fingers over his arms. I poured the amber liquid. His chair creaked, then footsteps approached. Yet I didn't pull my focus from the liquor as he loomed nearby. I gripped the snifter, a mix of annoyance and foreboding furling within my gut.

"There will be no wedding," he said. I dug my fingertips into the crystal.

Had he lost his wits? He couldn't change his mind now. We had paid the bride price, and we would hold our nuptials tomorrow evening, once Arianna arrived.

I downed the amber liquid. The contents burned my throat, and I turned to hold my father's stare.

"Arianna will be mine no matter what you or Mother think. I'll have no other."

His eyes flared with indignation at my impertinence, and menace filled his countenance. I resisted the urge to flinch.

"Arianna fled Krella last night. It seems she couldn't stomach marrying you. Her mother sent word via messenger, and it just arrived."

I clenched my teeth, my mind reeling at this unbelievable information. Arianna couldn't leave. Wasn't that half of her appeal? To sit locked away, part treasure, part pet, to complete my collection. But more so to be bound to me no matter what?

"Then where is she?" I asked through my clenched jaw.

He rolled his shoulders back, his barrel chest nearly pushing into me, but I wouldn't cower before him.

"Hallowhaven, Krella, dead on the side of the road." His tone would be mistaken as nonchalance by strangers, but I knew better.

"I'll not have this girl embarrassing us, tarnishing our family's good name. Goddess. All the progress I've made over the years to garner connections in Hallowhaven, all undone because your dick required a masked monster." His anger flare with each word.

He stepped closer, looming far too near. His hot breath, laced with port, rushed over my face. "And you, dear boy, will fix this. You'll locate her and wed her on the spot, or I am going to..."

He pulled back, and a malicious sneer crossed his face. Silence stretched as he allowed my imagination to run wild with the possible consequences. "You don't want to see my true wrath if you fail. Your punishments hence far have been mere child's play."

My stomach dropped. Unwilling to show him a hint of my unease, I huffed through my nose.

"I hope the men of Hallowhaven have fucked her senseless. Wouldn't it be funny for you to be forced to marry a whore you desired because of her chastity and tie to the goddess? A hilarious turn of events indeed."

I stood still, tilting my jaw instead of answering.

"You'll head to Hallowhaven in the morning." Father's gregarious nature returned as he withdrew. His heavy footsteps echoed as he exited and clicked the door closed behind him.

I seethed in the silence. How dare she think she could escape me, our marriage, my destiny? Hadn't I taught her what would happen if she disobeyed me? I chucked the glass to the floor and watched as it shattered into a million pieces. I was no simpering idiot. I turned to the drink cart and flipped it over, relishing in the clatter of the expensive glasses and liquids crashing around me. They soaked into the red rug, ruining the carpet. Shards of glass crunched beneath my feet. I would find her, and we would wed, no matter the consequences.

CHAPTER 34

SILAS

MY FIST HOVERED ON Arianna's door. I hesitated to knock, fearing that entering her suite would upend our unspoken understanding. Over the fortnight, we had settled into a rigid routine, with her as my apprentice and I as her teacher. We went about our lives in the manor separately, except for spending each morning training together, which she excelled at. She spent her days working at Layla's while I managed Presspin. In the evening, we never crossed paths, and despite the letter in my pocket, perhaps tonight should be no different.

Unwilling to cause upheaval to our harmonious situation, I turned to leave, but nearly crashed into Mrs. Potter.

"My lord!"

The dinner tray she carried shifted in her hands. The steaming soup sloshed in the bowl. She righted the tray, avoiding calamity. Settled, her eyes darted between me and the entrance to my wife's chambers. Her flabbergasted expression softened to one of optimism.

"Are you here to dine with my lady? Thank the gods! I can fetch a plate for you at once."

She made this same inquiry daily. Though I had refused in the past, she never rebuked me. However, the glimmer of excitement in her gaze made me uneasy. She likely misunderstood my intentions, and I needed to snuff out this misguided hope. I straightened, pulling against my mantle as Lord Belmont. This formality served as a reminder that I was the overseer of this manor and not simply the boy she had helped raise.

"No, but I need to speak with her about an important matter. Have her meet me in the library after her meal."

"She isn't with child, if that's what you are keen on discussing. You are aware that you need to share your wife's bed to establish your lineage, are you not?" she reprimanded through a tight smile.

For a heartbeat, I slipped from the role of Lord Belmont and felt akin to a green lad. Gods, why hadn't I considered the risk of a potential offspring when we consummated? But in the core of my soul, I had burned too deeply with desire to care. I had savored Arianna like a delicacy I could never partake of again.

A wry smile pulled on Mrs. Potter's lips; she was likely satisfied by momentarily ruffling me. Then her demeanor and tone smoothed back to that of the dutiful housekeeper.

"My lord, is that all?"

I wiped a hand over my face, attempting to clear the thoughts of Arianna writhing under me from my mind.

"Yes, that is all. Have her be quick about it."

Mrs. Potter bobbed a curtsy, and I strode away without a glance back.

Minutes later, I entered the library and breathed in the scent of ink. My chest ached as I flicked my gaze to the leather chair by the hearth that Beatrix had often lounged in while reading those damned romance novels. I ignored the pang of loneliness and strode to the table, then occupied the seat where I used to play chess with her. The space felt empty without her, but the warm, woodsy colors soothed me. I pulled the correspondence from her out of the breast pocket of my black jacket and reread it.

Dear Silas,

I hope my letter finds you well. I miss you. With Duncan away on business in Seaside, I am expiring from boredom. There isn't even any interesting gossip or excitement happening here in Krella to occupy my thoughts. Alas, I will have to spend the autumn delving into my novels for entertainment. Please write to me with stories about home soon.

Love,
Beatrix

I folded the letter and shoved it into my pocket. I scrubbed a hand over my face and leaned back into the seat. Had Mrs. Park's neglect of Arianna been so horrendous that her absence had gone unnoticed for nearly two weeks? Arianna's failed wedding date had likely already come and gone, since the post between Krella and Presspin was slow.

However, this note eased some of my concern. With each passing day, my anxiety that they would find her lessened. As long as she remained hidden, we would both be safe. But Brielle's distress clung to my mind. Did I fear they would find her? Could I protect her? There were dangers that even our marriage could not shield her from. I dwelled over the looming consequences that stretched far beyond Arianna's knowledge if our ruse was discovered. A half hour passed, and I considered leaving the library, but finally the door burst open.

"Silas." My name pierced the air, and Brielle sauntered in as if summoned by my recent thoughts.

A critical Mrs. Potter followed her in. Brielle swished her hips past me, moving to the armchair beside the hearth. She splayed upon it, uncaring as Mrs. Potter glared at her. I smoothed my momentary uncertainty, applying my aloof façade. I wouldn't allow Brielle's antics to rankle me.

"Ms. Brielle is here to see you, my lord." Mrs. Potter shot me a disapproving stare.

Did she think I would invite my ex-mistress to my home for an interlude when I was married to someone else? The thought caused my brow to furrow, but it didn't matter, did it? Arianna was my wife in name alone. But why, then, did Mrs. Potter's censure rile something within me?

"I see that. You may leave." I flicked my wrist at Mrs. Potter. Her lips pulled into a tight line, making her displeasure more severe. She bobbed a hasty curtsy and left.

Brielle giggled in amusement. "That woman has never liked me."

She folded her arms across her chest, where her green dress clung to her curves. A grin spread on her rouged lips.

"What are you doing here?" I stood from the desk, dragging a hand through my hair, confused by her sudden appearance. "Is one of my staff in need of your remedies?"

"No. I have something for you." She rose to her feet and moved toward me with seductive ease. Her face lit with amusement. She stopped, leaving only a handbreadth between us. I held a stony countenance, tipping my jaw skyward and arching a haughty eyebrow. She pouted, likely displeased that I wasn't giving in to her sultry stares, which would crumble another man or woman to their knees. Brielle was a beauty, and yet my desires had been elsewhere.

"Oh, Silas, so serious this evening. Should I help you relax?"

My calculated facade slipped, and I paused, considering her offer. I hadn't occupied anyone's bed since my return to Presspin. Perhaps that was why thoughts of Arianna haunted me. Why, despite myself, I stole glances at her as we trained, hoping those moments would be the antidote for this yearning my body and curse craved. Would sharing pleasure with someone else alleviate the lust for Arianna that bubbled beneath the surface?

A click sounded, and Brielle pressed her mouth against mine. She tasted of apricots and sweet wine, but it didn't dampen my yearnings. Her lips parted to deepen the kiss. Uninterested, I placed my hands on her shoulders and disengaged.

Thud.

A chill prickled along my spine as I turned toward the sound. I gaped as I beheld Arianna standing at the entrance, a heavy novel at her feet. Shock colored her face. Her mouth hung agape, then snapped shut. I released Brielle and stepped back, creating distance between my former paramour and myself.

My words caught in my throat. I shouldn't have felt guilty about being caught with another, but I did. The terms of our marital relationship, or lack thereof, was abundantly clear. So why, then, was I hit with a niggling desire to rush to Arianna and clarify that this fleeting kiss meant nothing?

Brielle recovered first and moved forward. She flourished a deep curtsy, the sage gown billowing about her.

"My lady, it's a pleasure to meet you. I've heard so much about you from Silas."

I watched the scene unfold, paralyzed. Brielle rose and rolled her shoulders back, dwarfing Arianna's petite frame. The pair stared at each other, and I expected Arianna to flee. Instead, her eyes flared with determination. Arianna glided closer until they were mere feet apart. That spark I had seen smoldering within Arianna ignited. Yet her expression remained cool, like an icy wind snapping through the space.

"Who are you?" Arianna's words rolled off her tongue.

Brielle didn't answer. Instead, she began pacing around her like a predator circling its prey, sizing up my wife. Arianna straightened to her full height, many inches shorter than Brielle or me. Since I'd met her, she'd often vacillated between the mousy miss she used to be and the bold lady she was becoming. Tonight, she embodied the lady of Belmont Manor in the dark blue garb with an elegant gold embroidery. Curls sprung from a simple twist, and she looked every bit a gentlewoman instead of the simple farm girl she had once been. Perhaps these past few weeks of training and no longer bearing the weight of the mask had made her bolder. Arianna tilted her jaw skyward, as if unaffected by this awkward situation.

"What a pretty little thing you brought home with you," Brielle said, but her gaze locked with Arianna's, and a battle of wills played out between them.

"This is Brielle. She is a friend," I said, trying to break the tension. Arianna held a haughty, disinterested stare with my ex-mistress. The perfect cupid's bow of her lips puckering as she pursed them.

"Friend," Brielle said as she pivoted to me. She tilted her head as if I had mis-categorized our relationship. Then she returned her attention to Arianna.

"Maybe we can be friends, too." A sensuous tone coated Brielle's implication-laden words. My inexperienced wife blinked, missing the innuendo that made me clench my jaw.

"It seems you have your hands full being my husband's friend," Arianna said.

She pivoted to leave, but before she could, Brielle grabbed her hand and slid something onto her finger. As if she had been burned, Arianna yanked out of Brielle's grip. Her nostrils flared as she glared at my ex-paramour.

"Now your bride has a proper wedding band." Brielle withdrew, giving Arianna space.

Arianna flexed a fist at her side, the delicate band and onyx stone glimmering in the candlelight, but she didn't peer at the ring.

"I'll leave you to your...amusements," Arianna said instead.

I flinched at her nonchalant tone. It was as if she didn't care if we proceeded with the perceived dalliance.

"Whatever you planned on discussing, Silas, can wait until tomorrow morning." Arianna flicked a disinterested glance at me, turned, and headed out the door. My blood ran cold.

But I didn't move, shocked by this turn of events. The past two weeks had been free from entanglement. I fought the urge to run after her. But to do what? For some strange reason, her indifference to seeing me with another unsettled me.

"She is lovely."

Brielle approached, but I didn't focus on her. My stare burned on the closed door.

"I see she has captivated you."

"She means nothing to me," I said, but I still couldn't turn my attention from where my wife once stood.

"I would be more than happy to take her off your hands," she said, her tone filled with sensual meaning.

My head snapped to her, and her emerald-green eyes danced with delight as she purred, "I can teach her so many things."

"No. You are not to go near her," I growled.

My head throbbed at the statement, and my power thrummed in response. Brielle had a variety of preferences in partners, and I would be damned if she lured Arianna into her bed. I glared, and she raised an eyebrow in challenge.

"Perhaps you want to reconvene our arrangement, then, since she means nothing to you?" She scrutinized me.

I opened and closed my mouth, but no answer came. Given the nature of our marriage, there wasn't a reason to forgo a tryst, but it felt wrong. I glanced at the floor, where the book sat and picked it up. A romance Beatrix used to love. I placed it on the table, my fingers tracing over the leather. Brielle watched me with unconcealed fascination.

"Will you at least tell your wife the truth about why she is here?" Brielle's features softened.

"No. There is no reason to worry her. She has been through enough." I flicked a glance from the book to her.

"You are being foolish. She deserves the—"

"Haven't you caused enough trouble for me today?"

She didn't cower at my terse tone.

"Very well. I will see myself out." She sauntered away, uncaring that she had left destruction in her wake. I moved toward the leather chair at the hearth, thumbing through the pages. A hint of lavender clung to the novel; perhaps it was a salve she wore that gave her that soothing fragrance, I thought absentmindedly. Part of me hated the event that had just unfolded. However, I wouldn't explain to Arianna the truth of my relationship with Brielle, or lack thereof. No, it was best that she kept her distance from me, and this new misunderstanding only added to the growing chasm between us, keeping us both safe.

CHAPTER 35

ARIANNA

SILAS STRODE AHEAD, AND my gaze drifted over his black coat straining against his broad shoulders. For a heartbeat, I was fascinated with the wavy raven locks that flipped along his collar. My heart fluttered, and an icy chill whipped across my face, cooling my one-sided yearnings. As I did every morning, I buried the desires threatening to bubble to the surface. With a sigh, I shifted my attention to the vibrant colors coating the world. Autumn had taken hold of the forest, covering the path in vivid yellow and orange shades as the foliage floated to the ground. I inhaled the scent of damp soil as we neared the wooded area where we trained. Birdsong in the distance cut through the deafening silence between us, which had been our constant mode of being.

Our feeble master and apprentice relationship had become even more strained since I had caught Silas kissing that woman a fortnight ago. We had never broached the subject of his mistress, nor had we spoken of anything outside of him providing me instructions toward honing my control over my curse. However, her appearance had reaffirmed my resolve to be his wife in name alone. Though he hadn't brought her back to the manor, and that provided me some solace. Yet an aching emptiness penetrated my soul and permeated deep within my bones, as if it were a corporeal part of me.

A howling wind whipped through my thick cloak. It numbed me into submission, so I could endure each day here as one bled into the next. I trained with Silas, worked at Layla's, ate alone, and wrote endless letters to Naomi that she would never see. Then Theo chased me in my nightmares, and I feared being found would bring these terrors to fruition. The cycle repeated daily. I worried that my life would be condemned to this pattern. A branch crunched under Silas's boot, jolting me from my thoughts.

Moments later, he halted at the clearing surrounded by evergreens and aspens. He unfurled the quilt from under his arm and laid it out. We sat. A warmth radiated off him, but it wasn't strong enough to dissipate the cold consuming me. Without being prompted, I closed my eyes as I had done every morning since arriving in Presspin a month ago, and his voice guided me through our exercise. His commands were firm and lacked any hint of gentleness.

Eventually, his prompts stopped, and his breathing steadied into rhythmic beats. My vacillating emotions no longer flooded me. Instead, I relished in the air's coolness and the wind rustling the leaves as they swayed in the trees. The thrum of darkness swelled inside me as I achieved stillness. I concentrated on the core of my power. The flow of time shifted, minutes skittered by. Despite myself, I felt relief at being so near Silas.

"Arianna." My name came from him as a command, pulling me from the ease of my practice.

I turned my attention to him, taking in the line forming between his knitted brows. A weariness clung to him that I hadn't noticed, like water constantly washing against a stone, creating cracks in his façade. He rolled his shoulders and smoothed his demeanor to that of the composed teacher.

"I may regret this, but I think you are ready to learn to wield your curse. Watch closely."

He opened his hand, and I leaned over, studying the lines along his skin. His lip twitched. He shut his eyes, and on an exhalation, a crackling orb formed, floating above his palm. I marveled as he released another breath, showing no sign of discomfort. Then it flickered out of existence in a second, controlled by his will. He closed his fingers, yet I continued to stare at his fist with a sense of wonder.

"Intense emotions trigger our curse: rage, sadness, loss, loneliness. To wield the power, focus on what..." He pulled his hand through his hair, and it settled on the nape of his neck. His countenance softened for a fraction of a second, and remorse filled his gaze. "Focus on what pains you."

I shuddered, uncertain if I wanted to delve into the unsettled emotions brewing just beneath the surface, barely tethered by my resolve. He studied me for a moment, rubbing the back of his neck. Then he released it, folding his hands in his lap.

"It is best to immerse yourself in a sole memory. You don't want to lose your control by being flooded by an onslaught of triggers. If you do, the curse will overtake your body, making you its conduit. You will have no authority if you fully succumb to its predilections, and you will lose your consciousness in the darkness." Though his tone remained even, his knuckles blanched, a sign of his lurking unease.

I nodded in acknowledgment at his warning. Then I closed my eyes and inhaled, easing into myself and finding center with the exhale.

"Use a recent memory to access the potency of your emotions while not allowing it to consume you. As you delve into the pain, the curse will swell, feeding off the despair. Channel the building power by envisioning the energy like clay, melding its shape with your mind until you form an orb in your hand."

Despite my uncertainty, I summoned the memories, tapping into a well of anguish caused by the isolation in Presspin. The guard I held against the melancholy slipped away like sand through my fingertips. A bitter taste laced my tongue, and I licked my lips in a futile attempt to clear the flavor. I let out a shaky exhale and delved deeper into the darkness swirling in my soul. My pulse surged, and a cold sweat washed over me. Threads of energy flickered within, ignited by the painful recollections. I lingered on the heartbreak that coursed through my body at seeing Silas kiss that woman. Yet dwelling on that singular moment triggered a cascade of sorrows to topple over me without my permission. Tears threatened to fall as the overwhelming loneliness consumed me. But I wouldn't relent. Instead, I breathed through the discomfort.

Minutes passed, and finally, the pain flowed with me, no longer a sharp pang in my gut, but a part of my being. I opened my palm and exhaled. The pressure in the air thickened, as if I were the storm. I tugged against the well within until raw inky power flickered into existence.

Sweat beaded down my forehead, and I melded the crackling energy with my mind. It swirled into a floating black orb the size of a child's ball. I panted, exhausted in the effort of allowing the darkness to linger while not letting it overtake me. The whispers from the blight intensified, beckoning me to submit to release this devastation into the world.

Fatigued, I choked out a sob, breaking my concentration. The darkness dissipated into the air as if it had never existed. Hot tears washed over my skin. My tunic, laden with perspiration despite the cool weather, clung to me. I folded over myself on the blanket, gasping.

Unlike the moment in the carriage, he didn't reach for me in comfort. Instead, he sat stone-still as I willed myself to regain my composure.

"What did you focus on that has caused you such distress?" he whispered.

I straightened and turned my attention to him. His hard expression softened. I wiped away the remnants of the tears that streaked my cheeks. I felt like a raw nerve from the uprooted emotions. However, denotations of strength pulsed in my blood, as if, through this training, I had unlocked a newfound courage. I lifted my chin in defiance as my words tumbled out of me.

"I focused on my soul-crushing loneliness, Silas. It has been my only companion since arriving in Presspin."

His mouth twisted into a grimace, and he shifted his gaze to the woods. My brow furrowed, and tears welled anew as I waited for him to say something, anything. But only silence remained. I clenched my hands, chiding myself for speaking my feelings. They had only fallen upon deaf ears. I stood, no longer willing to stay in his presence. Without a glance back, I left him in his discomfort to think about the woman who lived with him, the wife he thought so little about.

CHAPTER 36

ARIANNA

I CLENCHED MY JAW as I glared at the shimmering silk that matched Silas's eyes. Yet another reminder of my uncaring husband. I shoved the golden-hued textile between two similar shades. Stepping back, I admired my work. I had spent the afternoon shelving the bolts in the backroom of the tailor's shop. The structured task brought a sense of calm to my chaotic emotions and order to the cluttered storage area.

"Arianna, have you seen my measuring tape?" Layla called out from the storefront.

I sighed and scanned the space, finding it draped over the sage material she had been perusing for today's appointment.

"Coming!" I grabbed the tool and pushed through the swinging door separating the two rooms.

"Put it on the desk," Layla said, but she didn't turn her attention from the young woman on the pedestal. She paced around her, calculating her form as she did with all her clients.

I rushed forward and placed the tape on her workspace. Then I turned to leave. I didn't want to interfere with the appointment, nor did I possess the energy to make awkward small talk.

"Are you Lady Belmont?" the woman asked before I could retreat.

I froze mere feet from making my escape and gazed longingly at the rear of the shop. I fought the gnawing desire to flee, as I always had. My attempts at friendliness with customers and Layla had been stiff. I lacked the skill of conversing easily. However, I couldn't ignore being addressed directly.

I pivoted toward them. Yet Layla offered no help. She continued her assessment of the lady, taking in her lithe figure, her copper hair, and a smattering of freckles across her nose that drew attention to her brown eyes.

"I am." I fiddled with the onyx ring, and a long silence sprawled over us. The interaction reminded me of my sheer inability to form connections in Presspin. Not only with Silas, but the townspeople. My stomach sank. Today had already been fraught with emotions since my training session with Silas this morning. Uncomfortable, I attempted to back away slowly, hoping neither would notice.

"I knew it. Oh, you are lovely. No wonder Lord Belmont eloped with you. I am Elizabeth. My older brother is Vincent, your steward."

I nodded dumbly at the woman. Even if her brother was Silas's steward, I wouldn't know. The only member of the staff I had conversed with was Mrs. Potter. She was a kind lady, but she flitted about the estate, occupying every free second of her time in keeping Belmont Manor running smoothly. While I often found myself alone in my room or the library. Though I had the freedom to roam the estate, my habits of staying secluded were deeply ingrained. I wrung my hands. Perhaps my actions over the past month had also played a role in my loneliness.

Elizabeth smiled, as if waiting for me to respond, but no words formed on my lips. Layla finished her evaluation, then flicked a glance at me. Her brow furrowed, then smoothed as she focused again on the customer.

"Elizabeth, did I tell you about the new books that arrived at Jamie's? I'm hoping to go there tomorrow evening."

I turned and strode to the rear room until their conversation drifted off. My heart hammered and my mouth grew dry. A prickle of tears threatened, and my nostrils burned. It was silly to be flabbergasted by a simple chat with a stranger. Yet the raw emotions from my morning session remained like an open wound in need of tender care.

To soothe myself, I returned to organizing the bolts. I picked up a crisp floral pattern and froze. The details reminded me of the wildflowers that Naomi often brought me. I clutched the material to my chest. For a heartbeat, my mind drifted to Naomi. I missed her terribly, but she wasn't here, nor did I know when she could visit. My heart ached, and I put the fabric away, much like my thoughts of my sister. I focused intently on sorting through the colorful silks, and an hour slipped by.

"You seem off today. Is everything all right?"

I flinched, having been so lost in my task that I hadn't heard Layla approach.

I pivoted to her, but I couldn't repress the weariness that likely coated my expression. Her smile faltered.

"I'm a good listener. I promise."

I worried my lip between my teeth. We hadn't delved into my past, nor had we spoken of anything beyond frivolities. I picked up a bolt and ran my fingers along the crisp fabric. The texture soothed me as I debated whether to return to sorting or to divulge some of the truth that weighed on me. A long pause lingered, and her steady gaze fixed upon me as she waited.

I gave a reluctant sigh. An internal battle raged between my inclination to remain on the outskirts of society and a need for connection. However, I couldn't continue as I had. Silas would never be more than my sullen teacher, and I wouldn't survive this isolation. I had to try.

"My life in Presspin is complicated."

I clutched the bolt to my chest, taking courage from the softness.

"I've been lonely. Silas and I...we...our marriage is one of convenience. We rarely interact with each other outside of our daily...engagements."

She held still, as if afraid that any movement or noise would terrify me like a skittish animal.

"When I was home, I at least had my sister, but now...I am alone." A lump formed in my throat.

My mind wandered again to Naomi, and I wondered for the thousandth time about how she was faring. It killed me to not know how my impulsive decision affected her. But I pushed these thoughts away before they consumed me.

"It sounds like your marriage is...complicated."

Layla picked up a green bolt and shoved it haphazardly between shades of red. I flinched and placed the material I clutched in its correct spot near similar hues. We worked in tandem, sorting through the fabric. She didn't push for more, yet the bitter truth burned on my tongue, desperate to be heard.

"Silas helped me out of a difficult situation. Our hasty wedding was nothing more than a means to an end. I'm just a burden to him."

She paused, processing the information as if replaying memories with the updated detail. She tilted her head, assessing me in a new light.

"This is why you didn't want Silas to pay for your wardrobe. Oh, Arianna, it all makes sense now."

I nodded and my shoulders slumped. To my surprise, she moved closer and embraced me in a tentative hug. I stood ramrod still, uncertain of how to engage in this unaccustomed affection. But my body loosened, enveloped in her warmth. Tears welled as I wrapped my arms around her in return. The gesture brought a relief I hadn't realized I needed. With a quick squeeze, she released me and stepped back. Her effervescent smile returned.

"Come, let us sit for a while. The work can wait," she said.

We sat on the crimson sofa, and for the first time since arriving, I talked about my old life. I told stories of the farm where I had grown up; my sister, whom I missed dearly; and my unusual relationship with the husband I barely knew. Though I evaded many details, fearing she might divulge sensitive information that could put me at risk of being discovered.

She shared about her past as well. She had inherited this shop from her father after he'd passed years prior. Since meeting her, I realized Layla was a pillar of the community and a friend to everyone. I just never suspected she would want to be one to me. Eventually, she recounted tales of her childhood, which shifted to those of the Belmont siblings.

"Beatrix was my best friend, and we were inseparable until Duncan came to Presspin to help Silas transition to becoming the overseer of Belmont Manor. After their uncle's death, a hole formed in both of them, and Duncan swooped in to fill it." Her soft smile flattened, and a sadness filled her demeanor.

"I miss her. But if I'm honest, our friendship changed after Duncan came to Presspin. I never understood her loyalty to him, but perhaps I'm just being bitter."

"You haven't remained close since she wed?" I asked.

"No. I sent letter after letter to her with no response. I thought we were best friends. Apparently, I was mistaken."

I lingered on her lack of contact with Beatrix, which struck me as peculiar. Beatrix brimmed with kindness, and it seemed out of character that she wouldn't return the letters of a once dear friend.

"I've known Silas for many years, too." Mischief filled her expression. I fidgeted as she searched my face, a wide grin stretching upon her lips.

"I'm certain there is more to this story than you are telling me. Silas possesses a chivalrous streak, but he is also very sensible. Marrying someone suddenly is rash, and he prides himself on being level-headed. He rarely acts on impulse. I doubt Silas truly intended on having a loveless marriage. Hopefully, he will forget about this marriage of convenience nonsense." She winked at me.

A blush crept across my cheeks. I shook my head in disagreement and changed the subject to her frequent visits to Jamie's bookstore.

CHAPTER 37

SILAS

"MY LORD, FOR MR. Johnson's roof, shall I procure the supplies from the timber yard?" Vincent, my steward, asked as he held a notepad, occupying the chair on the other side of my desk. His dark brows furrowed, and his lips flattened into a straight line, the harsh look making him appear older than his twenty-four years. I blinked at him, taking a moment to register his words. I shifted my ruminations from this morning's training to the present in the study.

"Yes, obtain the lumber. It's best that we fix the issue prior to the winter storms." I flicked my wrist. Then I leaned back in my chair and rubbed my weary eyes, exhausted by this day.

"Silas," he called out tentatively. The use of my given name gave me pause. Vincent was a rigid believer in social hierarchy; this slip in decorum caused me to sit up and focus.

"What is it? Needing a few days off?" I asked.

Perhaps he wanted a much-needed break after managing my estate flawlessly while I visited Krella. His usually neutral expression pulled into a hint of a frown. A long silence stretched as I waited somewhat impatiently for my straitlaced steward to speak.

"It is none of my business, my lord, but are you feeling well? You haven't seemed yourself today. To be more accurate, you haven't seemed yourself since you arrived home with...well...with your new wife." He scanned my desk and furrowed his brow.

My usually tidy workspace appeared unkempt. Stacks of unopened letters were strewn over the space, and my typically immaculate ledgers were flipped open, riddled with mindless mistakes. I gritted my teeth. I had struggled recently to keep atop of the responsibilities that had once been like second nature.

I ran my fingers through my hair. Instead of delving into the task before me, Arianna's words from this morning looped through my mind again, as if she were right in front of me.

"I focused on my soul-crushing loneliness, Silas. It has been my only companion since arriving in Presspin."

I willed away the pained expression that haunted me. Yet with each time I recalled the conversation, I felt as if a knife stabbed me in the heart.

"I'm fine." I shook my head in denial, but my shoulders tensed.

"May I offer you an observation?"

Vincent removed his wire-framed glasses and cleaned them. For a moment, I assessed him, curious about what my serious and often shy steward could be thinking.

"Proceed." I crossed my arms over my chest.

"Despite your recent return with such a lovely new bride, I dare say you have spent more time with me over the past few weeks than with her. Perhaps, if you found some balance between your duties and Lady Belmont, then you would have a greater ability to focus."

He smiled sheepishly. Then he returned his glasses to the bridge of his narrow nose. The motion drew my attention to his russet-colored eyes and the speckling of freckles that lay just beneath them. He didn't flinch as I assessed him. Instead, he held my stare, not withering under the haughty demeanor I upheld.

"I would be more than happy to spend my days off working if you need extra assistance to allow you more time with your wife," he said.

I tilted back and stared at the ceiling, exasperated by his observation. Gods, now him, too? Had I truly abandoned Arianna? And did everyone realize this truth except me? The awareness made me sick. I understood, far too well, the loneliness of leaving one's home.

Beatrix and I had struggled in our first weeks at Presspin. Unlike Arianna, we were surrounded by those who cared for us. My days were filled with companionship from Beatrix, the affection of my uncle, and Ophelia's love. Even the staff paid particular attention to my sister and me as we settled into Belmont Manor. The sadness and grief of losing our parents had been heavy, but those around us lessened the anguish. In time, we slipped into a comfortable life because of our uncle's care. Yet I hadn't helped Arianna in her transition to living in Presspin, and guilt consumed me. What would Uncle Oliver have done in my situation? My fingers moved to his ring, dangling from the chain around my neck, having been returned from Arianna the morning after the incident with Brielle. I knew that if he could, he would chastise me from the grave, lecturing me for my recent behavior. He would have been ashamed. I'd placed her under my protection, but then I had forsaken her.

"My lord." Vincent's words pierced through my churning thoughts. I sat up and flicked a glance at him. His pale skin appeared even lighter than usual. "Perhaps you're right. You are excused for this evening. Please stop by the timber yard in the morning."

His color returned, and a small smile lit his good-natured face. Without another word, Vincent rose from the seat he had occupied across from me, gave a quick bow, and left.

Overwhelmed, I stood and walked to the windows, taking in the setting sun. What should I do? I needed to rectify this situation with Arianna, but we couldn't have a typical marriage. I didn't have the capacity for love, and it was best that I kept my distance. Yet no matter how hard I tried to deny it, we shared an unusual connection, and something about her enchanted me. My aloofness toward her served as a barrier of protection against any burgeoning feelings. I could help her settle into Presspin while keeping this attraction at bay. Couldn't I?

Monster, my mind whispered to me. I pushed the voices that haunted me aside. I left my study and strode through the hallway until I reached her suite. I paused, not knowing how to proceed. Exhaling through my uncertainty, I knocked once, twice, and a third time. No answer came. I opened the door.

"Arianna."

The room was empty. The space seemed untouched since the maid's morning cleaning. Panic seized me as my gaze caught the setting sun through the floor-to-ceiling windows. The color was fading behind the mountains as dusk fell over the town. A flicker of my stirring emotions threatened to take hold as my ring grew hot against my skin. Had she, too, finally abandoned this manor, her training, and me as I had feared all along?

ARIANNA

I walked out of Layla's and toward Belmont Manor. Flecks of orange faded behind the mountain range as the sun set. Despite the night settling around me, I felt confident in my ability to find my way home. I clung to my coat and couldn't help but smile, feeling lighter after my hours-long chat with Layla. A hush settled on the previously bustling streets as the once lively shops in the town square closed for the evening. Lights flickered in the apartments above, where townspeople nestled in their warm homes for supper with their families.

My stomach growled, and I hastened my pace, making my way through the town quickly. Yet as I turned the final corner, I nearly bumped into a man. He leaned against the last brick building on the outskirts, his legs kicked out in ease. His presence felt odd, since no one ventured to Belmont Manor after dusk unless they were a servant. However, his clothing did not match the black livery bearing the Belmont crest.

"Excuse me." I shuffled to avoid him. But he grabbed my arm, halting my progress.

"Lady Belmont?" the man asked, but he didn't release me.

I pivoted and assessed his unfamiliar face, thin lips, narrow nose, and brown hair slicked with streaks of gray. His short-cropped beard made him indistinguishable from the other townspeople. The shadows lurking from the low lamplight highlighted his thick, menacing brow, and a sense of foreboding churned through me.

"Yes?" I asked tentatively.

He said nothing. Instead, a malicious smile cracked his face.

Tension crawled along my skin in the silence. Anxiously, I yanked my hand, but it didn't budge. His fingers dug into my flesh. I winced, and my pulse surged.

"Unhand me at once!"

He didn't. I gulped down panic and tugged my arm once more to liberate myself. His grasp felt like unbreakable iron. I struggled for freedom, but his hold remained unyielding. I stared at the shadowed path just ahead that led to Silas. My heart sank as my feet shuffled helplessly along the cobble. He yanked me closer, and I tumbled against his barrel chest.

"Aye. Ms. Park, I dare say. I caught myself the prize of the century."

I froze in shock as my given name rolled off his lips. An eerie heaviness sprawled through the atmosphere, as if sticky syrup coated the air. My heart raced. I scanned the empty street for help, but there was no one. The shops on the outskirts were darkened. Only the faint lamplight overhead burned through the night sky.

He laughed with amusement, like he had just won a round of cards.

"My gut has never been wrong. Not in my whole thirty years as a runner in Hallowhaven. They all thought me a daft fool, but I was right, and here you are. I've been watching you, Lady Belmont—or should I say, Ms. Park."

My momentary haze cleared. Dread filled me, and I attempted to flee again. He sensed my desire to bolt and pulled me closer. His hand wrapped around my waist as he held me flush against him, pinning me in his embrace. I wriggled, but his thick arms and bulky frame subdued me with ease.

"You have caused quite a commotion, disappearing into thin air. And what a mystery you have been. The other runners are all chasing their tails in Hallowhaven, Krella, and Daviel, but not me. They laughed when I said I would venture to Presspin. They won't be laughing when I return with you and claim my reward. But I still can't figure out how you freed yourself from the mask. I suspected you might have stowed away in a spelled room. I remember rumors of a cursed in this area many years ago. But this? Even I could have never predicted this."

I flinched as he released my wrist and the back of his hand skimmed across my chin.

You'll have plenty of time to spill your secrets on our long trip to Daviel. Now be still, and I won't have to hurt you."

A cold sweat washed over me as my nightmares came to life. My ears buzzed, and I gulped down the bile rising in my throat. Theo, despite everything, had found me. I squirmed with all my might to be free. Yet his thick arms were like a vise, stilling my movements. His stench of sweat made my stomach roil.

"Let me—"

The hand that had clutched my wrist was now cupped over my mouth, muffling my cries.

"Shh. We will go quietly to Daviel, where you belong." His hot breath, reeking of ale, rushed over the nape of my neck.

Fear swelled, and my curse bubbled internally, like the steam of a boiling teakettle, whooshing into the air and feeding off my terror. The world fell away piece by piece as the darkness began to overtake me. My senses intensified, and crackling energy crept beneath my skin, churning in my blood.

The inky well of power within me whispered of destruction. It wanted me to surrender myself wholly. It yearned to use me as its conduit for the devastation it promised. It would kill this man. However, I was uncertain I could remain in control if it was freed. Unleashed, it would burn this town to ash, and I couldn't destroy the people of Presspin. But my panicked gaze flicked to the top of the hill as the stranger began pulling me toward a shadowed alley...back to Theo.

"Come now, don't fight the inevitable." He continued dragging me to my demise.

My darkness churned, eager to be released as it clawed at my mind. But I forced my breath to steady and clung to my resolve as I attempted the impossible.

"That's a good girl," he said when my body stilled. He likely assumed I had given up my fight and resigned myself to my fate. But I hadn't.

Instead, I willed myself to focus, though not on the impending doom, not on his hands, nor on my panic. No, I concentrated on inhaling the icy air and slipped into my training. I closed my eyes, breathing through the clunking of his boots on the path as he dragged me. The string of my curse tightened within me, and I plucked it like a taut bowstring. It snapped under my control, submitting to me. Exhaling, I melded the crackling energy with my mind, forcing it to leach from my core and through my skin.

"*Ahh*!" The man pushed me away.

Off balance, I stumbled forward. I should have run. Yet his cries were the most horrific sound. I turned toward him. He sobbed, crumpled on the cobbled path. Dim light washed over his anguish, highlighting the deepened grooves in his face. He wailed. Blisters protruded from the raw flesh of his palms, as if he had placed his hands in boiling oil. I gaped in horror. What if someone heard his cries? But no one came.

Stumbling, I gagged. Vomit crawled up my throat. The man's sobs, the stench of burnt flesh, and the thoughts of the fate that had awaited me bombarded my tenuous command over my curse. The world grew hazy, and the darkness that had lain subdued within me for weeks clawed at my wearing mental reserves.

Kill him! Kill him! my curse hissed in my mind.

My once centered breath shifted to ragged pants as the energy I previously commanded threatened again to unleash its fury upon this town.

"No!" I cried and clapped my hands over my ears, blocking out the sound of the man's shrieks.

Darkness coated the edges of my vision and flooded my mind. But I didn't want to harm anyone, so I clung with all my resolve to a sliver of reality. My remaining consciousness dwelled on the beautiful architecture, the cheerful children who played in the streets, and Layla's kind smile. I wanted to make this place my home, and I could not allow the curse to overwhelm me.

My fingernails dug into my scalp. I wanted to rip the whispers from my skull. I fell to my knees, gasping. I battled for purchase against the power. A flicker of my consciousness held on and repeated like a mantra: *I will not destroy these people. I will not destroy my home.*

I curled into a fetal position. My strength waned. The taste of ash danced over my tongue. I screamed. My skin burned from the effort to resist what felt like second nature.

"*Arianna...Arianna...Arianna,*" a voice called out to me, piercing through my soul.

Strong arms wrapped around me. I felt buoyant as they lifted me from the cold street and tucked me against a solid chest. My once rising curse capitulated in response to this presence.

"You are safe. I promise you are safe." Silas's lips brushed over my hands, which I still held against my ears.

I inhaled and exhaled, calming myself, as my fear slipped away and the internal storm dissipated.

"I should kill you this instant for daring to lay a finger on my wife."

My captor whimpered in response.

Silas's shoulders shook with rage. "Did they send you?"

A moan escaped the stranger.

"Answer me!" Silas snarled.

"I'm no one. A spice trader. I got lost. Drank too much. Stumbled on the woman. The *monster*. She's a monster!"

My head lolled against Silas's chest. I tried to speak, to tell him that the stranger was lying. No words formed. My head pounded.

"How dare you. That is *my wife,*" Silas growled, and he shifted me in the crook of his arm, freeing one of his hands.

A heartbeat passed, and I expected the man's cries to intensify or for him to beg. But only an eerie silence and the scent of ash washed over my senses. I gulped down a knot and wanted to move, but Silas pinned me against him. His presence soothed my raw nerves, and my eyes grew unbearably heavy until the exhaustion from the day overtook me.

CHAPTER 38

SILAS

I PACED ALONG THE soft silver rugs in Arianna's room. My fingers ran through my hair in a feeble attempt to quell this internal agitation. My shoulders shook with ragged breaths, fueled by my fury. Who was that stranger? I should have dragged him into the cellar and questioned him further. However, in those seconds, her agony seeped into me as if we shared the emotion. Her anguish riled my curse's inclination toward destruction, clouding my judgment. I hadn't hesitated when my darkness flowed through me and I turned the man into ash. No guilt weighed on me. I'd vowed to protect Arianna, and I would, no matter the cost to my already broken soul.

I peered at her, where she lay nestled in the silver and blue quilts of her bed, her face relaxed as she rested. She had been asleep for hours while I paced this room, unable to part from her side as I lamented over my poor choices.

Restless, I walked to the window overlooking the town below. The view didn't soothe me. Instead, it reminded me that my disregard for her had not only caused her pain but also put Presspin in danger. Her control over her curse was tenuous, and we were lucky that the incident that occurred today had not been catastrophic. I had been in a false sense of security for the past month, pretending that Ariana's presence hadn't altered my life. My actions put everyone, including myself, at risk. Everything needed to change. I couldn't keep her safe and continue distancing myself from her.

"Silas."

I pivoted toward the bed, and Arianna attempted to sit up. However, weakness took hold, and she collapsed against the cushions with a groan.

Swiftly, I moved to her side. A mound of shimmering silver pillows swallowed her. I frowned, taking in the fatigue etched on her face from the exertion of the evening.

The mattress shifted under my weight as I sat beside her. For a heartbeat, a flicker of a memory of our wedding night surfaced. How many times had memories of that evening, of our bodies entwined and powers enmeshed, wormed their way into my mind? Yet I pushed away the desire, chastising myself for the inappropriate moment to dwell on carnality.

Unaware of my lusty thoughts, her crystal-blue eyes pierced into my soul, searching for answers. She winced, breaking the connection, then rubbed circles around her temples. A hint of a pout formed on her lips. I grimaced at the pain I suspected she experienced, the burning sensation within her skull from holding her curse at bay. My fingers itched with the need to stroke her hair to provide some sort of comfort to both of us.

"What do you remember?" I asked instead.

She paused, and her brow furrowed in concentration, as if replaying the memory.

"A man, he grabbed me and..." A deeper crease formed on her forehead. She frowned, and her lower lip trembled. "He was a runner from Hallowhaven. Theo hired him. He came here on a hunch. He has been watching me. I...I hurt him to get away."

I hesitated for a heartbeat, but the overwhelming need to comfort her outweighed reason as I placed my hand on hers. At the touch, her expression smoothed, and her gaze locked on mine.

"Don't worry about that man," I said without offering the whole truth—that in my rage, I had killed him without hesitation.

She flicked a glance at my hand on hers. Her breath hitched, then she shifted her eyes to mine. Uncertainty crossed her expression as I rubbed my thumb against her smooth skin. I should have released her then, allowed her to rest and discuss this situation more in the morning. Yet I remained rooted to the spot. My heart pounded, and I choked back a truth hidden behind the walls where my emotions lived. Despite my effort, this woman haunted me.

"How did I get here?" She broke the silence, and her brows knit together in confusion. A weariness clung to her features as she fought off the dregs of exhaustion.

"I came to speak with you, but you had not returned from Layla's. The sun was setting, and..." I paused, not wanting to divulge the fear which had consumed me when I realized she was missing. Her gaze urged me to continue. "Concerned over your well-being, I left to search for you."

How had I found her? My soul had seemed to be guided by a compass straight to her, as if a piece of me knew her whereabouts. Something primal connected us. I gulped down the reminder of the terror that had dug into my gut as I galloped down the hill.

"You were fighting off your darkness, holding your power despite the circumstance. Somehow, you found control, and I brought you here a few hours ago. You did well."

My thumb never stopped its smooth caress against her hand. However, I was uncertain whether the motion was to console her or myself. The touch moored me to the present. It kept me from drifting to the moment panic had flooded me and my world briefly fell apart from seeing her harmed.

She let out a sigh and closed her eyes, shifting amongst the pillows. She relaxed as exhaustion began overtaking her. Yet shame enveloped me. Her features were fragile and etched with discomfort in the soft candlelight. My lips drew into a straight line of displeasure. Gods, I had been so stupid. Had I been more attuned to her, we could have avoided this incident. This wouldn't have happened if I had accompanied her. I would have noticed a stranger lurking. I should have predicted that someone might infiltrate Presspin. Yet my aloof nature played a large role in the occurrence of this incident.

"I should have kept you safe. I will not forsake you again," I vowed.

As she drifted back to sleep, I should have left, but I couldn't. Instead, I leaned toward her, my face so temptingly close that I contemplated brushing my lips against hers. I didn't.

"As long as I draw breath, you will never be alone." The promise forced my heart to beat wildly. Despite myself, I wanted to confess the feelings I harbored. Even though I denied it, I craved the taste of her, the touch of her skin, the release my body and curse desired. But I couldn't delve into the overwhelming yearnings I had for her.

Instead, I said, "I will be your friend and companion from this day forward."

"Friends," she whispered in half sleep, her face pale with exhaustion from the exertion of the incident. For a moment, I deliberated whether I should remain here in her room. Near, in case she needed me. Her breath took on a steady cadence, and I dared not push my resolve in her presence. Not tonight, as my emotions and power felt untamed.

"Good night." I withdrew, forcing myself away from her.

I slunk out of her quarters. The door closed. I leaned against the frame and scrubbed a hand over my face. It pained me to leave her alone in her suite, but at least she was no longer alone in her life in Presspin.

CHAPTER 39

Arianna

My thumb absentmindedly rubbed along the handle of my cup of coffee in a feeble attempt to soothe my disjointed feelings. Yet tension prickled beneath my skin as I sipped the beverage, hoping to wash out the metallic tang which had lingered on my tongue since last night. The scent of bacon drifted to me, and my stomach churned. I leaned over and covered the plate with a silver serving lid, unable to view the bountiful breakfast Mrs. Potter had provided. Instead of eating, I curled my weakened limbs into the armchair. I leaned back and closed my eyes, hoping for a moment of solace. However, my mind conjured images of the man's blistered palms and his shrieks of horror. My breaths rushed from me as panic blossomed in my chest.

My bedroom door clicked open, dragging me out of my ruminations. I stared, perplexed, at Silas. Unfazed by my confusion, his countenance exuded concern as he strode into the suite. Without hesitating, he occupied the chair beside mine, as if he were accustomed to joining me in my private quarters.

"How are you this morning?" he asked.

His sudden appearance in my room rattled my brain, and shock replaced my panic. I gaped, dumbfounded, at this unfamiliar man who spoke complete sentences unprompted. I shifted in the armchair, unfurling from my comfortable position to a more ladylike seat. I peered at him in confusion. Hadn't he avoided me since my arrival? Yet I vaguely remembered telling him of the stranger, and a whisper of a memory about being friends prickled in my hazy mind.

"I am...well," I said, not daring to admit my persistent panic.

He surveyed my face, searching for the truth. I lowered my cup to the small table and focused on its silver swirling pattern.

"I suspect last night took its toll on you," he said.

"I should have trained this morning. I need to gain complete control over my curse to prevent another incident from occurring. I almost..."

My stomach sank at the words I couldn't utter. *I almost killed someone. I almost destroyed Presspin. I am a monster.* I averted my gaze to the fire, unable to look at him. But I sensed him searching me, his stare drifting over my profile.

I glanced sidelong at him, taking in his unaccustomed attire. He donned a well-tailored black coat and a crisp dress shirt, sans a cravat. His usually askew locks laid slicked back. My mind hitched, caught on his formal appearance.

"No, you need your rest. It takes time for our bodies to recuperate after using our curse or fighting against its callings. Besides, I had other issues to attend to." He pulled a small leather notepad out of his pocket and handed it to me.

"I went to the inn this morning. Your attacker stayed under an alias as a spice trader from Hallowhaven. He had been tracking you for a few days. He likely saw last night as the perfect opportunity to capture you without drawing attention."

My brow furrowed as I flipped through the pages filled with notes detailing my comings and goings. The man had headed straight to Presspin after being hired by Theo. I lowered the notepad to the table beside the cup as my stomach roiled and a flashback of last night crashed upon me. Yet my fingers trembled as I traced along the name etched into the leather: *John Timmons*. To my surprise, Silas placed his hand over mine, steadying me. I peered over at him and couldn't avoid the pull of his gentle gaze.

"He must have heard rumors of my uncle's curse and pieced together from your visits with Beatrix that I assisted you. At least that is what I gathered from his notes. You needn't worry. He is gone now." Silas stroked his thumb over my hand. My heart fluttered at the tenderness, soothing my welling anxiety. Yet the gesture sparked a hazy memory. However, it didn't materialize, but it lingered in the recesses of my mind.

"How do you know? I hurt him. Seared his flesh. I am certain he is halfway to Hallowhaven to tell—"

"He is not."

Silas grabbed the leather booklet from beneath my hand, then chucked it into the fire. The pages crinkled and smoldered as it caught ablaze. The notes of one John Timmons disintegrated into ash. The scent prickled a memory, and my mind pieced together what I had missed the night prior. Silas had dispatched of the man. I stiffened at the realization, uncertain of whether I felt relief or remorse.

Sensing my understanding, Silas stood and moved to the hearth, watching the last dregs of the pages flitter into nothingness.

"I did what I had to do. I do not relish taking a man's life. However, when the choice comes between our safety and the lives of those who wish to harm us, I will always choose to protect us. To protect you." He didn't turn to me as he gripped the mantel, his knuckles blanching from the force.

I opened and closed my mouth, but no words formed. Yet, despite Silas's certainty, a heaviness clung to his shoulders. He acted nonchalant over the incident, yet a prickle of something sour dwelled in my soul. I could almost taste the bitterness of his guilt.

"Was he the first man you—"

"No."

I should have been frightened or disgusted, but Silas had saved me. Had he arrived seconds later, the man's death would have weighed on me instead of him. My mouth dried at the horrific thought of killing someone. However, had our roles been reversed and Silas was in peril, what would I have done? Pondering over the moral quandary didn't matter now.

"From his notes, the other runners are searching the underbelly of Hallowhaven. He told me they all thought him a fool for coming to Presspin. Hopefully, our secret died with him," I said instead.

Silas's shoulders rose and fell from his heavy breaths, and I sensed the unspoken grief rolling off him. Even if he had killed before, I doubted he took pleasure in the act. The grandfather clock in the corner of the room ticked minutes by, and I anxiously twisted my onyx ring, uncertain of what to say. Finally, he released the mantel and straightened his posture. As he pivoted to me, he plastered on his aloof expression and returned to his seat.

"You did well holding your power at bay," he said, changing the subject.

I shook my head in disagreement. No, had Silas been a minute later, Presspin would have likely burned to the ground in my curse's wake. Its whispers had tempted me, and it fed off the man's cries, crumbling my resolve. How could I describe the mix of panic and self-doubt I had choked upon?

He slumped into the chair. "No, I was in a similar situation and lost control once. Compared to me, you did exceedingly well."

"No, I almost destroyed everything." I clasped my hands together, but my fingers still trembled.

His focus remained on the dancing flames in the fireplace.

"I snuck out of the manor once. At the ripe old age of fifteen, I decided I was a man and should be able to roam Presspin freely, despite my uncle's frequent warnings. I had gone into town with my sister and met three young men who just reached their majority. They were wild yet seemed like fun. It shocked me when they invited me to sneak out late one night for some raucous adventure. Since I didn't have friends, it elated me to venture off with this rowdy group."

His brow furrowed, and a frown twisted on his lips. "When I arrived, I discovered I was the amusement for the evening. They ganged up on me and..."

A shudder crossed through me at the implication. He thrummed his fingers on his thigh, as if the motion would coax the story forward.

After a long pause, he continued, "They were violent, and as the heir to Belmont Manor, they believed I thought myself their better. Since I had never ventured into town alone, they assumed I was weak and an easy target for their misdirected anger."

A grimace twisted on his face, and my heart sank at the story. His pain leached from him, so dense I could almost sense it creeping along my skin.

"With each blow, I grew angrier, and my curse fed upon it. I could sense its pull, the instinct threatening to take over. To burn the world to the ground. Like you, I tapped into the well, using it to protect myself. I was rash, lacking control, and when the darkness seeped out of me, the two who held me..."

His words trailed off again. However, the implication was not lost on me. He heaved an exhale as he unburdened himself of the painful truth.

"Their ringleader survived. The darkness had burned his body and scrambled his brain. He fled, but my curse tasted the carnage and yearned for more. Gods, I fought tooth and nail in that forest, trying to hold back the blight from destroying the town. As dawn crested, I had caged the threat within myself against the thick walls of resolve I'd formed. When I awoke, covered in sweat on the forest floor, I feared I'd be ostracized.

However, no one found out. Most assumed the gang had left for Hallowhaven. The evening prior, they had boasted in the tavern about the departure for the city. No one knew they intended to beat me within an inch of my life as their fun farewell. The guilt ate at me for years. I never told a soul: not Beatrix, nor my uncle. I am telling you this so you truly understand how well you did last night."

I scanned his profile. Despite his stony features, a slight crack appeared in his haughty façade. He stood to leave, as if what he'd divulged was too heavy for either of us to bear. We were both suffering, he from his memories, and I from what could have happened if Silas had arrived seconds later. My heart raced in panic as his boots clinked against the wood floor, heading toward the door. Something within me yearned not only for his comfort, but to comfort him. Our emotions were jumbled together, and I couldn't endure being alone in the silence. Not now.

"Please don't go. Stay with me." A soft whisper cracked through me.

He froze halfway between the door and the chair, his focus on the exit just a few steps ahead of him.

"Even after what you know of me, you wish me to stay?"

"Yes."

In the core of my soul, I didn't care about his past, which was likely rife with as much anguish as my own. Though he hadn't lived under the suppression spells, he'd suffered in his own ways. We were both cursed beings living in a world not meant for us.

He turned and walked toward the rear wall. He perused the shelf that held a few books from the library. Then he settled back in the chair and offered one to me. I blinked at the book.

"That was Beatrix's favorite. It's a romance novel."

I took it, placed it on my lap, and watched in fascination as Silas began reading the other book he had picked. His brow softened as he relaxed into the chair. I scanned the title of the worn novel, realizing he held my favorite from home. How many times had I thumbed through those pages since being here? I missed Naomi, yet last night had shown me exactly why I couldn't write to her or see her. Anxiety swelled within me as I contemplated an uncertain future.

Sensing my welling panic, he flicked a glance at me, and gentleness entered his expression. He lowered the novel to his lap. The crinkled pages frayed out, a sign of my years of use. Then his amber eyes held mine, attempting to pry my secrets from my mind.

"I fear I made a terrible mistake in coming here. I was selfish. Had I stayed in Krella, everyone would be safe." My fingers rubbed along the soft leather cover.

He ran his hand through his hair, the dark locks springing every which way.

"That isn't true. Had you stayed in Krella, you wouldn't have been safe, and I couldn't bear the horrors that awaited you."

He held my gaze, and something sparked. An aching tenderness that hid behind his stony demeanor pierced through me, causing a ripple of something to stir in the depth of my soul. But before I focused on whatever beat between us, he shifted back to the book and began reading.

I lifted the novel and tried to focus, but my attention drifted to him. Despite the turmoil of my life since residing here, a sense of comfort settled within me. We eased into the quiet companionship, no longer alone in the world.

CHAPTER 40

Arianna

I buttoned my coat and hastened down the stairs leading to the foyer. I expected to see Silas waiting with his arms crossed over his chest in impatience. Yet he wasn't there. Only the refractions of light that often danced along the marble floor from the chandelier above filled the space. As I reached the last step, I pursed my lips in confusion, contemplating my options.

Moments later, a maid, Hannah, approached with a stack of linens.

"Have you seen Lord Belmont?" I asked, and Hannah furrowed her brow.

"My lord said you were recuperating. He instructed us not to disturb you. We all assumed you needed your rest after entertaining the lord all day." She snapped her mouth shut, as if she'd said too much.

I shook my head, wanting to argue at the implication. However, the staff didn't know about the terms of our unorthodox marriage nor about our tenuous relationship. They didn't realize that yesterday we sat in comfortable silence reading rather than engaging in carnality as Hannah's deepening blush hinted toward.

"As you can see, I am quite well. I will find Lord Belmont myself." I pivoted and left through the massive doors.

I entered the grounds and ran past the topiaries, a gazebo, and trellises covered with vines as the gardens gave way to the woods. My feet crunched along the brambles. My lungs burned, but the sensation soothed me as I rushed forward. Panting from the exertion, I stopped as I entered the small clearing of trees where Silas sat.

His shoulders rose and fell with his steady breaths, pulling my attention to his jutting collarbone peeking out from beneath the tunic. The thick coat clung to his broad back, and his wavy hair lay rumpled, as if he had just rolled out of bed. I approached.

Crack.

I winced at the twig beneath my boot, but he didn't open his eyes. His brow remained smooth, with his chin tilted skyward as he inhaled. I remained fixed to the spot. Seconds passed.

"You should be resting."

I flinched as his voice boomed through the silence.

"I have rested enough." I squared my shoulders.

He turned his attention toward me and raised a haughty eyebrow. I wondered if my unaccustomed defiance shocked him. However, last night, as I pondered over what had occurred, I'd decided that my patterns of behavior had to change. I could no longer hide away from the world, and to feel safe without the mask, I needed to master my curse quickly. To achieve my goals, I would have to return to my routine despite my fear.

A brief smirk cut through his stony expression, then disappeared as quickly as it had come. Despite myself, that quirk on his lips made my heart flutter. Yet I remained unmoved in my resolve.

He stood and ran his hands over his pants, smoothing the fabric. Then he prowled toward me. He scanned my face, and he paused with only a handbreadth between us. My pulse surged at the closeness, and the root of attraction I kept buried blossomed. My tumultuous emotions ebbed and flowed around him; his aloof nature had angered me only days prior, yet I was drawn to him against all logic. Silas had a mistress, but I couldn't stop the feelings that churned in the pit of my belly as his gaze locked on mine.

"You will not be training today. However, we must address something. In addition to mastering breathwork, you need to incorporate a way to release...tension."

He paused, and his lip twitched in a near smirk but smoothed quickly.

"I've considered the options all morning." His hot breath, laced with a hint of chamomile, washed over my skin.

I gulped. My curse swirled within me, and heat billowed in my core. His lips parted as he held my stare, and my heart beat wildly. He inched closer, and I wished he would kiss me.

"Running would help you build stamina and endurance. From your wheezing, I dare say you haven't run in an age."

I blinked at the statement. His earnest gaze drifted from me and onto the path. I chastised myself. Of course he didn't want to kiss me. Yet yesterday had rekindled the smoldering embers of attraction that I had kept dowsed. As we had sat reading in silence, my glances had often drifted to him, and I couldn't help but slip into memories of our wedding night. I genuinely had no idea what the book was about when he left with the setting sun.

"Fine, I will add running to my daily regimen." I moved past him and toward the quilt. He placed a hand on my shoulder, stopping me.

"I am serious. Give yourself at least another day. You need time to rebuild your stamina after holding your curse at bay. Now go back to your—"

"No." I spun to face him, moving out of his grasp.

"No?" He quirked an eyebrow at me, as if I were a petulant child.

But I had stood my ground with him only a few days prior when I told him about the loneliness I suffered, and he had taken my statements to heart. A spark of something alive swelled within me, fueling my resolve.

"I'm training, then I'm going to Layla's. She is likely worried sick about me." I crossed my arms over my chest.

"Fine, you can go to work. However, you shouldn't access your curse today. Your body needs time to recuperate, and I don't want you to suffer any long-term ramifications."

I wanted to argue, but my body already feeling fatigued from the short jog to this spot. Reluctantly, I nodded in agreement. He walked to the quilt and gathered it. He let out a long exhale, then pivoted toward me.

"In addition, I'll be accompanying you to and from work indefinitely."

I gaped, but he didn't wait for me to respond. Instead, he strode past me. Exhausted, I fought the urge to collapse. If I did, he would likely drag me back to my room without a second's hesitation and insist I stay in bed. How odd, that only days prior we were not speaking, and now we were falling into some sort of companionship.

With a sigh, I followed behind him, the man who confused me to no end.

CHAPTER 41

ARIANNA

SOMEHOW, I MADE IT through the day without incident. My earlier bolster faded with each hour at Layla's. My fingers continuously trembled as I stitched the hems of the trousers, fearing that something would occur to provoke my curse. Yet all remained calm despite my worries. Layla had overlooked my shaky demeanor as a symptom of my migraine, which was Silas's excuse for my absence. The usually chatty Layla resigned herself to humming throughout the day as we worked. I half feared that if I spoke, the truth would tumble from me.

The bell chimed overhead, despite Layla having just turned the sign from *Open* to *Closed* only moments prior. Silas stood at the doorway. My fingers froze mid-stitch. I had intended to finish the trousers on my lap before leaving. However, his presence muddled my brain. Shaking my head, I finished the seam, and he stepped farther into the space. I lowered the pants to the sofa beside me and shifted to stand, but Silas cleared his throat.

"Finish. It's fine. I can wait."

He pivoted with his hands behind his back, assessing the tidier storefront. I returned to the task, willing myself to steady despite my pounding heart at his palpable presence.

"Silas, is that you?" Layla called out as she entered the front of the shop. Her smile radiated. "Well, I wasn't expecting to see you this evening."

A whisper of a wry grin pulled on Silas's lips. "Arianna didn't tell you I would escort her from now on?"

"No, she did not," Layla said.

I flicked a glance from my work to Layla, who shot me an accusatory look.

"*Ouch*," I hissed as the needle pierced straight through the fabric and into my skin. I dropped the pants onto the sofa, then moved my finger into my mouth to catch the blood, hoping it would not leach into the pristine material.

Silas closed the distance between us within a heartbeat. "Let me see."

I stood, and he grabbed my hand. The moment bubbled with an unaccustomed intimacy as his eyes trailed over my pin-pricked finger.

"Layla, fetch a bandage," he commanded. Surprisingly, she obeyed without protest.

His gaze lifted from my fingers to my face. He studied me, taking in every facet of my countenance. "I knew you needed more time to recuperate."

I didn't have a retort as the warmth from his touch soaked into my skin. A flush crawled over my cheeks from his intense assessment. He inched closer. My breath hitched and my knees buckled. I feared I would swoon, half caused by fatigue and the other by the heavy weight of the moment that lingered.

"Please don't let me interrupt," Layla said.

Silas flinched and withdrew, returning to his perusal of the shop. Layla rushed to me and wrapped my finger, even though it had already stopped bleeding.

"Come, Arianna. I have an idea." Silas walked toward the door.

I looked at Layla in confusion, but she, too, seemed befuddled by Silas's sudden interest in me. In answer, she shrugged. With a sigh, I waved goodbye and exited the shop.

I stepped onto the walkway. The sun had begun to set, and shades of pink and purple filled the sky, reflecting off the snow-capped mountains. The air turned crisp as the warm autumn light faded. I waited for Silas as he spoke to the carriage driver, but instead of getting into the conveyance, he pivoted toward me.

"Follow me." He strode toward the center of town, but unlike in the past, he slowed his steps to accommodate my shorter gait.

"Where are we going?" I slowed my pace, no longer needing to scurry to keep up with him.

"Somewhere I like to go when I am agitated," he said.

"You must visit this mystery place often." I snapped my mouth shut and regretted the absentminded comment. Yet to my surprise, a hint of a grin pulled upon his lips.

We ambled along the cobblestone streets. The last dregs of light washed over the heart of Presspin in shades of deep orange, coloring the stone buildings and their wooden signs in rich hues. Candlelight gleamed in the windows above the shops, where the owners dwelled. I breathed in the chilly air as lamplighters began their nightly job of illuminating the streets. Flames flickered into life, keeping the path well lit despite the darkening world. I mused over the architecture that melded brick and basalt into a masterpiece of neatly lined stores. For a heartbeat, I paused, noticing yet again the lack of any mention of Aralia. There were no vendors selling children's books with her tales, nor figurines, nor the appearance of a single Aralian in town. I shivered. A chilly wind whistled through the ancient evergreens on the outskirts surrounding us like massive sentinels, pulling my attention toward the mountain range. The moon crested over its peaks, signaling the fall of evening to the valley we were nestled within.

A few townspeople bustled by, nodding in acknowledgment. I smiled as we walked toward the square and lingered beside the fountain at the center of the town. It depicted a couple in the white stone. Perhaps they were parted lovers? I assumed it was some ancient story that I hadn't inquired about. Water bubbled from the three-tier fountain. It served as part decoration and part water source from the bubbling underwater springs that kept Presspin lush. Silas continued forward, and I followed in tow, unable to consider the carvings any longer.

A few streets later, we stopped at a small brick building with a sign reading *Thomas's Teas*. Silas held the door open, gesturing me in. I walked into the establishment, and the bell chimed overhead. A multitude of scents of tea and cakes wafted through the air. The quaint shop displayed rows of tins and teapots along the wall. At the large window overlooking the town sat two pine chairs and a table. On the other wall sat a faded sofa. The space felt homey without being cramped. As Silas entered, I glanced sidelong at him, disbelieving that this was a place he frequented.

"Sorry, but we are closed," a male voice said. Seconds later, a man stood from behind the solid wooden counter, lifting a tray of cups. His eyes widened as he took us in.

"My apologies, Thomas. Lady Belmont and I will head home since you—"

"Nonsense, my lord. You are my best customer. I would be happy to prepare something for you and Lady Belmont. Please have a seat, and I will bring out your usual." Then Thomas hoisted the tray of cups and pushed through a door I assumed led to the kitchen.

We sat at the small table by the window that overlooked Presspin. Starlight glimmered, and townspeople strode by, heading home for the night. A woman rushed from the swinging wooden door leading from the kitchen. She began lighting candles around the shop, illuminating the space before the last of the sunlight whispered away.

"Thank you, Jane," Silas said. She curtsied, then scurried off, leaving us alone.

Tap. Tap. Tap.

Silas thrummed his fingers on the pine table.

I released a sigh. Though we were on amicable terms, we had yet to find our footing in conversation. Anxiousness bubbled in my belly. For a heartbeat, I hesitated in speaking, remembering his words in the carriage on our way to wed. However, the last month had brought many changes.

"You must come here often if you are friends with the shopkeeper," I said.

His focus remained on the window, and a flicker of a frown twisted his lips. "They, like everyone in Presspin, are my responsibility. I don't have friends, nor have I experience in making them. I have those who rely on me. I try my best to treat them with mutual respect, and I do so by learning the names of each of the residents under my care."

A heaviness exuded from him, and I resisted an urge to hold his hand, to show this sullen man that I understood his deep loneliness. Though we experienced it differently, I knew he had been separated from the world.

Before I could inquire about his responsibilities, Jane returned with a teapot, two teacups, and saucers. Steam billowed from the pot as Jane poured the tea. When she was finished, she left us alone in silence again.

My fingers traced the rose pattern on the delicate cup. My mind drifted to the past. However, my lingering memories were cut short as Silas asked, "Do you not enjoy tea? It is chamomile with honey. Ophelia used to brew it for me when I..."

His too-large fingers held the dainty cup. "She made this for me when I felt distressed. It still soothes me."

I focused on the crease etched in his forehead and the clench of his jaw, and I felt the immensity of the statement. He was allowing me to see a piece of the man he hid away.

"I like tea well enough. It's just that my mother had teacups like this. As a girl, before my curse awoke, I used to play with her fine dishes and pretend I was a grand lady. One day, I chipped a cup on the corner of our table. She didn't scold me. Instead, she insisted it would be mine from then on. Last year, she had to sell the set after my father died. We needed the money to make it through the winter, but the cup I damaged remained. I think it served as a reminder to her of a time before I became a monster."

"You are not a monster. Please never call yourself a monster. I can't bear it." His words were soft, like a caress.

My tight shoulders loosened as if his gentle words unfurled a knot that settled between the blades. I sipped my beverage, unsure of what to say as the honey coated my throat and the chamomile soothed my jagged nerves.

We savored our beverages in silence until the pot ran empty. Before leaving, Silas purchased a few additional loose-leaf teas for the manor and one, in particular, he thought Mrs. Potter would enjoy. He handed Thomas more than enough coins to pay for a month's worth of tea. Thomas's mouth hung agape as Silas thanked him for keeping the shop open well past closing.

As we entered the chilly night, a slight breeze rushed through me, sending a shiver down my spine. Yet Silas walked beside me, his warmth radiating off him as his voice cut through our footsteps on the path. "We should begin having dinner together. It seems prudent to prevent the staff from having to serve us separate meals."

Uncertain whether it was the soothing tea, the honey on my lips, or the beautiful night sky, I couldn't resist his request.

CHAPTER 42

Arianna

I knocked on Silas's bedroom door, and a nervousness fluttered in my belly. When he requested that we dine together, I hadn't anticipated having supper in his room. I gulped down the wave of nerves and smoothed my hands along my skirts. I'd forgone the exquisite gown Layla had pleaded with me to wear. She had assured me that as Lady of Belmont manor, there would be expectations to adhere to. However, in my gut, I suspected Silas would not desire pomp and circumstance. Thankfully, my assumptions were correct. I would have looked ridiculous entering his suite in the lavish attire. Yet Mrs. Potter had insisted I change into my finest sky-blue dress. Unlike the modest styles in Krella, the fitted bodice accentuated my waist and the square neckline drew attention to my cleavage. To my surprise, after a month of consuming many hearty meals, my bony frame had blossomed into a more feminine figure. Seconds passed, and I twirled a tress near my face, then tucked it behind my ear. I should have worn my typical plait, but Mrs. Potter had coaxed life into my curls, which sprung around my shoulders.

The door clicked open, and I froze. Silas wore a crisp black dress shirt with the top button left unfastened. It drew attention to his jutting collarbone, while his matching trousers highlighted his long, muscular legs. I bit my bottom lip, resisting the urge to gawk at this roguishly handsome man. A wisp of a smile cracked his usually stony façade, as if he were amused by my staring. For a heartbeat, we stood in the doorway, taking each other in.

He cleared his throat, stepped back, and gestured for me to enter. "Come in."

I crossed the threshold and stared at a mahogany four-poster bed that lay prominently ahead. A crisp green quilt covered the mattress, and a few bronze pillows were arranged beside the headboard. A flash of our wedding night flickered in my mind, causing goose bumps to prickle along my flesh at the sheer memory of the ecstasy. I wetted my lips but forced my focus to shift to the floor-to-ceiling window, where starlight glimmered. I stepped forward, onto rugs the shade of the evergreens that softened our footsteps. Shelves brimming with books and different types of rocks interspersed throughout the tomes lined the rear wall. A desk sat in the corner, with stacks of papers and a discarded cup I assumed contained his afternoon tea. Earth-toned wallpaper with flecks of gold shimmered in the dim candlelight.

"This way." He gestured toward the small table nestled beside the hearth, where dinner had already been set out on fine silver plates. As we approached, my stomach rumbled over the fresh bread with globs of rich butter, roasted trout, and asparagus. To my surprise, Silas pulled out the chair for me, and I gaped for a moment before taking my seat.

As he sat across from me, an uncomfortable silence filled the air. I fiddled with my napkin as I placed it on my lap, but only the ticking clock above the hearth made any sound. Though we were finding a comfortable, quiet companionship, dinner seemed insurmountable. I opened my mouth to speak but closed it. I remembered my previous efforts at building a connection with this man on our way to the inn, and how he'd chastised me for speaking of frivolities. However, things between us had changed in these last few days.

I willed that spark of courage within me to ignite and asked, "Why are we dining here?"

Silas, who had just raised his fork to his mouth, lowered it to the plate. He leaned back in languid ease. His posture lacked its usual rigidity, as if being in this space unfurled his tense demeanor.

"At my request, the staff have not served my meals in the hall since Beatrix wed earlier this year. Now I eat here or in my study."

He lifted his fork and picked at the asparagus, and it rolled over his plate. I squared my shoulders. Even though he didn't ask, I felt a compulsion to fill the stagnant quiet.

"I have always dined in my quarters. After my curse awoke, it became my sanctuary. I rarely left my room, but Naomi would tell me about the gossip in Krella." I grabbed a piece of bread and slathered it with creamy butter, but continued chatting mindlessly, lost in my memories of home. "One of my favorites was about a hog who caused havoc. Farmer Tanner brought him to the town square to sell at the market, and somehow, he got loose..."

Lowering the knife to the dish, an uneasy self-awareness flickered through me. I stopped and said instead, "Sorry, I am prattling on. You wouldn't care about this silly story."

His focus shifted from his plate to me as he lowered his fork yet again. My cheeks flushed in embarrassment at my foolishness over sharing these secondhand tales. But he tilted his head, his eyes locking on mine, and a wisp of a grin tugged on the corner of his lip. "And what happened to the hog?"

I gaped in shock but couldn't help mirroring his tentative smile. "It barreled through the entire market, knocking over the stands. It was a disaster! The men chased it through the square, tumbling through the muck and grime, but he evaded capture. He now roams the outskirts of Krella, and the village children have named him Harry."

Silas let out an amused chuckle. I froze, so unaccustomed to the sound of merriment coming from this stoic man.

"That is quite the story." He raised his goblet, then sipped.

I smiled in return as I grabbed my fork and cut into the pickled asparagus, which reminded me so much of home. I had expected us to eat in silence, but he spoke.

"I never let a hog loose in the square, nor in the manor. But Beatrix and I slipped a frog into Mrs. Potter's shoe when we were children. Beatrix swore the frog would turn into a handsome prince if Mrs. Potter kissed it. Then she could remarry and no longer need to serve our home. She cajoled me into catching it when we snuck off to play at the creek on the eastern border of the woods. Obviously, it wasn't a prince. We were both scolded for the prank and for venturing to the stream alone." Silas's countenance lit with amusement, but a flash of sadness quickly replaced his lightheartedness. He flaked the fish off the bones.

"I never imagined I would miss Beatrix so much. She pestered me to no end, but since she wed, it has been unbearably quiet. Her chattering stories and questions used to agitate me, but in honesty, they often filled the loneliness. I didn't appreciate her fully until she left. That is why I ventured to Krella under the guise of procuring supplies. It was a partial truth. I could have easily done so in Daviel, but I used it as an excuse to see her. The silence in the manor has been deafening these past few months. I'm haunted by the memories of joyous dinners with a family that is gone." His brow furrowed. He shifted his focus to his shredded trout and grimaced.

"I understand. I miss Naomi and write to her every night. The letters are collected in my desk drawer. Hopefully one day she will be able to read them. Perhaps when everything has settled, she can visit." I glanced at him, and he clenched his jaw.

With a sigh, I took a bite of asparagus, but my mind dwelled on my sister. Not knowing when I would see Naomi again caused an ache within my soul. However, the appearance of the runner had only strengthened our need for secrecy. As I chewed, I recalled Peter's words from our wedding: *Those under the council's control in Hallowhaven do not always view our ancient practices as binding.* Maybe our consummated marriage wasn't enough. Silas shifted in his seat, and the motion pulled me from my ruminations. I forced the thoughts to drift away and focused on this time with him. I glimpsed through my lashes at my morose husband as he picked at his food.

We ate our meal with only the clink of silverware cutting through our conversational lull. I should have made an attempt toward building familiarity, but something else crested in the back of my mind, distracting me. Despite myself, my eyes continuously drifted from Silas to his bed. Memories flooded me, and the wine tasted so similar to that of our wedding night. I could almost taste the sweetness of his kiss on my lips. With each passing minute, my skin flushed as a wanton desire pulsed through my blood. I resisted the urge to fan myself with my hand as heat sweltered within. Even my curse whispered for me to give into the carnality I craved.

Instead, I forced my attention on my meal until I had savored the last bite of trout. Satiated, I licked my lips, and a soft sigh of pleasure escaped me.

A rough cough rattled from Silas, and my glance flicked from my empty plate to him. He sputtered on his wine and cleared his throat.

"Are you unwell? Do you need something?" I asked.

He held up a hand in response as heat rose to his face.

"I'm fine. How about we...maybe you should... Gods! Tell me anything to distract me." He dabbed his mouth with his napkin, then settled it on his lap. He shifted his gaze away, focusing on the ceiling instead of me.

"I don't know what to say. I'm not accustomed to dining with anyone." I fidgeted with my napkin.

"You didn't sit with your family during dinner?" His brow furrowed as he looked at me.

I shook my head. "I attempted to join them once as they ate, but my presence made the situation awkward. In the stony silence, I realized I hindered their merriment and resigned myself to listening to their laughter from my room. My meals were a solitary affair, with no company but my favorite doll, Ms. Matilda. Then Naomi joined me when she was older."

Silas watched me with remorse etched on his features. I worried my lower lip between my teeth, and a truth burned heavy in my chest, aching to be released. "Perhaps that is why I agreed to wed Theo. I know I am a burden. At least chaining a man I hated into matrimony..."

I clamped my mouth shut before the words could escape me. Deep down, I feared that I was a blight that would bring ruin to Silas. A man who, despite logic, I could love. I twisted my onyx ring nervously and stared at it.

He reached across the table and grabbed my hand, stopping my anxious motion. The warmth from his palm sank into my skin, and my heart pounded. "Arianna, never refer to yourself as a burden. Do you understand? You are not a burden, and I will not allow you to disparage yourself because of your family's ineptitude."

My gaze shifted to him. He mesmerized me. In the intimacy of his bedroom, I was aware that a simple touch could lead to more. The golden flecks of his eyes glimmered in the soft candlelight on the table, beckoning me forward. His usually stony features softened. I fought the urge to release an audible gulp as his thumb traced along the back of my hand, a habit he had taken to when soothing me over the past few days. The intimate gesture lit a fire in me that was best left as smoldering embers. Yet a similar energy sizzled as it had on our wedding night. Something raw I couldn't explain. My curse fed off it, delighting in the tension between us.

"I won't," I said through parted lips, and his shoulders rose and fell in sharp breaths.

Pop.

The fire crackled behind him, and Silas shook his head, as if pulling himself from whatever thoughts lingered. He removed his hand, and my skin missed the warmth. He leaned back and crossed his arms over his chest. His chin tilted skyward as he stared at the ceiling for a heartbeat. Then he settled his attention on me. But his stiff countenance replaced the once present tenderness.

"Starting tomorrow, it would be best if we ate in the dining hall after all. The servants will expect the formality. Partaking in dinner here was..." He shook his head. Instead of finishing his thought, he picked up his wineglass and drained it in one gulp.

"Very well. Layla will be elated. She kept insisting I wear this gown—"

"*No.*"

I wrinkled my brow at the sternness of his tone.

He scrubbed a hand over his face. "There is no need to dress formally. You can save it for the upcoming harvest festival, Kesere."

I tilted my head in assessment at an oddly rattled Silas. Perhaps he did hate formalities.

"What is that?" I grabbed my wineglass and sipped the crisp, sweet liquid.

"Kesere is an ancient tradition. The entire town will celebrate the end of harvest that the gods provided. Families and friends who no longer live in Presspin trek here to attend. Everyone dresses in their best attire while they eat, drink, and are merry. It's the last festivity before the winter insulates us in layers of thick snow for many, many months."

I smiled. I had never been to a festival, and the idea of participating delighted me. Yet something prickled in my mind.

"I've never heard of this celebration. Who do you pay homage to during Kesere?"

He poured another glass of wine, which he sipped this time. His lips were straight-lined, and a furrow wrinkled his brow. But before he could answer, my curiosity outweighed my patience.

"Does Presspin worship the dark deities, then? The ones in legends that Aralia locked away? I noticed there are no Aralian temples here, so I assumed you must honor them instead," I whispered, as if the goddess would strike me down herself or an Aralian would burst in with a whip to punish me for my heresy.

"We have no love for Aralia here." I expected him to elaborate, yet a tense hush rolled between us as he drank deeply.

Uncomfortable, I picked up the goblet and gulped the last of the contents, and a warm, heady feeling washed over me. Be it from the wine or being in Silas's presence, I was unsure. My attention drifted again from him to the bed. My pulse surged as thoughts of an amorous Silas pleasuring me flooded my mental reserves, loosened by the alcohol. I squirmed in my seat, as if the motion could give me the release I desired.

I lowered my glass and shifted my focus to him. He seemed wholly unfazed by my proximity as he leaned back in his chair. His gaze lazily trailed over my face, my neck, my shoulders. But then he snapped to attention, his once languid posture replaced with a rigid tension.

"I think we should retire now." A huskiness entered his tone, and he lowered his goblet. His eyes flared with intensity as they locked on mine.

My stomach fluttered, and a flush crossed my cheeks. Goddess above, I knew he meant for me to leave and that he had grown tired of my company, but my brain felt muddled. In hopes of not embarrassing myself, I stood and took a step. But my heeled boot caught the edge of the rug, and I stumbled forward.

The wind rushed out of me as I collided with a solid chest instead of the floor. I gasped as Silas pulled me against his solid frame. My lithe form melded against the firm lines of his muscular body. My head rested against his pectorals, and I swore his heart thundered against my ear, beating as fast as my own.

"Arianna." A raw timbre entered his voice. His hands slipped down my shoulders, rubbing along the silken fabric covering my arms. My breath quickened, and a flutter of desire burned hot in my core. I closed my eyes, losing myself in this charged moment that would fuel my dreams. My lips trembled and melted against him. Moments passed, and I remained unmoved, trapped in his blissful embrace.

"It is best you retire to your suite now." His cold words yanked me from this foolish fantasy. I flicked my gaze to his stoic face, and my stomach plummeted. I knew better than to allow myself to hope.

Stung, I withdrew, shuffled past him, and exited without looking back. My heartbeat thundered, and I rushed to my bedroom. I closed the door and slid to the floor. I placed my head in my hands, mortified that I wished Silas and I could be more than friends.

CHAPTER 43

ARIANNA

THE LIBRARY DOOR CREAKED open, echoing through the empty hallway as I slipped into the dark room. I released an anxious breath, grateful to have not awoken the sleeping manor as I sought distraction. Shadows clung to the bookcases while only a faint flicker of light emitted from the dwindling embers in the hearth, causing a nip to linger in the air. My bare feet padded over the cold wooden floor, and I inhaled the soothing scent of ink. I ambled past the table where Silas and I often played chess. Then I moved deeper into the expansive space, weaving through the labyrinth of bookcases, and perused the shelves. I lifted the candle I clutched, illuminating the rows of novels. My other hand traced along the titles; the pristine leather bindings were smooth against my fingertips. I paused on a gold-flecked spine that I hadn't read yet. My lips pursed as I grabbed the book.

The novel should serve as a needed distraction on a night like this when my curse throbbed beneath my skin, yearning for release. I ambled toward the center of the room and lowered the candle to a small table and skimmed the pages. I paused, my attention catching on a salacious scene. I read the detailed descriptions of a carnal affair. With each phrase, my mind conjured a fantasy of Silas mirroring the act. My heart pounded from the vivid details. I wished Silas had his lips on my mouth, my neck, my breasts, even my...

I slammed the book closed, and a heat rushed to my cheeks. Hadn't I come here to distract my mind from the drugged slumber caused by the sleeping draft that led to vivid dreams of Silas?

I clutched the book to my chest and attempted to slow my frantic breathing. However, I couldn't ignore the fact that my longings for Silas had become more pervasive since we had embarked on this friendship a month ago. Each day, I grew fonder of our time together. In the mornings, we trained, and a camaraderie blossomed. Silas now treated me more like an equal and less like a pupil. Then on our journey to and from town, we discussed his endless work as Lord Belmont or the townspeople I met while at Layla's. He often encouraged me to engage with customers who came into the shop, and with each passing day, I found my footing in socializing. In the evenings, we dined together, sharing stories of our pasts, followed by games of chess or reading alongside one another in quiet contentment. The feelings I kept buried crept closer to the surface with each interaction, seizing me. This pining took hold despite my misgivings, unswayed by my knowledge that this affection was one-sided. Tonight, I didn't want to dream of him. Each smirk that played on his lips, each stroke of his thumb against my hand, and every moment of consideration he paid me stoked unbearable yearning. I couldn't awaken unsatiated again, and no amount of running nor breathwork could clear this ache.

I sighed, forcing myself out of my reveries of Silas. Yet a shiver crawled along my spine, and a flicker of awareness fluttered in my consciousness, triggered by my curse swirling within, delighted. I froze. My breath hitched from the intoxicating sensation, as if Silas loomed nearby. My head whipped to the entrance. The clinking of the knob turning echoed through the silence. Panic flooded me as I dashed to the candle and blew it out in haste. Then I pounced behind one of the tall bookshelves, out of sight. Energy prickled, causing goose bumps to wash over my skin. The door cracked open, and his soft footsteps strode over the wood floor. My pulse raced as I waited in the darkness.

I peered around the bookshelf and viewed him. The shadows clung to the strong lines of his jaw and the hollows of his cheeks while light danced within his gold-flecked irises, illuminated by the candle he held. A whoosh of breath left him as he raked a hand through his tousled, wavy hair. He didn't move. Instead, he peered about the space, a hint of confusion pulling in his knitted brows. My gaze trailed down the length of him, catching upon the opening of the soft tunic he wore, where a glimpse of toned muscle was exposed. I gulped as a welling surge of emotions swirled in me. My fingers gripped the shelf as I leaned against it, angling for a better view of this uncharacteristically rumpled version of Silas.

Suddenly, his attention shifted to where I hid; his voice boomed. "Arianna, I know you are here." I froze, not wanting to venture out and reveal myself. His tone became smooth as honey. "You couldn't sleep?"

Hesitantly, I emerged from around the corner, sheepishly moving to him like a child caught out of bed. "I'm just looking for something to read...I'm not ready to fall asleep yet."

He arched an eyebrow in response, but intrigue rather than reprimand colored his expression. A shiver crossed through me as his eyes drifted to my body. The thin nightgown and flimsy robe I wore left little to the imagination. I wrapped my arms instinctively around myself, and a blush heated my cheeks. Layla had sewn my night garments more for style than practicality. The white, feather-soft fabric skimmed across my skin but did little to guard against the bitter air which cut through the sheer material. I clutched myself tightly, and goose bumps formed along my arms as Silas's gaze flickered back to mine.

"Why are you here?" I asked.

Instead of answering, he cocked his head as he took me in, momentarily lost in thought, before he shifted his attention to the dying embers in the hearth. Silas moved toward the fireplace, where he stoked the cinders and removed wood from the box. I watched in curiosity as he blew the flames to life. The once smoldering embers were now ablaze in a roaring fire. Heat emanated, and the soft scent of smoke filled the space. He focused upon the blaze. "Why couldn't you sleep? Are you out of the sleeping draft Brielle made?"

The woman's name sent an icy chill down my spine, reminding me of why my desires should remain buried. I vacillated between running back to bed and remaining by his side. I spun the onyx ring on my finger, as if it held the answer. The unorthodox band matched our odd marriage. It reminded me that we were not a love match. Love was an impossibility, and the existence of his mistress was proof enough that his desire was elsewhere. I pivoted to scurry off, my decision made, but Silas's words halted my progress.

"She is my friend," he said, as if sensing my ruminations.

A friend. Friends don't typically kiss one another in libraries, but since that incident, she had not been seen in Belmont Manor, nor mentioned again. I pondered his words for a heartbeat, afraid to ask bluntly if she was still his paramour. Though I had become more vocal about my inner thoughts, I struggled with being direct when it came to matters of my heart.

"A friend, like we are friends?" I moved to the leather chair next to the hearth and sat, allowing the heat to consume me, wishing it would remove the chill settling into my bones. Despite myself and the answer I dreaded, I needed to know if he cared for her. Seconds passed. Perhaps I should have left and forgotten that I had ever broached the subject of Brielle.

"We had interludes before I came to Krella. But she is not my friend like you are. It is not the same. She is not..." He shook his head and didn't finish his statement. He poked at the coals with the iron, the flames swelling to life. A near truth lingered that neither of us acknowledged: that we would never have a relationship of a carnal nature. I expected Silas to leave. Instead, he asked again, "Are you out of the sleeping draft?"

Unwilling to focus on Brielle or their entanglement any longer, I said, "No, I still have plenty. My curse feels unsettled, and I..." My mouth dried, and the words caught in my throat. How could I tell him I didn't dare sleep because he haunted my dreams?

He turned from the fire, and his gaze pierced through me as if unraveling my soul to share in its secrets. My curse fluttered under his attention, and heat billowed through my body. The air filled with a thick tension, saturating every corner of the library. I exhaled shakily, lost within him.

His words cut through the density. "Is it because you miss your sister, or maybe you are still...lonely?" Tenderness crossed his face as his question sank to my core.

His care caused warmth to swell in my heart, and a small smile crept across my lips. "No, it's not worry or loneliness. It is the..." I gulped, pushing myself to admit my reasoning. "It is the dreams. They haunt me when I take the sleeping draft."

His features softened as he sat on the adjoining leather seat. "I see," he whispered to himself. He watched the dancing flames, and his face turned stoic. "The tonic helps to dampen our curse, as if trapping them within our bodies as we sleep." His mouth twisted into a frown as he pivoted his attention to me. "Yet it intensifies the nightmares. Especially when our emotions are unsettled. It can be...overwhelming." He adjusted in the chair as if remembering his own latent draft dreams.

Heat fluttered in my belly, and I was desperate to shift the conversation away from myself and my looming fantasies. "Why did you come to the library? Why not drink the sleeping tonic yourself?"

The question lingered in the silent air. Silas leaned forward in his chair. "I felt drawn here this evening for some reason.

I awoke from a dreamless slumber. I tossed and turned, but I was unable to find sleep again. Unsettled, I came here and..." He closed his mouth into a tight-lipped line, keeping his secrets locked within himself.

I stared at him, perplexed, but my curse thrummed as if it was alive in the silence. Energy rippled through me as my gaze drifted upon his profile, lit by the warmth of the fire, and my pulse skittered in response. Time lagged, the once quickening seconds slowing as if covered in honey. I wet my lips and ached to touch him. He leaned closer, his woodsy scent filling the closing space.

Yet reality loomed. The name of the other woman still tasted bitter on my tongue. My stomach dropped. I pulled back and couldn't allow myself to release into these longings. Unsettled by this blossoming emotion, I jolted from the chair and strode to the door. I gasped as a hand grabbed my wrist, halting me. I turned, finding Silas looming near. Tension crackled through the air as his eyes held mine. As if we were both half-possessed, his heaving breaths matched my palpitating heart. I gulped under the pressure of his stare, and something that lived deep within me came undone. The feelings I had repressed since I met him could no longer remain hidden.

I searched his face, hoping that he might reciprocate this longing. But as suddenly as he had grasped my arm, he released it. His words, a husky whisper: "Good night, Arianna."

Without awaiting my response, he fled the library, leaving me to dwell on the fact that my feelings were so much deeper than friendship.

CHAPTER 44

Silas

"Check," Arianna said triumphantly.

I peered at the board and thrummed my fingers along the wooden table. I had unwittingly stepped into a trap. I exhaled and raked a hand through my hair. She remained composed as she focused on the pieces, likely calculating her next move. But my focus, despite myself, was on the flicker of candlelight playing through her locks and the threads of amber curls framing the curve of her cheek instead of on the game. Yet she didn't notice as my stare drifted along her narrow chin and settled on the slight pucker to her rosy lips.

"Silas, it's your turn." She flicked a glance to me, her brow set in determination.

I fought a hint of a grin at the stern expression she bore when resolved to win. It was the same steely gaze she donned whenever we played. The idea had come to me after our nearly disastrous first dinner a month ago, when we dined in my room. It had been some inane mix of subconscious desire and complete hubris. However, we now ate in the dining hall and retired to the library to play chess or read every night. The space served as a halfway point between formality and intimacy. This arrangement suited us as we were no longer master and apprentice, but also something more than friends. Though I dared not dwell on the details.

I pursed my lips in thought, then moved the king out of harm's way, placing him behind the queen. But without waiting, her rook slid into attack, taking my queen out.

"Checkmate." She beamed with elation, finally winning a round. Yet her victory didn't surprise me. Arianna thrived in everything she tried, be it chess or training. She had an untapped curiosity that fueled her knack for learning. She even grew in speed and stamina as she ran every morning before dawn.

I chuckled and grinned with pride. I couldn't help the swelling warmth as she clapped her hands in excitement. She had grown from the broken girl I'd rescued into a fierce woman, yet an underlying gentleness remained. I let out a sigh of contentment. This month had gone smoothly as we had settled into this companionship. Fortunately, no strangers lurked in the shadows, nor had any new dangers loomed. She was finally safe.

"Shall we play again?" I began resetting the board, but she shook her head.

"I dare not test my luck at beating you a second time." She rose and smoothed her hands over her black trousers, which clung to her hips.

I shifted in my seat as a surge of arousal flared from the view of her curved backside while she walked to the shelves lined with books. She perused the titles in languid ease, unaware of my lingering stares. Her fingers trailed along the spines, and she softly hummed to herself. I stifled an internal groan. This woman was disintegrating my resolve bit by bit without even trying. I should have retired, but I couldn't. Instead, I stood and approached her. I loomed behind her and reached for a book far above her head. She froze at my nearness, and I inhaled her intoxicating lavender scent. I was playing with fire and would likely get burned if I continued these antics.

"Silas," she whispered.

I stepped back, and she turned. Her eyes drifted to my face as she bit her lower lip. Gods, that damned gesture melted another piece of my stony heart. But I wouldn't give in to this attraction. I couldn't bear the consequences an entanglement with her would have, upending this pleasant friendship we shared. However, there was more than she realized, more secrets than I cared to share. I couldn't delve into these base instincts, no matter how much I burned with desire. Instead, I withdrew and held out the book. Her focus shifted to the gold-etched title.

"This is one of my favorites, about a monstrous beast who roams the woods. Be warned, it is not a romance, as you and Beatrix enjoy. It is more a mystery," I said.

As she took the novel, her fingertips grazed against mine. For a moment, we stayed, unable to break the featherlight touch. Heat billowed between us with an unspoken need, which intensified with each passing day. My damned incessant curse crackled beneath my skin, urging me forward toward destruction. Her chest rose and fell in ragged breaths. I inched closer, curious if the taste of wine from dinner lingered on her lips.

"My lord," a small voice called out.

A gasp left Arianna. My shoulders tensed and my jaw twitched. I smoothed my demeanor and pivoted to Grey, the servant boy. The brash lad should learn to knock, and I would chide him for it later. However, my attention caught on the envelope he clutched.

"I'm sorry, my lord. This arrived before supper, and I...forgot." He rubbed his free hand on the back of his neck.

"It's fine." I strode to him and took the letter. The boy bowed, then scurried off.

I scanned the correspondence and recognized Beatrix's scrolling handwriting. I broke the wax seal with the Archer Estate crest and read the contents. From the corner of my eye, I glimpsed Arianna approaching. My pulse climbed as she stood closer than usual. Her chin tilted toward the note in an attempt to peer at the words.

"Is it about Vincent recovering from his cold? Or perhaps Farmer Johnson? I was worried about his roof the other day during that sudden rainstorm." Her brow furrowed. The rough edges I held within me smoothed at her tender concern for the people in town, whom I had mentioned during our dinner conversations.

"No, it's from Beatrix," I said, then read the correspondence aloud:

Dear Silas,

I hope this letter finds you well and settled. I have missed you terribly. Duncan is still away on business, brokering the contract in Seaside to create a trade route. Sadly, we cannot correspond since Seaside is more remote than Presspin and is without an established post. Yet he should arrive home soon, and I long to see him.

Despite my loneliness, there has been plenty of gossip to occupy my time. Do you remember my acquaintance, Ms. Arianna Park? I assume not, since you only met her briefly before you left. She is the cursed sister of that charming Ms. Naomi Park.

There has been quite a scandal surrounding her. She was engaged to marry Theo Terrell, son of the wealthy Mr. Terrell of Daviel. An advantageous match for both families. They made the arrangement, and the engagement was set, and yet Ms. Arianna Park jilted her betrothed by running away from home. Can you believe it? Arianna fled a few nights prior to her wedding, leaving a note behind of her desire to live in Hallowhaven. I was shocked when her mother came to me after her disappearance and inquired about whether I had any relevant information about her daughter's whereabouts. Despite the unfortunate circumstance of her curse, she spoke quite highly of her betrothed.

That is not all. Apparently, her jilted groom has been searching for her since she vanished. Alas, they fear the poor girl might be dead. She is cursed and likely rotting in an alleyway somewhere. It seems the bride price has been returned, and the Terrells are ending their search. The Terrells are rumored to have another prospective wife in their sights. Such a scandal!

Alas, except for the gossip, Krella is dull this time of year. How is Presspin? I'm disappointed I will miss Kesere, but I'm certain Duncan will not be in the mood for traveling after returning from Seaside. Next year, we shall all celebrate the harvest together. Write soon.

Love,
Beatrix

I flicked a glance to Arianna, who bore an unreadable expression. One similar to when we played chess, as if her mind was piecing together the information in front of her. Before I spoke, a brilliant smile cut across her face, lighting her features.

"Thank the goddess above. If the bride price is returned and they are discontinuing their search, then we should be free. *Oh*, I can finally write to Naomi. Perhaps Theo will be wed by spring, and Naomi could visit. I swear she will love Presspin. Silas, I have to send word to her at—"

"*No*," I snapped, my voice cutting out far sharper than I'd intended. Gods, I should have been wiser and read the letter in private. But Arianna's presence jumbled my rational mind. A creeping panic seeped from behind the stony walls I held as she blinked at me in confusion.

"No? I don't understand." Challenge laced her tone, and she tilted her chin skyward. Over the past month, she had not only grown stronger but also bolder in her speaking.

I opened my mouth, but no words came out, and only raw anguish clung to my throat. How could I tell Arianna that if anyone found her, she would die? Wither into nothingness? Theo Terrell, though problematic, had only been the last proverbial straw that led to me whisking her away. How could I reveal that I never intended for her to speak with her family again? There was so much she was unaware of, so many secrets I kept hidden. I'd reassured myself that she didn't need to know the harsh and ugly truths about the fate that might still befall her.

But she strode past me, heading to the door. "Goddess. You are aware of how I have worried over Naomi. These last two months, I have ached with uncertainty. Wondered if my mother punished her for aiding me. I need to write to her."

Before she could leave, I placed a hand on her shoulder and spun her toward me. I studied her stern face, taking in the determination etched there. Gods, this woman was far fiercer than she realized, with an iron backbone. How else had she been so resigned to marry Theo despite his abuses?

"Arianna, you can't write to her. Please. I am certain they are looking for you. I can't let them find you. Please...please." I grabbed her hands in mine, clutching them as if she would flee not only from the library but to Krella and her doom.

"Please. They can't find you," I pleaded, afraid that she might slip through my fingertips forever.

I pushed away the horrible thoughts that crashed upon me. The same ones I'd feared as I walked into her home, the same certainty that death would beckon her. I tried to coax the words to life, the hidden secrets that tore within me. I should have told her long ago, or at any point since we met. Brielle was right. She needed to know the consequences of her curse. But as her gaze locked on mine, a bone-deep agony ripped through me. I wouldn't let her die, no matter what the cost. Even if it meant lying to her about a truth so egregious it would shatter her.

I was a coward and feared unraveling her entire world would sever this tenuous peace between us. I enjoyed this new life. My days were no longer denoted by loneliness, but with a deep friendship.

But even now, as my eyes pleaded with her to trust me, to not write, to not inform them of where she was hidden, I couldn't help but fight the bitter tang in my mouth. I had grown too close, and the crumbling walls that held my feelings back shook under her stare. The truth I had built my life upon whispered in the recesses of my soul: *You are nothing but a monster, boy. A monster no one will ever love.*

However, to my surprise, her intensity softened, and her brow smoothed.

"Fine. I'll wait until we hear of Theo's betrothal to someone else. Then I will write to Naomi. Our marriage is enough to provide me the protection I need, especially if he is wed to another." She tilted her head, as if searching for the secrets I kept hidden.

Relief should have flooded me. Instead, my heart raced. For a second, I yearned to pin her against the door and make her scream my name until she forgot about everyone but me. However, I remained unmoved. If I crossed this feeble boundary, I wouldn't have the strength to return. No, it was best that we remained friends and stayed the course. The door clicked open, and Arianna slipped out of the library, leaving me alone with my turbulent emotions.

CHAPTER 45

ARIANNA

I STOOD AT THE base of the butte, staring up the daunting slope that had served as the bane and the blessing of my morning routine. My gaze followed along the path I had carved through it from weeks of running up its side. I bounced on my toes, shaking off any hesitation. The air stilled around me, and the world lay silent as whispers of light crept over the hill. I sprinted, determined to reach the top before sunrise. Evergreens lined the way; I bobbed and weaved through them, following the worn track to avoid peril. Perspiration beaded down my forehead with each step forward. My pulse surged, but I didn't slow. Instead, I pushed myself harder. Torturously long minutes passed, and my legs stung under the pressure. My body wanted to relent, yet my will had become stronger than ever before. Sunlight crested, and I surged toward the top. My lungs burned as I reached the plateau. A sweet release filled me as my ragged breaths punctured the once silent forest. A smile cracked across my sweat-laden face as the dawn stretched across the white-capped mountains.

I gasped for air and collapsed, taking in my reward: the most spectacular vista. Oranges and yellows shot through the sky like a painter smearing bright colors along a dark canvas. My respiration slowed. I lay on the hard rock and watched the sunrise, as I had every morning since the incident in town six weeks prior. The darkness of predawn gave way to shades of light blue, and for a heartbeat, I wondered about Naomi. Was she awake now, too, watching the sun illuminate the apple trees likely half-bare as the end of the autumn neared? I thought of her often, hoping to receive word that Theo had proposed to another so we could share this beautiful view.

Today, like every morning, I chastised myself for not insisting on contacting her a fortnight ago when the letter from Beatrix came, but the genuine terror in Silas's expression had given me pause. Something within my gut twisted at his anguish, and I surrendered to his pleading to wait for the inevitable to occur. However, my impatience grew. I trusted Silas, yet he still kept me at arm's length. Over the past two weeks, I had inquired about his reasonings on dissuading me from contacting my sister, but time and again, my questions were cut off by his stony resolve. At my core, I couldn't help but agree with Naomi's assessment of him. Silas had many secrets, and despite our friendship, I was not privy to the inner workings of his mind.

I closed my eyes and pushed the ruminations away to begin my breathwork. Since the incident with the runner, I exercised, then practiced my skills independently before my sessions with

Silas. This intense routine soothed me and gave me a sense of control. As I inhaled, a desire buzzed beneath my skin, heating my blood. My lips twitched, and I forced away my curse's yearnings that vacillated between destruction and a coupling with Silas.

A chilly breeze cut through the air, cooling my skin. I steadied my breathing. Then I shifted my attention to the well within me as it pulsated in sync with my heartbeat. A grin tugged at my lips, and a sense of satisfaction washed over me at having found this new level of understanding. Since beginning my training, my curse felt more like an integral part of me than a separate entity requiring suppression.

Minutes passed, and I eased into my breathwork. Balanced in my emotions, I drew from my reservoir of power. A current coursed beneath my skin, desperate to be unleashed. But I held it at bay as I delved deeper into the murky depths, no longer afraid of what dwelled within. As I exhaled, my senses sharpened. I opened my eyes, and my vision intensified, allowing me to see details far sharper than before. Peering at my hands, my once blue veins transformed to coal black.

I stood, and a shiver crawled down my spine; the curse slithered through my body, feeding off the meager portions of anguish I supplied. I inhaled, pulling against the well. In seconds, an inky orb crackled into existence with ease in my palm. I focused on a boulder twice my size and flicked the energy toward it. It hissed through the air, then crashed against the smooth stone. An explosion echoed through the silence as the boulder disintegrated into rubble. I repeated this exercise, focusing on the speckling of targets to hone my skill.

Half an hour later, I panted from exertion, surrounded by a scattering of dust and broken rock. My head buzzed with a heady feeling from the power, and the curse crawled along my mind, whispering for submission. Before it could claw at my mental reserves, I retreated. I closed my eyes, centered myself, and shook off its pleadings for destruction. With an exhale, I forced my body to its baseline. My senses dulled, and my veins returned to their pale blue.

I unhooked the waterskin from my belt, then drank deeply and admired the amazing vista. Satiated, I re-secured the half-empty waterskin and wiped my brow. A keen awareness caused the hairs on the back of my neck to rise. I froze. My curse swirled, sending a surge of raw energy to prickle beneath my skin. I shivered with delight at this internal alarm signaling Silas's approach. This sensation intensified with each passing day. However, I didn't know why my curse often notified me of his looming presence.

I spun and viewed Silas. He leaned against a tree with his arms crossed over his broad chest and a crooked smirk on his lips. This grin had appeared over the last few weeks, which caused my heart to flutter. I bit my lip as he sauntered toward me.

"You've been busy this morning." He scanned the plateau. "You've pulverized most of the boulders up here. You might have to practice somewhere else soon."

"No, I like the view. I'll just have to roll some boulders or practice making the darkness more corporeal to grip them, like a whip. Either way, it will be excellent practice." I scanned the space that boasted of vast rock formations weeks prior.

Now only the faint dust from the pulverized stones covered the space.

"Always training. My uncle would have liked your work ethic." He let out a chuckle and stood beside me, taking in the vista. I pivoted toward the pristine view with him in reverent silence. I gulped under the magnitude of his presence, as if the air became charged whenever we were near one another.

Like a string had pulled my attention, I glanced sidelong at him. I trailed over his immaculate profile. His features were like that of a god's chiseled in stone. The breeze tousled his wavy dark hair, and I ached to run my fingers through his locks. Want pooled in my core, but I couldn't capitulate to this wanton feeling. He had a mistress, or as he had coyly called her, a *friend*. Yet I wondered if he felt this unexplainable tether, too. He peeked from the vista to me, and I forced myself out of this lust-filled haze.

The smirk twitched upon his lips. "You are quiet this morning."

He turned fully to me as the wind whipped past him. His woodsy scent enveloped me. His gold-flecked gaze bored into mine, curious, as if my silence concerned him. My mind froze as my focus drifted to his full lips, then back to his amber irises. I let out a breath but said nothing. He raised one eyebrow in question. As I drank him in, unable to speak, every part of me cried out to reach for him, to kiss him, to touch him. But I remained still.

"We better start our session. We shouldn't..." He let out a heavy sigh. "We shouldn't dawdle." Without waiting for a response, he started down the hill.

Paralyzed by my lust-laden brain, my eyes perused the outline of his broad back through the coat and the trousers that clung to his muscular legs. I stared as he walked away until his form was out of sight. I shook out of my haze, then jogged behind him to our training spot. However, the short run did not dampen my longing.

He sat on the quilt already situated on the ground, and I joined him. I no longer required his prompts as we practiced mindfulness in silence. Minutes passed, and my mind quieted. I focused on the song of the larks, the icy autumn air, and the warmth rolling off Silas beside me. However, my lingering desire sizzled. I inhaled in a feeble attempt to ignore my yearning. The curse, sensing my carnal need, whispered to me the most delectable offer. My breath hitched under the promise of the sweetest release—not of destruction, but of ecstasy. I capitulated to its will, unable to withstand this unquenchable ache that no amount of running could satiate.

This unspoken yearning thrummed through my blood. My curse, as if corporeal, whispered his name, and it echoed through my being: *Silas, Silas, Silas.*

As I relinquished control, a loose line that felt bound within my soul pulled taut. It connected me with a raw power that was so familiar yet separate from my own. I instinctively enmeshed myself in the warmth of this bond as it crashed over me, leaving denotations of a spark similar to our wedding night. I sensed Silas's presence within the depths of my consciousness, in the marrow of my bones, in the core of my being. As if our souls and curse entwined as we breathed in unison.

A heady sensation washed over me at the entanglement. Delicious heat prickled beneath my skin as I succumbed to the combined well that lived between us. An ancient instinct took hold, and the energy bent under my will. Darkness sparked from my fingertips, and wisps of power surrounded us, creating a cocoon of crackling tendrils.

My once steady respiration accelerated as a shiver crawled along my spine. His energy crept through me, causing my blood to run hot. A delighted sigh escaped my lips as my senses heightened, sinking deeper into the bliss of this merged entanglement. Goose bumps raised along my flesh, and I licked my lips, tasting the ghost of his kiss.

"Stop!"

My breath hitched at Silas's command, and our once synchronized curses unfurled. My haze broke. Yet all that lingered were delicious denotations of the shared connection that had crackled between us. I steadied my mind and dissipated the inky tendrils until no trace of our enmeshment remained.

Silas stared at me in disbelief. A shaky exhale pressed through his clenched jaw. I couldn't focus on anything but the after-waves of the rhythmic flow of energy coursing through my body.

Without a word, he stood. That stony demeanor, which had lessened over our time together, reemerged. Without waiting for me, he stomped away. Twigs snapped under his boots. I could almost sense the frustration rolling off him. Yet something within urged me forward. I fumbled to my feet and followed in pursuit.

His quick, long strides cut across the terrain with ease. I propelled myself on a mix of need and unaccustomed forwardness.

"Silas, wait." I scurried after him.

He ignored me. I should have stopped as raw tension practically rolled off him, but I couldn't. My feet pushed me forward.

"Please, stop," I said through a ragged breath, uncertain if it was from the exertion of chasing after him or the heady sensation that dampened my better sense.

"Don't come near me," he growled, whipping toward me until his gaze finally locked on mine. However, something cracked in his stoic resolve, a plea in his eyes that spoke to my soul.

I didn't heed his warning. Instead, I approached, unable to ignore the pull any longer. An eerie silence fell over the woods. The once singing larks paused their chipper tune as the palpable tension densified the air, drawing me to him like a planet in his orbit. He released a shaky breath. We stared at each other, and with only a hairsbreadth between us. An eternity passed under the pressure of my unspoken need, which I'd harbored for him since the moment we met.

I gasped when his mouth crashed upon mine. His arms wrapped around me, and he yanked me against him. With the thrust of his tongue, he parted my lips. He licked with hungry strokes, as if he could steal back the power that had entered me and swallow it whole. I moaned in pleasure, and his kiss intensified with a desire that burned far hotter than our wedding night. I languished in the delight of his taste, desperate for more. I pressed my body against his hard flesh, and heat pooled within my core. Goddess above, I wanted everything from this man. I prayed to whatever deity would grant me my wish that he would ravish me against this tree and claim me as his.

"Silas, please." I moaned.

But as suddenly as the interlude began, it ended. Silas's mouth froze, and as if burned, he released me. He stumbled back, creating distance between us. His eyes blazed with something I didn't understand. He grimaced before settling to his aloof countenance.

"*Why*? Why did you kiss me, then stop? Why torture me this way?" I choked down the lump in my throat and blinked back the tears threatening to fall.

"This should have never happened." His bitter words pierced through my soul.

I flinched at the statement and the displeasure that lingered within his gaze. As he walked away, the once taut line untethered, like woven strands of a braid coming undone. I stared at him as he skulked through the woods. The wind whipped through my heated body, now growing cold from the lack of his touch. As I watched his form disappear in the distance, I anguished over the lust I could no longer keep contained. I yearned for Silas, despite his flagrant disregard for me.

CHAPTER 46

SILAS

"BRIELLE!" MY FIST THUDDED against the door to her apartment. With each passing second, my knocking intensified from civil to frantic. She didn't answer.

For a heartbeat, I contemplated fleeing, but where to? I couldn't return to the manor, nor did I have the mental reserves to appear like the composed Lord Belmont. A few people opening their shops had already viewed my bedraggled state. Their confused stares indicated that I likely looked a fright. I had shirked off my coat somewhere in the gardens after I made my way through the woods. Arianna's lavender scent had clung to the fabric, tempting me to rush back and ravish her against a tree with reckless abandon. Instead, I sprinted down the hill in a mindless haze to create as much distance between us as possible. My hair lay askew from the whipping wind, which did nothing to cool the blazing fire within me.

The door flung open. The wood came flying toward me. I leapt back, barely avoiding being smacked in the face by the heavy oak.

"Sweet mercy! Do you know what time it is?" Brielle raised an eyebrow, and her usually sensuous smile pulled into a thin line.

"Are you going to let me in? Or shall I stand here a fool for the whole town to see?" I ran my fingers through my hair, attempting to soothe this feeling burning beneath my skin.

A line of caution creased her forehead, and her jaw twitched as she held firm, blocking my entrance. I expected her to slam the door in my face. I deserved it, having come to Presspin married without a word, ending our agreement, then ignoring her. She ground her teeth.

"Please, let me in." My shoulders slumped in defeat. I had nowhere else to go.

She paused, taking in my ragged state, and her features softened. She huffed a sigh. "Fine."

I followed her into the living space. However, I didn't have a moment to settle. She turned to me with her arms folded against her chest; the motion rumpled the crisp white blouse she wore when working downstairs in her shop.

"Why are you here?"

"I need a drink." I clutched the back of the chair I had often occupied, steadying myself.

She pursed her lips and tilted her head. "Isn't your manor filled to the brim with plenty of expensive spirits? We shared an excellent vintage before you visited Krella."

I opened and closed my mouth, but no words formed. This had been a horrible mistake.

Agitated by my lack of an answer, she unfurled her arms and smoothed her hands over her tan trousers. "I don't have all day. Why are you here?"

I didn't speak. Instead, my fingers squeezed into the chair. I couldn't tell Brielle that had I remained, I would have taken Arianna against the tree, or on the desk in my study, or on the rug in my bedroom. Damn it. I stifled a groan, and my knuckles blanched from the force of my grip.

As if sensing my inner thoughts, a seductive grin spread across Brielle's lips. "Did you hope I would satiate the lust you harbor for your pretty little wife? I doubt anyone could quench your thirst for her, and I wouldn't dare try. Even so, I have another bedfellow. He is quite skilled, and the way he uses his mouth..." She let out a hum of satisfaction.

I glared at her, and she chuckled. "Poor Silas. I shouldn't brag about a feast to a starving man."

I wanted to argue but couldn't. That kiss had nearly been my undoing. I had ached to claim Arianna, but then what? Nothing had changed. I still had no ability to love, and taking her in the woods would have only complicated our relationship further. I wouldn't spoil the friendship we had finally formed by allowing lust to overrule better sense. I shook my head. Yet my wild emotions disagreed with my logic. The wood backing buckled under my fingertips as a hint of my curse seeped out.

"Calm down or you'll ruin my furniture." Brielle threw her hands in the air.

"A drink. Please," I said through gritted teeth and released my grip. I pursed my lips at the fingerprints burned into the frame.

"*Fine.*" She stormed off, frustration rolling off her in palpable waves.

Minutes passed as I breathed through my roiling emotions, forcing them behind the brick wall of resolve. Finally composed, I took a seat and rubbed my forehead, hoping I could scrub away the memories of this morning. I shouldn't have kissed Arianna, but I couldn't resist the sweetness of her lips.

"Here." Brielle thrust the snifter of whiskey forward, jolting me to reality.

I grabbed the glass, then swallowed the contents in one smooth gulp. The amber liquid burned down my throat, loosening the tension in my shoulders. I placed the cup on the small table beside me with a clink.

With a sigh, she lounged on the floral sofa and sipped her drink, despite it being only an hour past dawn. The clock ticked seconds by as we sat in stilted silence. My eyes drifted over the painting above the crackling hearth of women dressed in white dancing in a circle, their hair askew.

"You are testing my patience. Again, why are you here?" Brielle asked, cutting through my numb haze as I shifted my gaze to her.

"It's...Arianna. I wouldn't have come to you, but..." The words caught in my throat, and my leaden tongue struggled to speak.

She downed her whiskey before gesturing for me to continue.

"There is something occurring between us that I don't understand. Our curses are entangling somehow, and the closer we become, the more palpable the pull toward her is. It is unbearable. I try to fight it, fortify my mind against her. Then today, I...Gods. What is happening to me?" I clutched my head in my hands and stared at my boots.

"Sweet mercy. You are *such* a fool."

I flicked a glance at her, expecting her to say more. She didn't. Instead, she stood and took my glass. I gaped after her as she sauntered to the kitchen. I sulked in this miserable silence, lost in my confusion, and debated leaving. Yet minutes later, she reentered with two full glasses and handed one to me, then settled on the sofa.

"I have my theories about what is happening to you." She swirled her drink, the amber liquid sloshing in the snifter.

I leaned forward, giving her all my attention, and waited as she drew out the moment by taking a long sip of her whiskey.

"My first suspicion is that you are besotted with your wife." A smug smile stretched across her face.

I downed the spirit. The smoky flavor of the two drinks washed over the taste of Arianna still clinging to my tongue. I lowered the glass to the table, careful not to slam it, as not to give Brielle the wrong idea.

"Impossible. What is your next theory?" I asked, unwilling to dwell on whatever lay between Arianna and me.

"Since you are not in love with your wife, then my other suspicion is pointless. Cursed beings do experience emotions in such a unique way." She cocked her head, assessing me. However, she didn't continue with her train of thought. Instead, she sipped her drink.

I thrummed my fingers against the wood table, punctuating through the quiet. Though Brielle and I had past interludes, the entanglements now felt hollow. I hadn't been her only paramour, nor had I cared about the aloof nature of our connection. Yet, in this silence, I noticed the ease that we lacked when compared to my time with Arianna. We had formed a comradery over the years, but neither of us showed our true selves. My stoicism and her allure served as our personas to the world and each other. She finished her whiskey and lowered the glass to her side table. I stood to leave. Coming here had been pointless.

"*Wait.* There is another matter, and it's best we discuss it while spirits have numbed both of us." She took a long breath, steeling herself to bring up whatever vexed her, as I sat back down.

"A raven arrived last night, bearing a message from Martha."

My jaw clenched. She only spoke of Martha, another ex-Aralian disciple, when the woman sent warnings. Brielle fiddled with the edge of her braid, her cavalier persona slipping.

"What is it?" I asked in a calm manner despite my lack of patience, since Brielle, too, seemed a bit rattled.

"She has informed me that they are searching for Arianna. They have been scouring Hallowhaven since she disappeared, and they are intent on finding her." Her soft features tightened in distress. She often referred to those who hunted her as *them,* and neither of us dared speak their names.

"Do they know she is here?" I curled my hand into a fist, dreading my worst fears were coming to life. That runner had already pieced together my impetuous plan to bring Arianna here; would they, too, find her and take her to her doom?

"No. Martha often notifies me of missing cursed beings or of other runaway disciples. I sent the raven back, informing her that there was no one matching Arianna's description here. Though I trust Martha, I will not risk the message being captured with damning details. She didn't mention Arianna's current whereabouts, nor a connection to you. You have concealed your curse well, and they have no reason to search here." Brielle released her braid and smoothed her palms over her pants. However, a hint of fear lingered in her expression. Brielle, too, would suffer if discovered hidden away in Presspin.

I sagged deeper into the chair. My head pounded from trying to sort through these overwhelming emotions and looming threats to Arianna's well-being. My life felt like a runaway cart barreling through the coal mines of the Presspin mountains, uncertain where the track would lead. All I could do was brace myself and hope for the best, yet in my experience, the worst often occurred.

"Silas," Brielle said with a steadier voice. "She needs to know—"

"I *can't*. How am I supposed to tell her that everything she knew was a lie? I need more time." I shook my head, nearly choking on the fate that likely still awaited Arianna.

I rubbed my eyes, overcome by these untethered feelings that coursed through me like lightning. Brielle approached, then stood in front of me. Worry no longer filled her features. She now looked akin to a mother preparing to lecture a misbehaving child.

"It's time you go home to your wife and tell her the truth." The clock chimed over the mantel, drawing her attention. Her jaw ticked with agitation as I remained unmoved. "Fine. I have work to do. When you finish sulking, let yourself out."

I stared at the ceiling, paralyzed with indecision. The click of her footsteps drifted away as she left. I scrubbed a hand over my face. Overwhelmed, I stalked to the kitchen in search of the whiskey to fortify me as I dwelled on these additional complications.

CHAPTER 47

ARIANNA

"MY LADY, CARE FOR a loaf of dark rye bread? It's fresh out of the oven," Jacob, the baker, called out as he swept the walkway leading to his door. As I neared, he came forward and cleared the light golden leaves off the path before they could crunch under my boots. I paused and inhaled the scent of baked goods wafting from the shop.

"That sounds lovely. I'll send Grey to pick up a few loaves. I'm heading to the herbalist, but before I forget, has little Genevieve recovered from her cold?" A grin cut across the man's face at my inquiry. Despite my frustration this morning, it warmed my heart that my attempt to learn the townspeople's names and needs had been met with friendliness. Though I hadn't acquainted myself with everyone yet, I strived to build a life in Presspin. Even if my title as Lady Belmont was honorary, given my precarious marriage to Silas.

"Yes, my lady. Genny is doing well, thanks to Ms. Brielle's tonics. I hope you haven't taken ill." Jacob stopped sweeping, leaned on the doorframe, and wiped the sweat from his brow. My jaw ticked, and I withheld a bitter laugh; something ailed me, but nothing her herbal remedies would cure. But I didn't divulge my tumultuous feelings to the kind baker.

"No, just needing assistance only Ms. Brielle can provide." I forced a smile, and he nodded before popping into the bakery.

I strode forward, approaching the bookstore, and my nostrils flared. I had avoided the space because of Brielle's business being its neighbor. After today, I wouldn't stay away in fear of crossing paths with Silas's mistress. I squared my shoulders and walked toward her storefront. The gray building appeared like the others on this street, a melding of basalt and brick to create a façade uniquely its own. Wild vines crept up the front, seeming as untamed as its owner. I drew in a breath for courage and pushed back any uncertainty. I couldn't cower from my problems any longer. Determined, I stepped over the threshold, and a bell chimed overhead.

A mix of sweet and spicy scents hit me all at once, and my nose wrinkled. I moved forward. My boots clicked against the gray tile floors, and with each step, the smell became less pungent. Flora grew along the interior brick walls, and clay pots with a variety of herbs hung from the wooden rafters overhead. The oversized hearth in the corner near the entrance roared, keeping the space overheated. Sweat beaded across my brow. I unbuttoned my wool coat, allowing the light from the many windows to wash over the violet day dress.

"Coming!" Brielle's voice echoed from behind a partially closed door I assumed led to a rear room.

I scanned over the wood hutches with tiny drawers that lined the walls. Each one was labeled with different components. Yet I couldn't focus on the words. With each passing second, the indignation that bubbled within me grew, strengthening my resolve.

Yesterday, I'd waited for Silas, but he did not accompany me to work or home. Nor did he join me for dinner. After supper, I lingered in the library for hours. Then, at midnight, I heard his heavy footfalls on the steps. I watched through the cracked door with gritted teeth as he swayed, appearing inebriated. Initially, I had assumed he had been at the tavern. He hadn't imbibed in excess before, but I didn't know all his habits. Then, this morning, I overheard two maids whispering as they scurried down the halls, unaware as I eavesdropped around the corner. The first maid recounted how she saw Silas entering his mistress's apartment while she was on her way to collect a bakery order. The second maid giggled and corroborated the story. Apparently, the driver, a man she often cavorted with, was summoned to pick him up at Brielle's. I rushed off before they could spot me snooping.

"How can I—"

Brielle entered the main shop, and her lips pursed, catching the rest of her sentence. Then they flickered into a sensuous grin. I straightened and pushed away the thoughts of my gabbing servants.

However, confusion knitted my brow. For a second, I didn't recognize the woman, given Brielle's less ostentatious appearance. She donned a crisp blouse, cotton trousers, and a white apron. Her plaited auburn hair snaked down her shoulder. My brain strained to reconcile the two diametrically opposed versions of this woman. But that catlike aura permeated the room as her professional demeanor dropped. She approached and stood before me.

"Lady Belmont, to what do I owe this pleasure? In need of a draft for headaches? Perhaps an elixir to prevent pregnancy?" She smirked. Yet I wouldn't allow the undercut to hit its mark.

Instead, I lifted my chin, feeling every bit of my title as Lady Belmont settled upon me like a costume I wore for this act.

"Ah, Brielle, we both know I don't require a contraceptive. I am certain it is your bed my husband has been warming." My venomous tone cut through the air, and a sense of pride filled me from the callous statement.

She did not react as I'd expected. Instead, she tilted her head, taking me in as if for the first time. "Ah, I see it. The woman who has Silas so unsettled. Bravo." She clapped her hands, but I didn't shrink under her condescension.

"I don't care what you think of me. I am here to inform you that your liaison with my husband ends now. If you dare find your way back into his bed..." I loosened the leash against my curse. Power crawled under my skin, turning my blue veins an inky black. The air pressurized, and the pots overhead swayed. My fingertips blackened as a hint of darkness eked out.

"Are you threatening me?" She stepped forward, daring me. For a moment, we held each other's glare as the atmosphere densified from my cresting power.

"It's not a threat. It's a promise." Despite being inches shorter than the woman, I stood to my full height.

She didn't cower. Instead, she laughed. I held firm, seething that Silas had run to her after kissing me. I should have confronted him, but I couldn't bear the heartbreak of hearing the truth from his lips. No one desired me; hadn't that been abundantly clear my entire life? Theo only wanted me as a piece for his collection. Even now, I had become Silas's friend at best. For a heartbeat, I had thought maybe he yearned for me, too. However, his words had been like a dagger to my heart. That the kiss should have never happened. Despite my growth, it felt easier to confront the person I hated than the man I longed for.

"Put your threats away. There really is no need. Silas and I haven't had a dalliance in months. Our last interlude occurred well before he left for Krella. I swear he can endure a dry spell like no other. He came to my apartment yesterday, but not for a tryst. He drank himself into a stupor after telling me about your moment in the woods."

I gaped in shock. Uncertainty replaced my righteous indignation, and my curse dissipated. The air stilled, and my body returned to its baseline. I stepped back. Why did everything about my relationship with Silas muddle my brain? A desire to rip this woman to pieces had surged through my blood. My curse had fueled my rage, pushing me toward town to seek my revenge, as if Brielle had trespassed on something that belonged to me. Before I could turn to leave, she spoke.

"It is time you and Silas have a serious discussion. Not just about what lives between you, but about the truth of your curse." With a catlike smirk, she leaned closer and whispered, "Haven't you wondered about your curse, or why there are no mentions of Aralia here? Perhaps you are so enthralled by Silas that you haven't noticed the difference in Presspin compared to your home. No? Open your eyes. When you stop and think about it, the truth is blatantly obvious."

I wanted to argue, but her questions planted a seed in my mind. I had wondered why there were no Aralian temples or Aralians here. No temple existed in Daviel or Krella either. However, in Presspin, not a soul mentioned Aralia. I hadn't seen a single golden book with her stories, nor any figurines in remembrance of her. Silas's words echoed through my head: *We have no love for Aralia here.* My heart pounded. I suspected Silas kept many secrets, and my impatience with them had finally reached its boiling point.

"What are you not—"

A bell chimed, halting my question.

"Everette, come in. Lady Belmont was leaving." Brielle purred to the handsome farmer, a strapping young man in his early twenties, with a sultry smirk.

"And Lady Belmont, we will chat soon. For now, have a lovely day." She flourished a ridiculous curtsy, then turned her attention to the dark-complexioned gentleman.

The bell chimed once more as I exited, followed by the subtle click of the lock. Fuming and confused, I hastened home, ready to finally confront Silas.

CHAPTER 48

Silas

Shadows cut across the study as the once warm sunlight faded behind gray clouds. I blinked at the numbers, now obscured by the darkening room. With a sigh, I leaned back in my chair and rubbed my weary eyes. My head pounded from the migraine induced by the copious amounts of spirits I consumed yesterday mixed with hours hunched over this desk. I gritted my teeth and pushed myself forward. I needed to finish tabulating the food stores. Winter neared, and I doubted the supplies from the Parks' farm would last through the snowy months.

I picked up the pen, and ink leaked onto my fingertips. A frustrated growl escaped me. Everything, down to the most minor details, had gone awry today. I grabbed my handkerchief and wiped the smudges from my hand. I froze mid-swipe. My covered fingers were midnight black, the same shade as that horrible day that had frequently repeated in my mind. My throat tightened as my father's voice echoed in my soul: *You are nothing but a monster, boy. A monster no one will ever love.*

I attempted to push the slew of emotions away, but they no longer remained locked behind my stony resolve. Frantically, I blotted the fabric square into the water cup on my desk and washed my digits clean, then discarded the ruined kerchief. However, my hands were still stained.

I breathed through my unease. Emotions were a nuisance, yet Arianna had chipped away at my fortifications, weakening me to memories that were best left repressed. Thinking about her brought on an onslaught of complicated feelings, replacing thoughts of my past. I could no longer deny that our relationship burgeoned into something undefined. My pulse skittered as I peered down at my stained fingertips. I was a monster who destroyed, who killed, and who didn't deserve love. But the pull to her felt unavoidable. With each of these interactions, my curse grew more unyielding, more enticed by her, beckoning me to relent to my suppressed ardor.

I had avoided Arianna, lingering at Brielle's until the late-night hours, drinking whiskey until she returned from her new paramour's home and kicked me out of her apartment. I expected Arianna to be asleep, but I sensed her watching me from the library. Her presence was palpable, like my heartbeat. I didn't go to her, nor apologize. Instead, I staggered off to bed. Then this morning, I avoided training and hunkered down in my study. My head throbbed, and I couldn't dwell on Arianna, nor my father's words, any longer. Before I could return to my calculations, an eerie sense washed over me. My heart raced, and a flicker of awareness tugged within me. I straightened in my seat, my focus on the entryway as silent seconds passed.

A knock echoed, then the door opened. I applied my most rigid façade as Arianna entered. A whisper of light cut through the window. It highlighted the violet day dress that deepened the shade of her crystal-blue eyes. Her face remained unreadable. I held my breath as she stepped closer, her boots clicking against the wood floor. She settled into the chair across from my desk and rolled her shoulders back. Her chin tilted, and she looked every bit a refined lady as she donned a haughty air.

"I spoke with Brielle."

I gaped, slack-jawed, then snapped my mouth shut. A sudden choking sensation overwhelmed me, and I loosened my cravat. Arianna did not flinch at my discomfort. Her lips remained straight-lined, unamused. Seconds stretched, and I tried to reconcile why she and my previous paramour had conversed. What had Brielle told her? Gods, this was a disaster.

"Arianna, I—"

She held up her hand, halting me.

"She clarified the confines of your relationship. Moreso, the lack of intimacy since we have wed. However, we have other matters to discuss. Brielle insinuated that you are hiding something from me. Though I didn't believe her at first, her questions sparked my curiosity. I spent the day exploring Presspin. As I perused the bookstore, I noticed there were no stories of Aralia there, nor in our library. Not a single townsperson I spoke with has ever seen an Aralian here. Even the mere mention of the goddess brought a distaste. They were all vague and oddly unwilling to chat when I asked about Aralia. Why is that?"

Of course Brielle had planted the seed in her mind. She had encouraged me to inform Arianna of the truth, no matter how painful. I wanted to avoid this conversation, yet a storm churned in her eyes. My mouth dried, but I had to tell her.

I stood and walked to the window, taking in the mountain range as I searched for words. The clouds loomed over the town. The faint whispers of light that had crested through disappeared, and the world darkened. I clutched my hands behind my back.

"You are curious and clever. I should have known you would have pieced together the facts. The history, you know, is a lie. Aralia is not the Goddess of Light, but the Goddess of Darkness. She cursed us."

"No, that's incorrect," Arianna said through a shaky breath.

I stared out the window, unable to look at her. Instead, I remembered the tale Ophelia had recounted. She'd stroked my hair, offered me a sleeping draft, and told me this story before I drifted into a deep slumber. I channeled her tenderness as best I could and continued.

"Long ago, Cassius, God of Light, and Aralia, Goddess of Darkness, lived in harmony. Cassius brought life, and the world praised him for it. While Aralia, the harbinger of death, was reviled. After generations in which she had been loathed, the balance between life and death became skewed by Aralia's displeasure. Famine and plague swept the land, only evoking more ire from the people. Spurred on by their hatred, she concocted a curse. She damned Cassius's followers, the Cassiulls, with a darkness that would destroy everything it touched. Yet Cassius cared about his worshipers. He marked them with a blessing; the will to control the blight. A war broke out between the Cassiulls and the Aralians, who believed that their fealty to the goddess would spare them from her wrath. However, because of Cassius's interference, Aralia's desolation did not come to pass. Enraged, she conjured another strategy to plunge the planet into chaos. In order to carry out her plan, she needed to eliminate Cassius from aiding. She knew the God of Light loved her despite her dark delights. Cunning Aralia seduced Cassius, hoping to kill him in a moment of weakness. He suspected her wicked intent and imprisoned both of them somewhere within this world before she could carry out her last scheme. With both deities gone, the Aralians enacted their failsafe to overpower the Cassiulls. Then they twisted history and burned most of the ancient text regarding Cassius. I only know this because Ophelia had served as a scribe for the High Disciple, translating texts from Aralian into our tongue. When she learned the truth, she fled."

I paused, uncertain of how to proceed. Yet the ominous sky and looming shadows covering the valley offered no help. I jolted at the sound of a chair scraping against the floor.

"I don't understand. Why lie about Aralia being the Goddess of Light?" She stood behind me, and the hairs prickled on my nape. My stomach sank from the next harsh blow I had to deliver.

"It was all part of the Aralians' master plan. They weren't helping you suppress your curse. Instead, they were stealing the energy from you and harnessing it for their use. The etchings on the windows, on the doors, inside the masks, are ancient spells connected to enchanted onyx rings just like ours, which the Aralians don. They store our energy in the spelled onyx using the ancient word bindings that Aralia bestowed upon them. However, these spells don't work on their own. They need power, and our curse is their supply. These wards have been draining you dry for years. The Aralians are not magical. They are ordinary women who have learned from their forbearers how to steal power and wield it as if it were their own."

Silence ticked by, and she said nothing. I pivoted to her. Her face turned a sickly shade, and I feared she would vomit on the hardwood floor. I reached out to steady her. "Arianna, I—"

"Don't touch me!"

I recoiled.

"Why didn't you tell me this immediately? Why hide this from me?" Her words pressed through her clenched jaw. Anger laced her features as she stepped forward.

"What should I have said? 'Nice to meet you, Arianna. You are bound to wards that are killing you.' Or perhaps, 'Arianna, you might succumb to an early death like my uncle, because the Aralians have been depleting you of your vitality since you were six.' Or maybe just my deepest fear? I hope to the gods that I intervened soon enough that you would not suffer a similar fate as my uncle."

My composure shattered as my unstated and tumultuous feelings bubbled within me. I huffed in a breath, furious at myself for lying to her, at Brielle for forcing my hand, and at Arianna for making me—*No.* I couldn't love her. I couldn't love anyone. For a moment, the seething anger between us consumed me. My cursed swelled, fueled toward destruction or an incessant need to claim her.

"You should have told me sooner. I deserved to know." Her shoulders rose and fell with her ragged breaths.

"That is not all. The Aralians are looking for you. Since your disappearance, I am certain they have scoured Hallowhaven and its territories. They likely would not suspect that you are here. That is why I insisted you contact no one. I can't let them find you. My family hid my secret well. My uncle had no children, and after he perished, anyone who knew of his curse assumed it died with him. All I want is to keep you safe."

She shook her head. Tears welled in her eyes. She turned away and fled the room. My knees buckled from the weight of the last few days, and I staggered to the chair. I held my head in my hands, uncertain of what to do about Arianna.

CHAPTER 49

ARIANNA

I PEERED DOWN THE long hallway leading into the abandoned east wing that I hadn't explored. However, it felt like trespassing because this area housed his uncle's quarters. I ambled down the corridor, and plush rugs dampened my footsteps. A sparse number of lit candles illuminated my way, casting shadows along the copper-toned wallpaper. A shiver cut through me, as if ghosts dwelled in this eerie silence. Perhaps his uncle's looming presence had been why Silas had forgone occupying the master suites. Though I dared not ask him, since we were avoiding each other.

I slowed, perusing the paintings of past generations lining the hallway. As I reached the last one, my breath hitched. I lingered over the portrait of Silas. His stoic countenance showed no hint of the gentler man beneath the façade. My heart raced, and my conflicting emotions churned. I missed him, but I was still livid. It had been a week since we had last spoken. When he divulged that the Aralians were the ultimate manipulators.

Since then, I had filled my days with anything to occupy my time. I trained on my own, worked at Layla's, planned the Kesere festivities with Mrs. Potter, and scoured the library, evading Silas. Yet at night, he haunted my dreams.

With a sigh, I continued down the hallway. Minutes later, I stopped at the etched wooden door and hesitated, uncertain of what I would find. However, I needed answers. Slowly, I entered the previous Lord Belmont's bedroom. The expansive space was decorated in an outdated gold and copper motif. Against the wall was a sleigh bed, and the nightstand beside it housed an empty water pitcher. Two armchairs were nestled near the fireless hearth, with floral throws draped over each. In the rear corner lay a desk with a neat stack of correspondence. A pang of sorrow tugged at my heart. The pristine quarters served as a monument, as if the late Lord Belmont would return at any moment. Yet a faint scent of musk wafted through the air, indicating disuse.

I walked to the bookcase with shelves that stretched beyond my height which covered the back wall. My fingers traced along the spines, scanning for any book that might divulge the history of the god and goddess. I had already rifled through the library for information on the Aralians, but the search had been fruitless.

I grabbed a few promising titles, then moved toward the leather armchair by the empty hearth. Sunlight flickered through the floor-to-ceiling windows, barely heating the chilly room. Fortunately, I had left Layla's early enough to investigate before nightfall when the suite would become unbearable without a fire. I shivered and yanked the throw off the back of the seat, wrapping myself in its warmth. Comfortably settled, I flipped through the pages, hoping that any of these tomes would provide guidance.

Two hours passed, and I still hadn't found the reassurance I sought. Though I'd located fascinating details about the mining system in the mountains of Presspin, where the town derived its wealth from gems and coal. I lowered the third book to the side table. The fading sunlight began making it difficult to read. I leaned deeper into the chair, uncertain of what to do next. However, a prickle of awareness caused goose bumps to form, halting my thoughts. A knot formed in my throat as the door opened.

"Why are you in here?" Silas asked through gritted teeth.

I gaped at an unfamiliar Silas and couldn't form words. Instead, I took in the changes in his appearance since last week. Dark circles rimmed his eyes, dulling his luminous amber irises, a wrinkle creased his forehead, and his hair lay askew. Despite myself, I wanted to reach out and straighten his locks and smooth the crease on his brow. He remained rooted to the spot, glaring at me.

"How did you find me here? I assumed you never stepped foot into this wing." I unfurled myself from the blanket, then rose and smoothed my hands over the navy day dress.

A whisper of sunlight washed over him, highlighting his exhaustion in the orange glow of the setting sun. He brushed his fingers through his hair. His features softened. "I just knew."

Seconds passed as my mind tried to reconcile this phenomenon that occurred between us. It felt like we were each other's true north, constantly directed to one another. Yet the light shifted, casting him in shadow. His expression hardened.

"Why are you in my uncle's room?"

"I thought something might be hidden here to confirm your story about Aralia and Cassius. I have found nothing." I held his stare.

He gritted his teeth and grimaced with each step forward, as if the movement pained him. He loomed near the other armchair, keeping feet between us.

"If I had a book in my possession, I would have brought it to you after our conversation. If you require further verification, I can take you to visit Peter and Agnes after Kesere. They are old believers and can recount the oral history shared with them by their forbearers."

I nodded, waiting for him to usher me out. Instead, he crossed his arms over his chest. He scanned the space, and he spoke as if lost in memory.

"It is strange to think every Lord Belmont, myself excluded, has occupied this suite. To me, it is still my uncle's room."

I dared not move or speak, afraid of snapping Silas out of this rare vulnerability.

"I wish I'd had more time with him, but decades under the suppression spells had weakened him." He shook his head, and his lower lip trembled, then pulled tight. I didn't ask how long his uncle suffered, fearing that despite Silas's intervention, a similar fate awaited me.

"I'm glad I don't occupy this room. It wasn't just my uncle's but my grandfather's once. I never knew the man. Thank the gods. But he had been a pious follower of Aralia and was appalled when my uncle's curse awoke. He unwittingly sentenced his son to an early grave when he allowed the Aralians to place him under the wards. Even after my grandfather died, my uncle was trapped."

A shiver crawled along my spine, and a frown pulled on my lips. He stepped closer, as if the story had loosened some of his tension.

"Then when Ophelia came to Presspin, everything changed. She freed my uncle and spoke of the truth she uncovered about Aralia. Unbeknownst to him, many of the townspeople worshipped Cassius in secret. Presspin had once been a stronghold for the god's followers, but they had hidden their beliefs from my grandfather, who favored the goddess. After he died, any love for Aralia had waned. Uncle Oliver searched for answers, much like you are, but the only ones he found were through the town elders. Each one confirmed Ophelia's tale. Eventually, any dwindling loyalty to the goddess diminished. Now we practice the old ways."

Silas's shoulders slumped. Despite his massive frame, he seemed small in his uncle's former lodgings. Darkness stretched across the suite as the last dregs of sunlight faded away. However, we didn't leave. Instead, he walked to the hearth and lit the candelabra on the mantel, illuminating the space. "But this is not why I came to find you. A letter arrived for you."

I approached, waiting impatiently as he fished the correspondence from his pocket. I grabbed the paper and scanned over the familiar handwriting. My fingers trembled as I read the contents.

Arianna,

We direly need help. All has gone awry over the past few weeks since Theo ended his hunt for you. Yesterday, Mr. Terrell stormed into our home and demanded that Mama reimburse him for the engagement ball attire and the expense of the failed wedding. He was unsatisfied with the returned sheep and the little coin we had left from Lord Belmont's purchase of the harvest. Mama used the money to repair the damaged roof and spent a ridiculous amount on frivolities, despite my protests. Mr. Terrell took our meager savings as a deposit toward the sum of ten thousand Aralian Crown he believes we owe him. We have a month to repay him, or they will file a claim with the High Council for us to be imprisoned for our unpaid debts. I fear he is more nefarious than we realized. Why else would a wealthy man threaten debtors' prison to an impoverished widow and her daughter?

The only bright spot is that no one knows your whereabouts. Luckily, Mama was engrossed with visiting the modiste in Krella and bragging about her good fortune to notice you were missing before your wedding. There have been no whispers as to your connection to Lord Belmont. It is fortunate that our ruse worked, and he appeared to leave a fortnight prior to you running away. At least in Presspin you are safe from being found and out of their clutches, for I fear that their wrath would fall upon you far more harshly. Please send aid.

Naomi

I released the letter, and it drifted to the ground. Short, panicked breaths escaped me, and my chest tightened. Tears welled, and guilt filled my soul. I shouldn't have abandoned my sister to deal with the burden. I rushed to leave, but Silas grabbed my arm, halting my movement.

"Let me go! I must go to Naomi. Immediately. I have to fix this." My eyes bored into his, pleading, but his lips remained straight-lined.

"Don't move, Arianna. Just wait." He released me, stooped to pick up the letter, and scanned its contents. His brow creased as he read.

With Silas distracted, I sprinted for the exit. Moments later, my fingers wrapped around the knob. I opened the door a fraction, but a force behind me slammed it shut. I yanked it again, but it didn't budge. Silas's hot breath tickled the nape of my neck, causing goose bumps to trail along my skin.

I spun and met his gaze. His arms were on either side of my head, caging me in while simultaneously holding the door closed. He leaned forward. His head dipped to my ear, and his voice came out in a snarl.

"How do you intend on resolving the issue? By wedding Theo? Did you forget you are my wife? We consummated this marriage at your request, and no one can tear us asunder now." His lips whispered over my lobe, and the wisps from his unshaven face brushed against my skin. "You expect me to allow you to flounce off into danger without a plan?"

My pulse skittered, and my cheeks blazed from a mix of frustration and ill-timed lust. I splayed my hands on his chest in a feeble attempt to push him away. He didn't move.

"And you just expect me to sit here and wait?" I glared at him.

"Listen to me. I can secure a solicitor to provide the Terrells with the funds to cover your mother's debts from an anonymous benefactor. The Terrells will assume it is from distant kin."

He let out a ragged breath, his muscular form looming only inches from my own. I fought the instinct to meld my body against his. As if sensing my desire, he pulled back. The gesture cooled me, a reminder that even if an attraction dwelled between us, he would never capitulate. His eyes locked on mine as if they pleaded with me to hear reason. "I am certain this is a bluff. The Terrells are after money, and once the debt is paid, they will relinquish this ridiculous claim of carting your family off to debtors' prison."

I shook my head. "How can I trust you anymore? You've lied to me too many times. How do I know you are telling the truth? I'm tired of these games. Let me go to bear the consequences of my actions."

His face dropped, and he withdrew as if I had slapped him. I shivered, my body chilled from his absence.

"I'm sorry. I've made many mistakes since our hasty marriage. I should have told you everything before we wed. Before letting you tie yourself to me." He stumbled toward the chair and slumped into it. The flicker of the candelabra pierced through the darkness, highlighting the exhaustion in his features. He lowered his head into his hands.

With him distracted, I had the perfect opportunity to leave, but I couldn't. I remained paralyzed, practically drowning in the guilt that radiated from him and crested over me like a wave.

"I don't want you to die, too. Please, I can't bear losing you. I know you're angry. Rightfully so, but please do not go. Let me fix this," he pleaded.

I leaned against the door. Long seconds passed as I mulled over Naomi's letter and Silas's plan. I could run home, but then what? I couldn't marry Theo, nor did I possess the funds without Silas's help. The small savings I had built since working at Layla's wouldn't be near enough. Moreso, what about the Aralians? I shuddered. They had whipped me for the slightest infraction. What would they do if they caught me? I didn't have an alternative. I gritted my teeth in frustration. Irritated that perhaps Silas was right.

"Fine. You have a fortnight to fulfill your plan. If you fail, I will return to Krella."

Before he could object, I slipped out, leaving him alone to be haunted by his uncle's ghost and the decisions we've made.

CHAPTER 50

Silas

"Mama! Mama!" Beatrix cried. My father lifted her into his arms, and she burrowed her face into his chest.

I shook my head, as if answering Beatrix's pleas. Mama was gone. I stood beside my mother's bed and peered at her lifeless body tucked into the quilt. The soft candlelight illuminated the sallow pallor that had washed over her once olive complexion, caused by days of fever that had ravaged her. Her once vibrant brown eyes stared at me, unseeing. My lips trembled, and I fought back tears. I closed my eyes, and Beatrix's cries faded into the distance. The world slipped away.

Time felt irrelevant. Mere seconds or hours could have passed as I stared at my mother's lifeless form. My pulse raced, and my chest ached, as if molten steel burned within my heart. This roiling agony shattered my body as the heat unspooled through my skin like black tar oozing from my pores. I shrieked, my voice not sounding like my own as an inky energy crackled to life. The wood floor beneath me buckled, and black fire consumed the room around me, destroying everything. Muffled screams swirled around in indistinguishable noise as if I were underwater. I fell into this endless pit until the darkness consumed me.

I gasped, awakening to the night sky, covered in ash and soot. A rock poked into my back, and I shifted, sprawled on the hard ground. Bile crawled up the back of my throat, and unease seized me. Where was I? I stood and scanned the devastation before me. Our home had vanished and was replaced by a heap of scorched brick. My skull burned, and I grabbed my head. The buzzing energy filled my ears and crawled over my skin like ants biting my flesh.

"Beatrix! Beatrix!" I spun around but couldn't find her.

My breath hitched in the core of my soul; I knew I had caused this. I could feel this entity crawling along me, and it whispered its desires for destruction into my mind.

Oh, gods, had I killed her?

I collapsed in the ruin and wept, wishing the darkness would take me, too. I wanted to join my sister and mother in death. Nothing else mattered as my tears washed over the soot covering my cheeks.

"Silas!" Beatrix's frail voice pierced through my agony. The sweet sound anchored me to the world. I blinked, and my father came into focus with my little sister wrapped in his arms. Disgusted, he glared down at my weeping, grime-covered form.

"Look what you've done." Ash and fury lined his countenance. I trembled, afraid of his rage and of myself.

"Father, I am sorry. I am sorry. Please help me." My words came out between ragged gulps of air.

"How am I supposed to help you?" He paused, his lips trembling, and Beatrix sobbed into his shoulder. Not a soul ventured out, likely too afraid to offer any aid. His head whipped around the dark night; the sliver of a moon illuminated his furrowed brow. An eternity

passed as I wept. For a heartbeat, as I peered up at him, his expression flashed with a bone-deep sorrow, then hardened. "You are nothing but a monster, boy, a monster no one will ever love."

"My lord! My lord!"

I jolted awake and peered not into my father's face, but into Vincent's. His brow knit together, and for a heartbeat, I felt uncertain of where I was, my mind trapped between the past and the present. I blinked, taking in his worried expression.

"Why are you in my quarters?" I pressed my lips into a thin line, confused as to why my steward would overstep such an obvious social boundary.

"You are in your study, my lord. You must have fallen asleep here. I was bringing you the reports for the recent produce I procured. I would have left it on your desk, but you seemed distressed, so I woke you." He stepped back.

I bolted upright and took in the space. Sunlight washed through the windows, and the embers from a dying fire crackled in the hearth. I groaned. My back ached from the miniscule hours of sleep on the stiff leather sofa. I rolled my shoulders and smoothed my wrinkled dress shirt. At least I slumbered, even fitfully. I had run out of sleeping draft days prior.

Last night, unable to sleep, I had paced the study trying to conjure the names of solicitors to handle the Park family's issue without divulging my identity. However, most were of the dishonorable sort whose loyalty was to the highest coin. A list of men laid on my desk, each one scratched out because, in the end, I couldn't trust them with Arianna's life.

"My lord, do you require my assistance? I'm heading to the farms on the edge of town to check on the harvest preservation process, then to Liam's boxing club for a round. However, I can postpone my sparring practice if you need aid."

I gaped at my straitlaced steward, surprised that he, of all people, took part in fisticuffs. As if sensing my shock, he gave a lopsided grin. I rubbed my eyes. Had the entire world turned upside down? Was I so blatantly unaware of those around me that I missed these key components to their personalities?

Even last night had not gone as I expected. I had been unnerved when I found Arianna curled up in my uncle's favorite chair and reading his books in the room I avoided. She had a knack for stumbling into my most hidden depths, areas that I buried deep within myself. Then the daft woman insisted on running straight into peril. At that moment, I felt as if she'd cleaved me in half, determined to leave me and walk straight into danger. Yet she begrudgingly remained in Presspin, for now.

I was a fool. I should have chased after her and confessed that the week without her had tormented me. The comfort of her company and the light she had brought into my world were highlighted by the isolation I'd suffered as we evaded one another. Last night, my curse thrummed, drawing me toward her, which was how I intrinsically knew her location. It was as if we were magnets being constantly pulled together, unable to stop this unbreakable force. However, after our conversation, I skulked away and found myself here.

"My lord, shall I assist you with whatever this is?" Vincent asked, pulling me out of my memories.

"What?" I peered at my steward, who held out the list of names. "It's nothing. I will manage this task on my own."

A seriousness entered his countenance, the same expression he wore when working on troublesome problems. "Silas, you seem unwell this morning. I dare say this week. Let me help you."

I softened at my steward's earnest expression. Over the past year, he had done an immaculate job assisting me in running the manor and the town. However, I couldn't relinquish this duty to him. He was too inexperienced, and I didn't know him well enough. I needed someone I trusted with my life. I jolted from the sofa, as if struck by lightning, and rushed toward the desk. I collapsed into my chair.

"I do need your help after all." I gestured to the seat across from me.

He sat and cleaned his glasses, waiting for me as I began the correspondence I should have written from the very beginning.

Duncan,

I hope this letter finds you well. Please know I have missed you, my brother. I know when we parted we were not on the best of terms, and I'm sorry. However, I desperately require your aid. I need you to arrange for a solicitor to deliver a large sum of money for me. Immediately. You must handle the situation with discretion. I cannot go into further details. Please trust me.

Sincerely,
Silas

I folded the paper and heated the wax, then stamped my seal on the back. I blew against the solidifying liquid to cool it faster. My shoulders loosened, and the tension I held from last night unfurled a fraction. Beatrix had said Duncan would arrive in

Krella by harvest's end. Yet I didn't dwell on the possibility that my request would go unanswered. I had to believe that he had returned, for I had no one else to handle this delicate matter. Despite our argument, I trusted him with the two people I cared for the most, Beatrix and Arianna. He had guided me since my uncle's death a decade ago, when I was a lad emerging into my majority saddled with the responsibility of an entire territory. He had been my closest friend, my teacher, and now my brother-in-law. Our relationship had survived our previous disagreements, and we always reached a resolution. Once we told him the truth about me, about Arianna, he would understand. Our family could no longer live under these secrets.

The seal solidified. I flipped the paper and scrolled Duncan's information on the front. "Run this to the post immediately. It is of the utmost importance. See that it is rushed to Krella without delay. Let the rider know I'll double their fee if they can deliver this by nightfall."

Vincent took the message, and a twitch of a frown pulled on his lips as he scanned the name. My brow wrinkled at this unaccustomed grimace on my typically good-natured steward's face.

"Is there a problem?" I leaned into my chair and crossed my arms over my chest.

He flicked a gaze from me to the letter, then back to me. He pursed his lips and rose. "It's nothing, my lord."

Vincent gave a hasty bow, then rushed off on his tasks for the day. I grabbed the thick ledger for the newly procured produce and thumbed through the pages. The ledger amounts blurred into one another as my addled brain attempted to make sense of the numbers, but they swirled and danced. I forced the information to steady as I wrote in the new total, but my delayed mind miscalculated the balance. Agitated, I crossed the incorrect number out with a thick line, piercing through the paper with my intensity. Gritting my teeth, I scrubbed a hand through my hair. My curse throbbed, burning like fire under my skin. Despite my fatigue, I needed the solace only nature could provide. I rose from my desk and stalked out of the study to spend the morning training alone.

CHAPTER 51

ARIANNA

I PUSHED THE DOOR open and tiptoed into the foyer. My footsteps slowed to avoid the clicking of my boots along the marble floors. However, my attempts to sneak to my room were futile as Mrs. Potter rounded the corner.

"My lady, welcome home. Are you dining in your quarters again, or will you join his lordship for supper?" Hope brimmed in Mrs. Potter's expression.

Every night, she asked if Silas and I would reconvene our meals together. She believed that returning to the status quo would lift the malaise that hung over the manor like a dark cloud.

"I'll have dinner in my suite. Alone," I said, my tone coming out firmer than I intended.

"Very well." Her face dropped, and the soft wrinkles around her mouth hardened as she pulled her lips into a tight line. My shoulders sagged from her sullen expression.

I ambled up the stairs, and she followed in tow. As we entered the hallway, two maids lingered near a closet, whispering. Upon seeing me, they halted their hushed discussion and bowed hasty curtsies. I gave a curt nod of acknowledgment while Mrs. Potter flicked a disapproving stare at the pair. They gathered the linens, then scurried away. I rolled my eyes. They need not stop their gossiping on my account. I had been aware of the staff warning one another about the scorned lady and the cantankerous Lord Belmont. They believed our estrangement was due to him spending the day cavorting with his mistress.

As if sensing my ruminations triggered by the two women, Mrs. Potter spoke. "Shall I have a bath drawn? Or would you prefer dinner first? I had Grey fetch the rye bread you enjoyed a week ago. I thought it would go well with tomato soup. Also, I dare say you haven't been sleeping either. I'll reach out to the herbalist for a remedy." She snapped her mouth shut.

I huffed a sigh, yet I couldn't explain to Mrs. Potter the real reason for Silas's and my estrangement. Despite our discussion in his uncle's suites and his apology two days prior, I still had not reconciled the lies with the man I cared for.

"Sorry, I didn't mean to mention her." Mrs. Potter wrung her hands.

"It's fine."

However, she must have felt the need to recompense, as she continued chattering. "I'll add extra lavender oil to your bath tonight, or I can have chamomile tea prepared as well. My lord has been drinking pots full this last week."

I glanced sidelong at her. She fiddled with the buttons on her sleeve, as if I wouldn't notice the subtle mention of Silas's habits. Yet she acted akin to a mother hen fussing over us. My heart warmed. Perhaps this was what it was like having a loving parent.

We reached my room, and I pivoted toward her. She waited for instructions.

"Yes, tomato soup and rye bread would be lovely first. Then a bath." I smiled.

"Of course, my lady." She gave a quick curtsy.

I grabbed the knob and froze. The fine hairs on the nape of my neck rose, and goose bumps trailed along my arms.

Arianna

My heart raced, and my body ached not with lust, but with deep sorrow. I gulped down the heaviness of the crushing emotion, but my knees buckled under its weight. I swayed and pushed my palms against the door, catching myself from falling.

Mrs. Potter grabbed my elbow, stabilizing me. "My lady? Are you unwell? You truly are exhausted. Perhaps you should..."

But her words faded into the background as the connection that lived between Silas and me surged, more powerful than before. Since the kiss, the sensation had been dampened. Yet now it blazed like a fire beneath my skin, urging me forward as it had that day in the woods. Whatever lingered between us snapped taut, akin to a cord being pulled, binding me to him.

Arianna...Arianna...Arianna, something whispered to me, and I whipped my head toward the beckoning.

"My lady, are you—"

"Shh."

I looked beyond her to the opposite side of the corridor. My feet moved of their own accord, drawn in a near trance as I strode down the hallway. I could sense Mrs. Potter's stare as I followed the magnetic pull to find Silas. The call intensified with every step, causing my heart to pound, and my curse thrummed in acknowledgment of his absence.

"Arianna." My name was a mournful plea reverberating in my mind as I reached the study. My hand lingered on the knob. I hesitated, but the bitter taste of sorrow drowned my uncertainty. A need to see Silas burned into my soul.

Unable to withstand the compulsion any longer, I entered. A low fire crackled in the hearth. I blinked, my vision adjusting to the dim space. The sun had set recently. Yet candles were not lit. Perhaps the maids feared entering and invoking his ire, given his recent irritable mood.

With each step forward, the grief thickened, as if it covered me in tar. I approached a sleeping Silas. His head lay on the desk, cocked to the side on top of sprawled ledgers. His forehead creased, and dark bags lined his closed eyes. He gasped for air, trapped in his nightmare, and the unbearable anguish surged through me.

I shook his broad shoulder, urging him out of the darkness that consumed him. "Silas, please wake up. Silas."

He jerked to sitting. Startled, I stumbled back, bumping into the corner of his desk. His gaze darted to me, then around the room.

"Did something happen?" He peered at me with a mix of panic and confusion.

"Were you having a nightmare?" I asked instead, not wanting to divulge the overwhelming pull that had led me here, then faded once he awoke.

He crossed his arms over his chest and leaned back. Exhaustion played on his face, highlighted by his thick stubble and rumpled state. I doubted he had left the study in a few days. Scattered ledgers covered the desk, his coat lay over the chair, and wrinkles lined his dress shirt.

"When was the last time you slept?" I asked.

"Obviously, I was asleep when you woke me." Agitation laced his tone.

I shook my head at his sullen mood and moved toward the sofa. I settled on the seat and peered at the disregarded tray on the side table. My lips pursed at the untouched food. I grazed my fingers along the teapot and frowned because it, too, had grown cold.

He lowered his attention to the ledgers, ignoring me. My jaw ticked. The tactic might have worked when I first arrived, but not anymore. I suspected a piece of him wanted me here. Why else had I felt drawn to him like a moth to the flame? Or perhaps my hope to bridge the gap between us kept me rooted to the spot. Sensing I would not leave without an answer, he let out an exasperated sigh.

"I ran out of sleeping draft, and I have little desire to chat with Brielle." His focus remained on the ledger as he wrote with tight, fluid motions.

"Hmm. I am out, too. And I haven't slept well either," I said, hoping that my admission would prompt him to unburden himself. Despite my agitation, I saw the toll the last week had taken on him and felt a pang of sympathy for this disheveled version of Silas.

"Worried about your sister and mother?" He lowered the pen and flicked a glance at me.

"Yes, I try to keep myself occupied during the day, but at night, I lie awake and question my choices. My heart aches to be by Naomi's side, and I worry your plan will fail, leaving me with little time to amend my mistakes. I've racked my brain for other solutions, but none have come. I hate waiting, but the alternative is less palatable. However, if there is no other choice, I will go back to her, even if it means my death." I slumped onto the sofa, grabbed the throw pillow, and clutched it.

He rose, walked toward the couch, and settled beside me. "It will work. I promise. Just be patient a little longer. Please."

My gaze trailed over his stubbled jaw, causing a swell of yearning. The shadow of a beard made him appear more rugged, and it suited him. Despite our issues, I longed to touch him. But I couldn't allow myself to give into my desires. Instead, I asked, "What were you dreaming about?"

He raked a hand through his hair and glanced sidelong at me. Seconds ticked by, and an internal battle seemed to wage within him. I gripped the pillow tighter as I waited for him to relent.

"I have had chronic nightmares since childhood. In one, I am lost in the darkness and cannot find my way out. The other is of the day my mother died and my curse awoke." He tilted his head back and stared at the ceiling, studying the pattern in the plaster.

"I remember little about that night, but I burned my house down. I rose from the haze, yet there was nothing left but scorched brick. And Beatrix. Gods, I thought I'd killed her and wished for death to take me. But when I heard her, I wept from fear and relief. Until I finally saw my father. I will never forget the disgust in his expression."

His Adam's apple bobbed, and he blinked rapidly, as if fighting off tears. He inhaled and clenched his fists. Agony radiated off him, and the dense sensation I had experienced through this unexplainable connection knotted in my stomach. Overcome by his grief, I grabbed his hand and held it, my thumb stroking his wrist.

"I'm a monster, Arianna. I am a monster no one could ever love," he choked out through gritted teeth. His words hit me, their full meaning heavy on my shoulders. Silas was arrogant, stubborn, and could not communicate directly to save his life, but he wasn't a beast. We sat silently for a long moment.

My breath hitched as his fingers wrapped around mine. His gaze shifted from the ceiling and locked on to me. They pleaded, as if willing me to confirm the lies he told himself.

"That is not true. Are you challenging to live with? Of course. But you are not a monster. Though we have had our difficulties, you saved me, and I am grateful for that. But beyond me, how many others have you helped? You take your responsibilities seriously as Lord Belmont, working tirelessly for those under your care. Are those the actions of a monster?"

His lips pressed into a thin line, and his brows knitted together. Seconds passed, and his expression softened. His eyes filled with appreciation and something else I couldn't identify.

My heart pounded as he took me in with an unspoken intensity no longer associated with nightmares, Naomi, or worries about the future. A passion pulsated through my body, binding me to the present.

He removed his hand from mine and stroked my cheek. His fingers gently caressed along my chin. My body blazed from the coursing curse, mixing with lust and power. However, the sting of rejection accompanied the longing. His touches confused me. The tenderness warmed me, yet he had regretted our last kiss. I was afraid to ask, to make myself vulnerable again. Instead, I stood, breaking the moment.

"Let's have dinner. I am sure you are starving." My glance darted to the untouched tray of food. He hesitated, but a hint of a grin pulled on his lips.

"Mrs. Potter will be relieved to see us dining together. I am exhausted from her pestering me." He rose.

We walked out of the study and back into our previous routine.

CHAPTER 52

Arianna

Layla's giggle flittered through the air. She beamed at Jamie as he spun in the well-fitted jacket he planned on wearing for Kesere. A lopsided grin pulled on Jamie's lips. Layla blushed, and a heated silence lingered between them. However, Jamie turned away, rubbing his hand on the nape of his neck.

I watched the oblivious couple from the comfort of the sofa. Goddess, when would they get a clue? Jamie, the bookstore owner, had been visiting with increased frequency over the past few weeks. At first, he had requested a new winter coat, then hemmed trousers, then buttons to be resewn onto the cuff of a dress shirt. He seemed to concoct any excuse possible to find himself in Layla's company. While Layla, a lover of books much like myself, visited the bookstore daily. I had suspected our shared passion for reading had been the sole reason for her increasing collection of novels. Yet, her continuous mentions of the adorable Jamie had made me realize that something was blossoming between them.

Suddenly, a brilliant idea came to me. I lowered the beaded material to the couch, then rose. I squared my shoulders, adorning myself with the mantle of Lady Belmont. Their giggling chatter faltered as I approached.

“Jamie, that coat fits you well. It is very flattering.” I gave a regal smile, but the comment had not been a falsity. Layla had worked painstakingly to tailor the cut to fit Jamie’s slender frame. The navy color she had chosen made his blue eyes look like a river on a summer’s day and highlighted his tan skin.

In response, Jamie smiled and fidgeted with the cuff, then glanced away. Despite his obvious regard for Layla, he seemed to need a push.

“I'm sure you will have a row of ladies lining up for you, unless you already have your heart set on someone?” I raised a haughty brow.

“I um...well...Layla...I hoped maybe you would consider accompanying me to the festival.” A blush crept across his cheeks.

Layla beamed. “I would be honored.”

"It's just about lunchtime. Why don't you take a much-needed break, Layla? Perhaps Jamie could escort you to Thomas's Teas?" I gave her a wink, and her eye crinkled with amusement.

Jamie nodded, removed the coat, and placed it on the cutting table. He offered Layla his arm, and the pair headed out the door.

I settled back on the sofa. Yet the brief levity departed as silence replaced the once lighthearted laughter that had anchored me to the present. In the quiet, my brain spun with the worries I had been avoiding. I sighed. My looming fears for Naomi overshadowed the fleeting joy at seeing Layla escorted by her potential paramour. I picked up the needle and thread but couldn't focus as my mind shifted to last night. After Silas and I reconvened our dinner, he told me he hadn't received word from the solicitor. Though he reassured me that all would be well, I had decided I needed to secure Naomi's safety no matter the cost. As I endured another sleepless night, I concocted a plan to depart for Krella the morning after Kesere if a solicitor couldn't be procured before then. Hopefully, I could persuade one of the visitors in town for the celebration to take me home. Until then, I would relish in these moments of a life I might have to leave. No longer willing to dwell on the uncertainty of the future, I switched my focus to the last gown to be completed for the upcoming festival only three days away.

The bell chimed overhead, halting my progress on the garment once again.

"Can I help—" My lips pulled into a tight line, catching my sentence, as I stared at Brielle.

She sauntered into the storefront, clad in a vibrant red day dress that hugged her curves. A catlike smile cut across her face.

"Ah, Lady Belmont. You are working on my gown for Kesere. How delightful. I hope it isn't causing you too much trouble." She walked toward me but kept her distance, lingering by my cutting table. She leaned forward and peeked at the material that would take hours of painstaking beading to complete.

"Why are you here?" I placed the black lace on the sofa. Crystals shimmered along the intricate swirling pattern. I scrunched my aching fingers and glared at her.

"This morning, Mrs. Potter came to my shop. First, she chastised me for my loose morals in creating strife between her lord and lady. But she assured me that my wiles couldn't tear your marriage apart. Then she demanded I provide a bevy of remedies for the manor. The gall of the woman." Brielle dug into a concealed pocket and withdrew two vials.

I recognized the deep purple sleeping draft, but I had never seen the green tonic before. My brow knit in confusion.

"She did mention you were exhausted. I assume it is from late nights of cavorting with Silas and that you might need a contraceptive." A smug smile crossed her lips.

She placed the drafts on my workstation. I glared, wishing I could throw a pincushion at the woman's head. She had a propensity for saying everything in the most outlandish ways. I waited in silence and expected her to leave, but she remained. She leaned against the table, the curve of her hip jutting out. Seconds passed, and I bristled under the expectant stare. Her smirk flattened into a line of displeasure.

"*For the love of the gods.*" Her sensual demeanor dropped, again showing me a hint of the Brielle behind her act.

I glared at her, having no desire to have a heart to heart with Silas's former mistress. Instead, I picked up the beadwork and began sewing the crystals into the pattern. She tapped her foot in impatience, and I wholly ignored her. She growled in frustration, and a whisper of a smirk tugged on the corner of my lips at her agitation.

"Must I do *everything*?" She ran a hand down her face. Her auburn hair swayed, and she shook her head. "Did he not tell you the truth? I swear, if Silas avoided yet another conversation, I am going to—"

"He told me everything. We are friends the same as before. Not that it is any of your concern." I put down the lace and stood. I strode toward her, ready to see her out or perhaps find that pincushion to chuck.

"Then why are you not together? The man loves you, and since you confronted me at my shop, I assumed you love him as well." She peered down at me.

"You really are cruel. He doesn't love me. Do you truly enjoy tormenting me? I didn't know he had a mistress when we wed."

"Sweet mercy. You can't be serious." She rolled her eyes. A second passed, and when I didn't answer, her expression turned impatient.

"First, Silas and I had a casual arrangement. Did it shock me that he married suddenly? Yes. However, when he told me about you, I knew you enamored him, and I had hoped that he had finally found his beloved. Since you arrived, I have tested his resolve and feelings for you. I am certain that he loves you, even if he doesn't realize it." She moved past me and settled on the sofa, making herself comfortable. Her red skirts billowed, and she leaned back, lounging in the seat.

I huffed a sigh. I would rather be stricken by lightning than share that tiny couch with her. Instead, I crossed my arms over my chest. "I have work to do."

"Pfft." She waved a dismissive hand at me. "It is my gown, and looking at the lace, I'm certain it doesn't need more beadwork, so consider yourself free for the afternoon."

"Excellent. I'll head home then," I said.

"Why are you making this so difficult? Do you think I enjoy these little chats with my ex-paramour's wife? But I had to confirm that you and Silas had finally pieced everything together. Yet blockhead Silas couldn't navigate through his emotions even if I provided a map."

A chuckle escaped me at the ridiculous imagery. I clamped my mouth shut, unwilling to let her see that she had correctly assessed Silas. I cleared my throat, and a long silence passed between us. She sighed, slumping her shoulders.

"You know, I once loved a cursed woman. Wren. That's what lead me here to Presspin—our ill-fated ardor for one another." She paused and lowered her gaze to the lace. She picked it up and ran it through her finger.

"Nothing compares to being loved by a cursed when you are their mate. The all-encompassing emotions are undeniable. However, I'm not here to talk about my lost soulmate, but yours." Her tone softened, and I gaped at her.

A heartbeat passed, and the vulnerability vanished, replaced with a forced smirk. I clutched my arms tighter around myself, waiting with bated breath for her to continue.

"The curse you bear is a unique entity. It lives in a symbiotic relationship with you, its host. It can heighten your senses, intensify your strength, and provide you with a devastating power. It also heightens your emotions and has the innate ability to identify your soulmate. That is how Wren found me. She said that the curse compelled her to be by my side." A forlorn expression crossed her face, and a twinge of pity plucked at my heartstrings.

"On the rarest of occasion, two cursed are soulmates. There are legends of their immense combined power. They are formidable, with the ability to access one another's energy, sense the other's presence, and feel each other's emotions. The curses also call out to one another, beckoning them to consummate and accept the bond to use the full breadth of the power between them. This is why the Aralians keep you bound in your homes and sanction marriages to ordinary people. To prevent the possibility of two cursed soulmates finding one another. Even the suppression spells could wane under the shared well between a curse-bound pair. I'm certain that this is what has occurred between you and Silas." She flicked a glance at me.

"Why should I believe you?" I asked, yet my body trembled and my heart raced.

"I don't relish in sharing my past with a woman who despises me. Nor do I have a reason to lie to you. I want Silas to be happy because he saved me, too. And I owe him my life. I hoped that the two of you would have stumbled upon this yourselves. As always, Silas needs a bit of a push." She stood and smoothed her dress.

I struggled to accept her words as fact. Yet, given her recount of our situation and the lack of Aralian texts, I had little to corroborate her story. However, my curse whispered, acknowledging the truth. *Soulmate.*

"Does he know?" I asked. My hands shook at the knowledge, fearful of Silas keeping another secret from me.

"No, I wouldn't dare tell him. I've never broached the depth of my relationship with Wren to him. Based on his confusion about his reaction to you, I doubt his uncle ever divulged this facet of the curse. I've wondered recently if Oliver didn't speak of the connection he felt toward Ophelia because she left."

Brielle grimaced. "To be without your mate is a gruesome, hollow fate. I suspect Oliver thought he was protecting Silas. Hiding the truth to shield him. Lies as protection must be a familial trait."

She rose and sauntered forward. "It's best I be off and allow you some time to think."

She reached for the contraceptive tonic, but I stopped her and grabbed both vials.

She smirked. "A swig every morning before breakfast. I will add the remedy to your monthly inventory. Good day, my lady." She flourished a ridiculous curtsy and winked.

I clutched the tonics as she exited. My mind swam, dizzy from all the information. I scrambled to the couch. My heart pounded. How would I tell Silas that we were destined? And how would I leave him if his plan to help Naomi failed?

CHAPTER 53

Silas

I lowered my pen, finally satisfied with the reserves. Vincent had procured additional produce from farms on the southern border of Presspin, near Agnes and Peter's inn, to fill the gaping holes in the cellars. I leaned back in the chair. With the food preserved and stored, my people would survive through the cold season. Sunlight filtered through the study window, and the fireplace crackled with a warm glow. Winter would settle upon our town, and snow would blanket Presspin. A thought flashed through my mind—Arianna enjoying her first snowfall, wrapped in thick wool, with rosy cheeks from the crisp wind. I smiled, relishing the daydream.

"My lord," Grey called out as he peeked in from the doorway.

Pulled from my musings, I gestured for him to enter. He strode forward with a crooked smile spread across his face.

"My lord, this just arrived from Krella. I ran as fast as I could," Grey said with pride. Over the past few days the boy had been running frequently to town to check the post. He dashed toward the desk and handed me the letter. Youthful energy emitted from him as he waited for further instructions.

I recognized Duncan's familiar handwriting. Thank the gods. Had I not received word from him, I would have trekked to Daviel myself to settle the matter. However, I didn't want to draw attention by connecting myself to the Park family. Thankfully, Duncan would provide aid.

"Well done. There are treats in the kitchen. The staff prepared them for Kesere. Go and enjoy one of your choosing." I waved my hand, dismissing Grey.

His smile intensified. He bobbed a final bow and scurried off to the kitchens. Mrs. Potter would likely scold me for sending the boy for dessert before supper, but he had done well and deserved a reward. Without hesitation, I ripped the seal and read the letter.

Silas,
I have arranged for a solicitor to be in Presspin at week's end to assist you. He will handle your dealings with discretion and will send word when he has arrived. I am confident he can help with the situation.
Sincerely,
Duncan

Relief washed over me, and the tension I had been holding left my shoulders. The obstacles I'd worried about were fading into the distance, and with the Parks cared for, we could finally live our life in peace. *Our life.* I paused over the words. We had settled back into our previous routine, but something new blossomed in these moments, a tenderness toward her. I smiled, and an intensity swirled within me as I thought of Arianna.

I shoved the letter into my pocket, then strode out of the study, searching for her. With Kesere two days away, Arianna had opted to remain at home to assist Mrs. Potter. As I walked down the hallway, maids curtsied with bright smiles. The smell of apple cider and cake drifted from the kitchens, while the staff chattered excitedly. For the first time since my uncle had died, the manor felt alive. I felt alive.

My body propelled me forward, that magnetic pull guiding me toward Arianna. I no longer resisted this thread connecting us. Instead, I basked in the subtle warmth. I paused at the open doorway of the sitting room and lingered. A botanical aroma wafted from the line of floral arrangements on the table between the sofas. Arianna sat on a cream-colored sette, clutching a teacup. She beamed at an animated Mrs. Potter, who, surprisingly, lounged on the taupe fainting couch, describing the time Beatrix and I were caught in a rainstorm and came back drenched from splashing in mud puddles. I leaned against the doorframe and absorbed the moment. The manor no longer bore the hollow ache of loneliness, and it was all because of Arianna's presence. As Mrs. Potter finished her tale, I coughed, grabbing the attention of both women.

"My lord!" Mrs. Potter bolted from her relaxed position to standing, then curtsied. She flushed at being caught lounging and taking tea.

"I'm glad to see you resting, Mrs. Potter. You've been working too hard keeping this house together." I smirked, and the flustered housekeeper's eyes widened like saucers. "However, I need some time alone with Lady Belmont."

Arianna glanced at me but remained seated, sipping her tea. Despite our renewed friendship, she had seemed tense this morning during our breathwork. Even now, she clutched her cup and studied the flowers with fascination.

Mrs. Potter flicked a glance between us. She beamed and curtsied, then scurried off. The door closed behind her, leaving us alone so I could share the excellent news and hopefully dissipate the last of these troublesome issues.

I approached and settled on the sofa beside Arianna. She shifted, providing me more room on the narrow seat. My shoulder brushed her, yet she continued focusing on the arrangements. Her nose wrinkled from her intense consternation. I withheld a chuckle at the adorable expression and studied the curve of her face. As if sensing my intent stare, she turned her gaze to me, her pupils dilating. I inched closer. For a second, I fell under her hypnotic spell, relishing the connection instead of fighting it. However, we had matters to discuss. I cleared my throat and shifted my attention to the table.

"You should pick these. The prescar flowers. They are vibrant and full of life. They remind me of you—blossoming in even the most difficult of experiences. Also, the color matches your eyes." I stroked the soft petal. She sighed beside me, her tension loosening.

"Silas, I—"

I held up a hand, halting her. I needed to get this interaction back on track before I fell under her spell again.

"I have something for you, and it couldn't wait until dinner." I removed the correspondence from my pocket. My fingers brushed hers as I handed her the paper. For a heartbeat, her gaze locked on mine, filled with an unspoken apprehension. Then it flicked to the letter. She opened the note and scanned it.

"Thank goodness. Now I won't have to depart from Presspin." Her lips closed shut, and she snapped her attention to her tea.

My softened features hardened, and I stared at her profile, dumbfounded. "You were going to leave?" The words burned like acid, but she didn't disagree.

A sinking feeling akin to being pulled underwater overwhelmed me. I placed my fingers on her chin, turning her head to me. "Arianna, look at me."

She huffed a sigh and pivoted, her knee knocking into mine. I released my hold and clenched my hands into fists as betrayal dug into my gut.

"It's not what you think. I needed a plan to make sure Naomi would be safe if you failed. I couldn't risk her suffering on my behalf." Her features softened, her expression pleading with me to understand.

I pursed my lips, a bitterness lacing my tongue. She was just like everyone else. No one ever remained. Gods, I had been a fool to believe she could be different. "I would have found another way. I would have gone to Daviel myself if I had to in order to keep you safe."

Her expression dropped. "I didn't know."

I rose, but she grabbed my hand, her fingers interlacing with mine. My pulse skittered as the warmth of her palm leached into my skin. A tentative emotion filled me, pleading for me to remain. It loosened the knot forming in my gut, as if a warm energy coursed into me, unfurling the anxiety that came with the thought of Arianna abandoning me. The sensation anchored me to the spot, reassuring me.

"Silas, stay." She squeezed my hand, but my focus remained on the exit. "Please sit down."

Reluctantly, I sank onto the sofa next to her. I lounged back, and she released her hold. I focused on the prescar flowers—the ones that reminded me so much of the woman beside me.

"I'm relieved that Naomi will be safe and that I can remain here with you. Perhaps it is best that we start being honest with one another to avoid these misunderstandings. From now on, we will navigate problems together," she said.

Her statement softened me. Perhaps I had overreacted. Resigned, I nodded in agreement. "No more secrets."

"There is something else I need to tell you, but I haven't found a way." She picked up her tea and took a sip. Her knuckles blanched white, and fear coursed through me. Gods, what other secrets could she be harboring, aside from an intention of running headlong into danger if I couldn't save her sister? I gulped.

"This is challenging, but you deserve to know the truth about our curses and what is happening between us. Brielle came to me yesterday with some tonic." A blush crawled along her cheeks, and she bit her lower lip. I stifled a groan at the gesture.

She lowered the teacup to the table, and I thrummed my fingers on my thigh in impatience.

"She said that the curse has a facet beyond the power that courses through our veins. It also heightens our senses and our emotions, and it has the innate ability to identify one's soulmate." Her eyes searched mine. Paralyzed, my brain slowly unfurled the words and hitched on their meaning.

"Soulmates? I think Brielle, once again in her flair for the dramatic, has stirred the pot. That is fairy-tale nonsense my sister might read in her romance novels." I rose, uncomfortable as a sense of awareness prickled beneath my crumbling mental reserves and my pulse surged.

I strode to the door, yet she grabbed my hand, halting me. I should have pulled away. Instead, I pivoted toward her. She slowed her breathing, similar to when we trained. Seconds passed, and my heart raced. A flicker of awareness crawled over me, caused by an invisible featherlight touch.

Silas...

My name filled my ears, but her lips remained still. My temperature rose as she stared at me, urging me to understand, and my curse prodded me forward to capitulate to these desires, to entwine myself with her in every way possible.

Silas...

My name pierced my soul the same way as it had that day in the woods when Arianna had unwittingly entangled her curse with mine.

I shook my head. "This is impossible. I would have known. My uncle would have told me. I can't. We can't. I don't have the capacity to love."

Yet her eyes bored into mine. The storm that often roiled within them beckoned me forward. Her brow creased, and a pang of sorrow cut through me. That was not my own. My lip trembled at the anguish I had caused her. I lifted my hand to her face, and she rested her cheek against it, melting under my touch.

"Arianna, I—"

"My lady—oh!"

I withdrew from Arianna and pivoted to Mrs. Potter, who was gaping at the doorway.

"I'm so sorry to interrupt, but the florist is here waiting for our decision." She wrung her hands and peered down at them.

"It's fine. I'll leave you and Lady Belmont to your important matters." I strode past the women and out the door. A well of emotions rose, clouding my mind with questions. Yet something tugged within my soul, a truth that I attempted to ignore.

CHAPTER 54

SILAS

ARIANNA PEERED OUT THE carriage window, but I couldn't focus as we bobbed down the path to the Kesere festival. Instead, my gaze trailed along the curve of her bare neck. And despite my attempts at restraint, it drifted farther to the plunging cut of her gown. The fabric covered her arms, yet her shoulders jutted out in a modern style. A pool of shimmering sky-blue satin flowed out from the cinched waist. She regarded me, her crystal eyes settling on me with a mix of uncertainty and hope. As she batted her long eyelashes, her bow-shaped lips curved into a tentative smile.

For the first time in two days, I wished we had discussed this preposterous idea of *soulmates*. However, I had endured endless visits to the townspeople to ensure that each family was prepared for the winter. Each night, I fell into bed, exhausted. Yet Arianna's voice calling my name in a wordless plea haunted me. The phenomenon must have an explanation.

"Silas."

I shook myself out of my haze and peered out the window, not acknowledging that she had caught me staring at her. She sighed.

"We haven't had a chance to discuss...what I told you. However, for tonight, can we pretend, for the sake of the town, of course, that we are a happy couple? Everyone will expect a jovial Lord and Lady Belmont. Let's not ruin this evening for them by acting aloof to one another." She fiddled with her ring as she waited for my answer.

I couldn't help myself as I reached out and halted her nervous fidgeting. "Yes, for our people, we will play the role expected of us." My thumb stroked against her sensitive skin and heat washed over me, as warm as a summer's day, despite the chilly late autumn night. My pulse surged, and I fought the urge to pull her into my embrace and ravish her. Her breath hitched, as if she sensed my thoughts.

Silas

My name echoed like a plea from her soul. I slowly exhaled, dislodging myself from her spell. To my relief, the conveyance halted. Seconds later, the door opened, and a footman assisted her out of the carriage, his gloved digits wrapping around hers as she stepped out. A pang of jealousy cut within me, and I flicked a withering glare at the servant, who shrank. I exited and grasped her hand in mine. She peered down at our interlaced fingers, then at my face.

"We have a part to play," I said. However, in the depths of my soul, I knew I lied to her as much as to myself.

When we entered the town square, it shone with thousands of candles. The scent of mulled cider and spiced wines filled the air, mixing with roasted meats on spits. Prescar wild-flowers adorned archways and buildings, as if the wilderness of Presspin had taken root for one night. Villagers huddled around tables lined with a copious variety of dishes. Their plates brimmed with breads, vegetables, wild game, and sweet treats. Children weaved about the adults with raucous laughter, playing games of tag, uncaring about their formal attire. Men sipped the ale, seated at the benches on the outskirts. The center remained empty, serving as a space for dancing once the celebration began.

As I led Arianna forward, the townspeople, all dressed in their finery, greeted us with bright smiles. At my side, Arianna flashed a brilliant grin at each person, addressing them by their names. I nodded, unable to speak. I was too entranced by her to form intelligible sentences. Instead, I gave nods of acknowledgment. Yet none seemed to notice my restrained demeanor. No, they were too engrossed in Arianna. She glowed beside the steel fire pits that kept the space warm despite the icy chill of an approaching storm. As we meandered through the throng, she flicked a glance and smiled. My mouth dried under her full attention. I clutched her hand tighter, and a wave of sweet emotions enveloped me, causing my heart to pound.

"My lord," Mrs. Potter called out as she approached. She wasn't in her usual livery, but in a dark green dress, which made her appear years younger than sixty. She bobbed a quick curtsy, but I shook my head in reproach. Tonight, she was not my housekeeper, but a member of our town, here to partake in the festivities freely.

"My lord, I must steal my lady. She has prepared a surprise for the servants' children, and they are waiting a bit too eagerly for her," Mrs. Potter said.

"A surprise, you say?" I raised an eyebrow and peered at Arianna. Her smile widened. She released my hand, then followed Mrs. Potter.

I flexed my fingers, missing her touch. Despite myself, I watched on with fascination. A mound of wrapped packages covered the table, and the servants' offspring circled around in awed wonder as Arianna began passing them out. The children squealed in delight as they unwrapped dolls, books, balls, and paint sets. For a moment, I melted under her warmth. Gods, when had she become this woman? She, at some point, had turned from the mousy miss into Lady Belmont, someone I admired more than I cared to admit.

"She really is lovely this evening," Brielle crooned beside me, but my gaze never left Arianna. Her face was alight with joy while Grey showed her the leather ball he had unwrapped. But irritation overwhelmed the sweetness of this moment as I glanced sidelong at Brielle, displeasure crossing my expression.

"We need to talk about this foolish nonsense you put in Arianna's mind." Even as the words tumbled from me, they felt wrong.

"Nonsense?" She snorted.

A group of women passed by, tittering and flicking a glance at us. Their gossiping whispers were unmistakable as they giggled about the lord and his mistress. I gritted my teeth in frustration. We couldn't have a private discussion here.

I gestured for her to follow. We walked in silence toward the outskirts of the festivities until the temperature plummeted from the lack of the blazing fires. The chatter drifted away as we stood in the shadows of an alley.

Brielle crossed her arms over the black lace dress she wore. "Let's be quick about it. I'm going to freeze to death."

"Why did you fill Arianna's head with such drivel as soulmates? It's preposterous," I said.

"Of course you would think it's ridiculous. Why else would I tell her first?" she asked.

I leaned against the cold stone building and feebly attempted to sort through my muddle of contradicting thoughts. Nothing made sense.

"Just stop inserting yourself where you don't belong. Arianna isn't..." The sentence halted on my tongue, too heavy to speak. A long silence passed between us.

"Exactly, Silas. You can't even force the words out. Deny it all you want." Her teeth chattered, and she moved to return to the celebration.

"*Wait.* This is ridiculous. My uncle would have divulged this facet of our curse to me." The thought had plagued me for the past few days, and in the pit of my stomach, I suspected a truth I dare not speak aloud.

Brielle halted. Her shoulders slumped with an exasperated sigh. "Are you certain he would have told you after Ophelia left him? Trust me, a life without your mate is not something anyone should endure. Perhaps he hoped to shield you from a similar fate." She didn't wait for my acknowledgment as she walked back to the festivities.

My mind swam with possibilities. He had never divulged why Ophelia abandoned us. Could he have kept this from me? I closed my eyes, and his sorrowful pleas for Ophelia echoed in my soul as he slipped away to the great beyond. Yet thoughts of Ophelia triggered another memory of bedtime stories of destiny and love. Nighttime tales that Beatrix swooned over and I once believed were hogwash.

I scrubbed a hand over my face, but I couldn't remain here much longer without drawing notice to my absence. Confused even more than before, I walked toward the festivities. I hovered on the outskirts, searching for Arianna. She chatted with Layla and Jamie. Her features lit with amusement as Jamie spoke. My heart warmed at the expression. Something within me clawed against the flattering mental fortitude that I held against Arianna's allure. I pushed down the swell of emotions that threatened to consume me.

Minutes passed as I watched with rapt attention, unable to move to her side or walk away. I flinched as Brielle sidled beside me once again. A smirk replaced that flicker of vulnerability from only moments ago.

"Maybe you are right, Silas. Perhaps I am mistaken about this silly fairy-tale nonsense. Don't worry, I won't push the issue any further, and I have a feeling she won't either."

My muscles tensed as a group of young men sauntered up to Arianna and Layla. They smiled at Arianna with flirtatious grins. My jaw ticked as they circled her. Her warmth drew them in like moths to a flame. She giggled, unaware of their admiration. I clenched my hands into fists.

"You won't have to worry after all. I am certain one of those strapping men would be happy to take her," Brielle said with amusement lacing her tone.

My curse boiled at the thought of someone else touching what was mine. I whipped my head to Brielle and scowled. "I don't think a man here would dare touch my wife."

The cluster of men postured, hoping to snag Arianna's attention for the opening set. Everyone knew of my hatred of dancing, so it shouldn't surprise me that they would toss their caps to secure the honor. However, she seemed delighted, and I fought every inclination to claim her for the night.

"She is quite popular. I mean, in that dress, maybe I'll take her for a spin." A seductive tone entered Brielle's voice.

I clenched my jaw hard enough that I feared I might break a tooth. My fingernails dug into my palms, anchoring my billowing curse to remain locked tight under my control. However, the idea of Arianna entangled with anyone nearly sent me into a blinding rage.

"Oh, don't pout, Silas. Why would you care if someone else wanted her? If you continue to deny your feelings, then she is your wife in name alone. Right?" Brielle winked, then sauntered into the crowd, searching for a partner for when the dancing commenced.

I forced myself to steady, taking long, slow breaths until my swelling curse simmered under my skin. I stepped forward to claim Arianna for the inaugural dance. However, Mateo, the turnip farmer's son, bowed to her in a flourish. She took his hand, and he escorted her to the center of the square. Before I could make a scene, the fiddler struck a merry tune, and the country jig began. I glared daggers at the boy, who grinned, intoxicated by Arianna's vibrant nature. He guided her through the steps, and her cheeks were rosy with delight. The beat quickened, signaling an exchange of partners. Mateo released her to David, the butcher, but relief eluded me. His grasp lingered too low on the small of her back. She giggled as he spoke to her. I tapped my foot impatiently, ready for the set to be over. Yet the music played on. The tempo changed again, and David whirled her into a stranger's arms. My brow wrinkled at the man adorned in a deep green coat with gold buttons and thread. His wealth rolled off him. He must have been a distant relation of one of the townspeople. Even I didn't know all their kin.

Every muscle within my body tightened, like a taut bowstring ready to snap. A rakish smirk crossed his lips. His intentions were not that of a townsperson dancing with their lady. No, this man's intent was abundantly clear. Their interaction shifted from lighthearted to an unsettling intensity. I ground my teeth as he whispered and a blush colored her cheeks. I found myself unwilling to endure this torture any longer.

Tittering chatter from onlookers filled my ears as I pushed through the crowd, uncaring that the set had not concluded. I entered the dance space, nearly bumping into a swaying young couple. The fiddler plucked a shrieking cord, halting the music abruptly. A murmur of whispers replaced the once chipper tune, and I sensed the gawking stares. I didn't care. Instead, I focused on Arianna and the stranger.

The stranger bowed and placed a kiss on her hand. His fingers lingered on her skin, causing my blood to boil. I closed the distance in three quick strides. With his back to me, I gripped the man's shoulder. Arianna gaped at my feral state.

I tightened my grip. "That is my wife."

Menace flowed from me toward this rapscallion, and my curse whispered to dispatch him. Arianna was mine. Her lips pursed with displeasure, her eyes pleading with me to calm down. I ignored her. My frustration from weeks of these unsettled feelings focused on this individual alone. Seconds passed, and I didn't release him, nor did he wither under the pressure of my grasp. Instead, he peeked over his shoulder with a cavalier smirk.

"Silas," Arianna hissed, and I released the man.

The stranger tipped his head in acknowledgment to Arianna, then strode past her, disappearing into the throng.

"Have you lost your wits?" Arianna's biting comment snapped me out of my jealousy-laden trance. Yet my shoulders remained tense. The staring villagers whispered amongst themselves.

"Let's continue the merriment with a waltz." Arianna smoothed her composure, as if nothing of note had just occurred.

The fiddler twanged a slow tune, and the dancers paired off. I pressed Arianna's body against mine, and we whirled to the beat of the music. An overwhelming hunger consumed me. She bit her lower lip, and desire pulsated, reverberating along the tether between us. A hint of a blush flushed upon her cheeks, and a ragged breath pushed through those beautiful lips of hers.

I gulped, that beckoning call to devour her a whisper in my soul, and a heady sensation buzzed within me as her curse called for me to relinquish the wobbling mental fortress I hid behind as pieces fell, brick by brick. But I tried in futility to settle my thoughts, which still beat with primal jealousy. We whirled with the rhythm of the tune, locked in each other's gaze. With each passing second, the world fluttered into a distant memory. The air practically crackled with energy consuming me from the sheer intensity of the bond.

Her soft, sweet lavender scent drifted to me. Instinctually, I tightened my hold. My heartbeat quickened, and I lost myself to the humming desire I had ignored for too long. Gods, she was beautiful. My curse ached for me to capitulate to the carnality it craved, and I felt akin to a starving man ready to devour a feast before me. A sigh left her lips as they parted, and it took all my resolve to not crash my mouth upon hers.

Thankfully, the tune ended, and our bodies stopped swaying. The dancers switched partners, but I would not relinquish Arianna to anyone else. No, she was mine. Unable to control myself any longer, I lowered my head to her ear. "Follow me."

CHAPTER 55

ARIANNA

VILLAGERS GAWKED AS AN unaccustomedly embolden Lord Belmont cut through the crowd, pulling me in tow. We weaved through the tables where people ate and drank. Some raised their glasses to us in salute as we passed. We strode by a group of men who cheered with boisterous merriment as if this feral version of Silas amused them. However, Silas paid them no heed. An untamed passion rolled off him, thick like honey that I could practically taste.

I had stayed away from him these past few days since revealing Brielle's suspicions, allowing us each time to sort through what this revelation meant for us. I spent many hours delving within myself, searching for answers. Yet the phenomenon that occurred between us was undeniable, and this facet of our blight served as the most likely explanation. Perhaps we should have discussed our bond prior to this evening. However, I desperately wanted a night of pretending that we were the in-love couple the town expected. My gaze trailed over his black-clad form, and my mouth watered at the sight of him. Being near him lit a fire within my belly, muddling my logic.

The music of the beautiful festival drifted away as he guided me into a darkened alleyway illuminated by soft lamplight that cast us in half shadows. He turned toward me, his gold-flecked eyes barely visible. He let out a shaky exhale, his shoulders rising and falling in quick succession.

"Silas, I—"

His mouth crashed upon mine with a hunger so fierce my knees buckled. He wrapped me in his embrace, pinning me against him. His tongue traced the seam of my lips, coaxing me to open for him. The heady feeling thrummed, fueled by my curse's pleadings for the connection it had craved since our wedding night. His grip tightened, and I half expected him to take me against the side of this building and satiate both our needs. However, he ended the moment with a whisper of a kiss.

His fingers skimmed along my jawbone. "You are driving me to madness tonight in that dress, dancing with those men. Then I nearly lost my mind when that stranger kissed your hand and flirted with you. Gods, I'm tired of fighting this."

"Silas, we need to—"

He hungrily pressed his mouth upon mine again, sealing my protest in my throat. His hands roved over my breasts and trailed down to my hips, locking me in place. He took a heavy step forward, pinning me between him and the stone wall. My mouth opened, and his tongue entered with greedy strokes. A mewl of pleasure escaped me. I blazed under the fervent kisses trailing down the plunging neckline of my gown, and my resolve to discuss our bond swam.

"Silas," I sputtered through breathy sighs.

But he didn't relent. Instead, his tongue slipped to the edge of the gown's neckline, inching closer to my décolletage. His fingers traced over the hem, then slipped it farther down, exposing the pebbled nipple. Goose bumps rose along my flesh, caused by a mix of lust and the chilly night air. His lips found their target, drawing the apex between them. He nipped against my taut peak. Heat pooled in my core, and I pushed my hips against him. My breath hitched as the evidence of his arousal pressed against me. I threw my head back, arching to give him better access to my half-exposed chest.

He continued his ministrations, lavishing kisses from the tip of my breast to the hollow of my neck, then nipped on my earlobe. A moan of pent-up frustration left me.

His hot breath whooshed as he growled, "I know what you want."

My languid, melting body turned rigid, because I wanted more than a romp to satiate this hunger. My passions waned as a thought snaked through my lust-addled brain. After tonight, would he avoid me or simply act as if we hadn't burned with ardor? Despite destiny thrusting us together, Silas had fought the call tooth and nail. Even if fate guided us to each other, I needed him to desire me beyond this thrumming bond that drove us into wantonness. I wouldn't tolerate his vacillating disposition any longer, and the realization strengthened my resolve.

"Silas!"

As if drawn out of a trance, he snapped out of whatever spell he was under. He stepped back a hair. His shoulders rose and fell with his quick, shaky breaths, and an unquenchable desire filled his eyes. I straightened my gown, covering myself. Yet I squirmed under his hungry gaze, centering myself, and asked in a firm voice, "Who am I to you?"

His face dropped, and confusion replaced yearning. He inched back, breaking the entrancement of his carnal haze. His panting mixed with distant music, punctuating that we had almost entangled only blocks away from the public. I inhaled through the agonizing seconds, pleading that he would answer me, but he did not. Lust gave way to a boiling frustration.

"I will not play this game with you." I pressed my hands to his chest, pushing him away, creating distance between us. Goose bumps rose on my skin from the absence of his warmth against me. Yet he remained wordless. His heart pounded under my palms, but I was tired of misunderstandings and secrets. I needed clarification before I could move forward. "Tonight, we are lovers. Then what about tomorrow? Friends, apprentices, companions, what?"

His stare shifted to the darkness of the alley, as if the answers to his feelings lay there. I withdrew my hands and crossed my arms over my chest. A shiver cut through me, as if the fire within me had been doused.

"I cannot continue ignoring what beats between us. Soulmates or not, I love you, you fool." I clamped my mouth shut, the words overwhelming me. My heart fluttered with a truth I couldn't deny. When had I fallen for this man? In the quiet seconds, I suspected it had started the moment he saved me from stumbling into the muck in Krella. Yet he gaped at me like a fish out of water.

Strengthened by my words, I stood straight and squared my shoulders. "I'm not the same woman who married you, unsure of whether I deserved a life beyond the mask, beyond the scraps of affection given by those around me. I deserve to be loved wholly, and I will settle for no less."

He snapped his mouth shut, and his softened features hardened with an undistinguishable emotion. Yet he remained speechless. However, I couldn't abide by his taciturn behavior. He either loved me or he didn't.

A hollow ache pierced through me as his jaw tightened and he withdrew. His wordless answer was enough. Energy crackled beneath my skin, drunk on Silas's touch. Yet I leashed my building frustration with a steadying breath and pushed past him. I stormed off, unwilling to linger here with the man who couldn't verbalize his feelings.

Silas

Arianna stomped off, leaving me bewildered. One moment, I had held her, and the next, I was alone, encompassed by the dark night. The connection panged within me, as if my soul was a thread wrapped around her delicate finger. She left me breathless, unable to speak when she uttered the words *I love you*. For some reason, she cared for me, despite my aloofness, my rigidity, and my past. She loved me. Shocked, I had frozen, staring at the beautiful woman before me until she had run away as I puzzled over my swirling emotions.

I heaved a shaky sigh and leaned against the icy stone wall, willing the chill to soak into me and soothe this ardor boiling in my blood. Moments passed as I tempered my burning desire, a sight which would have been far too obvious had I chased after Arianna through the town square like a green boy appearing a bit too eager.

Music amplified, pulling me from my thoughts. I had no desire to return to the festivities and was in no mood for Brielle's teasing antics or to don the role of Lord Belmont. Instead, I left the alley and strode toward the bay of carriages, only to find that mine was gone. A mirthless chuckle escaped me at the long, cold walk ahead of me.

I trudged up the path until the music from the festival faded. In the silence, Arianna filled my mind. Her determined expression when we played chess, the sighs of pleasure when she enjoyed her meal, or how she squared her shoulders when pulling upon her courage. I admired how she pushed herself past her limits in training and in life. She ingratiated herself to the entire town, not for clout, but because she cared. It hadn't eluded my notice that I wanted nothing more than to see her the second I awoke, dressing and rushing out the door in haste for a glimpse of the coy smile that brushed her beautiful lips. I had hoarded these moments like precious gems, milling through each one. Unknowingly, she had brightened my once dull existence.

My heart pounded with an intensity that shattered the last fragments of my resolve. I froze mid-step, and a truth hit me like a blow to the gut, nearly bowling me over. Gods, I loved Arianna.

It was a fact that could no longer remain hidden, no matter how much I tried. She had captured my heart without me even realizing it. Soulmate our not, my love for her had taken root long ago. I had just been too stubborn to see it.

I stared up the hill and sprinted home to Arianna, the woman I loved.

CHAPTER 56

Arianna

I leapt out of the carriage and ran to my suite. Silence lingered in the empty hallways, with the servants all enjoying the festivities in town. I entered my room, tugged at the buttons of my dress with little care, and shimmied out of it. The garment slipped off me into a pool of discarded fabric. Then I dressed in my nightgown and perched myself on the sofa, focusing my attention on the red embers in the hearth.

The night had been so hopeful. The evening I planned had come to fruition, and yet Silas's befuddlement dampened my mood. However, in those brief moments, I relished being embraced by the people of Presspin with open arms. There had been joy as the children laughed while opening the presents I had procured for them. Elation as I danced amongst the crowd. Desire as Silas kissed me in the alley. I felt alive, and that sense of otherness I once carried melted away.

I curled on the cushion, grabbed the soft cashmere blanket, and nestled into it for comfort. But my heart still thundered as

I closed my eyes, remembering the feel of Silas pressed against me. My body ached from the unsatiated hunger. To soothe myself, I pictured a brooding Silas trudging up the cobblestone path in the bitter darkness, left behind by his lady and carriage. I released a wry chuckle. However, an aching frustration replaced the levity. Silas desired me, but it hadn't been enough.

I sulked, uncertain of how to proceed in our relationship. But I was too exhausted to dwell on the future. I curled deeper into the chair like a cat and watched the embers diminish.

I stared at the smoldering logs for half an hour, contemplating forcing myself to bed. Then, suddenly, the hairs on the nape of my neck rose, but the usual gentle tug of Silas's presence surged akin to the opening of floodgates. My breath hitched, overwhelmed by the swelling emotions that were not my own. The sweet taste of affection coated my tongue, similar to the wine on our wedding night. Longing skimmed over my body, akin to feathers floating over my skin, sending a shiver to snake along my spine. In my throat, a tight knot of remorse settled there, so painful that unshed tears welled. I inhaled, yet my quarters smelled of Silas, of the Presspin woods on a crisp autumn morning.

"Silas," I moaned to myself as an aching ecstasy crawled over me, my curse drinking in the swell of lust emblazoning me.

A sweet song filled my soul, beckoning me, my name a reverent plea. *Arianna...Arianna...Arianna...*

"Silas." I trembled, and warmth pooled in my core, stoked by his phantom touch.

A tantalizing sensation crashed over me in rhythmic ebbs and flows. Energy coursed through me, as if it mixed in my blood, heating my yearning to a boiling point. Silas's curse beckoned me like a siren's song. In my soul, I knew it was to complete the binding our curses had desperately desired for so long.

I forced myself to stand as the sensations surged through me. His whispers grew to booming bellows, and the power between us writhed through me. My legs shook as I walked to the door.

Arianna...Arianna...Arianna...

I stepped into the hallway, transfixed by our connection. I hastened the few paces to his room, my trembling limbs barely holding me upright as pleasure coursed down my spine. A moan escaped me as I reached his quarters.

I flung the door open, panting from the exertion.

He sat in the middle of the floor near the fireplace, immersed in breathwork, unfazed by my lust. I drank him in but couldn't move, mesmerized, as his chest rose and fell.

"There you are." He opened his eyes and fixed them on me.

I shut the door and strode to him, my knees wobbling from the denotations of pleasure. He stood and stalked toward me with purpose, never dropping the taut line of connection between us.

My body hummed with anticipation as he grabbed my hands. He placed a gentle kiss on each. "Only I will kiss these. Do you understand?"

I nodded. He stroked my cheek, then kissed me possessively. His lips melded over mine with vigor. I moaned for more, but he pulled away.

"Only I will taste of your lips, delight in your body, and hold your heart. For you already possess me wholly. You are mine, my mate, my destiny, and I love you."

I trembled against him, my pulse surging and blood rushing to my ears. He stroked the curls from my face, and his eyes blazed into me akin to molten amber. "Say you are mine, beloved."

My skin sizzled from his touch, and any resistance to him melted away. "I am yours. I have always been yours."

He lowered his mouth to my ear. His hot breath sent prickling shivers over my skin. "Good."

I throbbed with desire from nights of longing. He nuzzled down my throat, nipping at the hollow, and I pressed into him. I moaned as he kissed and licked my collarbone.

He lifted me up in one swift motion. Instinctively, I wrapped my legs around his waist, kissing him greedily, pulling his tongue deeper into my mouth. My head swam with ecstasy. I hit the soft surface of his bed, and I languished in being absorbed in his woodsy chamomile scent.

My core thrummed with liquid heat, and I pouted when he pulled away just long enough to remove his shirt. Yet delight filled me at the sight of him. Lean muscles worked along his form. His broad shoulders and chest were accentuated by toned arms.

He joined me in bed, then hovered above me. His mouth trailed down my collarbone to my breasts, which were covered by the cotton nightgown. He let out a grunt of frustration, then ripped the fabric, exposing my flesh to the night air. I gasped.

Before I could speak, he lowered his mouth to my nipple, biting the tip. My mind buzzed, and my skin flushed. I writhed beneath him, raking my fingers through his silky, wavy hair, securing him to this delicious spot as I arched into him, greedy for so much more.

He pulled the sensitive flesh into his mouth, sucking and stroking it with his tongue. My core ground against his hardened length. He paused as I rotated my hips in urgency, my need for release overwhelming me.

He stretched toward me and captured my mouth with his, tasting me. A groan escaped him as his fingers drifted down toward my sex. Heat pooled within me as he teased me, skating his thumb over my undergarment. A flush crossed over me. I inhaled, covered in his scent. My pelvis pushed against his digits greedily. He pulled away for a second, then shifted me to remove the tattered nightgown.

He returned. His mouth traveled to my neck, sucking and licking, causing exquisite delight. His lips skimmed down my breasts, to my stomach, then lingered upon my hips. With a grin, he removed my undergarment.

I lay bare and trembling from excitement before this intoxicating man. His gaze trailed over me, and gooseflesh prickled. He sank his head between my thighs. His hot breath tickled between my damp folds, and I squirmed.

"Be still for me, beloved." He grabbed my hips, pinning me to the bed. His thumbs traced soothing circles over my skin.

My breath hitched as he lowered his face, tracing gentle kisses along my inner thigh. My pulse skittered as his mouth inched closer to my aching core with slow, methodical licks. I gasped as his tongue swirled within my intimate folds; the sensation was intensified by the cascade of crackling energy within me as his curse interweaved with mine, like threads binding. My breathing turned ragged as his lips caressed the apex of my sex with pressured strokes.

"Silas."

He paused and smiled seductively before returning his mouth to the delicate folds with fervor. My heartbeat quickened, and a mewl of desire left me as he lapped the bundle of nerves. I bucked at the intense sensation, uncertain whether I could withstand this building pressure. I attempted to squirm away, but he held my thighs apart and feasted upon me like a starving man. A fire burned in me, and I nearly lost control of my curse at the intensity. The tension amplified as Silas slid two fingers inside my wet depths, pulsating with fluid strokes and curling into a delicious spot. My hips moved of their own volition, pulling his digits deeper into me. He sucked the apex of my sex, edging me closer toward release. My head buzzed. My muscles tensed. Heat washed over me as I tumbled over the edge of ecstasy as waves of euphoria and power coursed through me.

As I stilled, he lifted his head and smirked. He licked his lips as if he savored me like a rare delicacy. I panted, riding the high of the shuddering bliss racking through me. His face lit with mischief as he stood. Then he removed the remnants of his clothing, revealing his arousal. He moved to crawl over me, but I held up a hand, halting him.

"I want to touch you." I flushed at my wanton statement, despite Silas having just settled his mouth upon my most intimate flesh.

He slid into bed beside me, unclothed. Before I could think, a carnal desire overcame me as I pressed my lips against his neck and inhaled his woodsy scent. I trailed my tongue down a path to the jutting collarbone I had admired so often. He let out a guttural sound, driving me deeper into my frenzied passion. My fingers grazed over his chest, passing over the dusting of hair. I reached farther down the hard planes of his stomach and settled on his stiff erection. His breath hitched at my featherlight touch as my hand grazed over the sensitive flesh. I worked over his shaft with tantalizing touches and strokes. Uncertain of what I was doing, I allowed my curiosity to guide me, but my exploration was short-lived.

"Arianna," he growled out with desire. He rolled me onto my back, pinning me beneath him. His hungry gaze bored into me.

He spread my legs, then his fingers rubbed within my folds. I arched against him as the pleasure built again, desperate for the coupling that had occurred on our wedding night, for the fulfillment of my longing.

He hovered over me as he guided his thick erection into my depths. His length sank in without resistance, filling me to the hilt with his exquisite hardness. There was no brief pain, nor did he pause like on our first coupling. Instead, his strokes were swift and powerful, pushing into me repeatedly with an intensity that made my toes curl.

He undulated with each intense thrust, and tension coiled in my belly. I rocked my hips against him. I yearned for more. The building pressure swirled, our breaths ragged and needy as the scent of our sweat-ladened bodies filled the air.

"Silas, please," I moaned, so desperate for him in every way that it caused all care to leave me.

His full lips found mine in a fervent kiss, and his tongue slipped into my mouth. I mewled. The thrusts of his hardened length intensified to a breakneck pace, and my core throbbed with each quickened stroke. My hips bucked beneath him to match his manic rhythm, arching for deeper purchase. Tension coiled in me as I tried to crest over another orgasm.

He nipped at my ear. "Come for me again, beloved."

His hand snaked between us as he placed pressure against my sensitive nub. A jolt of molten heat coursed through me, and I shattered into a million pieces.

"Silas!" I threw back my head, arching against him as I drained every ounce of pleasure from the delicious friction.

He kissed me as he pulsated and pumped into me with a desperate need until his release came seconds later.

As we fell into the euphoria, the crackling sensation swirled and sang within me. The once tentative bond between us laid thick, like a braided cord that no one could tear asunder. On a sigh of joy, trembles racked my body as Silas rolled off me and pulled me into his embrace. His lips trailed along my hairline. "I love you, forever and always. This is my promise to you, my beloved, my wife, my mate."

CHAPTER 57

SILAS

ARIANNA LAY ON HER stomach, propping her chin on her hands while I dressed. Sunlight danced on her bare skin through the window, tempting me. However, I had work to complete, despite my beautiful wife, who had already kept me occupied throughout the night. I flicked a glance to the clock on the mantel. We had missed the breakfast hour long ago, yet no one had interrupted us. Luckily, the staff were behind schedule because of last evening's festivities.

"Come back to bed." She patted the empty mattress. Her shoulders slumped as she sulked.

"Still not satisfied?" I buttoned my shirt, but my gaze drifted over her naked body rumpled in my sheets. She bit her lip. Gods, I could spend a week entangled with her to make up for the nights we lost fighting our desire. However, we would have a lifetime of languishing in each other's bodies. I fastened the cuff links on my wrists, and she tilted her head with a flirtatious glance.

"Just eager for more." She gave a coy smile, but lust filled her eyes.

I approached her and leaned forward. My lips brushed hers in a gentle kiss while my hands cupped her delicate face. Yet she deepened the connection with fervor. I wrapped my arms around her. Perhaps work could wait for a day. But a knock echoed through the room. I groaned and withdrew, stepping away from the bed.

"Give me a moment," I called out.

Arianna's alluring countenance dropped as if she were about to be caught doing something quite mischievous. I smirked as the blush crawled up her cheeks. I grabbed my dressing robe and tossed it to her, and she slipped it on in haste. Then she smoothed her hair and folded her hands demurely. I nearly chuckled at her rigid posture as she lounged in my sheets, dressed in my clothing.

Before I could slip out of my quarters to attend to whatever matter awaited, the door clicked open. Mrs. Potter stepped in with her focus on a letter and not the scene before her. I held back a hearty chuckle as Arianna shrank into the mound of pillows, her cheeks flaming.

"My lord, we received a—" Mrs. Potter stopped mid-sentence as she lifted her gaze and finally registered Arianna tucked within my bed. Her mouth gaped open until I cleared my throat.

She stammered out, "My apologies, my lord. I was unaware you were...that my lady..."

"It is fine, Mrs. Potter," I said and resisted the urge to give her a wink. Gods, who was I this morning?

"Of course. I mean...well...when my lady wasn't in her room, I expected that she may have been with you in the woods. But gods above, why am I standing here like a fool? You should return to...your...activities." She blushed and began backing away, forgetting about why she had come to my quarters.

"Is that a letter for me?" I asked, my glance catching my name in a tight scroll on the paper she clutched.

"Yes, of course. Here you are." She pushed the correspondence into my hand and scurried off.

The door closed behind her, and I bellowed a laugh. "That reaction was better than when I placed that frog in her shoe."

"Silas!" Arianna pouted, then threw the covers over herself, mortified by the incident.

"I am sure Mrs. Potter is delighted to see us spending quality time together." I cleared the chuckle from my throat.

She emerged from the blanket, and her face lit with merriment at my response. "Who is the letter from?"

I broke the seal and scanned the note. "It's the solicitor. He is here, thank the gods. I'll leave immediately. He would like to meet at the inn's tavern. Then I'll have a few tasks to complete this afternoon in town. But I am assuming I can't persuade you to stay in my bed until I return?" I asked, half in jest, half in hope.

She fiddled with the robe, her fingers trailing over the black silk, pulling my attention toward her barely covered cleavage while she spoke. "Layla is likely waiting on pins and needles to talk about her night with Jamie, and I'm certain she's curious about how I fared as well." She pursed her lips and stilled her hands. "After breakfast, I will leave for Layla's, but I won't stay for long." She winked.

I strode to the bed, leaned over, and placed a kiss on her head. Her soft tresses tickled my nose. My pulse raced, and I contemplated devouring her before I left.

"You'd better go. We don't want to keep the solicitor waiting." She shimmied out of my reach with a sigh.

I nodded. My gaze lingered on my beautiful wife for a heartbeat before I forced myself to withdraw and exited the room. However, as I walked down the hall, I couldn't help but smile at the giggling maids. Finally, everything was right within my world.

The clock on the wall ticked by as the inn's tavern filled with villagers entering for their afternoon meals. The scent of ale and stew wafted through the air as farmers chatted about the Kesere festival. Gossip swirled over newly formed couples and connections made.

An hour passed, and the once boisterous chatter died down. The townspeople came and went while I waited impatiently for the tardy solicitor. I thrummed my fingers over the oak table and considered departing. However, finding someone else to handle this delicate matter in such a short time would be impossible. I urged my growing agitation to settle as Farmer Johnson, the last of the dwellers, tipped his hat to me and exited, leaving the once bustling tavern empty.

An unfamiliar blonde barmaid sauntered toward me with a snifter of whiskey and a toothy grin. She reached the table and slid the drink to me as I raised one haughty eyebrow.

"It is on the house, my lord. Compliments of my grandmother. Since you've been waiting for a while," she said.

Before I could answer, she sauntered away. I paused, my mind trying to remember Mrs. Jenkins's granddaughter's name, but I came up short. However, Mrs. Jenkins had a brood of grandchildren who lived in other areas and often visited for Kesere. Resigned, I drank the amber liquid, feeling its welcome sense of relief wash over me.

Minutes later, the last drop crossed my lips, and a man in a cloak entered. He strode toward the back corner with purpose, heading for me. He took a seat across from me but didn't remove his hood. I squared my shoulders to reprimand him for the wasted time.

"Silas," the familiar voice said.

I froze in recognition.

"What are you doing here, Duncan? Where is the solicitor?" I asked in confusion.

He sighed and pulled back the covering, revealing his annoyed expression. He raised his hand and snapped his fingers, gesturing for a drink.

"What is going on?" I asked in exasperation.

Within seconds, the buxom woman sauntered up and slid a glass to him with a wink.

Yet as he turned his gaze to meet mine, the brotherly affection I expected to see was missing. His lips curved into a malicious smile, and disgust coated his features. Fear prickled beneath my skin at the menace radiating from him.

"You put me in the worst position," he said through gritted teeth. I stared at Duncan, and a sense of foreboding filled my soul. He gulped the whiskey, then slammed the glass on the table.

He sneered, and his fingers clutched into the empty snifter. "You nearly ruined everything. You stupid boy."

I flinched, willing myself to make sense of this man before me. Rage dwelled in his gray irises, like smoldering ash. However, in the pit of my soul, hadn't I known that this piece of Duncan lingered just under the surface?

He leaned forward, his teeth clenched. For a moment, I wasn't the grown Lord Belmont, but his pupil, frozen and awaiting his lecture.

"The Terrells were furious when they learned of Arianna's friendship with Beatrix. When I returned from Seaside, I had no choice but to clear my name and my involvement with this whole mess. I couldn't lose the funds from my wealthiest backer for the Seaside trade route. My years of planning would have been wasted."

I clenched my fists, but I couldn't move, my mind unable to reconcile what was happening. My body and reasoning were sluggish.

Madness entered Duncan's tone. "You almost fooled me, boy. I thought it impossible for the girl to be with you, but I had my suspicions. Your face that day in my study showed the depth of your affection for her. You are far easier to read than you realize. But I hoped you were not dumb enough to entangle with her.

However, when you reached out about the solicitor, you all but confirmed that you harbored Arianna here. Why else would you need to send a large sum of money anonymously?"

I clutched the table, willing my swirling anger and curse to dampen. The wood buckled beneath my fingertips, and the scent of charred ash wafted into the air. I leashed my fury, unwilling to burn this tavern down and identify that I carried the blight within me.

He cocked his head, and a smirk crossed his lips. "What did I find when I arrived? You wed a woman named Arianna, who somehow managed to parade around town unmasked, as if she were not a cursed monster." His expression twisted in disgust.

"What have you done?" I asked as rage bubbled beneath my skin.

His smirk grew in malice as he said in an even tone, "I couldn't let you and your whore ruin my standing with the Terrells. Not only will I partake in the handsome bounty for finding her, but my name will be restored."

I growled in frustration and lurched forward, grabbing him by the collar. He remained unfazed.

"I have been cleaning up your messes since your Uncle Oliver died. I even took your sister off your hands, but her little backwoods title hasn't strengthened my station in Hallowhaven as I thought. Don't worry, I'll take good care of her. She is locked away as we speak." A smug smirk cut across his expression.

My curse blazed. I might have killed the man on the spot. Yet a pang of terror pulsated through the taut connection to Arianna, wavering my resolve for bloodshed. My eyes widened in horror as her fear swirled within me.

My curse flared under my skin in answer, sounding an alarm. I released Duncan and pivoted to sprint to her side. I stepped forward, but my knees buckled beneath me. My fingers clutched the edge of the table, and the world tilted on its axis. However, I couldn't hold up my weight as my limbs weakened. My waning strength faded, and I collapsed onto the wood floor. The scraping of a chair filled my throbbing head. Then Duncan loomed over me, his boot near my belly. He jostled my limp form and said with mock sympathy, "I think you drank too much, brother."

I fought for consciousness, but everything faded to black.

CHAPTER 58

ARIANNA

I AMBLED DOWN THE path to town, and the afternoon sunlight washed over me. I breathed in the sweet smell of pine from the forest that reminded me so much of Silas. He would likely chide me later for walking instead of taking the carriage, which he'd left behind for my use. However, the beautiful day beckoned me, and I planned on soaking up every bit of happiness, including this glorious weather. My soul brimmed with fullness as I replayed the events of last night and this morning.

Silas loved me and was likely already speaking to the solicitor who would settle my mother's debts. Life would finally settle into bliss. My heart swam as I daydreamed about my mother and sister coming to Presspin to reside here.

Midway to town, a cawing crow flew overhead, jarring me out of my blissful trance. My attention darted toward where the bird had emerged. I jolted, surprised, as I spotted the stranger from last night. He was the rakish gentleman who had asked me about my recent marriage and then placed a kiss on my hand, fueling Silas's jealousy. Perhaps I should thank him for his roguishness.

"Arianna Park," he called out as he glided to me with catlike agility.

My stomach lurched, and on instinct I inhaled, readying my curse to activate on the exhale. However, before I could unleash my wrath upon him for knowing my true identity, he spoke. "Maybe you should listen before doing anything foolish. Or do you truly not care about your family's misfortune?"

"What do you know of my family?" My face remained neutral despite the churning panic.

His feline smile smoothed into an expressionless façade as he threw a small pouch to me, which I caught.

"Open it," he said.

I looked inside, and bile rose in my throat. I choked down vomit as one blue eyeball peered at me, the same crystal color as my own. I collapsed to my knees, sickened, and fought tears threatening to overtake me. The satchel fell beside me as I touched the hard ground, hoping the feel of earth would center me.

"It's your mother's," he said.

I sensed the man's gaze on my back and flicked a glance to him. Ash coated my tongue and rage boiled my blood. My vision intensified, and energy coursed under my fingertips.

Kill him, kill him, my curse urged.

I willed the blight to fall under my command. It sizzled under my skin, but I couldn't get answers from a dead man.

He stepped forward until his boots were inches from my hands. My palms itched to shoot darkness up his leg and melt his flesh. However, I didn't have time to waste with a whimpering stranger when my loved one's life hung in the balance.

"I am glad I have your attention now," he said.

I stood and brought myself to my full height. I wouldn't cower, despite him being a head and a half taller than me. His stare held mine, but a hint of pity filled his countenance, taking me aback for a heartbeat. Then he paced around me, as if sizing me up, unaware that I could destroy him with the flick of my wrist. I glared at him.

"It's truly a shame. You seem like a nice lady. At least from what I can tell. Alas, you displeased Mr. Terrell when you jilted his son. He is intent on unleashing his revenge. The choice is yours, whether it is upon you or those you love."

A thin layer of sweat formed on my brow, and my heart thundered. Goddess above. I should have suspected that the Terrells would take my fleeing personally and that Theo wouldn't simply wed another. In this safe bubble of Presspin, I had forgotten about the harsh truth of reality. I had been foolish.

He placed his hands in his pockets, and ease swept across his face. "You can't outrun this. Other hunters, or worse, the Aralians, will come for you. They will cut through this town and harm anyone in their way, like your husband. If you leave with me, Mr. Terrell will release your family from the confines of his home. But based on his actions with your mother, I am certain a much more gruesome fate than debtor's prison awaits them if you remain unfound."

My fingers trembled at my sides, but I knew where Naomi was and could reach her. I needed to find Silas. Without hesitating, I inhaled to pull against the well within me.

As if sensing my intention, the bounty hunter, in a blink of an eye, pulled a dart from his pocket and sent it sailing toward me. I summoned my curse, but the dark aura surrounded me too late. A sharp sting pierced my neck, and cold liquid rushed into my veins. The crackling darkness vanished.

Panic filled me, and I stumbled. My knees buckled as if I were a newly born foal. He approached and wrapped his arms around my waist, lugging me to my feet. "Sorry. Deary. You're a bit too slow."

My body grew heavy, as if my limbs weighed a thousand pounds, and anxiety swelled within me. Panicked, I used my last remnants of consciousness to send my emotions through the bond to Silas.

My head lolled as I fought to stay awake, but I was so weary. Then he lugged my limp body over his shoulder, and I fell unconscious.

CHAPTER 59

Silas

I jolted from the black haze, gasping for air. My vision adjusted to the dimly lit surroundings as fading sunlight filtered through the gossamer curtain. I was no longer in the tavern, but in an unfamiliar bed. I attempted to sit, but my arms were bound by a thick rope tied to the headboard. Enraged, I surged energy forward, and the fraying cords snapped within seconds. Freed, I sat up, but my head swam as if I had spent the day drinking. I gulped against my dried mouth, then forced my heavy body off the mattress. However, my legs buckled, and I grasped the nightstand for stability.

From my weakened state, I ascertained that Duncan had somehow drugged me. I would kill the man, yet my worry for Arianna superseded revenge. My stomach sank. Had he captured Arianna, too? Perhaps she had been wise and stayed in my bed after all. Yet that horrible panic that had surged through my soul as the darkness overtook me flickered into memory.

I searched internally for a wisp of the bond between us, which had felt thick as a braided cord this morning. Yet only a gaping hole in my heart remained, as if a piece had been ripped out. My curse screamed within me, a blood-curdling sound that reverberated through my skull, intensifying the ache.

I needed to find Arianna. I trudged forward at a snail's pace, making slow progress to the other side of the room. As I reached the exit, a thin layer of sweat clung to my skin. I gritted my teeth and yanked the door open. My vision swam, and I used the wall for leverage as I stumbled toward the stairs. My hands clutched the railing, and I gingerly walked down the steps, afraid I might tumble to my demise. Many minutes later, my feet touched the landing.

Laughter floated from the tavern brimming with townspeople who were unaware that I struggled mere feet away in the foyer between the inn and bar. My stomach churned as the scent of roasted meat and stale ale wafted through the cramped space. Despite my nausea, I released the banister, but swayed. I clenched my jaw, frustrated that my body did not register the urgency of finding Arianna.

"My lord, are you unwell?" Mrs. Jenkins scurried from behind the inn's desk, her features soft with concern as she rushed toward me. Despite being a woman of sixty-five, she was built like an ox. I wrapped an arm around her, unafraid of crushing her solid frame, as she led me to a chair.

"Where is he?" I spat out in frustration as I leaned into the wooden seat, panting from the exertion of getting down the stairs. My body burned as if I had run miles. She knitted her brow in contemplation, but then it smoothed.

"Ah, yes! He was looking for you, too. Just give me a moment; I think I can catch him." Mrs. Jenkins said.

Then she rushed out the door, leaving me seated by the desk where she greeted patrons. My hands shook with frustration, and I tried to stand, but my knees buckled beneath me. Minutes passed as I coaxed life back into my limbs, rolling my ankles until the numb, heavy feeling dissipated.

Moments later, Vincent barged in, his face filled with panic as he approached with Mrs. Jenkins in tow. "My lord, what happened? I have been searching for you for hours. I assumed you were having a late morning after...well..." He cleared his throat. "After your interactions with my lady at the festival. But when I arrived, Mrs. Potter said you had already left. I went to the farms, hoping you were there, but you weren't. I was heading to Layla's to—"

"*Yes*. Go and check on Arianna immediately." I flicked my hand in command.

Vincent pushed his wire-framed glasses up the bridge of his nose, but he didn't bristle at my terseness. Instead, he opened the door and left.

"My lord, can I get you anything?" Mrs. Jenkins smoothed her hands over her stained cream apron. I forced myself to stand but still required the leverage of the chair, so I clutched the backing.

"Your granddaughter. Fetch her for me at once," I said, needing to speak with the woman who had served Duncan and me. Yet Mrs. Jenkins's lips pulled into a frown.

"Granddaughter? My lord, my granddaughters do not live here. Nor was any of my family able to visit for the Kesere festival." Concern filled her face.

"The blonde who served me and my brother-in-law, Duncan Archer, after the lunch rush," I said through gritted teeth.

Her eyes widened in shock, and I leashed my boiling rage, the energy ready to course from my fingertips. I wouldn't divulge my secret or scare my people. Instead, I took a long breath and let out a shaky pained exhale.

"I was taking my meal in my quarters, as I do every day when the afternoon rush ends. I didn't have any help until Fiona showed up for the dinner crowd." Her lips pursed, highlighting the laugh lines around her mouth.

I shook my head in frustration. The woman must have been with Duncan. Gods, he knew the townspeople and their habits as well as I did. However, I needed to focus on finding Arianna.

As if summoned by my thoughts, Vincent burst through the door. Panic etched his face. "My lord, my lady never showed up for work. Ms. Layla assumed she was with you."

Those horrific words confirmed my fears. But I couldn't allow terror to overwhelm me. I snapped into my role as Lord Belmont and issued orders.

"Mrs. Jenkins, have a stable boy prepare the quickest steed you have. Go now."

The woman nodded and scurried away. I straightened, but my legs still wobbled as I took a tentative step. Vincent grabbed my elbow, steadying me as we walked into the tavern. Fiona, the barkeep, pivoted toward us, confusion lacing her features.

"Water and bread." I lowered myself onto the barstool. My brain spun as I attempted to straighten my thoughts.

"My lord, what is going on?" Vincent sidled beside me.

Before I could answer, the barmaid slid my order to me. I chugged the liquid and forced the food into my unsettled belly, knowing that tonight I would ride until either the steed broke or I did.

"It's Duncan. He abducted Arianna to return her to her former betrothed." The words tumbled from me before I could register that I'd revealed a fraction of the secret to my steward.

However, he didn't ask any further questions. Instead, he pulled off his glasses and wiped them with his handkerchief. He pushed them back on and held my gaze. A stony resolve entered his usually good-natured face. "I always hated that man. I'll assist you, my lord, while you take care of that trash."

I opened and closed my mouth, shocked at Vincent's assessment. The two had never worked with me concurrently, but they'd crossed paths over the years while Duncan served as my estate adviser. Then when he came to formally court Beatrix. As I thought back on their interactions, I realized that Vincent had acted even more stoically than usual when around Duncan. However, I'd assumed it to be because of his shyness, in contrast to Duncan's boisterous nature. I wanted to pry, but a young boy tapped me on the shoulder. "My lord, your horse is ready."

Thankfully, the dregs of the drugs left in my system had finally dissipated. I raced outside as the darkness of night covered the town. I mounted the steed, and the lad handed me a satchel with water and an apple. The groom lit a lantern for me and attached it to the black stallion's bridle, lighting my way. Pushing a heel into its side, I rushed forward toward the mountain range and Daviel, where I hoped Arianna would be.

Daylight broke, and my exhausted mount panted. Fortunately, we were only feet away from the inn at the base of the mountain range. I yanked the reins, slowing the horse as its hooves clicked over the cobble path.

"Thank you," I whispered to the fatigued stallion, then dismounted. As soon as my feet hit the ground, I sprinted for the entrance.

I swung the door open and shouted, "I need a horse!"

Despite having ridden through the night, I was wide awake. My curse had fed off my rage, urging me forward, as if the hysteria that settled within my blood displaced exhaustion. I stomped toward the stairs. "Agnes! Peter!"

Seconds later, Peter bolted down the steps with shock etched upon his face. "Silas, what's going on? Why are you here making a racket?"

"I need a horse immediately." My eyes darted frantically, searching for a way to cut the distance between Arianna and me. Agitated energy billowed at my fingertips, and I fought for control. My curse buzzed with the desire to overtake me. It had rippled beneath my flesh as I made the agonizingly slow descent in the dark through the winding mountain range.

"Calm down and tell me what happened." Peter approached, then placed a hand on my shoulder, but I seethed with fury at the situation. I wanted to destroy anything that came between me and my path to her. Yet his features softened as he waited. I let out a sharp exhale, focusing my mind on the present and cooling my boiling blood.

Before I could speak, a servant boy entered from the kitchen, likely curious about the commotion. Peter turned to him. "Go to the stables and have a steed prepared for Lord Belmont. Then gather fresh water and food for his travels."

The lad sprinted out the door.

"Now, tell me what happened." Peter's voice cut through the swirling madness that I fought desperately to contain.

I withdrew from him and paced. My thoughts were an entangled mess, and my need to find my mate consumed my mind. Any instinct toward protecting Arianna I had prior to last night amplified exponentially, as if an ancient, unspeakable rage had taken root within me.

"He took her." I pulled a hand through my hair, yet the motion didn't soothe the riling anger.

Peter crossed his arms over his chest, waiting for me to form a coherent explanation.

My shoulders sagged in sorrow from the fullness of the truth weighing upon me. "Duncan kidnapped Arianna to return her to her former betrothed."

Peter's expression twisted in horror, but before he could interject, the cry of my name came from the doorway. "*Silas*?"

I turned to see my sister. I gaped, baffled that she, too, had made her way to the inn. My temper dampened as she ran toward me and wrapped me in a warm embrace. Her tears pooled against my coat, rekindling my frustration at her blackguard husband.

"What are you doing here, Beatrix?" I pulled her away and scanned over her. My jaw tightened at her dulled features. Purple rings clung to her brown eyes, and the merriment that once danced within them had diminished. An odd pallor colored her now-sunken cheeks, as if she hadn't eaten in some time. Either illness or heartsickness had taken hold of her since I last saw her. She swayed near collapse, and I moved her to a sturdy chair.

"What happened to you?" A knot formed in my throat.

"Duncan, he..." Her shoulders shook with sobs, halting her speech. She gulped for air. I patted her shoulder to soothe her. Yet my blood boiled with disgust for the man I used to admire. A minute passed, and she steadied herself.

She reached into her pocket for a handkerchief and wiped her face, then continued in a faint voice.

"I bribed a servant to help me escape Archer Estate last night since Duncan had left on business." Fresh tears welled as she struggled through hiccupping breaths. "Since his return from Seaside, he has become paranoid that my friendship with Arianna would reflect poorly on him. He became obsessed with the route, drunkenly telling me about all the money and power it will garner him. He changed into a man I didn't recognize, so I started snooping around his study. I found many horrible things. His investments in Seaside with the Terrells, his gambling debts, and his mistress in Hallowhaven." She gasped a sob and crumpled in the chair.

She wrung the handkerchief in her hands. "He caught me investigating his ledgers and locked me in my room a fortnight ago with barely any food or water. I never thought he would treat me this way."

I looked upon my broken sister, who had been betrayed by the man she'd loved for so many years, and I swore if I ever saw Duncan again, I would delight in killing him slowly for the anguish he had caused the women in my life.

"I want you to head back to Presspin as soon as possible. Have Peter and Agnes accompany you. I have to go. He abducted Arianna," I said.

"Your horse is ready, my lord," the boy called out.

Beatrix's sobs reconvened as I hastened out the door. I noticed heavy storm clouds beginning to form over the Presspin mountains and felt a pang of relief, knowing snow would soon cover the world. The promise of protection filled me.

CHAPTER 60

THEO

I AMBLED ALONG THE abandoned hallway, making my way to Father's study. Faint sunlight cut through the windows, but not enough to illuminate the dark corridor. Instead, it cast ominous shadows over the carpet. A knot formed in my gut. What horror awaited me today at Father's hand?

I walked too quickly and winced as the wounds on my back tugged under my loose tunic. Sweat beaded on my forehead, and I wiped my brow with my shirtsleeve. I gritted my teeth and pushed forward. Yet I couldn't ignore the stinging pain from the lashes, one for every day I had avoided his summons home after giving up my search for Arianna.

Yet my weeks of cavorting, drinking, and gambling had been well worth the agony. The runners I hired had been fruitless, and a few had taken their deposits and never returned. Instead of hiring a bounty hunter, I had used the last of my coin to enjoy my life to the fullest, knowing that Arianna likely lay dead in a ditch somewhere.

After agonizingly long minutes, I reached my father's study but stopped as Edgar approached.

"Wait, young sir." He placed a gentle hand on my shoulder, halting me from entering.

His face filled with sympathy. My spine stiffened at the tenderness. It was the same expression he wore when applying salve to my wounds. My lips pressed in a harsh line. I stepped away, creating distance between us.

He recoiled. "Sorry, young sir. I wanted to warn you. Your father is in a peculiar mood. Something is amiss. He has ordered me to fetch the finest brandy from the distillery as soon as they open. He is too jovial. Please be cautious."

I clenched my jaw at Edgar's warning and shooed him away. However, I squared my shoulders and plastered on a smirk, despite the welling terror. I sauntered into his study, as if being summoned at the crack of dawn only days after being delivered a brutal beating was normal.

I blinked, adjusting my vision to the dark room. The curtains were closed, smothering any sunlight from entering, and a few candles lit the space. An aching cold lingered in the air. I glanced at the unlit fireplace and pursed my lips, fighting the shiver crossing over me.

"Come in, my boy." A manic smile cut over Father's face, but malice radiated in his gaze. Yet I didn't pause. I couldn't show weakness or he would destroy any last remnants of my soul.

My attention shifted to the blond gentleman seated on a velvet chair across from the oversized desk. Within seconds, my mind registered that the man was Duncan Archer, the odious connection chaser who was married to that woman from

Presspin. The lady who had befriended Arianna. Why was he here?

"Come have a drink with us."

Father gestured for me to take a seat in the chair beside Duncan's. I straightened to my full height, but the motion pulled at my unhealed flesh. I fought the urge to wince.

I didn't follow his instructions. Instead, I sauntered to the beverage cart, as aloof as possible, ignoring the agony slashed upon my back. I forced my trembling hands to steady as I poured two fingers of whiskey. With a steadying breath, I took the snifter and joined Duncan in the adjoining velvet chair facing my father. I hovered on the edge, balancing my weight in order to keep pressure off my wounds. Sweat beaded on my forehead from the effort.

I plastered on a smirk and held the glass out in salute. "I am never one to turn down a drink, even at this early hour."

Father arched an eyebrow, but I didn't relent. Seconds passed before he raised his snifter in return. "A toast to Duncan Archer. Not only is he a fine business partner, making me more money than I could ever dream by securing connections for the trade route in Seaside, but he has also returned Arianna to us. I don't know how you accomplished this feat in such a short time since arriving home."

I gulped the drink. Yet hope mixed with the burning alcohol, loosening my tension. Arianna was here, thank the goddess. My life could return to normal; we would wed, and my little pet would be mine. She would be bound to me, forced to love me, and unable to leave my side.

However, something ominous loomed in the air, souring my momentary relief. My father's stare darted to me with cold calculation while he sipped his brandy.

"Gods, Duncan, you are ruthless. I like that about you. A wolf in sheep's clothing. When you suggested I threaten the Parks with debtors' prison, it was a genius move. Then hiring a bounty hunter to bring them here? I knew your wife had Arianna over for tea, but when did you suspect she had been cavorting with your brother-in-law? She must have a magical cunt to sway him into marrying her." My father chuckled.

I clutched the glass, willing myself not to chuck it at the floor. Arianna had wed someone else? *Impossible.* No one wanted her but me. A feral grin pulled across Father's face as if he sensed my discomfort. In the depths of my soul, I knew this conversation served as yet another punishment.

Duncan beamed like a puppy being praised by his master, as he said, "I didn't know they had met until I returned from Seaside. If I had, I would have surely warned you. However, when I arrived home my staff approached me about an incident that occurred. It seems they were in bed together before she ran off. At first, I assumed it to be impossible for him to assist her in any meaningful way because of her condition. Yet if he had helped her, his poor bleeding heart wouldn't be able to resist assisting her family. I just never would have imagined that he would have wed her. After being notified by my staff about their interlude, I sent a bounty hunter to investigate. When he told me my brother-in-law was married to a woman named Arianna, I concocted a plan to retrieve her under the guise of visiting for their harvest festival. Silas had no clue I had infiltrated his town, which created the perfect opportunity to snatch her. What I can't figure out is how she lived there without her mask. It is still a mystery, but not one I care to dwell on."

Frustration bubbled in my stomach. I had been right all those months ago when I was at her home. She had lied to my face about not knowing Duncan Archer's brother-in-law, and I had fallen for her flattery like a damned child.

Father turned his attention to me, and my mouth dried. "Obviously, Arianna is no longer a viable option. She is a better bargaining chip with the Aralians. Apparently, they too have been eagerly hunting for her since she disappeared. Their stretch of power is far more vast than I realized. They have promised a vacant seat on the high council to the person who returns the girl to them. I sent word to the Aralians last night when Duncan arrived. Perhaps, ironically, her leaving you at the altar was more beneficial than her actually marrying you."

Fury blazed in my belly, but I remained silent, my lips twisting into a grimace. Gods, even a masked creature didn't want me. I let out a snide chuckle at my self-loathing.

"What are you smirking about, you stupid boy? You embarrassed the lot of us choosing her as your betrothed. But you can still be useful to me by marrying her sister, Naomi, when she comes of age." Father sipped his drink, as if the information were not life changing.

I gripped my glass so tightly I thought it would shatter like my soul. My fingertips blanched from the pressure. I wanted to scream, but even in Duncan Archer's presence, I feared Father's wrath, with his wild eyes and the deep stench of alcohol fuming off him. Father let out a chuckle of amusement, knowing he was dooming me to a lifetime of misery wed to someone I loathed.

"It is the perfect arrangement. Mrs. Park will probably not survive her captivity here—a nasty infection from that missing eye." He laughed.

Duncan sipped his whiskey, but a rigidity entered his posture, as if he had just realized the monster he'd entangled with.

"I'll be exalted as a hero, taking on the daughter of a deceased widow and the sister of the girl who jilted you. With her bloodline attached to your name and the backing of the Aralians, the high council seat will be mine."

My blood pulsed in my ears, and bile crawled up my throat.

"What if I refuse? Do you plan on beating me to death? I would rather die than be bound to that shrew." I clamped my mouth shut, but my true feelings had escaped me.

Father bellowed a mirthless laugh, and a shiver snaked along my spine. "Your death would be a waste of your use to me. If you refuse, I'll kill Edgar and make you watch. You seem to have a soft spot for the servant."

I gulped. Goddess, despite the distance I attempted to keep, the aloofness toward those around me, he had still found someone I begrudgingly cared about.

"Kill him. He is just a servant," I said, but my words came out a shaky mess, showing my affection for the man who had tended to the wounds inflicted by my father since childhood.

He cut a toothy smile, knowing he had already won. He swirled the snifter, his menacing stare locked on me. "You will marry the girl. It is time you realized that life is about winners and losers. You will never win, boy. Now go before I become less magnanimous."

I clenched my teeth and rose. My hands shook and my stomach sank from the nightmare of being wed to Naomi Park. I closed the door behind me. Defeated, I sulked away to find comfort.

CHAPTER 61

ARIANNA

MY HEAVY LIDS BLINKED open. Where was I? I attempted to move but remained paralyzed, staring at the ceiling. Many long minutes passed while I focused on the impossible task of wiggling my toes. Eventually, they scrunched in my boots. After that, I spent an eternity flexing my fingers. Then I willed strength to flow through me, focusing on one extremity at a time. Finally strengthened, I shifted on the overly soft bed. My head lolled as I took in the rose-colored room. I groaned at the familiar spelled suite in Terrell Estates.

I gaped at the exit and registered the absence of my onyx ring. My stomach sank. Without it, I was trapped, and I needed to formulate my escape to rescue Naomi, then return to Silas.

Determined, I forced myself to a sitting position. Yet my body ached from the weight of the spelled quarters that I was no longer accustomed to. How had I lived under the pressure of these vitality-draining wards?

I reached for the cup of water on the nightstand, brought it to my nose, and sniffed the liquid. Was it laced with a tranquilizer? But it didn't have any scent, and extreme thirst overruled my logic. I chugged the contents. Still parched, I grabbed the pitcher, but my arm strained to tip the heavy crystal as I refilled my cup. I sipped and rolled my shoulders. Satiated, I returned the glass.

Hesitantly, I stood, and my knees wobbled. I swayed into the nightstand, clutching it for balance, and knocked the ewer over. It rattled and tipped over, spilling water onto the carpet. I ground my teeth and leveraged my weight against the wood surface, forcing myself to stand. I wiped my damp palms on my pants and leaned against the bed for support.

A throat clearing caught my attention. I whipped my head toward the rear corner of the suite and saw Mr. Terrell lounging on the sofa. Had he been sitting there watching me stumble through this haze this entire time?

"Glad to see you are finally awake, Arianna." He smiled, but a predatory gleam in his gaze gave me pause. He was a wolf in sheep's clothing: amiable on the exterior, but ruthless to his core. I should have suspected, given Theo's rotten behavior, that the apple hadn't fallen far from the tree.

Instead of cowering, I forced myself to my full height, lifting my chin in defiance. "That is Lady Arianna Belmont to you."

His amused smile flattened. I wasn't the meek bride he'd purchased for Theo all those months ago. No, I was Lady Belmont of Presspin, wife of Silas Belmont and a cursed being who could kill him in an instant, given the right circumstance.

He stood and bellowed a laugh. I winced from the malice laced within the tone. He assessed me as if I were nothing more than a little girl playing dress-up. Yet he didn't respond. Instead, he downed the contents of his snifter and threw it against the wall. It shattered to pieces, scattering over the carpet in a speckling of glittering crystal. It took all my will to remain still. I wouldn't give him the satisfaction of seeing my fear.

He rose and stalked toward me. I didn't cower, despite his hulking size. His heavy footsteps crunched over the fragmented glass. My heart raced, and anxiety coated my tongue. I held his stare as he approached and left only inches between us. He towered over me, and his empty brown eyes bored into mine, akin to a pit of death that would swallow me whole.

He grabbed my chin and assessed me like Theo had that day in my room. He scanned over my face, then lowered his hand. His lips pursed as he leaned back, perusing my figure. I resisted the urge to cross my arms over my chest, disgusted by his ogling.

He raked his fingers through his short, graying beard, scratching his jaw. "I don't understand what the fuss is about. Theo is a dullard, swayed by his cock, but how did you convince a lord to wed you? You are not ugly, but you are not pretty either. It makes no sense to me."

I attempted not to flush at the insult, but I wouldn't let this man rattle me. No, I needed him to ramble on while I regained my strength. I squared my shoulders and held his glare.

"Though you have filled out nicely." His stare roved my body, my well-tailored trousers and shirt highlighting the weight I'd gained since arriving in Presspin.

I sneered at him, my lips twitching in disgust as his focus lingered on my breasts.

A chuckle left him, as if my vitriol amused him. "You may have temporarily derailed my plans, but in the long run, I really should thank you. Teresa hated the idea of her precious son marrying you. She kept insisting you were beneath him. But I thought you were a perfect fit for that little shit. How wonderful to pair such a cursed creature with that wretched child. Your lineage would have given me the needed connection to an ancient bloodline, especially when none of the gentry wanted Theo near any of their daughters. I couldn't have arranged another marriage for him if I tried. Then you ran. But something unexpected happened. The Aralians started searching for you, and how eager they were to find you. I was elated to help."

I flexed my fingers as the strength slowly reentered my body. I remained silent, buying myself time by being the captivated audience he desired.

"Did I mention the best part? Theo will suffer even more. I have grown tired of his antics, his drinking and cavorting, his fuckery. And to think he isn't..." He stopped and flexed his jaw. His tongue rolled over his teeth beneath his lips, as if whatever he was going to say was too distasteful to speak.

"He is to wed Naomi. They despise each other. It will add to the sweetness of the punishment. You should have witnessed the scene they made at your engagement ball. Oh, he will be miserable. While you, my dear, are to be handed over to the

Aralians. They are eager to have you, so much so that they plan on backing me to assume the currently vacant seat on the high council. Imagine, Counselor Fletcher Terrell. It really has a nice ring to it."

I breathed deeply as he leaned forward, readying to grab me. Yet during his monologue, my stamina had returned. My body lagged under the spell but was no longer lethargic from the drugs. In a flash, I lurched for the pitcher on the nightstand. With one fluid motion, I smashed it against the side of his head.

He hissed from the impact and stumbled. I sprinted past him and searched for a weapon but found nothing of use. I glanced at the door and gritted my teeth. Without my ring, I was bound to this suite. However, I would not give up. I couldn't allow Naomi to wed Theo, and I would rather die than be imprisoned under the wards. I had no choice but to fight.

I grabbed a floral vase off the side table. In my momentary distraction, Mr. Terrell ran for me and lunged. But from my training on the mountain, I had become agile, and I pivoted around a chair, using it as a shield between the two of us.

"You little *bitch*. You will pay for that. I have been nothing but kind to you, and this is how you repay me?" His fingers touched his head, where blood seeped from the wound.

I lurched forward and threw the vase at his nose, but he dodged the projectile. It shattered against the wall. He growled and grabbed the chair as if it were light as a feather. He flung it across the room, the pieces cracking as it snapped on the floor. His shoulders rose and fell with rapid breaths as he lunged. I whirled away, grateful to be in trousers and not a dress. I sprinted for the broken piece of the armchair, hoping I could use it as a weapon. However, my forward motion stopped as Mr. Terrell yanked me back with full force by my hair. He spun me to face him, then dug his nails into my scalp. I peppered him with ineffective blows to his barrel chest, but I was still too weak to fight him off.

No hint of the jovial man from my engagement dinner or the ball remained. No, he was pure evil. He grabbed my throat with his free hand and lifted my feet off the ground. I kicked and wheezed, but my legs found nothing but air.

"I think I know just the punishment for you and Theo. Maybe your cunt is magic, after all. Oh, he will hate that I had you when he could not." He licked his lips, then slammed me to the floor.

I tried to squirm away. I couldn't escape as he landed on top of me, pinning me between the carpet and himself. I wheezed out a painful breath from the impact of his heavy weight pushing into me.

"Theo should have snuffed out this fire in you long ago, but I dare say the boy enjoyed it. Foolish. I'll fuck the fight right out of you. If you are still, it won't hurt. But if you move...well, I can't make any promises."

I kicked and fought, to no avail. Terror bubbled within my throat. I would have vomited had it not been for my empty stomach. I closed my eyes. Mr. Terrell's hands roved over my blouse, tugging at the buttons. I shuddered. He reeked of alcohol, and an oil permeated from his skin as his chin skimmed along my cheek.

My mind drifted, dissociating from the external world. I entered the place where the darkness dwelled and searched the depths within me for a whisper of my power. However, I felt as if a wall separated me from the dark well.

My skin crawled as the present circumstance attempted to shift my focus. I steadied my breathing using my training. Unrelentingly, I dove into my emotions, and they crashed against the boundary, keeping me from my power like a wave against rock. The whispers of my curse lurched forward, eager to feed off the agony. However, it still lay trapped beyond my reach, locked behind the wards. I dug deeper. Thoughts of my loved ones juxtaposed against what would happen if I did not overcome this man, this suppression spell. If I didn't succeed, Silas would be alone in Belmont Manor, my mother would be sent to debtors' prison, and Naomi would wed Theo. My fury surged, and a hair's width crack formed. A black thread snaked between the fracture, and I wrapped my will around it. With each passing second, I found purchase, and the once miniscule rupture in the enchantment spread into a gaping hole.

Arianna...

My pulse raced as my name rang through me, and an energy that wasn't my own washed over me. The once absent connection between Silas and me snapped into place, intensifying with each heartbeat. A well bubbled before me with our shared energy. I dove into the depth, falling into the abyss, becoming a conduit for destruction. The wavering boundaries faltered, and the ward crumbled under the immense combined force.

"Goddess damn buttons. Why the fuck can't I..."

I opened my eyes, the world snapping into sharp focus as my senses heightened. Mr. Terrell's soulless gaze flicked from his fumbling fingers to my face. He gaped in horror at the monster he had pushed too far.

My crackling aura rippled from my skin, and tendrils of darkness tightened around the bumbling man's stomach. It sizzled. He screamed. The scent of burning flesh wafted through the air. Within seconds, his weight was off me as he hung in stasis, hoisted by my dark power.

He writhed in pain, tears pouring down his cheeks as the crackling tendrils melted through his clothing and skin like butter against a hot knife.

"*Where are they?*" My voice boomed.

"In...in...in the cellar! The key is in my pocket. I'm sorry. I'll do anything. You can have anything. Please, just let me go!"

Kill him...kill them all! my curse pleaded.

The chant was a battle cry for the pain I had suffered, and nothing anchored me against its destructive delights. The blight slipped into me, making me its willing puppet. I held on to a whisper of consciousness, looming in the recesses of my mind.

"*Tsk, tsk, tsk.* Didn't you know there is no mercy for a monster like you?" My voice echoed with an otherworldly timbre. I flung him with full force at the broken chair. His head collided with a spiky piece of wood, impaling him through the soft spot at the base of his skull.

"Shame. I wanted to take my time with you."

The disgusting man lay sprawled on the floor akin to a lifeless doll. His blood spilled out, drenching the rose-colored floral carpet.

I let out a maddened shriek. The windows shattered around me. Glass covered the once pristine prison. The door flew off the hinges. I walked out of the ruined suite and stepped into the corridor.

Servants screamed as the floor beneath me crumpled with each step. The once immaculate marble fractured from the pressure of my dark aura, marking a trail of destruction in my wake. Broken shards swirled as if my power had defied gravity itself. As I stalked down the steps, the foundation of the home trembled. The atmosphere densified, thick like tar. The chandelier above swayed, then snapped. I remained unfazed as it sailed toward me.

Boom!

It collided with my dark aura. Crystal scattered into a million pieces, shooting every which way. Shrieks spun around my cyclone of destruction. Yet I didn't care about the servants' screams as they fled, avoiding the shrapnel.

I stalked the corridor. The wallpaper melted off the walls. An acrid scent skated over me, and I licked my lips, delighting in the devastation.

"*What have you done?*" a whimpering voice called out from behind me.

I whirled, and Theo came into view. He had always been a bully, tormenting those weaker than him. This insignificant boy couldn't hurt me, even if he tried.

"*Shut up!* Take me to my sister. *Now*!" My aura intensified, and a wave of darkness crawled to him, snapping at his feet. "Don't think I won't kill you."

"This way." His green eyes were wide in horror. Yet his disposition leaned toward self-preservation.

"Good boy," I said.

His lips tightened to a straight line, and he walked in the opposite direction from where our engagement ball had once been held. The golden wallpaper turned to ash as I passed. The sconces melted as my dark aura touched them, and the paintings disappeared into nothingness. My curse washed this place clean of its wealth, leaving the once glittering manor dilapidated. He stopped in front of a door and jiggled the handle. I stood behind him, impatient with his antics.

"I...I...I don't have the key," he stammered.

I raised my hand, and darkness built. A black orb surged toward Theo and the door. I didn't care if I hurt the man-child. Yet he leapt away before the energy collided with him. The wood disintegrated, leaving nothing between me and my family. I peered down the murky step while Theo trembled on the cracked marble like a cowering dog.

"Go get them!"

Power rattled from me, causing the windows in the house to shatter under the pressure building in the atmosphere. Glass rained down from the end of the hallway.

He sprang to his feet and ran down the stairs.

I waited impatiently, my curse feeding off my wrath as the surrounding space decayed. The once beautiful home was now marred by my presence. After a few moments, two sets of footsteps echoed through the narrow passageway. I peered below as my sister and my mother came into view. Naomi dragged Mama up the stairs. A dirty bandage was wrapped over her missing eye, and her face had a gray pallor. Anger seared through me as they ran into the hallway. Before Theo could emerge, I shot crackling energy into the cellar; the braces buckled as the entrance collapsed. I smirked. He would wither away in that prison where my family had been kept.

I laughed as I walked to the door, taking in my handiwork. I had been the harbinger of doom to this house, the beckoner of death. But I stopped as a voice beckoned through my haze, loosening the destructive urge.

Arianna...Arianna...Arianna...

My name cut through the chaos swirling in my mind. I halted, and Naomi turned to me, her face etched with exhaustion.

I blinked at her, my surging power waning as I rushed past them. I could feel him guiding me homeward. My body moved of its own volition to my mate.

"Silas," I said, as if he could hear me.

"Who is Silas?" Mama asked between ragged breaths.

Naomi grunted as she pulled her forward. "Her husband."

Mama gasped as they hobbled behind me. "Who would marry her?"

"For once, shut up, Mother," Naomi said, as she trudged at an achingly slow pace, dragging Mama along.

Yet I ignored them as the cord of our bond drew me closer to Silas.

CHAPTER 62

ARIANNA

SUNLIGHT BLAZED AS I blasted through the door of the Terrell estate. Servants screamed, sheep bleated, and horses' clopping hooves swirled within my heightened senses. Yet they could not drown out Silas's calls reverberating throughout my soul. He beckoned me forward, and I didn't care about the chaos I left in my wake. The stone steps crumbled beneath my feet, crunching under my boots. The scent of ash and decay licked off me, mixing with the chilly air. Freedom was just beyond these lush, rolling hills.

Arianna...

My name drowned out the world around me.

Silas...

However, the fury and power within me did not relent. Instead, this distance between us intensified my curse's longings, and a willingness to turn the rolling hills to a barren wasteland to get to him rang within my soul.

"Arianna," Naomi called out, and I wrestled within myself for a modicum of control.

"*What?*" I pulled myself from the trance, guiding me toward Silas.

"Look ahead." Her voice trembled as I focused on a wall of onyx approaching. The sun glinting off the smooth black shields nearly blinded me, but the symbol of the goddess of Aralia etched onto them ignited my fury. But they didn't relent at the sight of me. Instead, they marched down the cobbled path at a brutal pace.

"The Aralians! Go back to the house," I ground out through clenched teeth.

The once opulent manor barely remained. Glass from broken windows peppered the once pristine gardens, cracks webbed over the stone pillars, and the awning leading to the massive door sagged. Decay and ash lay where my darkness had touched, and the sound of creaking wood and groaning foundations made my stomach twist.

We could flee, but my mother wouldn't be able to outrun them, not when she hobbled forward, barely making her way back to the stone steps. The Aralians grew closer, only fifty yards away now.

I gritted my teeth and let out a shriek of rage. They did not cower. No, they were not meek disciples, but warriors in their twisted battle for righteousness. I flung orbs of crackling darkness toward them, but they ducked behind onyx shields that absorbed the blow. Not even a dent formed on the smooth, stone-plated armor. The women moved in a strategic formation, covering each other in a battle stance.

They marched on but halted at the cobbled drive, keeping a gaping distance between us. They paused, as if waiting for me to react. Naomi and my mother cowered, frozen. I stared down the dozen Aralians donning pristine armor akin to knights in a twisted holy war.

Kill them all, my curse hissed.

I fell deeper into my repressed emotions. I had endured years of anguish at the Aralians' hands. Today, I would repay them for their transgressions.

I shot out a barrage of inky energy. It crackled forward, rolling like tar toward them. They huddled together, their barriers taking on the onslaught of my attack. Even under the dense pressure, they did not recoil. Instead, the darkness dissipated as if it had been leached from the atmosphere.

"Arianna, do you not see the destruction you are causing?" Ester asked.

I clenched my jaw. I would recognize Ester's voice from the great beyond. Hadn't she been the disciple whose supervision I had been under, the warden to my prison?

An unhuman shriek left me. The group parted, and Ester stepped forward. She, unlike the others, was not in armor but in fine white robes, unmarred from traveling. She pulled back her hood, and her eyes held mine with mock sympathy.

"We want to keep the world safe. That is why your curse is suppressed. Do you not care about the people you killed or this manor you destroyed?" She gestured toward the crumbling building and the servants who fled in the distance. Her face remained unwavering. "You are out of control. Let us help you, Arianna. Look at your family. Do you really want to harm them?"

I shook off the haze that enveloped me and glanced at my mother, who wobbled against Naomi. Her head hung as she fought for consciousness. Then I gazed at my sister, expecting fear, but anger blazed in her blue irises.

I whipped my attention to Ester and laughed. With the flick of my fingers, darkness coursed from me and straight through Ester's chest. Inky waves encompassed her, and the scent of sizzling flesh wafted in the breeze. A horrified scream cut through the darkness, then it dissipated, leaving a pile of ash where the woman once stood.

My tongue was bitter, not sweet, as I suspected revenge would taste. For an instant, my killing instincts dampened as concern poured through the taut line between Silas and me.

"*Formation B!*" an Aralian shouted, undeterred by the death of their comrade, who was now nothing but dust in the wind.

Yet I cared little for their antics as I felt Silas pull closer. My sharpened vision caught his descent as he raced down the path like a prince on a white steed.

"*Fire!*" the Aralian shouted, pulling me from my hopeful moment. A heartbeat later, crackling arrows peppered the sky. Energy coursed from me in response. The air densified like a thick fog, but they flew true, unfazed as if they were enchanted. Shocked, I dodged behind a pillar just before an onyx head pierced through the spot where I once stood.

Luckily, Naomi had dragged our mother to a mound of rubble on the other side of the entrance. The stones took the brunt of the onslaught, which continued to fill the afternoon sky like flocks of black birds searching for their mark.

Yet the sound of hoofbeats followed by shrieking screams caused a satisfied smirk to tug on my lips. I watched as two women near the rear collapsed to the ground with seer marks wrapped around their broken necks at the spot unguarded by their armor.

"*Formation C!*" an Aralian yelled, and they shifted again, their shields encompassing them. Time slowed as the Aralians pivoted away from me and to Silas on a white steed, galloping at full speed.

Arrows careened toward him. A dark aura surrounded him, but the projectiles penetrated. He attempted to dodge the onslaught when a gut-wrenching sound emitted from the horse. Blood soaked its pale hair as it stumbled. Silas was flung off the animal, and my stomach lurched. Unable to protect himself, he rolled into the gravel, the mare almost collapsing on top of him. He bounced to his feet and leapt behind the thick beast. The Aralians were uncaring as they continued their barrage, turning the horse's white body crimson as onyx shafts stuck into its side.

I shrieked, ramming inky tendrils against their barrier, searching for purchase. But there was none. Their attack returned to me. I bolted behind the pillar, yet the arrows continued eating away at the stone. The once sturdy hiding spot was now riddled with holes, making me an easy target. I flicked a glance to Naomi and Mama, who trembled, their faces white with terror.

"You need to leave," I said, my voice inhuman.

Naomi nodded in agreement. However, the manor was crumbling from the damage I'd enacted. If I distracted the Aralians long enough, Mama and Naomi could run for the hills to safety. But there were too many arrows to elude. One whooshed past me toward where my sister and mother stood. Their bodies were in the open, stuck between running and hiding. Time slowed down, as if I could catch the arrow with my hands and stop it from finding its mark in Naomi's chest. But in a heartbeat, Mama stumbled in front of her, and a horrific thump echoed through my soul.

A chilling wail cut through the chaos. My mind shattered into a million pieces as I beheld Mama and the onyx protruding from her heart. She coughed out blood with a horrible gurgling sound. A tinny scent filled the air, and her blue eye caught on mine. She stumbled back into Naomi, blood oozing around the arrow lodged in her chest.

"No!" Naomi screamed as Mama slumped against her. They dropped to the ground. Tears streaked Naomi's cheeks as she held our dying mother in her arms. "Mama! *No*."

She reached a hand up to Naomi and stroked her face. The chaos stilled. Arrows careened past me in slow motion. My surging energy knocked them off their path as they scattered around us, unable to permeate the pressure my curse emitted, feeding off this frenzied panic.

"I love you, Naomi," Mama said through sputtering breaths.

Her gaze flicked to me, and she reached out a hand, unafraid of me. I wanted to grasp it, but I couldn't cause her more pain, not as energy pulsated through me. Instead, I knelt beside her.

Her expression softened, and she looked at me like she had when I was a little girl, curled on her lap.

Tears streamed down my cheeks. She wiped them away, her fingers marred by my darkness, uncaring as she stroked my face free of the mask.

"I'm sorry," she said through a gurgling wheeze. Her head slumped backward, and a final shaky exhale escaped her. Her stare fixed on the sky as she peered into the great beyond.

The last remnant of myself, the core of my soul I clung to, melted away.

"I will kill you all!" I unleashed a barrage of fury against the Aralians. Their shields buckled but did not break as sorrow consumed me.

SILAS

Uncaring about my safety, I bolted from behind the mangled mare. Arianna moaned as I reached her. Naomi sobbed on the ground, and their mother stared, unseeing, into the sky. Anguish roiled through our connection, fueling the manic energy coursing off Arianna. Black flames licked and crackled at the stone steps as they buckled beneath the pressure. The ground shook and cracked, but the Aralians did not waver as whatever control Arianna had over her curse disappeared. Her darkness lapped against their shields like waves upon the rocks, crashing against them. But they did not falter.

She shrieked again, the sound unholy in nature, no longer possessing an ounce of the woman I loved. Another onslaught of arrows flew, and Arianna dodged them with an agility more animal-like than human. She sent blow after blow toward the disciples. Her curse whispered to mine of nothing but mindless destruction, akin to a beast on a rampage. My stomach sank. If she continued, she would not only obliterate the Aralians, but everything in her wake. She would not survive the guilt, even if the blight didn't destroy her body.

Her breaths were ragged. She was waning from the full force of her power, akin to a dying star about to explode. Black blood oozed from her nose and the corner of her mouth. Her tears poured down her face like inky tar. The scent of ash filled the atmosphere. A maddened laugh escaped her, and the soulless black orbs where her eyes once were glared at the Aralians, who didn't cower under her onslaught. They knelt behind their shields as her energy rolled off them, leaving nicks and scratches against the once smooth onyx.

"*Fire!*" an Aralian shouted as arrows flew forward.

Arianna knocked them off their course with the pressure of her power. She laughed wildly, her soul consumed by the curse. She had become wrath incarnate. There would be no stopping her from destroying everything. Her hand raised, and as crackling energy shot out of her palm, my attention caught on her empty finger.

"Arianna," I yelled out to her, but she didn't hear me, her mind trapped in the curse's clutches.

I yanked my uncle's ring from around my neck. Her hand whipped as she expelled more waves against the disciples' defenses. I pulled her coal-veined wrist toward me. She squirmed. I slipped the onyx ring onto her thumb.

She jolted away. "No!"

Yet the ring dampened her curse, pulling Arianna back into control of her body.

"Silas," she whimpered in her voice as grief washed through our connection.

CHAPTER 63

ARIANNA

I INHALED AND FORCED myself out of the trance, which had possessed me, mind, body, and soul. I pushed the curse back, leashing it under my control. It burned under my skin as the world came into focus. However, I would no longer serve as a conduit for the blight. Yet the well within me seemed shallow since the ring had diminished my ability to access the full breadth of the curse.

I grimaced and summoned whatever I could muster, pushing power against the Aralians' defenses. However, the coursing energy lacked the same intensity, fizzling against their shields. To my dismay, they marched in unison, closing the distance between us.

Silas sent wisps of darkness toward them, searching for purchase, but none could be found. The cocoon of onyx protected the Aralians from our attacks.

Panic filled me as I spun to a wailing Naomi, who clutched Mama. She was seemingly unaware or uncaring of the looming danger. Silas panted in exhaustion as he continued his onslaught against the disciples, who were closing in at an alarming rate. I let out a shriek of rage, pulling against my drying well, sending darkness out of myself. Yet it rolled off their defenses. Our previous training focusing on control felt futile. Neither of us was prepared for a battle against the group of Aralians with unfaltering armor.

"Stop this madness and come with us. If you do, we will spare your sister," a woman's voice called out from behind the stronghold. "Our quarrel is not with her."

My glance flicked to Naomi, and I considered the offer. I stepped forward, but Silas grabbed my shoulder.

"*No.* You cannot have her. I will not allow it." He seethed beside me, his face laced with coal lines, his fingertips black with energy. I expected fear to radiate through our bond. Instead, I was enveloped in a soothing tenderness so sweet it lulled me into a false sense of hope. The Aralians inched forward but didn't assault us with an attack, as if they knew we were nearing surrender.

"Arianna." He spun me to him. His gold-flecked gaze held mine as he traced his fingers over my chin. Remorse washed over his expression and his lips trembled. My heart sank as a heaviness lingered in our bond. "I wish I hadn't fought my love for you. Then we would have had more time together, beloved."

"Wise of you to give up," an Aralian said from the sidelines as they edged forward. Their presence loomed, yet Silas remained unfazed.

He pressed his lips to mine in a quick kiss. As he pulled back, his eyes shifted to wholly black. I choked back the bitter taste of his resolve. A knot formed in my throat, and I feared my heart would shatter.

"Don't do this. Please...please...please don't." I shook my head.

"What about Naomi?" His tone turned otherworldly as I shifted to my sister and the horrible choice in front of me.

"Archers at the ready!" the Aralian screamed, no longer willing to wait for us to forfeit.

Yet I sensed his overwhelming desire to protect me, no matter the cost. I choked upon his intentions, screaming down the connection, pleading for him to reconsider.

Seconds later, we were bombarded with arrows. He pulsated with energy, scattering a few. The rest peppered the ground around us, nearly hitting their mark. It was only a matter of time before we were captured or killed. Our diminishing defense could not withstand their barrage.

"I love you. Forever and always. May I find you again in the next life," he whispered as he slipped his onyx ring into my hand.

A gentle smile formed on his lips, and for a heartbeat, the world fell away, and I was caressed by the deep sense of peace emitting from him. But tranquility gave way as he sank into the dark depths. He pulled against every ounce of pain, every memory of horror, and every moment of despair. The agony sparked through our connection, so thick it threatened to drown me.

I sobbed, but the remnants of his soul sent emotions of love, reassurance and, most of all, hope. Hope that his sacrifice would not be in vain.

"Run," he shrieked as the whispers of his essence faded into the blight's depths. As he became its conduit.

I didn't hesitate. I pivoted to my sister, yanking her away from Mama. Naomi moaned as she scrambled to her feet.

"Run, *run*," I yelled, and her eyes widened with understanding as my hand gripped hers firmly and I pulled her onward.

"*Change formation!*" the Aralian shouted. Their arrows surged. Darkness rolled off Silas, as if he were night itself. The projectiles scattered around him.

We sprinted for the hills, focusing on the lush grasses and blue sky, as if desolation were not mere feet away. The contrast sickened me.

But I ran and dragged a teetering Naomi behind me. My head whipped back to the scene unfolding. Agony clenched my throat as I felt every ounce of Silas's anguish pulsating through our bond. Darkness shot out of him and into the sky, a beacon of his intent. The Aralians stumbled, but they were too late. We were all too late. Menace drowned the connection between us. Silas was no longer the man I loved. Only a vessel for his vengeance. Anguish filled the connection. It bloated like a balloon with too much air until it burst.

Boom.

Power exploded from him, and darkness rolled forward. The explosion enveloped the estate and the Aralians. Their shields bent and broke like twigs, unable to withstand the sheer magnitude of the release. The massive eruption surged only seconds behind us. Panic flooded me. Silas's curse would view me as its own, as its kindred, but not Naomi. I cried out in terror as the black fog edged closer.

I pulled her forward, clinging to her hand in desperation. She moved too slowly. The energy pulsed forward. The once green fields disintegrated behind her. The sky blackened as if night had fallen. She stumbled out of my grasp. She reached for me, her eyes blazing with terror as crackling energy nipped only inches from her feet.

Her demise was only heartbeats away, and in those seconds, my mind flooded with Naomi. Memories of our childhood, her bright face as a baby, her companionship, her brilliance, my deep, unbounded love for her. I couldn't let her die, not like this.

I ripped the ring off my finger and dove into the depths of the curse's well. I drank in Silas's pain, coating myself in our shared agony. It consumed me yet again. Power coursed through my veins, and my body throbbed as if it would be torn to shreds as the curse took hold. But I would sacrifice myself for Naomi a thousand times.

I called upon my terror as wisps of energy formed a cocoon around my sister, who lay prostrate on the ground, a second before the darkness crashed over her.

"Don't move," I yelled in agony as I surged my will, which encased my sister. My body ached as I held the protective shield against the onslaught. Silas's power wafted past me and the barrier surrounding Naomi. It sensed me as its mate, its beloved, its own.

Time was irrelevant as a second, or centuries, passed while I protected her. My head pounded as the curse called for me to release my feeble hold. Eventually, the dense black air shifted to shades of blue, as if the dawn had pierced through the night sky. I dropped the shield, and sunlight glimmered off Naomi's hair, her pale face unmarred. But my vision swam as I collapsed beside my unconscious sister. The world around me faded away as I was embraced by nothingness.

CHAPTER 64

ARIANNA

I GASPED, AWAKENING IN my bed. The familiar setting filled me with a sense of peace. What a terrible dream. I reached my hand for Silas, searching for comfort after the dreadful nightmare. My fingers grazed over the cold, empty space, unrumpled by his sleeping form. Dread tugged in my belly. I sat up, but my head swam from the motion.

Silas, I called out through our connection, but I was met with silence. It no longer pulsated with intermingling power. Only a hollow chill filled the absence of the bond, as if nothing remained.

"Silas!" I screamed. Sobs racked my body. As I shook uncontrollably, the memories of that terrible day flickered into existence one by one. I gasped for breath, hyperventilating from the crushing wait of the loss. I grasped my head in my hands, rocking back and forth as if the motion could soothe me. Nothing would ever bring me comfort as I walked around with this gaping hole in my heart.

The door slammed open, and the quick click of boots approached.

"Arianna." Warm arms embraced me as I wailed against a soft body.

I peered at the woman through my blurry, tear-filled eyes, and another burst of shock hit me. "Beatrix?"

"*Shh.*" She smoothed her hands over my hair. "It's all going to be all right. It's all going to be all right." She repeated the mantra almost as much to herself as she did to me.

"Silas, he's..." I choked on the words I couldn't say.

"Alive. Barely, but alive," Beatrix whispered.

A sob broke from me, and we cried in each other's arms. Minutes passed before our weeping dissipated into hiccupping gasps.

"I'm so sorry. It's my fault. Duncan—he betrayed us. I was a fool." She pulled away and searched her pockets for a handkerchief. She blotted her face, but the damp fabric square didn't absorb her tears.

I wiped my sleeve across my face. "No. Don't blame yourself. We must worry about Silas and keeping him safe."

I tried to scoot out of bed. I needed to see Silas, but she placed her hands on my shoulders, anchoring me to the spot. "You are still too weak. You've been unconscious for days. We worried that both of you would..."

She shook her head, as if dislodging the thought. "Fortunately, you are awake now. Thank the gods for Brielle. She has been administering remedies while I've been spoon feeding you and Silas broth. However, I doubt you will be able to stand without proper nourishment."

Beatrix stood and moved toward the bellpull to summon Mrs. Potter. Before she could, the door burst open.

"You nearly scared the entire manor screaming Silas's name and wailing. They thought he died." Brielle walked in, her brow knitted. Her auburn hair popped out of her unkempt braid. She rushed to my side and grabbed my wrist, taking my pulse.

"I'll give you two a minute," Beatrix said, then exited.

I stared at my once enemy, who now acted more like a friend. Her lips pursed as she looked at her pocket watch. "Hmm. Still sluggish. You need to rest."

I expected her to leave, but she seated herself on the edge of the bed. "Did Beatrix tell you about his condition?"

I shook my head, then bit my lip; the sting kept my welling tears at bay.

She sighed. "He's not well. His body somehow survived that blast that should have blown him to smithereens. At least that's what I gathered from the destructive radius Beatrix described and his wounds."

Bile rose in my throat as memories of the carnage we caused flashed through my mind. I shuddered.

"Sorry," she said, pulling me back to the present.

"I don't know what will happen if he recovers. Since arriving, he has been unresponsive, much like you were. However, I'm hoping that he might rouse in a few days." Her uncharacteristically sweet tone made my skin crawl. Whatever was happening to Silas wasn't good.

"Lying doesn't suit you," I said, peering at the haggard woman, who looked as if she hadn't slept in days.

She gave a weak grin. "You're right, Arianna."

She didn't say more. Instead, she fussed over me, pulling vials from her pockets and demanding I drink the horrid concoctions. Then she examined every cut and scrape for possible infection. She poked and prodded at me for at least half an hour. Finally satisfied, she withdrew.

I plopped back on the pillows, exhaustion threatening to overtake me, when the door clicked open again and Beatrix entered with a tray of food.

"Excellent. I'm certain you are in good hands now. I will go check on my other patient," Brielle said.

"Thank you." I gave her a watery smile.

She winked.

"What, no curtsey?" I asked, needing something to feel normal.

She let out a short, wry chuckle, then exited. The brief levity lightened the heaviness of the looming situation.

Beatrix approached and settled the tray on the bed. But before she could speak, I held up my hand. "I know I must eat every bit."

A flicker of a smile twinged on her lips. However, she didn't seem like the Beatrix I had once known. Her once round apple cheeks had sunken, her dress hung around her waist, and the glimmer in her eyes had diminished.

"How did you end up here?" I reached for the spoon and took a tentative sip of the soup. The weak broth washed down my throat, and my stomach growled.

"I ran away from Krella after I escaped Duncan."

I paused to ask her to divulge what happened, but as if sensing my questions, she said, "That's a story for another day."

I returned to eating the flavorless broth in slow sips.

She lowered herself to the corner of the bed and folded her hands demurely. "Silas and I crossed paths at the inn. He pleaded with me to return to Presspin with Agnes and Peter. Luckily, for you both, I didn't listen. I had to help you, so Peter and I followed in a wagon. But we couldn't keep up with Silas's breakneck speed, which, in retrospect, was in our favor. When we arrived, only you, your sister, and Silas were alive. Other than the three of you, only scorched earth, ash, and rubble remained. Then when we reached Presspin, I sent for Brielle. She has been by both your sides ever since."

I dropped the spoon into my soup. Liquid splashed over the bowl and onto the tray. "Naomi. Where is she?"

"She is here, but she has not spoken to anyone, nor left her room. I believe she is in shock. Mrs. Potter is tending to her as best she can." Beatrix frowned.

My stomach churned. My sister's life was turned upside down. Would she ever forgive me for what I'd caused her? I truly had been a curse upon her since her birth, and the awareness sank within me, heavy as a stone.

I pushed the meal away, but Beatrix arched an eyebrow. My heart panged at the expression that was so similar to Silas's.

"Eat your soup. When Silas wakes up, I don't want him to chide me for not taking care of his wife." Her lips tilted in a forced smile, and I relented.

I ate in silence, absorbing Beatrix's company. Thankfully, neither of us wanted to divulge what had happened on our paths to lead us here. I begrudgingly finished the broth and a slice of buttered bread. I yawned, surprisingly weary after having slept for days, and she took the empty tray.

She paused before she left with her eyes on the window, watching something. I turned my attention and blinked, taking in the thick blanket of snow covering every inch of the mountains. "I've never seen this before."

She pivoted to me, and for the first time, warmth filled her expression. "It's lovely. In the past, I used to hate winters here. It blocked us from the outside world. The dense snowfall makes the mountain range impassable until the spring. Back then, I pouted about being unable to receive letters from Duncan, or worse, see him, until the ice melted. Now, with everything that has happened, I pray it falls for six months."

I gazed at her. My lips pulled into a thin line as she snapped out of her trance. "I'll take this to the kitchen. Get some rest."

She hurried off and left me alone with my thoughts. I let out a weary sigh as the snow fell. I hadn't pieced together before Silas's urgency in procuring supplies for the winter. Yet as white blanketed the world, I drifted to sleep, knowing that at least something had worked in our favor.

CHAPTER 65

ARIANNA

I PULLED BACK THE curtains in Silas's suite, illuminating the once dark space. Snow flurried and swirled against the windowpane, coating it with thick ice. The dim sun peeked through the clouds, and I prayed to whatever deity would listen that today, Silas would awaken.

Brielle had worked tirelessly on Silas, plying him with concoctions. Except for some bruises from the blast, he appeared to be healing. Yet his mind was lost. According to Brielle, when he'd arrived, his breaths had been shallow and his pulse waning. The herbal remedies and rest from being in a comatose state had strengthened his respiration. However, his muscles atrophied from lack of use, and his heart still beat a bit too slowly for Brielle's liking.

Once I became strong enough, a fortnight ago, I sat by his side. I rubbed my hand along his in soothing circles, yet he did not rouse. The manor slowed, waiting with bated breath for him to heal. Vincent had taken over the management of

Presspin, while Mrs. Potter busied herself tending to everyone's needs. Beatrix often joined me in silent vigil or to read in Silas's study. She found comfort in occupying the office where he once had thrived. Naomi floated through halls, a shell of the girl she had once been. She lingered in the conservatory, spending hours cleaning the space that had been neglected since Ophelia left. Mrs. Potter suggested we leave her be, as she seemed to take some solace toiling in the soil, as if she were at home. Daily, Peter and Agnes would trek here from the inn, where they took residence, despite my offer for them to stay in the manor. However, they liked to keep themselves busy, helping Mrs. Jenkins with the tavern since the winter chill was harsh on her bones.

Oddly, Brielle had become my closest companion during these weeks. In the silence as we hovered over Silas, she spoke of her time as an Aralian disciple and the abuses she suffered. She told stories of her beloved Wren and how she tried to help her escape her life in Hallowhaven, only to be caught by the Aralians. She had been punished harshly and had nearly died for her attempts to save the woman she loved. The disciples left her for dead in an alley, but a kind stranger saved her. He let her stay with him, and when she was well, he suggested she go to Presspin, where the Aralians' wrath wouldn't reach.

The door clicked open behind me, and I shook out of my thoughts. I pivoted to Brielle. She strode in without a knock or greeting, as she had every morning. She had dropped that sultry demeanor, revealing the real Brielle. Strong, dependable, and oddly tender as she applied eucalyptus creams to Silas's chest or tipped bitter concoctions into his mouth.

"How's he doing today?" She lowered her satchel to the nightstand and pulled out jars of salve and vials of remedies.

"The same." I strode to Silas's side and perched on the armchair beside his bed.

"Hmm..." Her brow wrinkled, and she pursed her lips. She tugged open his tunic and placed her ear against his chest, listening to his breathing.

I watched her as she spent half an hour examining his contusions, his reflexes, and his pulse.

However, my gaze lingered on his handsome profile. The bruises were fading, and a gray pallor no longer colored his skin. His chest rose and fell, the sign that life remained. Yet he seemed frail. A knot formed in my throat, but I promised myself I wouldn't cry any more. No, I would focus my energy on helping Silas recover.

The tinkling of glass drew my attention. Brielle rummaged through her satchel until she pulled out brightly colored vials and swirled them. She pivoted to the bed with a vial of green liquid and gestured to me. I tilted Silas's head as she poured the contents into his mouth. He swallowed instinctively. We watched him with bated breath, but his eyes remained shut. I loosened a bone-weary sigh. I sat and held his limp hand for dear life.

"Have you tried reaching out to him through your bond?" she asked, her voice cutting through my churning sorrow.

I stroked my fingers over his wrist. "All morning. There is nothing but darkness."

Her face fell at my answer, and hopelessness filled the suite.

She moved to the door and paused. Her words were soft as she urged me. "Keep trying, Arianna. I know he is still there. Just keep trying."

She left the room, and silence filled the space. I stroked Silas's hand, gazed upon him, and stifled the tears that threatened to pour out. Unwilling to give up, I exhaled and delved within myself, searching for that cord that had once lived between us.

Silas

"Silas, Silas, Silas," the voice cooed from the pitch-black landscape on this moonless night. I blinked in the lightless world, straining to see.

"Silas."

My feet acted of their own accord, pushing me toward the wraith who called my name.

"Where are you?" I shouted in panic, the darkness consuming me as I walked deeper into the void.

"Silas," the voice whispered, drifting farther away from me.

"Where are you?" I yelled. My heart raced as I sprinted, searching for whoever beckoned me. I gulped down my unease. I had to find the ghost to lead me out of this misery.

"Silas," it crooned in the distance, the sweetness of my name ringing in my ears. But the specter eluded me, no matter how fast my legs moved. I could no longer muster the strength to call out or give chase. The darkness leached the life from my soul.

Exhausted, I sat on this bleak space's cold, hard ground, lost in the abyss. I placed my head in my hands as fear consumed me. "Where are you?" I whispered through a shaky, disheartened breath.

"Silas," it crooned as warmth grazed my shoulder, radiating into my body. My mind reached for the woman who called to me, her voice a comfort to my aching soul. If only I could remember. If only I could find her. Silas...Silas...Silas... *My name crested upon my ears.* Come home, *she cried out repeatedly.*

Hopelessness consumed my world. I reached out again and again. Yet I could never grab hold of the ghostlike creature, no matter how hard I tried. An eternity passed, trapped here.

Each day, the wraith slipped through my fingers. Only her whispers brought solace to my endless torment. She soothed as my curse urged me to remember this woman. I need you, Silas. Please come back to me, *the voice bemoaned as if her hope was dwindling.*

Remember, *I urged myself.* You must remember.

I stilled and forced my mind to focus on the peace she brought. I searched for her and sensed a beating thread, like a line to life itself.

I love you, Silas. Come back to me. *Her words, a caress, warmed my soul. Memories crashed over me, filling my empty being.*

"Arianna!" I howled, reaching toward the voice. Her presence set the darkness ablaze, and I sensed home in the distance, until light flooded my being.

"Arianna!" I exclaimed. My eyes flung open, and I beheld her beautiful face. Heat radiated from her hand intertwined with mine.

"Silas!" she cried out and leapt into the bed. I stroked her hair as she sobbed into my chest. Her warmth encompassed me. "I thought you were lost to me forever."

She gazed at me as I wiped away the tears, my words were gravelly as I held the woman I loved. "I'll always come back to you, Arianna. Always."

EPILOGUE

SILAS

My shoulders loosened as I stepped outside for the first time since I had awoken from my coma. The storm clouds parted, and the setting sun blazed through the sky. My nostrils stung as the chilly wind whipped over my face, twisting snowflakes about. I peered at the vista ahead, only a few hundred feet away. I clenched my jaw. The once effortless walk seemed insurmountable.

Arianna clutched my hand, unwilling to leave my side as we trudged along the snow-laden path toward the grave markers overlooking the mountains. Flurries swirled around us, clinging to her hair, her eyelashes, her nose. Despite the somberness of the afternoon, I couldn't help but grin at my beloved. I gazed at her instead of focusing on the slick ground, and my foot slid a quarter of an inch, sending me off balance. She placed her free palm on my chest, stabilizing me.

"Slow and steady." She gave a watery smile that didn't reach her eyes. I knew the last few weeks had weighed on her shoulders.

We continued with sluggish steps that made me feel like an octogenarian. Everyone considered me lucky to be walking at all, given that only a fortnight had passed since I awoke. Yet I couldn't remain an invalid forever, and Mrs. Park's funeral had been the only reason the women in my life allowed me out of bed.

I breathed in the crisp air, but my lungs burned, and a rattling cough escaped me.

Arianna's brow knit in worry. "I knew you weren't ready for this. We could have waited for a few weeks, or months, since her body is gone. There is nothing to lay to rest."

I pursed my lips and steadied myself. "True, but this isn't about cremation. It's about saying goodbye to someone you loved."

She heaved a sigh and guided me forward. I could sense her grief, even though she acted as if she were unaffected by the ordeal. Instead, she focused her attention on my health and on her failed attempts to reconnect with her aloof sister.

We walked the rest of the way in silence, not needing words to express the feelings we shared through our bond.

Finally, we reached the vista, where the unlit pyre sat on the ledge. My glance shifted to the stone markers that held the names of those memorialized as members of the Belmont household. This morning, the gardener had added one for Clara Park. Arianna faltered and her breath hitched, and a swell of her grief washed over me.

"You can do this, beloved." I squeezed her hand for reassurance as we approached the waiting group.

Layla came forward first and pulled her black hood back, sympathy shining in her gaze. "I am so sorry about your mother. It's horrible that she passed so suddenly, then you and Silas became ill as well. I'm certain it has been a hard month for you."

"Yes, it has been." Arianna stared at her boots.

The lie we had given the townspeople had been effective. Beatrix had concocted the story, and she had told Layla. By the end of the day, the entire town believed that we had left Presspin the morning after Kesere because Arianna's mother had taken ill with pneumonia. She died right after we saw her. However, Arianna and I both became inflicted with the same illness, which explained my weakened state. While Beatrix, the dutiful sister, had ushered us home with Naomi in tow.

Layla withdrew, then sidled up next to Brielle, who remained silent. We made our way toward the group, adorned in black mourning hoods.

I nodded to Vincent, who stood at the rear of the gathering. He still seemed unaccustomed to acting as a friend instead of just my steward. However, he had become someone we trusted, as he managed the town in my stead.

Mrs. Potter curtsied from beside Vincent, her lips twisted in a frown. She had been one of the few people we could no longer lie to about our curses after she witnessed our battered bodies. Yet, to my surprise, she, Peter, and Agnes had always suspected that Arianna and I carried the same blight as my uncle. Our onyx rings had given our secret away. However, the town seemed unaware, and our fabricated tale spread like wildfire.

Without a word, we stood beside Beatrix and Naomi at the front of the group. I grimaced, observing that both of our sisters had become hollow versions of their past selves.

As we convened, Peter stepped forward. “Lady Belmont, Ms. Park, are you ready?”

Naomi crossed her arms over her chest, and that flat expression remained on her face.

“We are,” Arianna said, attempting to reach for Naomi, who flinched away. Arianna lowered her hand and scooted closer to me, giving her sister the space she required.

“We consecrate Clara Park, mother, wife, and friend, to the great beyond. May she find her loved ones in the next life.” Peter lit the empty funeral pyre.

Fire danced along the logs, and the smoke swirled in the wind, whipping around us. The scent of burning filled my nostrils, and my stomach sank, reminding me of the carnage of that day. Yet I didn’t want to dwell on what had happened, so I pushed the memories back. Instead, I focused on my wife. Arianna’s shoulders rose and fell as tears streamed down her face. I wrapped her in my embrace, and my heart broke. I couldn’t protect her from everything, even if I tried.

“I can’t do this.” Naomi threw her hands in the air.

Was this the first time she had spoken since her arrival? I gaped at the young woman, who scowled at me in return. Without another word, she turned and stormed off, with Mrs. Potter chasing after her.

“She’ll never forgive me,” Arianna cried into my chest. “Mama is dead because of me.”

"Shh...it will be all right. She'll come around in time." I pushed back her cloak and pressed my lips against the top of her head.

Arianna wept. Over the hour, as we stood beside the fire, our friends took turns comforting her. Yet their soothing affirmations didn't pierce through the guilt she carried. Eventually, her cries quieted, and the crackling pyre died down until only a flicker of light remained. The last wisps of sunlight faded into the horizon, and the temperature plummeted. The once soft flurries intensified to heavy snowfall.

Arianna shivered against me. "I'm ready to leave."

I nodded, but Brielle gestured for me to follow her. My shoulders tensed. Had she finally received word from Martha detailing what was happening in Hallowhaven?

"Go with Beatrix. I just need a minute," I said.

Arianna, too fatigued by the day, didn't question me. However, Beatrix turned and cocked an eyebrow. Even in her melancholy, she still possessed the sharpest mind. I shook my head. She sighed and walked Arianna back to the manor while the remaining group followed behind.

Brielle and I waited until they were well out of earshot. Then she pulled a letter from her pocket. My lips pursed, and a chill cut through the air. She handed me the folded note. I blinked at the tight handwriting, struggling to see the note as night fell around us. I strode toward the low light of the pyre and read.

Brielle,

I'm glad you are in Presspin and nowhere near the Aralians' reach. The disciples have infiltrated every town under Hallowhaven's control, searching for Arianna Park. They even offered a handsome bounty to anyone with information about her location. Fifty thousand Aralian crown. Can you believe it? But given the devastation she caused, eliminating one of their battle units and destroying an entire manor, it's not a surprise that they covet her power. At least that is the rumor.

Apparently, a servant who escaped from Terrell Estate returned looking for her husband after what she described as a horrific explosion. She watched an old farmer place Arianna, an unidentified woman, and an unidentified man in his cart. She considered following them but had witnessed Arianna's rage firsthand and feared her retribution. Sadly, it seems no one else survived. The woman shared this information with High Disciple Delphine, who rewarded her handsomely.

Luckily for you, the winter months are keeping the Aralians, runners, and bounty hunters at bay, all because of Counselman Xavier Veronin's firsthand knowledge of Presspin and its terrain. He has advised her that only death awaits those trying to cross the mountain range during the snow season. To your fortune, he has sway over the high disciple, making them bedfellows in more ways than one. I doubt she will send anyone to Presspin until spring.

I hope they find Arianna Park, so you, my dear friend, can remain hidden.

Martha

I clenched my jaw at the name of the man I hoped to never see again: *Xavier Veronin.* I crumpled the letter in my hand and chucked it into the fire. The paper burned.

Frustrated, I inhaled sharply, the crisp night air cutting through my lungs like a sharp knife. I wheezed, then hacked a wretched cough.

"Come on, let's get you inside." Brielle approached.

I nodded, but the fit didn't end. My chest constricted. I placed my hand on my lips as I sputtered. Seconds later, my respiration steadied, but when I pulled my fingers away, they were coated with blood.

ABOUT THE AUTHOR

Chelle Cypress is a voracious reader, mother, wife and anime enthusiast. As a child, Chelle dreamed of becoming a published author. Through hard work, many late nights, and copious amounts of coffee, she has finally achieved her dream of sharing the stories of her heart with the world. Chelle infuses her writing with themes from classic literature, regency romances, and fantasy. She enjoys blending the contents together in a novel that she hopes speaks to the hearts of her readers. Chelle has used writing as a therapeutic outlet which has helped her maintain her sobriety (7/30/21).

Follow her on her socials:

Tiktok: Chellecypressbooks

Instagram: Chellecypressbooks

https://chellecypress.com/

ACKNOWLEDGEMENT

WHAT A JOURNEY! THANK you to everyone who has supported me and lifted me up along the way.

First, I would like to thank my husband, Bill, for his continuous support. A round of applause for him for enduring many late night writing sessions, wrangling our two kids, all while encouraging me to chase my dreams.

To my mom, thank you for all the hours spent listening to me talk about this book and helping me with the kids so I could focus on meeting the never ending deadlines.

To my best friends, Alyssa and Haley. Thank you for listening to every version of this book, holding space for my hyperfixation and being the best cheerleaders a girl could ask for. When I doubted myself and this story, you were there and I am eternally grateful.

To my Booktok and Authortok community. There are no words to express my love for you. From the bottom of my heart, thank you for accepting me into this beautiful community. I am so blown away daily by each and everyone of you. I often thought about giving up, and so many of you encouraged me to just keep going.

A special thank you to my beta readers and editors who gave such amazing notes, which helped me become a better writer. Thank you to my sensitivity readers and Brittany Mack for her editorial assessment.

To Rebekah Sinclair, thank you for all your help, guidance, graphics and being a well of information. I truly appreciate all of your help.

Finally, a special thank you to Isabelle Olmo and Sabrina Blackberry for helping me figure out the title of my book.

Made in the USA
Columbia, SC
25 February 2025